WARLORD

OF THE UNRAVELING

DOC SPEARS

WARGATE

An imprint of Galaxy's Edge Press
PO BOX 534
Puyallup, Washington 98371

Paperback ISBN: 979-8-88922-066-4
Hardcover ISBN: 979-8-88922-067-1

www.wargatebooks.com

✠ ✠ ✠

Warlord Benjamin Colt and his fellow Green Berets have slain barbarian armies, toppled governments, dethroned gods, and forged the greatest fighting force to ever battle on the decayed and dying world of Vistara. Thanks to the transformative tactics and disruptive technologies brought by the displaced operators, for the first time in centuries, security and prosperity reign.

But just as their adopted homeland stands on the cusp of greatness, an unknown enemy steals undetected into the heart of the flowering civilization they've sacrificed to build.

This new evil's declaration of war—depraved murder and chaos. Their means and methods—asymmetrical and advanced beyond understanding. Their goal—complete and utter terror.

As surely as this cowardly assault on liberty colors his vision red as the sands of Mars, Benjamin Colt harnesses his drive to lead the fight from the front, once again prepared to bring total war to whoever threatens the peace he and his team have given their all to win. But when evidence points to a ghost-like tribe of primitives thought long eradicated, driven by an ideology so foul its source could only be the planet he'd left behind, against whom can Benjamin Colt wage this war?

If they're to save their society from extinction, the Green Berets and their peerless alien compatriots must discover whoever is behind the discord—jealous aristocrats, alienated comrades, devious criminals, vanquished enemies... or does all of Vistara wish them flayed to dust by a cyclone of vicious sands? And as their alliances and scientific innovations break down, a fabled land known only through a poem teases possibilities. Do they represent a new ally, or the wakening of a terrible giant?

What Benjamin Colt and his warriors are bound to do, they do for their worthy queen, herself locked in a struggle to balance the needs of a kingdom with the needs of her heart. They do it for their honor as soldiers sworn to liberate the oppressed. And they do it for a people fated by history to abandon reason, to harken the alluring song of a new and beautiful provocateur, ready to lead them towards crisis and slavery.

Of all of Benjamin Colt's many wars, this will prove his most challenging to win. But when all others are found wanting, a kingdom depends on the only man fit to bear the title—WARLORD.

✠ ✠ ✠

01

"*You*, Deacon Benjamin Colt, are 200 pounds of stupid stuffed into a 100-pound ruck. Brah, you don't know squat about racing horses much less arkall."

Dave busted my balls per team SOP. And normally I'd be giving some right back to him. But as he was quite right in his estimation of my arkall-riding abilities, I had my hands full. Literally.

The arkall I'd learned to love were huge and steady and even at full gallop, gave you the same confident glide of an M1 Abrams cruising over freshly laid asphalt. True, the youngsters chosen for racing were smaller, but they were still the size of a full-grown rhino and so far, no easier to straddle.

I'd just gotten one foot in the stirrup when my pony used its eight legs to gyrate like an out-of-balance washing machine, making me think arkall jiu-jitsu was a thing. With one leg mid-swing over the saddle, my body did a decent imitation of a flag flapping in variable winds. I managed to seat myself with all the grace of a duck crashing onto an icy pond.

Dave was a runaway machine gun fed by a thousand-round belt. "Brah, after all the knuckle-headed shit you've done, *this* is how you're finally gonna go out." I tuned out his tirade as he ticked off previous times that I'd narrowly avoided the coroner's pronouncement of death by misadventure.

Doug shined with his usual optimistic energy as he pushed in opposition against a rump as wide as a Buick.

“You’re gonna nail this like Tony Hawk hitting the 900! No sweat, Ben-dog.”

Also unlike Dave, Doug teased the arkall instead of me.

“This is happening, little dude, so stop fighting and get in the minivan, ’cause you’re going to the dentist, whether you like it or not.”

Khraal Kahlees held the bridle with his upper hands. For the moment, constrained on all sides and with me firmly on top, the arkall calmed. But he wasn’t strapped down like a kid on a papoose board getting stitched up in the ER, so I fully expected his tantrum to start again any second. When it didn’t, Khraal Kahlees carefully passed the reins up to me with lower hands.

“Good, Benjamin Colt. Now, brothers, do not let up on your pressure, for he will surely attempt to spin next.”

The arkall gave a disgusted snort, annoyed that Double-K blew his next tactic. The temperature beneath me rose to a sizzle and I braced for the volcanic eruption to come.

The race hadn’t been run in Filestra for centuries, and it was apparent my arkall couldn’t care less about the honor.

I tensed, not sure what to expect, when my pony pulled a move so slick, it was like he’d learned it by studying judo. He cocked his knees on one side to suddenly lean his full weight into Doug, breaking from Dave’s contact. As Doug naturally pushed back, the black belt pony blended with the push and slammed into Dave with the momentum of an iron locomotive.

“OOF.” Air gushed out of Dave as he was knocked back a step.

It was a trick that would’ve worked against a Tarn. But against a pair of Thulians gifted with the supernatural strength of our adopted world, it was an invitation to a lesson in humility.

Spewing expletives to turn an English vicar Vistaran red, Dave charged back like a sumo wrestler. He hit the wall of flesh with a slap that I felt through the saddle. We skidded sideways, the arkall's hooves leaving marks on the stone, until finally slamming into the immovable wall that was Dougie.

"Don't hurt him," I said. Trapped in a headlock by a green Hulk Hogan and its rump squeezed between the two jaws of a superhuman vise, its frenzied baying tugged at my empathy.

Until he took the only direction available for rebellion.

Up.

I found myself suddenly heading for Double-K, ass-over-teacup. Its buck reversed, nearly flinging me off in a backward somersault. With a molar-jarring impact, it bucked forward again, but to my amazement, I was still on top.

"Benjamin Colt!" Double-K called my attention with ferocity, corded muscles taut as he pulled the creature's head low. "Even a small second-summer youth as this is too large an animal for us to overpower. Do as I have instructed!"

He for sure knew his arkall. The warriors of the Korund were adept cavalrymen, and none more accomplished than our Double-K. He was riding since before he could walk. His reputation as Vistara's el numero uno badass was well deserved—and the day I knocked the king off the hill had been the wet mortar of a respect that cemented into our brotherhood. Soon came his nearly religious conversion to our ways of warfare, and he led by example to bring the rest of the Korund warriors along with him.

Until we showed up on Vistara, the Tarn had only ever gone to battle mounted on arkall, eschewing the Vistaran flying craft we christened flitters as "unnatural."

Now the hulking four-armed greenies we'd trained were as comfortable riding the deck of a flitter through the cloudless Vistaran skies as they were on arkall.

Or in our hardback gun trucks. Or our tanks. We still had good old-fashioned mounted cavalry. Gotta let a Tarn be a Tarn. But I also had a company trained as static line paratroopers. What we'd do with them I wasn't yet sure, but when the opportunity arose for a Tarn airborne assault, it would be glorious.

It was just another in a long line of firsts that us Thulians—Earthmen, that is; specifically, Green Berets—had brought to our adopted world.

Though the arkall bucked harder, still I hesitated. What Double-K advised seemed cruel. I did as my Gramps had taught me when dealing with his rarely ridden gelding, always frisky after long months at pasture. I squeezed my thighs and gave a slow but firm pull low on the bit to bring its head down in submission, prepared for it to spring like that old gelding did until, after a few bounces, it would settle down.

This was no twelve-year-old quarter horse who'd gone all winter without being saddled.

With power that reminded me of the local variety lion I'd once tussled with, my boy went for the full suplex, vaulting onto its rearmost legs and taking Double-K a full story high with him.

I had no way to stay on except to abandon the reins and death-grip its neck like a hippie on a tree. Double-K evaded a trampling by executing a crab walk at light-speed. Considering that on scorched Vistara he'd never seen any form of aquatic life, he nailed the impression. Six-limbs sure helped.

The arkall—its head as big as an engine block—turned sharply back and snapped at my naked knee. Hot spittle sprayed my kneecap. Frustrated at not being able to quite reach, he stretched lips and ground his grill full of flat teeth. The image of him Captain-Crunchin' my patella like it was Saturday morning cartoon time caused sensitive parts of me retract into my body.

Khraal Kahlees cussed in creative combinations learned from Dave and leaped up to grab the bridle.

"Benjamin Colt! You will not win this mount's obedience with kindness! TAKE CONTROL!"

I like animals better than most people, excepting gazraal, that is. They were permanently on my persona non grata list after nearly making a meal of me. But I despise cruelty to any animal. My puppy Apache and I started our relationship in a manner distinctively different from how Khraal Kahlees and I commenced our friendship. A gadron isn't a dog, not even close. They're about the size of a grizzly. So, at first sight you might not think "puppy" is a fitting way to describe him—but in every way save size, he was one. And kindness was the material that built our bond of trust.

But Double-K was right. That approach wasn't going to work here.

"GET IT DONE, BRAH," Dave pleaded as he and Doug clasped arms to make a weighted blanket over the bouncing haunches.

I balled a fist as the beast raised for another big drop. I followed the momentum and delivered a hammer blow between its front shoulder blades like I meant to split a boulder with a single swing of my sledgehammer.

The surging powerhouse beneath my thighs buckled to its knees and remained there, wilted like a willow tree after an ice storm. I hadn't given it all I could've, of course. The strength I possessed on Vistara meant a full-power blow would've broken its spine. In combat I'd grievously injured an arkall twice this one's size, splitting its ribs like brittle cordwood with a single punch.

It gave an injured bleat. My heart wrenched, but not so much that when it tensed to make another go, I wasn't willing to repeat the lesson. This time I used an open palm—a much different transmission of force—rising in the stirrups and dropping all my weight to land a firm clap on the same spot.

As Doug had so correctly called it—whether he liked it or not, junior was getting in the minivan.

The meaty slap produced a wide impact that rippled beneath my seat and down its muscled spine. It gingerly looked back over its shoulders with sad eyes that said, "I didn't ask for this, you know?"

I took that as its epiphany. Hopefully he now knew that had been my last word on the subject, and if he was good, there'd be a Happy Meal later.

I tightened the reins and my pony dipped his head to follow. I let slack just slightly, permitting him to test the limits I'd allow his nose to turn, and finally he snorted acceptance. My rough alchemy had transmuted the earthquake beneath me into pliant muscle, ready to be commanded.

I only hoped that after this much trouble, I'd drawn the arkall equivalent of Seattle Slew and not a glue factory reject.

Khraal Kahlees was dusting himself off when Doug joined him up front.

"Not laughing at you, Double-K. It's just..."

Dave met them. "It's just that it's been a while since we've been in this kinda Ben-dog predicament."

Khraal Kahlees gave a wet, throaty Tarn chuckle. "It is truthful. There has been rare opportunity for strenuous diversion as of late. Especially the kind the Warlord seems to attract."

Dave blew a raspberry. "Same panic, different disco. But, guess I'm glad to be on the dance floor again. I must be as stupid as him. Crazy haole."

From my newly settled horizon, I had the vantage to check out the other riders. Even though our mounts were assigned by a drawing—Talis Darmon pulled the tokens from the leather bag—the difficulty I had simply getting on top of my arkall had me suspicious the fix was in against the Warlord. That doubt evaporated as I registered the six other competitors were enduring the same ordeal, fighting for their lives just to get mounted. Like me, each had a retinue of helpers doing their best to avoid getting trampled themselves. But because we were the four strongest men on Vistara, I'd beaten the pack to be first to fully mount.

As befits a Warlord.

The crowd cheered my accomplishment and even Apache howled approval from the reviewing deck. I gave my arkall's shoulder firm pats of affection as I would my puppy. The same would bowl a man over but to both, the gesture was received like a tender caress. After a few massaging strokes alongside the thick neck, he nickered appreciatively. My mount had blown through the stages of arkall grief and arrived at acceptance, and our understanding afforded me a moment to reorient.

We'd only arrived outside Filestra the day before to a city under siege by flitters packed with a thousand Griswold families headed for Wally World. From all parts of the kingdom they'd come for the festival of the race—the reinstituted annual celebration that was the official proclamation of Filestra's rebirth.

We toured the city, amazed by the progress, pleased to see tourists ambling across the plaza where the course of tomorrow's race was being laid out between curving stone barriers like a NASCAR short track.

Center in the plaza, the once parched fountain sprouted plumes showering onto the blue basin as it had not in more than a thousand years. Bounding the bowl of the plaza were the towers of the innermost wards. Like my queen's capital of Shansara, cities were traditionally divided into districts associated with a family guild. The ancient emblems had reappeared in Filestra to mark the wards—stone reliefs bearing the likeness of animals real and mythical, floral designs, symbols of tools or the crafts a guild produced.

Ground-level cafes were cleared of canopies and tables to permit spectators to line the outer ring of the track as well as to crowd into the plaza. The business offices occupying the floors above the cafes rented window space to spectators for exorbitant prices, and the balconies of the higher-level apartments were festooned with bright banners of the respective guilds who cheered from the most expensive viewing spots.

The pageantry and spirit were all the result of Talis Darmon's grand vision to restore Filestra to its grandeur as one of the premier cities of her kingdom. Decorated in the royal colors, a stilted reviewing stand stood high in the central plaza to hold the people dearest to me in all the universe, my queen first among them.

Filestra's collapse into ruin was well underway before its abandonment and subsequent occupation by the Mydreen, who further hastened its demise into the decayed shell of the city I met on my first and nearly last stop on Mars. Now, the enemy had not only been driven from their former capital, but the nomadic Tarns had been made nearly extinct. If that alone weren't enough to encourage resettlement, Filestra held the first of our atmosphere factories rehabilitated to full function. And with the air works recently restored in Shansara and more on the way, the depleted atmosphere of our world was being revitalized and with it, all of Mihdradahl.

One thing I've learned about our people. Scratch the surface of a Vistaran—seemingly disinterested in anything but their narrow desire for constancy and calm—and beneath is a fervent partisan. From aristocrat to bricklayer, each held the conviction that their familial line traced the strongest connection to Mihdradahl's ancient history, back to a time when the Furrow of the Creator's Hand cradled the wide Amethyst Sea.

And as finely honed as any of her many skills, Talis Darmon knew how to shape wills. As surely as a bladesmith forges iron into sharp steel.

From across the kingdom there'd been a rush by the major and minor guilds to reclaim Filestra. But beneath the answer to the queen's patriotic call lay a pragmatism. Filestra was once a metropolis filled with all variety of trades, from bankers and merchants to artists and craftsmen. The city had once been a center of wealth—renown for the masters who cut and processed the energy stones and raw gems taken from the mines of the far eastern edge of the Korund mountain range—and could be again.

The first to claim their ancestral places in Filestra stood to profit greatly.

I was half nodding off in the council meeting while the historians described in nauseating detail the traditions of the festival of the race. It didn't sound like much of an event. Just four laps around the fountain. Seven riders chosen by lottery raced a narrow course for the victory pennant that would be hung outside their ward's seat until the next year. It was a race for pride and nothing else. It certainly was no Indy 500 or Kentucky Derby. It wasn't until the historian mentioned the next bit that I perked up.

Whenever the regent of Mihdradahl was in attendance, it was tradition that the Crown had a representative in the race.

Her reply when I volunteered? Silent skepticism.

"It's a given that as Warlord, I'm the one to represent the throne."

The pregnant silence and my queen's cocked eyebrow remained.

"Really, sweetheart, I'd like to. It'll be fun. And I haven't had the chance to do anything really Warlord-worthy in some time. I gotta represent."

She sighed. "I might remind you of another race in which you represented the office of my regency."

Right. That was one for the books. Disguised within the colloquial Annamerian festivity, the race I'd been blindsided into had been a murder-fest—its purpose to placate the proles of their society while making me very dead and leaving my queen embarrassed and weakened in the process. I was not the least bit sorry to have disappointed my yellow friends to the south by demonstrating my homicidal proclivities were more accomplished than theirs. Especially when I later harnessed my drive for total warfare to bring them a regime change.

If not ancient, it was at least history.

"This is nothing like that, Talis Darmon. It's just a horse race on friendly territory. It'll be fun."

She fought a quick internal battle, then relented.

"With the twin evils of both the Whites and Annamese defeated, the vigilance with which you keep yourself perpetually ready to wage war has perhaps become strained by disuse. Under your direction my mighty army is truly peerless. But we are without enemy against which you would direct my will. I know your warrior need, as you say, 'to represent' is important to your well-being. Very well, husband and Warlord. You have my dispensation to represent my throne on this auspicious occasion."

She made the slight, regal smile she reserved for use in the council, but did give me a tiny wink to go along with her nod. If we'd been alone, she'd have squealed with delight at the prospect of seeing me strut my stuff. I knew how to charge my wife's batteries. She was my number-one fan, like I was hers, but she didn't need to do anything at all to get my motor revving.

Anyway, with her seeing things my way, I put the race out of my mind. I was damn good on an arkall, and this was just going to be a county fair kind of horse race out in the sticks with the yokels, right? Nothing to worry about.

My talent for misreading a situation may someday stand among the greatest legends of Vistara.

This morning the air crackled with the electricity of thousands yearning for an excuse for madness. Overnight the serene plaza had filled to capacity with crowds come to stake out prime viewing territory for the event. They drank and partied like lifelong Super Bowl tailgaters. Banners waved, lovers lustily mauled at each other, drunken fistfights were fought in the crush of crowds so dense that the Guard didn't make the slightest overture to wade in break things up.

From atop a tall reviewing stand Talis Darmon drew our mounts, and as each tile was announced, the crowds oohed and aahed. People cheered for a favorite and jeered for the opposition. More fights broke out, the Guard all but helpless to intervene. Then began the process of us meeting and mounting our animals—and now, here I was.

With all riders mounted, at last the crowd's passion built to the kind of mass hysteria associated with revolutions or rock concerts. And though I sat on a giant beast, I didn't swell with the invulnerability of a tank commander standing in the turret. I felt like a nose-picking preschooler rocking on a wooden hobby horse beneath a leaky dam showing wider and wider cracks.

From his balcony, an official waved a white banner above the start line.

"Welp, that's the signal to line up," Dave said. "This is all coming together like two dirty butt cheeks. We're out of here. Good luck, dummy."

"Any last words of advice?" I asked Double-K, but it was Dave who answered.

"Advice? Okay. Don't kiss your mom on your dad's birthday."

I groaned. "Not from you, Davey-Dave!" Guess I set myself up for that one.

Khraal Kahlees shrugged four shoulders. "Do not fall, or you will surely be killed."

With that, Double-K became the point of the three-man plow headed for the reviewing platform. The crowds parted for Khraal Kahlees like the Red Sea for Moses, making me think we needed Tarns in the Guard as well as the army. Doug was last to follow, but before he did, he cupped his hands to yell over the din of the crowd, "Remember what Talis Darmon told you, duder."

Before we'd gone our separate ways that morning, my wife had pulled me aside.

"Husband, I am very proud that you are taking part in this day. It will surely be recorded as the pivotal event marking Mihdradahl's new age. But, Benjamin Colt..." She searched for the right words. When a master of rhetoric like my wife struggled to express herself, it could mean only one thing. I was about to be told to cool it.

"What?" I coaxed in as coy a manner possible. "I thought it got you all hot and bothered to see me flex on my rivals."

"It does. But perhaps, you would consider what it would mean to the people of Filestra and her pride if one of the guilds were to win? Hmm? Can you overcome your competitive nature and do this? For me?" She fluttered eyelashes.

I pointed at my chest and made my best "butter wouldn't melt in my mouth" look. "Me? Competitive? Why, whatever do you mean, wife?"

That brought a laugh, and a kiss.

"Do not make it too obvious that you allow another to win, yes?"

I gave her a peck in return and winked. "You know me."

"I do. Which is why your wife tells you that if you are good, later I shall give you a great reward." She winked back and gave the playful smile that always melted me.

There was more than one way to be a winner.

I guided my oversized pony to funnel in with the other riders moving toward the starting line. The safety walls marking the course were waist height for a man, barely above shin height to an arkall. If one of these critters went over the rail, there weren't enough sponges in Mihdradahl to soak up the partiers it would squash to wet paste.

At the center of the stilted platform sat my queen. Surrounding her, my closest friends. Through a gap in the towers and over the horizon, sitting on the plain in almost the exact spot where Dave and I first viewed Maleska Mal, I could just glimpse the top deck of the *Hope of Vistara*. The massive ship would be the floating embassy of our mission to explore the rest of Vistara—if we ever got all the bugs worked out.

Karlo and Cynar were presently not on speaking terms over the issue. They pretended to ignore each other though they sat side by side on the crowded stage. My wife's three bodyguards-slash-companions, Tranya Olan, Keshin Tellest, and Shasa Karin, stood behind her.

Perrin Halser sat beside the queen. He'd become one of her closest advisers, accepting her commission to investigate a transition of Mihdradahl's governance into some form of republicanism. The engineer was still discomforted by public appearance, but was eager to make the trip with us on the *Hope*, and had even tried to mediate some of the disagreements between Karlo and Cynar.

With Double-K leading, my three buddies finished their exodus to arrive at the platform. Doug joined his waiting lady friends, Dave moved to stand with Tranya Olan, and Double-K took the spot behind the chair to the queen's left. On it sat his daughter, my adopted sister, Beraal Kahlees. And on her lap bounced the light of my life.

My little girl.

Six months old and already four handfuls for her aunt, Tashara Colt was currently more fascinated by her toes than she was with the craziness around her. Tashara Wavecrest Darmon Colt Sylah was her full name, but to my wife's chagrin, she was my little Shara.

I was bought from distraction by the snorted protest of my mount as a pair of riders a few steps ahead worked their arkall in concert to squeeze us out of a place in the starting line. Both riders gave a grin to let me know it had indeed been done in coordination.

"You may be Warlord, but I am master of the ride, Thulian." He wore a neckerchief bearing the mark and colors of the banking guild, the three-headed gazraal on green. The other rider with the red scarf bearing the square, level, and hammer of a builder only sniggered in a particularly annoying way.

"I'll let someone else win. I promise," I muttered to myself. My pony turned his ears back and whinnied. Whether he agreed or disagreed, I could only guess.

"Riders, be ready," the official yelled, lofting the triangular yellow flag that was the start signal. When it dropped, the race was on.

I coaxed my mount to turn, nudging it sideways, and removed a foot from the stirrup. My target was almost in reach. The official raised the flag overhead, just as I kicked the banker's mount in the most sensitive region of any critter born on Earth or Mars.

His mount sprang forward and in sympathetic response, every rider spurred their mounts to explode ahead. All before the yellow flag dropped. A thrown red silk drifted down over the line.

False start.

"Hehehe." Cynar's trademark chuckle slipped from my lips. If anyone had seen me do it, word hadn't reached the official, and the order was given for our gaggle to line up all over again. Riders turned their nervous mounts back to the start, then turn again to face the start line, bumbling into each other as they crowded large animals into a narrow space. The excitable young arkall bleated and whinnied irritably while the crowd booed, their anticipation of the glorious release of the start ruined.

While I'd succeeded in paying back the banker and his conspiratorial buddy, I fared little better in the new lineup. Forced out and stuck behind a wall of closely pressed animal flesh, I was trying to wedge into a spot when a single beige leg cocked and snapped an odd angled kick at me, just like Grandpa's old gelding would when I'd try and saddle him. The hoof missed my thigh by an inch and smacked a thick rib. With all eight legs, my pony jumped sideways, taking us briefly airborne and filling me with dread that he'd come down in a parachute landing fall, me the dough to his rolling pin as he laid down his points of contact.

Fortunately, my arkall proved agile and recovered its balance with a hop, which atop even a small arkall is akin to being bounced on an amusement park ride designed to make you toss your corn dog. The builder looked my way, giving another of his stupid sniggers. I'd seen him tickle the haunch of his arkall, producing the near-fateful kick. Today was my Ph.D. in arkall studies. Noted for future use.

There was not just a conspiracy between the banker and builder to lock me out of the lineup. The whole line worked together and I was again trapped behind six other riders, with not so much as a glimmer of sunlight between them. The yellow flag raised high. At that precise moment, the leftmost rider leaned his arkall to shove the line right, producing a slight gap on the outside. I had a sense of the timing, and went for it. I kicked my arkall on both sides and, as if he'd read my mind, we took off into the hole. We crossed the line at a full gallop at the very instant the yellow flag dropped.

It was on.

By God, this guy was fast! But there was more to his talent than speed. I'd gotten lucky and drawn an arkall who had something in common with me.

Neither of us cared much for ass-clowns or their hijinks.

I may have been in the lead, but hot on our wide galloping ass chased a thundering stampede. I nudged us to the inside line and concentrated on relaxing and just letting my guy do what he was proving he could do so well. We hugged the inside curve like my boy was born to be there. Hoofbeats thundering on stone and the pounding of my heart were not enough to drown out the roar of crowds. In no time my steed was carrying us around to the starting line, ready to give us a second lap in the lead. Everything but the back of my arkall's head was a blur.

Everything, that is, except the look on my wife's face.

It was subtle, but there it was.

The frown.

She'd said not to make it obvious.

I drifted the reins a tiny bit left and pressed with my inside thigh and soon enough in my peripheral, the minor space we'd made on our right was occupied by the snorting nostrils of an arkall, the red neckerchief of the builder bouncing into view. Oh, well. I'd have to find another way to settle with him post-race for his cheap antics, lest knocking his teeth out make me look like a sore loser. I drew back on the reins ever so slightly, just the amount of a thought, and let the sniggering buffoon move a shoulder ahead of me. All I had to do was maintain this position, and I'd have a plausible second place loss.

Into the third lap, the builder's annoying cackles turned to curses as his arkall faded. I had to slow us a corresponding amount to maintain the fiction we didn't have the horsepower to pull ahead at will. On the outside came the green neckerchief-wearing banker. Ugh. Something about his stupid pencil-thin mustache made losing to the builder better than losing to him. Whether it was me or my mount that bristled at the sight of the banker, my boy burst ahead and, in a flash, we were side by side for the lead.

This is how we started the last lap. I diverted no attention to checking my wife's reaction. I already knew what it would be.

Nudging up along the inside came the frothy hot breath of an arkall on my thigh. In a frenzy, the builder slapped at his mount, beating it like a drum to go faster. Simultaneously the banker pushed down from the outside causing our mounts to rub, slowing us both and allowing the sniggering builder on my right to come fully alongside me. First one, then the other, threw backhands at my face. Both missed, but my vision took on that Mars-red tint.

You know. The one that taints my view just before I set to killing.

If we'd been stock cars, my front quarter panels would have black rub marks from the tires squeezing me on both sides. These idiots would rather have us all wipe out than lose to me. A disaster was imminent. Bystanders were packed as densely as the atoms of depleted uranium that tipped the Vulcan rounds of an A-10. And when the inevitable pileup sent animals over the painfully short wall... tragedy.

I could save us all—just by pulling ahead. All I had to do was let the reins out, give the nuclear-powered rocket beneath me a little of my heels, and the control rods in its reactor chamber would build the chain reaction to critical. We could leave them in the dust. But I'd made a promise to Talis Darmon to let this be someone else's day of days.

I coaxed the reins back.

The builder squeezed ahead. He fumbled something from his waist and threw a handful of whatever it was beneath our path. My mount broke stride with a lurch. I clenched, waiting for the Hindenburg-quality crash onto the hard stones and the trampling to come beneath the many eight-legged speed demons behind us.

Neither happened.

The builder had thrown a handful of pointed caltrops right beneath my boy's path. My mount broke into a staggering canter with at least one hoof successfully spiked, but refused to fall—saving us both. This wasn't cheating.

This was attempted murder.

Hell to pay didn't describe what was going to happen when the race was over.

The pack pulled around as my mount slowed into a lame hobbling gait, crying in pain. We came to a stop in sight of the official holding a green flag, ready to declare the winner.

The crowd roared its loudest yet.

Suddenly, my horizon of bobbing riders erupted in blazing yellow light, followed by a dull sizzling sound and a saddle-vibrating concussion. A dust cloud billowed, the same as from any bomb I knew, as people screamed, arkall cried, and blood rained.

I sprang from the stirrups. Two bounces took me nearer to the scene of carnage on the finish line, and I took an immediate course correction. Springing high for the reviewing stand, wounded littered the plaza, their bodies telling the story of frag spreading in a radius far beyond the blast.

Landing, I vaulted up the stairs to the platform.

Beraal was crouched with her head tucked and her arms wrapped tightly over the precious package in her lap. Talis Darmon knelt by Perrin Halser, clutching his arm. Between her fingers, arterial blood pumped in bright spurts. She resisted the women of her Guard pulling her away until Karlo was there an instant later, producing a tourniquet.

A cloud was open over Dave's wrist to the *Hope.* I placed a hand on Beraal's back. I had to be sure. "Beraal, it's me, it's okay," I said loudly, certain the shock of instantaneous violence made it necessary to yell. My sister raised her head.

"The princess is safe, dear brother." Beneath her, shielded like the gold in Fort Knox, was my baby girl, unharmed, her eyes wide.

Combat flitters launched from the deck of the *Hope* and in seconds were lowering from the cloudless sky to surround the platform. Green and red troops in desert camo rushed off to pass the royal party onto the floating craft. The queen flung her arms around Beraal and our child, and a protective ring of the smaller women joined her. All were painted with blood.

"Apache, go with them, boy!" My puppy was stoked for battle, but did as I asked without having to be told twice and leaped to Beraal's side. I pointed to the pilot. "Take off."

Flanked by more gunships, the flitter holding my family sped off for the *Hope*, vanishing in the blink of an eye. But in that brief instant before my queen and our child disappeared behind layers of loyal retainers, the last image I had of her burned into my mind.

Talis Darmon's clothes and deep red skin were streaked with Perrin Halser's crimson blood.

And the eyes of the most courageous woman I'd ever known held terror.

02

More combat aircars came, hovering above stunned crowds oblivious to the need to disperse. Only Doug, Dave, Karlo, Khraal Kahlees, and myself remained on the reviewing stand. One of our company commanders leaped from a hovering flitter and presented to me. "Orders, Warlord?"

Before I could open my mouth, Doug placed himself in front of the captain. "We have to get everyone out of the plaza as rapidly as possible. There could be secondary devices."

Karlo took the captain by a shoulder and pointed. "That building's the casualty collection point. Have all the wounded brought there. Nothing more than tourniquets as needed, then get them to the CCP." He turned. "Ben, I'm taking charge of triage. Send me evac flitters ASAP." I gave a thumbs-up, and he was gone.

My teammates had been there and done that, and the gestalt of their response was intuitive, like bloodhounds on a scent.

Unspoken was the obvious. An IED had done this. The location and timing of the explosion meant it had to have been detonated on command. And whoever had done so could be anywhere, waiting to choose the next best moment to unleash hell with who -knew-how-many more IEDs.

The next device could be waiting to kill responders aiding victims. Or to shred the morbidly curious gawkers fighting against the flow to see for themselves what had happened. Or at one of the many chokepoints where half-drunk partiers clumped like wet sand stuck in the neck of the hourglass. There were dozens of small plazas between wards where escapees might stop to catch their breath. When the densest numbers swelled against one of those dams—if maximum terror was the goal—that's where the next IEDs were going to be unleashed.

Other than wave a magic wand and gift the power of flight to every hapless spectator still in the plaza, the only viable option was to get them to scatter in as many directions as quickly as possible.

Because the math's as simple as it gets: if it looked to the bomber like he'd have settle for netting one or two fish instead of a whole school, we'd still end up with fewer mangled and dead, and more left alive to be tortured by the scars of today's trauma.

Ugly? Yes, but often a first line treatment can seem nearly as callous as the disease. Sometimes, you have to amputate a leg. Whether the patient ever learns to accept that it was the only way to save them, at least they had the rest of a life to dedicate to the process. How the actions we took now would be understood later, the armchair quarterbacks could debate.

Which they surely would.

"Dave, you're incident commander," I said. "Run it airborne." It was always a good idea to ensure there was no confusion about who was in charge. But as usual, Dave was already calling the ball. He gave me the thumbs up, barely breaking eyes away from the cloud over his wrist as he issued orders.

Like Karlo, Doug and Double-K were already gone. No sooner than Dave hopped onto the deck of his airborne command post, I sprang off for the epicenter of the disaster.

The finish line.

I landed at the edge of the blast crater, the scene littered with the bodies of indomitable beasts and frail men, their pieces scattered with the rubble of the street. And wandering through the devastation with a glowing slate held to his face was Cynar.

"Cynar! Get the hell out of here! There could be another bomb."

The grizzled old wizard ignored me. Had the blast wiped out what little hearing he had left or was his concentration so intense my words didn't penetrate?

"Cynar!"

He didn't look up from the slate when he said, "I must do my portion, Benjamin Colt."

How'd he get here so fast? The debris must've still been falling when he made his decision. It's not what I would've expected.

"You have to go, Cynar. It's not safe."

"Nowhere is, my friend. I am useful in no other way. Leave me to do my part. Now go do yours, Warlord."

So I left him treading the carnage of ground zero.

For fifty meters the broken bodies of the grievously wounded spread in a radius circumscribed by the protractor of a cruel mathematician. Peppered in with the bloody harvest and beyond, flocks of people milled like sheep caught in a lightning storm, their congealed masses clogging all avenues leading to safety. Unfortunately, our troops were having little success persuading the stunned crowds to spread and make the necessary space for landing zones, themselves having no choice to reach the ground but to drop from their low hovering craft.

Wading through the crowds like the colossus he was, Doug cradled a wounded woman. A tourniquet was applied high to her thigh and below her knee, little remained that resembled a leg.

"Make a hole. Coming through. Get the hell out of here!" He pushed his way through, aiming for Karlo's CCP.

I snatched one of the small red bags littering the street. Karlo called them speedballs. It had been at his insistence that all our vehicles were provisioned with the mini trauma kits, and they'd been thrown by the handfuls from the responding flitters.

Fizzle guns and K-specs didn't produce a lot bleeding—they burned things to a crisp—but we still used lots of sharp stabby things and good old-fashioned bullets as prime means of delivering violence.

Even on Mars, massive bleeding called for tourniquets and pressure dressings.

I pushed toward a pooling eddy in the human currents where two civilian men pivoted in place, pleading help from those around them with no effect. At their feet lay three bodies.

"I've got these two. You carry the last and follow me." I hefted a casualty onto each shoulder and checked behind me. The well-intentioned bystanders gathered the remaining casualty awkwardly by the arms and legs. There was no time to teach them different. I forced a path through dense crowds shifting and swirling in directions that took them nowhere useful.

As per everywhere—and I have two planets of experience to draw from—people are people. Some of the spectators had the instinct for self-preservation and hightailed it for safety, but the majority remained, as if the surrounding herd insulated them from further danger. Replacing those who'd successfully evacuated came two more sorts: the helpers and the gawkers. Of both, many had been drunk only moments before.

Traumatized and inebriated was a terrible combination of afflictions, regardless of the intent that drove them into the fray.

A familiar voice boomed over the plaza.

"I'll kill you all! I'll kill you all!"

Waving his sword and dagger overhead in theatrically large movements, Khraal Kahlees threatened the crowd with god-like menace, his thundering voice bouncing off the surrounding towers. He charged a stalled gathering.

"Scatter from here, or I will cut you down! Run!"

With wide-eyed screams, they took escape routes as divergent as the shrapnel of the IED. I'd been on the receiving end of Tarn doing likewise and damn near did the same getaway act myself. His method wasn't textbook, but it was effective.

Perfect solutions are the enemy of good enough.

Coming my way and headed back for more was Doug. "That's getting it done," he said, referring to Double-K. "Don't waste time on the finish line, dude. I've been over ground zero. No one's alive."

"I saw, but Cynar's there, doing his thing. Check on him, maybe," I said and kept moving.

Outside the casualty collection point, the troops were using techniques less successful than Double-K's to clear an LZ for the first medevac flitter, holding frozen at a hover because there was no place to set down. A Guard sergeant made stern pleas.

"Move aside and allow the aircar to land. We'll get everyone out, but first we must load the seriously injured and get them to the hospital. Move aside! Please!"

"Clear them the hell out," I yelled. "Whatever it takes."

The sergeant stiffened at recognizing me and nodded understanding. He brought his K-spec horizontal. "Like this, men." His Guards joined in pushing open a clearing and the first aircar set down.

Karlo waved to me from the door. "Bring 'em in, Ben."

I let him take a body off my shoulder and followed him inside. Restaurant tables were pushed to the walls and served as litters. Many wounded sat, grasping bleeding heads and appendages. My followers were relieved of their victim and, failing to find an empty surface other than the floor, I knelt and lowered the young woman I still carried.

She was covered in lacerations, but none had sprung into the gushers I checked for before hefting her onto my shoulder. Her eyes opened and before I could ask where she hurt, I was bumped aside by a trooper who started running hands over her limbs and trunk again to locate any bleeder that had been missed. Karlo had trained our army in the tactical combat casualty curriculum, and it had apparently stuck.

"The man you gave me's dead, Ben," Karlo said at my shoulder. "Go get me more."

Outside, the flitter loaded with the first of the stabilized casualties was lifting. Significant patches had cleared in the plaza thanks to Double-K. Combat aircars were finally landing to deposit more troops to carry out Dave's orders to further push people out of the city center.

But we were nowhere near the easy downhill part of this mountain hike.

Two competing likelihoods nagged at me like a yin and yang chasing each other's tail. The first—that somewhere from the towers around us —a murderer watched, satisfied the time had at last come to unleash the next IED. The second—that with every passing minute—it was also becoming less likely.

The probabilities were one in the same, until they weren't. Until an indeterminate number of minutes collected into the significant amount of time that put us past the IED that might, or would never, detonate.

It was from *Star Trek* and not Shakespeare where I learned that the future is an undiscovered country.

It was a place I very much wanted to visit.

We gathered the last of the wounded and dead. It may have been another hour. It may have been much less. I all knew was, the next IED didn't come. And from where we stood on the deck of Dave's command

and control flitter, in every unfortunate way, the scene below reminded me of a graveyard.

It was time. I opened my wrist link and in the cloud was Talis Darmon. She was clean and no longer the distraught mother I'd sent to the safety of the *Hope*.

"How is she?" I asked.

"Our daughter is perfect and unharmed, thanks to her aunt."

"Perrin Halser?"

"I do not know. I directed our black widow to fly him to Shansara."

Our small hypersonic ship would have him there in hours rather than the days of flight taken by any other conveyance.

"Who else is injured?" I'd seen a lot of blood on a lot of people I cared about.

"Keshin Tellest and Tranya Olan sustained lesser injuries, as well as one of Douglas Knoblock's companions. I am ashamed to admit I cannot keep their names in my mind. They are such kind and lovely creatures! That I have failed at such basic decency as it concerns someone as dear to us as Douglas Knoblock, it causes me grief."

This was the first time Doug's three companions had been invited along on a royal junket.

"This'll have them running for the hills next time we invite them to something, sweetheart."

She fell wearied. "Please do not make one of your jokes, husband. I cannot bear it."

"I apologize. How are you?"

"Stunned. Frightened. Relieved and thankful. Furious. Benjamin Colt, had your beast not stumbled, you would not be speaking to me now."

"But I am, and I'm fine. I'll be returning to the ship presently."

My wife hugged herself. "Benjamin Colt. Our daughter could have been killed. And those closest to us. Perrin Halser may be injured beyond repair or even dead. Who has done this foul thing? And why?"

"I'm going to figure it out, Talis Darmon."

She frowned, her eyes glaring razor sharp determination.

"Yes, Warlord. I know you shall. And then you will bring war to them. Return to us soonest, husband." She extinguished the cloud.

Dave stepped in now that I was done. "Just got off the cloud with Zaylin Twee. She's on the way with her people. She's anxious to talk to Cynar."

Zaylin Twee was the head of the Guard, the First Shield of the constabulary of our kingdom. She was a trusted friend and a part of our inner circle.

"Learn anything yet, Cynar?" I asked. I was still a little surprised by his bold move to spearhead the investigation before the dust and blood had even settled, but maybe I shouldn't have been.

I wasn't the same man I once was, either.

The old wizard's propensity for derision was gone. He'd taken on the persona of a grizzled homicide detective, consumed with finding the murderer, the heinous nature of the crime just so much rain beading off his trench coat.

"Precious little, Benjamin Colt. I have gathered all possible emanations but on first examination, nothing yet drives me to a useful conclusion."

Khraal Kahlees growled. "I have drawn a conclusion. This was a craven act. A desperate one. Its purpose seems clear—the death of Talis Darmon and her line. None but Mihdradahl's elite would benefit. Her pursuit of a new form of governance is as a blade to their throats. I would skin them one by one until they confessed their crime."

Dave shook his head. "Don't think so, brah. If that's what they wanted, they would've planted the bomb under the reviewing stand."

Cynar growled like a Tarn. "Incompetence is a characteristic common to most men, David Masamuni. Do not confuse results with intent."

"I'm tracking," Dave replied, "but I think Ben was their target. With him out of the way, the queen would be more pliable. That's what those last clowns who tried to kill Ben thought."

Doug spit on the ground. "The cojones on those chumps!"

In retrospect, the perpetrators of my nearly successful homicide by drowning had in fact been the most obtuse amongst the elites of the council. I still felt stupid how I'd blown off their constant barbs and disdain as being nothing more than hot air from stuffed shirts.

"I'm not ignoring Double-K's instinct that this could be the work of another cabal of aristocrats, but there's no one on the council giving off those kind of vibes."

Khraal Kahlees snarled. "Creatures whose sting holds the deadliest venom give no warning before their strike. But perhaps we overlook a foe even more obvious. Especially given where we are. The Mydreen are not extinct."

Though Khraal Kahlees truly hated the Mydreen, not even he could truly suspect the unfortunate remnants of their tribe had perpetrated this. Undoubtedly, small bands of able warriors still roved the vast deserts, but even so, any militant Mydreen wanting revenge was more likely to go berserker on a crowd of women and children using a pair of swords than he was to plant a bomb in one.

"I'm not sure we're on the right track, guys," I said. "We need to let Zaylin Twee do her thing. In the meantime, we do what we know. Security, security, security."

Dave said, "I've got foot patrols out everywhere in the city, but we all know that's mainly for show. I have an air and ground cordon in place around Filestra, but it's too little too late. The bomber's probably already escaped in the chaos, mixed in with everybody else who's hightailed it for home. We don't know even know who all was here, much less who's left. It's not like we got surveillance recordings to pour over. Zaylin Twee's people gonna have their hands full piecing this together, brah."

I had a grim thought. "The bomber could be on the *Hope*." If he'd been wounded in his own blast, he could have been inadvertently transported there.

"If a bomb got on board, it'd be worse than the USS *Cole*," Doug said.

A small boat had once made a suicide run at a US Navy ship in a foreign port, and the explosive results were no different than if a submarine had torpedoed the guided missile destroyer in an actual naval battle.

"Not to worry, brah. All casualties evacuated to the ship were run through a fine-tooth comb before being allowed below deck. And to make sure we didn't leave an opening for a bomber to get their shot at the grand prize by playing wolf hiding with the sheep, I've ordered that no uninjured civilians are to be allowed on the *Hope*."

"Talis Darmon's not going to like that," I said. "She'll want to offer haven to anyone who wants it."

"Then I'll take the heat and be the guy to tell her no, brah. We weren't prepared for anything like this. Gonna take us time to have all the measures in place we need for screening. Ain't enough to just order it. It's gotta be trained first."

As usual, he was right. "Spot-on, Dave. What else?"

"It was weird," Dave said. "I ran all this by Zaylin Twee. She pretty much rubber-stamped everything I was rolling out on the fly. Didn't have much to add."

"Probably because you'd already thought of everything," I surmised.

"I ain't so sure." Dave scratched the stubble that substituted for the beard he could never grow.

Meanwhile Doug was stroking his jaw, studying his feet, and making deep thought noises. Today was a kick in the balls, but after any good swift shot to the nuts, Doug always came back with double the hate aimed for whoever'd tried to show him some.

With a pang, I realized what had to be consuming him.

"Sorry, Doug. We can do this back on the *Hope*. I know you're concerned about... your girlfriend." I tripped on her name. I was about to ask which of his three companions got hurt when he gave a lopsided grin.

"S'okay, Ben-dog. I heard what Talis Darmon was frettin' about. Tell her no worries and no offence. We're private folks by choice, not necessity. Bandra Lang's fine. I've already talked to her and the girls. There's something else stewing in my kitchen."

"Spill, brah," Dave coaxed.

Doug was an easygoing giant. Like Dave—and like most all guys in SF—his analytical mind was always at work. But unlike every Ivy-leaguer, he had no need to constantly proclaim his intellect. He was a quiet professional who treated his many abilities like a pistol, concealed so well that not until drawn would anyone know it'd been there all along.

Doug gave his chin a final stroke before folding his tree trunk arms over a chest as wide as the Furrow was deep.

"Doesn't this bug you dudes as... being out of place?"

"Whatcha mean, brah?" Dave said, puzzled as I was.

"You were going there earlier, Davey-Dave. Like, how Mihdradahl's top cop isn't familiar with post-incident procedures for a terrorist bombing. We aren't cops, but we know the basics 'cause of who we used to deal with in the sandbox. Double-K, when's the last time there was a bombing like this?"

Khraal Kahlees shook his tusks. "I am unaware of a similar event, Douglas Knoblock."

Dave hmphed. "Can't ask Cynar. He was in a cave the last thousand years."

The old wizard looked unabashed. "That is true." Then he dropped the beat to his favorite mix. "And though isolated, in that time I built the greatest mind on Vistara. You have experienced a wealth of external stimulation since the day you hatched, and what has it brought you, David Masamuni? Have you apologized to she that laid your egg for the wasted effort?"

"All right, all right." I waved them both down, but I could sense Dave was readying his revenge.

See, we speak in a mixture—west coast surfer, hillbilly, mil-speak, correct English when appropriate, and more than ever, high Mihdra. When Dave asked Doug the next, he used pidgin.

"So wat da akamai ting you tink, brah?"

The deciphers hadn't heard enough of Dave's pidgin yet to translate it fully, leaving Dave his secret language—along with the occasional pig Latin he reserved for special occasions.

Dave did it because it infuriated Cynar, who balled his fists and shook with rage, just like the Cynar of old. The wizard's frustration brought an evil grin of satisfaction to his tormentor's face.

Doug translated, spoiling Dave's revenge. "Yo! What I'm thinking might not be smart, but here's what I got. This was an IED—stuffed with as much frag as a couple-dozen claymores. And it was employed *not* against a military target, but in a civilian venue full of touristas. *That* is undeniably a terror tactic."

I still didn't get what he was driving at.

"Obviously true, Dougie. And?"

Doug threw up his hands and shook his head. "Don't you get it? IEDs aren't in the local bag of tricks. That came out of a playbook written on *Earth.*"

✤ ✤ ✤

Doug continued laying out his case as we flew back to the *Hope.*

"Not my proudest moment, but when I was in charge of Thoria's defense, I laid in layers of claymores, JP-8 jellied with animal fat, pungi pits, toe-poppers—the Mydreen got a kick out of how devious and cruel it was. They'd never seen anything like it."

It was at the dawn of our history on Mars that my A-team suffered a schism. First, we lost our captain and team sergeant. Then our XO, the now deceased Brandon Bryant—the biggest piece of back-stabbing filth that ever lived—made a play to become the ruler of any and everything on our new permanent home.

With the Mydreen hordes as the fodder of his indigenous army and a warped faction of Mihdra troops, he'd nearly succeeded. But he spread himself and his army too thin. He just didn't have the competent help or the numbers he needed to pull off his try to become the Khan of a Martian Mongol Empire.

Plus, he never saw me coming until it was too late.

"It's no doubt we were sweatin' taking Thoria back, brah," Dave admitted. "We were expecting the worst. You're a wicked devious engineer."

Doug's expression looked pained as he recalled his dark days under Brandon Bryant's rule.

"We're all glad it turned out like it did, me most of all. But it's something I've pondered ever since. The Mydreen—we all know they aren't the most sophisticated bunch. At the time, I blew it off that the defense was just one more thing we had to teach them. But the Red army—heck, even when we were in Annameria and I saw how the Yellows did things—nothing I've ever seen about anyone else's methods and tactics has ever struck me as, well, as nasty as what *I* would do."

Khraal Kahlees bristled. "Do you bundle the Korundi in with your assessment of those fools?"

Doug blew him off. "I know you're just bustin' stones, Double-K."

The Tarn chuckled. "That I am, my Thulian brother."

"I get you, Doug," I said. "The Mydreen burned prisoners alive for fun. The whole dance of remorse thing the Yellows used was mainly a political tool to keep people in line. But no one we've tangled with so far has used a tactic as brutally sophisticated as an IED."

Dave said, "Someone's just figured out they need to go asymmetrical against us, 'cause there's no other kinda warfare that's gonna take us down."

Khraal Kahlees scoffed. "Lend this act no dignity by naming it warfare, David Masamuni. Rather name it villainy, and those who perpetrated it, dead men."

We settled onto the *Hope of Mihdradahl*.

She had a flat top, not unlike an aircraft carrier. We salvaged a goodly part of one of Bryant's death stars to build her. Cynar delivered on his promise to make something far more aesthetically pleasing. Her lines were beautiful, as though she could ride ocean waves as gracefully as she did the sky. But she was no speed demon. I'd compare her get up and go to that of a fully laden container ship on a trans-Pacific voyage from Seoul to Long Beach. If that.

Which was just one of the many issues vexing both Cynar and Karlo. It was difficult for either to admit that the Annamerians had built two craft much larger, and that they'd performed much better than our attempt with the *Hope*.

The cruise to Filestra was supposed to be as much of a shakedown as it was a show of the flag across my queen's kingdom.

We'd had delays on our way here, mysterious power fades when the *Hope of Vistara* literally stopped on a dime. Oh, there was no falling out of the sky or anything like that. The redundant failsafe to prevent that had been tested and tested again. But the force of the rays that provided propulsion simply dwindled at random times. Then, after remedy on top of remedy failed to put her under power again, she mysteriously resumed flight on her own without explanation.

It was a big hitch in our plans to start exploration into the unknowns of the Vistara we'd been teased with by a glimpse of the Whites' map system, the only real map of the planet we knew to exist.

So of course it malfunctioned and erased itself.

Ours was a world of mysteries.

Along with the *Hope*'s erratic propulsion, there were issues with the HVAC, random power fluctuations, and a waste management systems that sometimes made toilets reverse flow in geysers like Old Faithful.

We were no closer to becoming Martian Magellans than we were to getting a SeaWorld franchise on Vistara.

"Is Tranya Olan okay?" I asked Dave just before going separate ways below deck.

"I'm headed to the med bay, brah. She's still waiting her turn to get stitched up, her and Keshin Tellest."

"Do we know the casualty count?"

"Six riders at ground zero. Another thirty dead recovered from the immediate blast radius. Most of those were chest and head wounds—instantly fatal. The safety walls around the racecourse saved a lot of people, brah. There's about fifty severely wounded who got evaced here for treatment. More went to the local hospital. No idea yet how many minor injuries were sustained."

"And the wounded who went on to die afterward?" I asked, thinking about the man I'd carried to Karlo.

"Sorry I don't have an exact number yet, Ben."

His regret was unnecessary. "A thing like this—it takes time. Hey, it was another amazing job of command, bro. No one could've done better."

"Thanks. But you know who I was wishing was there?"

"I do." I purposefully hadn't said his name.

Kleeve Hartus was once the man we held in an esteem so great, his fall from grace was the bitterest of pills; a medicine concocted by Talis Darmon. "But that man doesn't exist anymore, Dave. He hasn't for a long time."

"I know, brah. Just sayin'." He yawned. Fatigue was catching up to him. And to me.

"Holler if you need me, Dave."

"Ditto, brah."

Outside the royal cabins stood two of my oldest friends. The older Sarkan Sell and the younger Jodal Jark both folded arms and bowed in the traditional manner of the Korund.

"Stand tall, brothers," I ordered.

"Warlord, we should have been at your side," Sarkan Sell said.

"It wasn't to be, and there was nothing you could've done anyway."

Jodal Jark expanded to his sternest position of attention. "All are things now past, Warlord. For what surely comes, it is best we be at your side."

Not being there to share in the danger and the opportunity to be useful afterward had injured their pride. I knew the feeling. And I knew how to restore their dignity.

"Get replacements up here and get some sleep. That's an order. At first light you're both with me." They saluted fist to chest in the manner of our army, and I left them.

Shasa Karin lay on the small settee in the cramped outer room. Space was a premium on the *Hope* and even the royal stateroom was not as large as a cheap room in a motor lodge.

She rose, giving no heed to my motion for her to remain reclined. "Warlord, are you well?"

"Fine. How are your sisters?"

"Their wounds were minor. They are feisty and ready to return to duty."

That made me grin. "Nothing minor about shrapnel. You all did an admirable job. I've never been prouder."

"Thank you, Warlord."

A good rule for leaders is to never give an order that won't be obeyed. If I sent her away, she'd just post herself in the hallway with the guards. So I gave her an order she could follow, one that came out as a reasoned suggestion.

"Remain, but get some sleep. Tomorrow's going to be a long day and despite your sister's insistence, they will *not* be back on duty. Are they awake?" I nodded to the bedroom.

"It is doubtful the queen sleeps," she said. "But the princess has made no sound in some time."

I eased the door open to find my wife awake, propped up in bed with little Shara held to her chest. Sweet noises whistled from her button nose. I moved to place her in the crib, but Talis Darmon shook her head and whispered, "Come lay with us."

"I'm filthy and bloody."

"Then hurry."

In minutes I was beside her and our daughter. "I don't want to wake her, but shouldn't we talk?"

My little girl made a sleepy giggle. I wondered what she dreamed of that amused her so. That's the gift of parenthood. How a child inspires curiosity, and a passion to mold the world around them into a reassuring embrace.

Today had been anything but that.

"My silly warrior, she is comforted by your voice, not disturbed by it. But more should wait, husband. Let us pass these few precious hours together as a family. For tomorrow, it is a queen and a warlord who rise to take to our fields of battle, you to yours, and I to mine. And together, we shall outwit and out fight any who threaten our peace."

Her eyes found mine and in them, fire.

"Any and every foe, Benjamin Colt."

03

The sun returned to a Filestra chastised and regretful for her attempt to transmute through merriment rather than the sacrifice Vistara preferred. The silence over the city was the sound of repentance. Save for soldiers saluting fist to chest as we passed their posts, the streets were empty.

Apache fell out of stride to sniff the uneven paving stones. His drive was no less pure than that of any intellectual—always in pursuit of that rarest tome which contained all the truths. He studied the remains of wisdom deposited on the ground, then trotted to rejoin. The nearer we came to the plaza, the closer to my side he stayed, eventually abandoning his compulsion to decipher scents. Whether he brushed my leg to reassure himself or me, he was not the happy puppy he usually was on a stroll.

The cool fountain rain no longer sang of life, restoration, and respite. Beneath the soft splashes permeating the empty plaza, I heard the faint voices of yesterday's violence. Felt the concussion, tasted the blood, meat, shit, and fear.

Near the misting fountain, Zaylin Twee beckoned, and we passed beneath the cordon to join her. Like the Waters of Persidia in Shansara, I'd witnessed how public fountains weakened wills and diverted to them even those on the most important business, teased by the satiation provided by even the tiniest hint of humidity. It was especially strong here, a phenomenon possible because of the greater miracle.

The curving exhaust pipes of the nearby air factory always reminded me of musical instruments designed by HR Giger. How the pipes twined around each other like vines of blue steel was almost organic. In the brief morning chill of first light, the vapor of atmosphere could be seen issuing from the trumpet mouths of the many tubes.

The First Shield of Mihdradahl saluted. Zaylin Twee could only have gotten here so fast by taking the black widow that had delivered Perrin Halser to Shansara. I held our few hypersonic craft in reserve for greatest need. A full flight from one of our two Black Bird squadrons would arrive by midday to carry out my order to return all of the royal party home—though I'd yet to tell Talis Darmon. She was asleep and holding our blissfully snoozing daughter when I crept out with Apache to meet Double-K, Sarkan Sell, and Jodal Jark.

I returned Zaylin Twee's salute, then took her wrists as she did mine in the crossed grasps of those who'd served together the way we had. "I'm glad you're here, First Shield. Any word on Perrin Halser?"

"Only that he was in the hands of the surgeons, Warlord. I have been otherwise occupied. We have only just commenced our inspection of the crime scene."

Three red-cloaked Guardsmen carefully picked through debris ringing the blast site.

"I have taken reports from those on duty during the incident. None were as proximate to the explosion as you, Warlord." She paused. "Save the two Guardians who now know all the answers but cannot reach us from the other side."

The Tarns joined me to cross arms over chest and bow to say, "A warrior now walks with his glorious ancestors in the underworld."

Though we'd demolished the underworld, old habits died hard. Our condolences accepted, I gave her my eyewitness rundown.

Khraal Kahlees said, "I have little else to add. Like most violence, it struck in the blink of an eye. Even with attention on the culmination of the competition from my high vantage on the reviewing stand, I saw nothing to presage the devastation that transpired just as the riders reached the finish."

Zaylin Twee's attention was over my shoulder, and she grimaced. "Warlord, would you please recall your pet?"

Apache was on ground zero, vacuuming the area with his snout. The nearest Guard tried to shoo him away to no effect. "Korundi, would you mind?"

Sarkan Sell and Jodal Jark were moving before I finished asking. They also dreaded the embarrassment to come if the big lunk away before he could roll in the grisly remains of an arkall or committed some other desecration on the site of the murdered.

But he did neither. With his nose held high, he followed a scent luring him on a winding course out of the blast area, all while ignoring Sarkan Sell and Jodal Jark who chased after him.

"Sorry, Zaylin Twee," I said.

"Think nothing of it, Warlord. It is unlikely the war hound would disturb any evidence, but there is a principle to observe."

"Of course."

"Warlord, I am anxious to learn of the Wizard Supreme's findings."

Khraal Kahlees snorted. "No more than he will be to impose his intellect on us all."

I thought not. Cynar had been extraordinarily humble since the incident. "I'm certain he's motivated for a respectful collaboration with your team, Zaylin Twee. He'll be at the morning meeting."

"Excellent," she said. "I also wish to request the services of Douglas Knoblock."

The look on my face brought her clarification.

"His expertise in energetic compounds and devices would be of great use in the investigation."

Like any great leader, Zaylin Twee knew what her organization knew, and knew what it didn't. When it seemed the army was soon to become a garrison force, Dougie had once expressed an interest in becoming a cop. But it turned out that the formation of an expeditionary unit attached to the *Hope* was challenge enough to keep him in desert fatigues.

"You'll find no one more capable, Zaylin Twee. See you on the *Hope* in an hour?"

"Until then, Warlord."

I looked for the rest of our party. "You see where they went, Double-K?"

"I did not."

"No time to look for them. We need to visit the TOC and catch up with Dave and Dougie before the big meeting." I thought of Sarkan Sell and opened my wrist link. "Where'd you go? We have to leave."

"Apologies, Warlord. The war hound leads us on a determined path eastward and out of the city. Benjamin Colt, if I did not know the loyalty of your gadron, I would think him undisciplined. But he lives to serve you. There is purpose to his obsession."

I hated to think he was just chasing after a meal. "All right. Sorry about this, guys. Stay with him and we'll pick you up when we're done with the morning report."

Back to the flitter and settled on the *Hope* again, we were soon in the tactical operations center where Dave and Dougie were at work with the staff. "Catch me up. Anything I need to know about?"

Dougie started. "A lot of folks set off for home during the night. The air and ground patrols have been collecting ID info so the cops can interview them later. Woulda made more sense if we'd sealed the city."

"It's a free kingdom," Dave said.

Doug continued. "Otherwise, nothing to report, Ben-dog. No one's seen anything suspicious. I've issued a FRAGO to maintain current operations."

"Right on, Doug. After the staff meeting, turn ops over to your second-in-command. Zaylin Twee's requested you join her investigation. She needs the help of the best demo man on Mars."

Dougie raised his eyebrows, intrigued. "Roger *that*. But I won't be gone long. I think I have a good idea how it was done, or I should say, that I *don't* know."

Doug had experimented with all sorts of Vistaran energetic materials, searching for local sources to substitute for our favorite explosive compounds. His efforts had produced some successes, but nothing to replace our old friend, C-4. Alfred Nobel's prize was funded by his penchant for explosive chemistry. Someday Mihdradahl might have a Knoblock Award.

Dave passed me a slate. "I've got the corrected casualty count from Karlo, brah."

The numbers were grim, larger than most any battle we'd fought against Green, Yellow, Red, or White.

"Karlo joining us?" I asked.

"You just missed him, brah. He's getting cleaned up now. He worked all night in the ship's hospital."

"Then we'll see him there. Let's be off."

The aft hold was an impressive sight, seeming especially vacuous with fully half of what was usually parked in her currently out and patrolling Filestra. A partial company of Kardan remained, our light armored ground hovers. Three sharply faceted tanks sat near, chained to the deck. Smaller fast attack sleds were on another side of the bay, along with the mobile ADA miniguns and mortar sleds. The arkall stables beneath this deck were empty, as all our cavalry were patrolling a perimeter around the ship.

In the center of the deadly storehouse, a long table had been set up. We were soon joined by the other invitees, including some members of the queen's council from Shansara—unharmed, but witnesses to the events viewed from their exclusive rented perches surrounding the plaza.

Beraal announced the queen and we all rose. Two of the trio of her personal guard displayed dressings on repaired arms and legs. There was just no forcing these women to rest. We took seats and I began.

"General David Masamuni is the critical incident commander. I would like him to brief us."

A single curt nod of royal approval and Dave proceeded.

"At approximately 14:32 yesterday, an explosive device was detonated in the central plaza. The epicenter of the blast was the finish line of the festival race. The nature of the device and how it was emplaced are yet to be determined, but it was constructed to produce a wide spread of fragmentation for purposes of wounding out to a great distance. To that, the current casualty numbers are contained on your slates." Dave indicated Karlo should speak.

He looked tired, but no more than usual. Karlo burned the candle at both ends as a way of life. He savored his Johnny-on-the-spot reputation, throwing himself at every problem in the kingdom, from military technology to aeronautical engineering to social science and of course, medicine, often simultaneously.

Karlo sat taller. "Treatment centers in Thoria, Clymaira, and Shansara are prepared to accept any patients the doctors prefer to transfer. There are currently six patients stable enough to transport."

"Have our hypersonic craft been sent for to act as transport?" the queen inquired.

I spoke up. "They're on the way, but I've ordered them here first to return you and the rest of the royal party and the council back to the capital for your safety."

She dismissed my plan. "Out of the question, Warlord. We will return together on the *Hope.*"

As gently as I could, I said, "That's a bad idea, Queen."

"Why is that, Warlord?"

We were getting out of order on the agenda, but it couldn't be helped. When she had a question, she received an answer. "I'm keeping the *Hope* here to act as my operations center. I'll be staying to coordinate the next phase of the investigation and to enable a prompt military response as necessary."

She wasn't having it. "I will remain to provide comfort to my people. I will visit the injured and their families, and demonstrate to all that the kingdom is strong and will never cower to an assault on our peace."

I chose my words carefully. "As I knew you would, Queen. After a visit to the victims currently on the *Hope*, it's our recommendation that for your safety, you return to the capital."

"Surely, I could not be in further danger surrounded as I am by the might of my army?" My wife tilted her forehead at me—our subtle body language that one thought the other was wrong, wrong-headed, or just plain dumb.

Dave took up my cause. "We don't know the full extent of the threat, ma'am. There's nowhere safer than the palace for you."

Talis Darmon shook her head. "So demonstrably untrue, David Masamuni. The touch of an assassin has nearly succeeded there, as you well know."

"Past history, Talis Darmon," I said.

Shaera Kōall made a seated bow and turned her palms upward in a most formal feminine manner. The aristocrat was from a family line similar to my wife's—born and bred to lead and even rule if so chosen. With platinum blonde hair and skin the shade of ashen rose petals, she was as light as my wife was dark, as fair as any Vistaran I'd ever seen. Enough so that it'd made me wonder if there were cosmetic treatments involved in achieving such perfectly pinkish skin. I once made the mistake of asking my wife about it.

"Why do you ask, husband? Do you find her appealing? Would you wish me to undergo such modification were it available? Hmm?"

Yikes! Teasing or not, I had to back out carefully before the teeth of this bear trap snapped shut.

"I would sooner have my eyes burned out than see you changed in any way. Then the picture of your perfection would be frozen in my mind's eye forever."

An approving smile told me I'd backed off the trigger plate in time, leaving it securely cocked for my next haphazard misstep. "Good answer."

Thus my innocent curiosity about the nature of Shaera Kōall's appearance remained unsatisfied.

The blonde aristocrat raised her narrow chin high and joined her palms over her heart.

"Queen Talis Darmon, please allow me to carry your beneficence to those laid low by this tragedy. I would be honored to spread your message of comfort, though I cannot hope to radiate the empathy you so genuinely shower on our people."

The council had always had its share of puffed up elitists, but since the day the Whites landed a surprise jab on our nose—followed by the Annamerians' hard right cross—we'd gotten some better corner men in our ring. The chambers of Talis Darmon's advisers included many more like Shaera Kōall, acting with an intention to serve the kingdom, rather than the other way around.

It was a refreshing change from prior councils.

I said, "I think it's a good idea. Don't you think that's a good idea? Take Shaera Kōall up on her offer. Please." Except I said it all to my wife via telepathic wave, a microwave-burst transmission sent through the delicate plea in my eyes.

Talis Darmon was an intuitive genius. She took every factor into consideration in seconds and always came up with the right call to balance her personal desires with her many duties—made more complex than ever now that she was also a mother.

"I would be grateful for you to do so in my name, Shaera Kōall. Thank you. Warlord, the plan for my visit to the infirmary followed by our return to Shansara is acceptable. But I insist the wounded are transported first."

With that settled, I moved us back on track. "I've ordered a heightened security posture across the kingdom. But until we have a more concrete target on which to focus our deterrence, it really means little more than increasing the visible presence of both the army and the Guard."

"A reasonable precaution," said the queen. "Is there no indication who this undeclared enemy may be?"

Zaylin Twee addressed this. "There are possibilities among the many bad actors known to us, Queen. However, the method of this attack is unlike any used previously by those malefactors. It represents a new tactic against peace and order."

My wrist link buzzed. I ignored it, until it buzzed again. I stepped away from the table, surprised and a little irritated to see Jodal Jark.

"We're almost done. We'll pick you up soon."

Jodal Jark was gravely serious. "Warlord, I do not abandon good sense to make communication brazenly. Sarkan Sell begs you come. He believes he has located critical information."

"So? Tell me!"

"Warlord, Sarkan Sell asks you bring Khraal Kahlees and meet us in the eastern desert. It is necessary."

Korundi were stoics and used few words, but he was holding back. Why? I could only guess that he didn't know the reason for the summons either. But if Sarkan Sell insisted on pulling us out of this meeting, I'd be a fool to ignore his request. His wisdom and rectitude were peerless among all races.

"On our way."

All eyes were on me. "Khraal Kahlees and I must evaluate a developing situation. Please continue without us." I moved to whisper to Talis Darmon. "Sweetheart, I'll try and return as soon as possible, but please take Shara and Beraal and go back to the capital on the first black widow."

Beraal leaned close. "It is best, Talis Darmon. Our counsel in this matter is correct."

She relented. "Yes, Warlord Benjamin Colt. Yes, Dosenie Beraal Kahlees."

I piloted the flitter, following Jodal Jark's directions to take an azimuth straight into the morning sun. After ten minutes and many klicks of flight, we picked the trio out amongst the desolation of the red sands.

Apache wagged his tail at sight of me, but stayed in place beside Jodal Jark. In a reversal of roles, the older Korundi was down on his knees and hands as I'd never seen another Tarn. He pressed his nose to the ground and breathed deeply, then sprinkled a pinch of sand onto his tongue like salt. He spit, then crawled to another spot before doing it again.

"What's he doing?" I asked Double-K.

"He is old," was all Khraal Kahlees gave for explanation.

We trudged through loose sand to where Jodal Jark and Apache intently watched Sarkan Sell at work. Khraal Kahlees broke the silence.

"What is it, old man?"

When the Korundi called someone old, it was not out of derision. The title recognized the honor due to one who had grown old in a tribe where most did not. To be called old conferred recognition their longevity came by qualities acquired, not the inheritance of good genes.

Sarkan Sell kneeled.

"There is spoor here. I ask that you evaluate it yourself, Khraal Kahlees. Perhaps you better remember the traditional ways. This one, I have failed to educate."

Jodal Jark flushed with embarrassment, his skin blushing a dark green. "It is true. Though I can follow month -old godahl trail trodden across a stony range, I detect naught here."

"So Apache *is* on to something?" I asked. I'd secretly wished we'd been called for just this reason.

My boy barked and wagged his big round butt, pleased his accomplishment was credited.

Sarkan Sell swept an arm across the desert horizon. "Tell me, Khraal Kahlees, what does the greatest warrior of the Korund sense?"

Double-K bristled. This was a challenge. And he took all challenges seriously. "You have tromped these sands mercilessly. I will make my own judgment."

Sarkan Sell grunted approval. "Do so."

Ten minutes passed. We waited patiently, permitting Double-K the space he asked for. He paced careful cloverleaf courses, dissecting the sands with his gaze, lowering frequently to test choice spots as the elder Korundi had done. He placed his lower hands on his hips as he spat the most recent sample away and returned.

"My skill is weak in comparison. You alone know the way to hear shadows, old man. I find nothing."

Sarkan Sell thrust his tusks forward. "I take no pleasure in shaming either of you. Come here, hatchlings. I will put you on to the spoor."

We followed behind as he led us to a patch of layered sands blown in shallow terraces by the rare winds from how long ago, no one knew. The desert's dead calm was rarely interrupted—thank God—by the massive dust storms the Tarn called Sand Blasters, because being caught in one could remove skin.

I thought of my teammate Matt, as fine a mantracker as there'd ever been. He would've loved this, and begged to learn an art so arcane not even Khraal Kahlees was its master. Sarkan Sell knelt. "Come here, both of you. Take it in fully to reach your deepest senses."

Both obeyed. After several committed efforts to extract something of value by nostril or tongue, Jodal Jark was the first to stand and admit defeat. "Still nothing, old man."

Khraal Kahlees frowned. "It is there, but so faint I cannot name it."

Lofting a single finger, Sarkan Sell lectured as if he were the chair of philosophy at Cambridge. "The eye sees only what the mind knows. The senses stir memory only of that which it has experienced. Though this gadron knows not what left this trace, I give him great credit. He at least knew it among the many scents of the city as one that did not belong. It was not until we removed ourselves far from the constructions of Filestra that I myself could sense it."

Sarkan Sell scratched Apache's neck, who showed appreciation by producing happy slobbers and wagging his stubby curled tail.

I'd strained my eyes over every square centimeter of terrain and saw not even a scribble left by a vereen—the rats found most everywhere on Vistara. "What?" I begged, bubbling with anticipation.

Sarkan Sell made his reveal. "It is the Pale."

The diesel engine rumble from deep within Double-K's chest gave me goosebumps.

"Sarkan Sell is correct, Warlord. I should have suspected. The Mydreen may be gone, but as it is ever so, the void left by one extinguished vermin is soon filled by another.

"The disease of the Vermeel have returned from eradication."

✠ ✠ ✠

Loaded back on the flitter, I paused before firing it up for the return. Instead, I kick-started a different machine—one I had faith in like I did Mom, the Stars and Stripes, or an M4 with a freshly lubed bolt carrier. The Team Round Robin. One of the defining elements that put the "special" in Special Forces. It's an open and free exchange of ideas as alien to the regular army as the four-arm men beside me are to Earth.

"This is all very interesting, but how could the Vermeel be connected to what happened? I thought they were some kind of aboriginal Tarn more primitive even than the Mydreen."

Sarkan Sell said, "The Vermeel are that, and more. I have witnessed the Pale practice cruelty to make even Mydreen take note. This craven act carries the stink of the Pale."

Double-K turned the tables on me. "As you yourself have oft observed, Benjamin Colt, there are no coincidences."

"I do say that, Double-K, but I may have only ever used the shortened version around you. The full saying goes, 'once is happenstance, twice is coincidence, three times is enemy action.'"

I'd learned that one in the SF Operations and Intelligence Course, and it's always served me well. It's funny how in any advanced field, the hundreds or thousands of hours of didactics and study so often boil down to some short aphorism that permanently lodges in your midbrain. An MBA reduces to 'Buy low, sell high.' Years of a doctor's training in dermatology condenses to, 'If it's wet, make it dry; if it's dry, make it wet.'

And I guess the PowerPoint slide with that quote from Ian Fleming had the same staying power for me.

Double-K thought it over. "Then I prefer the simpler version, Benjamin Colt. I need no further analysis to judge whether or not this is coincidence. And it is irrelevant, because regardless, we must answer—why now do the Pale reappear?"

He had me there. "Agreed. Say, why do you call them 'the Pale'?"

Jodal Jark snorted. "Even a hatchling knows. Their skin is a ghastly shade of death, much like a..." He hesitated.

"A Thulian?" I finished for him.

The young warrior cocked his tusks to one side. "Forgiveness, Warlord. The Vistaran sun has rendered you and my Earth brother's skins nearly indistinguishable from that of any Mihdra. I thought to make comparison to the Whites of the underworld."

Sarkan Sell shot him down. "You have seen neither Pale nor White for yourself, hatchling. You remain strong as an arkall and twice as smart, Jodal Jark."

Moe slaps Larry, Larry slaps Curly. Double-K was still a little embarrassed by Sarkan Sell making light of his tracking skills, and took the tag to heap some more on the junior-most of our inner circle. "Silence is always a choice. Use it more frequently, hatchling, and it will serve to make others think you smarter than you are."

I felt for Jodal Jark. He'd been taking a lot of abuse today for being the youngest. "In that case, I'm a hatchling too, brothers, because I did no better. Let's get back to the *Hope* and you can school the rest of the staff."

I'd no sooner lifted us and turned for the city when Jodal Jark cried out, "Movement on the sands!"

I snapped to look sternward. Jodal Jark pointed northeast to the tiny protrusions that were the farthest eastern peaks of the Korund range, barely poking above the horizon. I brought us around to the bearing he indicated and squinted.

"I see nothing," Double-K said.

Shading his eyes, Sarkan Sell squinted. "Nor do I."

"What are we looking for?" I said.

Jodal Jark said, "It is a rider."

Khraal Kahlees made a strained scan of the horizon, growled, then chuckled at his own failure. "It seems I must twice today admit a paucity of skill."

Sarkan Sell also made the wet cough of an embarrassed Tarn. "My years have brought me experienced skill, yet have lost me faculties. You have both the eyes *and* the sight of the hunter, Jodal Jark."

The Korundi were just like an A-team. They busted stones on the reg but also doled out recognition when it was deserved. And they knew when to rub it in. Jodal Jark sang in tones as melodious as a Tarn could achieve, "I take no pleasure in embarrassing my elders. It is a rider. I am certain."

"Keep me on course," I said, vectoring the rays. It was several minutes until I was able to pick out the black dot on the horizon, but it was still too tiny for my human eyes to resolve into anything.

"It is not an arkall," Double-K pronounced.

"Perhaps a sōkoon?" Jodal Jark said.

That was a new one to me. "Is it the Vermeel?" I asked.

Sarkan Sell chuckled condescendingly. "The Pale do not travel by day, nor mount sōkoon."

The old man sucked in a breath. "Forgive my bad manners, Warlord. You are a son of the Korund as true as any and a master of this land. But all are young compared to me when it comes to knowledge of the Vermeel. I may be the last remaining Korundi to have spilled their blood."

"It's okay, Sarkan Sell. Keep schooling me."

Staring straight ahead, Khraal Kahlees spoke with certainty. "It *is* a sōkoon. From the Veil of Seriata the rider must travel."

From deep in mines older than all the kingdoms of Oceania, the Veil of Seriata was the source for the stones we depended on for the rays stored within. Where the eastern Korund range dwindled into the endless wastes of the east, they dug gems of aesthetic value, the stones that powered our machines, and other useful minerals and metals.

I'd never been there.

All I knew was, every six months a barge with a hold stuffed full of our goods traveled to the Veil, then returned with a greatly smaller volume of treasures from the mines.

The Veil was not a part of the kingdom, but an independent polity. In the Veil were craftsmen of the highest order. They produced great riches, yet the society of miners lived in seclusion. They allowed no visitors nor did they travel from their domain. They harnessed few of the rays stored in the stones they mined, but were said to live in splendor.

And it seemed a member of their clan was aimed at reaching Filestra.

I'd only been playing devil's advocate earlier. Chiseled on my tombstone would be, "There are no coincidences."

This sojourner was part of a bigger picture we could not yet see.

I circled slowly over the rider halted on the strange animal, and set us down lightly. It's hard to make a true determination about the size of a man mounted on a large beast, but he struck me as short. From head to toe, he was draped in a costume as wispy white as the cheese cloth from my mom's cupboard. His knotted forearms sported geometric tattoos of silver and gold that disappeared up his wide sleeves. Very unlike the Vistarans I was accustomed to, his rough face was bearded.

The animal he rode was covered in curls like a poodle fresh from the groomer. Its head reminded me of a camel, but the rest of it was feline, especially its long tail. And of course, it walked on eight legs. The tack was woven, and small colored gems dangled from the shag trim skirting the saddle and bridle. These people prized their animals.

"I'll go meet our visitor," I said, and hopped off.

"He bears a sword and rifle, Warlord," Double-K said. "If he comes with challenge, allow me to accept."

A mistake repeated more than once is a choice. And I believed in learning from the mistakes of others. I'd watched my team sergeant and captain make a mistake they couldn't recover from. I never made the same, nor would my curiosity lull me into any kind of complacency now. "I know how the game's played, Double-K. But I don't think this guy's riding through the desert looking for a throw-down."

Nevertheless, I put a hand on my pistol to make sure it was where it was supposed to be and set off. As I neared, the man pulled a fold of his headdress across his large nose, leaving me a face of only deep set blue eyes to address.

"I'm Benjamin Colt, Warlord of Mihdradahl." I held my open hand high as I spoke—my non-dominant hand, that is. "You've come a long way. Am I correct that you come from the Veil?"

The rider clucked his tongue twice and his sōkoon bowed and folded its legs. The man's gossamer clothing billowed as he dismounted with a graceful swing over the creature's bent neck. I'd been right, he was short. The top of his head barely came to my chest, but he was as broad across the shoulders as Doug.

"I am Trayver Lomal. I come from the Veil with a message of urgency."

I speak Mihdra like a native (or so my wife says), though in private Beraal corrects my grammar endlessly. His language was foreign to my ears, and I understood him only by the decipher on my arm.

"Welcome to Mihdradahl. How may I be of service?"

My new acquaintance grumbled, "Curse not speaking Mihdra, as foul to the ear and tongue as it is." He pointed to my bicep. "Do you understand me?"

When I nodded, he gestured toward the flitter and asked, "Since you are in company of Korundi, does that mean I have found the Mihdra who now occupy Filestra? I come to seek the assistance of any who would show friendship to the Veil in our hour of need."

I made my big dumb nod again. "On behalf of Queen Talis Darmon, I offer every possible assistance."

The man grew gruff, not at me, but in frustration at his predicament. "I do not understand you, though hearing the name Talis Darmon tells me I have met a subject of her land."

I yelled back over my shoulder. "Do any of you speak his language?"

Khraal Kahlees answered. "We do not, Benjamin Colt, but you know one who does."

Of course! It was my turn to mumble a curse. I had my wife's face in the cloud in an instant. "Sweetheart, is Tranya Olan with you?" I could've called her directly, but this was killing two birds with one stone. "We've come across an emissary from the Veil of Seriata, headed for Filestra to seek our help. Our communication is one-way because he doesn't have a decipher."

Talis Darmon's eyebrows lifted. "Most interesting. Yes, husband, Tranya Olan is right here."

The stout man perked up. "Did I hear you speak name of Tranya Olan?" The way he pronounced her name was not how it sounded in Mihdra, but still recognizable.

The diminutive woman I often compared to a Tasmanian Devil stepped beside my wife. The visitor parted his headdress. Tranya Olan's eyebrows raised like my wife's had.

"I know you, Trayver Lomal, elder cousin." Her speech matched that of the traveler; guttural in an almost Germanic way, but spiced with a touch of Hindi lilt and topped with something approaching the rolling R's of the Scots.

"And I you, Tranya Olan, departer though you may be."

Tranya Olan turned sour. "Are you not departer yourself, hypocrite?"

"Tame yourself for once, child, and give service."

What's the story here? I wondered. For a guy seeking help, he was being an unapologetic dick to the only person who could speak his brand of babble. He returned the long headscarf across his face.

"We are two full cycles of the moons from the arrival of the next trade ship, and I leave the Veil and risk uncleanliness to deliver an urgent message. An old enemy has come hidden in darkness, bearing intent most murderous and breaching our defenses in ways unheard of. It is for that reason I have accepted exposure."

"Let me guess..." I started.

Khraal Kahlees gave me as much of an "I told you so" as I'd ever heard.

"Benjamin Colt, it would seem the Vermeel are now thrice evidenced. Enemy action it is."

04

We set off for the Veil with a company of troops from the *Hope* along for the ride. Our emissary demanded his flitter be empty save the pilot. It was the "uncleanliness" thing again. On Mars I'd navigated friendly and unfriendly relationships with a half-dozen groups, both human and not. I feel justified in saying my success in cross-cultural communication would be required reading in the SF Qualification Course.

But this guy was nothing like the crabby but loveable dwarves from the movies.

His attitude was wearing my sense of nobility thinner and thinner, and soon, I'd be rubbed raw to the bone. Whether he was a germaphobe, a racist, both, or something entirely different, for the sake of mission success I was trying to accommodate him.

"Best I can do is let Tranya Olan accompany you with General David Masamuni piloting."

He thought it over. "With my mount along for comfort, I accept."

"Sorry. A combat aircar won't accommodate your animal for such a long journey. He can be returned to you in the Veil at some point."

He spat his disgust. "Keep him."

I should've expected our uncleanliness would irredeemably taint even an animal. We were all very curious about what to expect once we arrived in the Veil of Seriata, but Tranya Olan volunteered very little, with my direct questions producing not much more. Finally, she testily painted a picture as undetailed as one of my stick figure renderings.

"You have seen holes in the ground before, Benjamin Colt. The people who populate it are similar."

I knew to leave well enough alone, for now.

Our mass formation of troop-laden combat flitters made us a cloud of wasps with more stingers than Carter's got liver pills. We flew close along the dizzying peaks of the Korund, following their range eastward. After two long days the mountain chain tapered lower and lower, indicating we at last neared the Veil.

Concerned his medical skills might be needed, Karlo volunteered to come along, and it'd given us more time together than any time I could remember since our first months on Mars. We reminisced about good and bad times on Earth and Mars, about armies, about life. We experienced the dawn and he pointed to the distant mountaintops.

"I'm old enough to remember when asking someone for directions meant writing it all down like your life depended on it," he said.

I laughed. "Where I come from, that always came with help like, 'Turn left when you see the house with the fallen tree. Not the one with the Chevy up on blocks; the one with the Ford.'"

Karlo kept reminiscing. "Heck, remember when being able to print directions from a website was a huge leap forward. GPS? Forget about it. I'd settle for a good ol' dependable compass and Universal Transverse Mercator map."

"If only compasses worked on Mars," I complained, not for the first or last time. "We've never asked Cynar if he could do something on a grand scale to duplicate a magnetic north for us."

My friend gave me "the forehead" in a big way.

"I know it sounds ludicrous, Karlo, but with Cynar, you never know."

More than once the old wizard had pulled off some totally inconceivable miracle, then berated us all for either doubting him or not thinking of it ourselves.

"Not to mention you," I continued. "You've made things once possible on Earth possible on Mars. Or even better! Like our K-specs and the black widows!"

Karlo rolled his eyes. "We don't need a new Ellesmere Island to be a magnetic north for us, Ben. I'm probably not that far away from being able to launch satellites and create our own GPS."

My eyes nearly popped out of my skull. "SAY WHAT? If you can do that, can you build us a satellite to do photo reconnaissance? Map Vistara from space?"

Karlo's grin turned into a wince. "Sorry, Ben. Our best bet's to stick to the plan to use the black widows for high-altitude recons of the images I saved from the Whites' map system. Then it'll be exploration time for the *Hope*. If we ever get her running right." He waved the annoyance away like a horsefly and returned to my question.

"When I said satellites aren't that far away, I mean probably ten years or more—if I work on it exclusively—and that's just to get something about as sophisticated as the first Sputnik into orbit. I'm thinking that an inertial guidance system for navigation is probably closer to a near-term reality. It'll still require navigating between known points—because it's basically dead reckoning—but it'll be way more accurate than relying on what we pried away from the navigator guild."

The kingdom we fought to win for Talis Darmon was one largely incurious about the rest of Vistara. Karlo identified it as a symptom of the societal malaise that was part of the world's decay. With no magnetic pole, navigation was mainly celestial—which restricted reasonably accurate long-distance travel to night—combined with some form of rate calculation. It was all dead reckoning at its most basic. Go in a direction at a steady rate for a set period of time, look for the landmarks (if there were any), and if you missed your destination—it was no different from messing up the directions Granny gave you to her second-cousin's niece's holler where the butchered hog was waiting to be picked up. Ask someone or backtrack and figure out where you went wrong.

Traveling *really* long distances was not so different than it was when Columbus searched for a route to Asia. Okay, maybe not quite that bad. In the army we made extensive use of aerial and ground scouts to make sure our main force was always heading where it was supposed to—still, hardly better than the way American Civil War armies bumbled around. When we retook Pyreenia, staging for our invasion was half the battle. The other half—killing the squid -god who ruled it. I won't recount the whole thing; I'm just pointing out how something taken for granted like accurate maps and a way to follow them is a really big deal when you don't have them.

The roads joining a Roman empire that spanned continents lasted for millennia. Mihdradahl's borders spread over an area we judged to be larger than North America, but the system that once joined all parts of our kingdom vanished in neglect about the time Roman road builders laid their first brick.

The navigator guild charted the way for the trade barges that flew back and forth to Annameria—many days' flight across the vast canyon known as the Furrow of the Creator's Hand—and also to all the rest of the kingdom and the Veil. The guild hired out navigators to all ships carrying goods or passengers, but not to the army or Guard. We had our own charts and navigation methods, but none were as accurate as what it seemed the guild used.

Because things were dull and looking like maybe they'd be that way permanently, Dave assigned himself the mission to investigate the why behind our predicament of efficient navigation. Davey-Dave knew how to build an agent net and in no time had our answer. Navigators are sailors. Sailors congregate in bars. Bars attract all sorts of service providers. Among them are those who not only take bribes, but some of them are downright patriotic.

When she heard, the queen blew her top, same as me.

The guild had a secret system of landmarks and hyper-accurate sailing directions, the Vistaran equivalent of the nautical rudders of the Portuguese explorers who were the envy of the Old World. And the guild's handbook had a permanent distribution list of no one, most particularly to our armed forces.

What really galled us? It meant that every time the queen made a plea to all citizens to pitch in during any one of several war efforts, the navigator guild had chosen to keep their secrets secret. When she called them on it, they took the traditional route—they played dumb.

Her recourse? Me.

If you'll forgive my lapse into a French I don't even speak, existential problems are my raison d'être and joie de vivre all rolled into one. She was still regent, and reserved her option to take the direct route without involving the courts. I was sent as her representative to... negotiate. I'll let your imagination do the rest. They taxed my patience, but I did not resort to violence. Okay, there was a little violence, but it involved a demonstration on inanimate objects.

I got what I came for.

Later, I apologized and sent a fruit basket.

But recently, a new wrinkle sprang up to make me believe the affair wasn't totally smoothed over. Someone was sabotaging the queen's project to rebuild the archaic marker system that once guided efficient routes between all the cities of her kingdom. Catching red-handed whoever was toppling the obelisks was proving elusive. At the top of my list of suspects—you got it—the navigators. Zaylin Twee's people were on it, but there are few cops and Mihdradahl's a big place.

I made a mental note to pay a visit to the guild house in the not too distant future.

Problems, problems, problems. Being Warlord's no picnic.

My wrist link buzzed and from the lead flitter Dave's face appeared in the cloud. "Tranya Olan says we're about two hours out."

"We should launch the CAP," I said. It wouldn't be much of a combat air patrol as we didn't have fighters per se, but we'd be detaching gunships from our flight to scout for opposition. Khraal Kahlees was running things back in Filestra from the *Hope*, so he wasn't here to scoff at the idea the Vermeel could have flitters. Trayver Lomal hadn't been able to tell us who'd raided the Veil, but whether or not it was the boogeymen Vermeel, the fact that, like in Filestra, they'd left virtually no trace in my mind made them the prime suspect.

"I'll give the launch order, Ben-dog. Oh, brother! Are you hearing this?" He canted his wrist. I was still waiting on the backstory to explain why Tranya Olan and her kinsmen played North and South Korea at the same table. Like with Double-K, Dave had expanded Tranya Olan's vocabulary, and she was employing her full repertoire.

"Feast on a platter of the unshaven scrotal sacks of your brothers!"

Trayver Lomal's exasperation tented the gauze covering over his mouth. "As if there were any other kind! Even when casting insults, you reveal your total lapse into degeneracy."

She spat back. "Xenophobe!"

He scowled. "I do not know the meaning, but as I am of a vastly superior culture, I choose not to take offense. That is the difference between you and I."

"Hey! Knock it off!" I yelled. "We're coming over." Soon enough, Karlo and I were on the deck with them. The emissary from the Veil remained at the bow's peak, the spot most distant from us he could be unless he grew wings. An embarrassed Tranya Olan stood beside Dave.

"Apologies, Warlord. I am a poor diplomat. I strive to serve you and the queen, yet Trayver Lomal taxes my ability to remain civil."

"You're doing fine," I assured her. "I was speaking to him when I yelled, not you. For a guy who says he's desperate for help, your kinsman's a jerk. What gives? This is more than a personal beef. I know you don't like talking about it, but it's past time you spill. What's waiting for us in the Veil?"

Tranya Olan was a loyal friend, but I'd been patient long enough.

"It will be challenging, Benjamin Colt. Trayver Lomal was sent by the Seniority of Twenty. They are indeed desperate for help, but my people are difficult. The first citizen of the seniority is the very embodiment of that character."

"Why are they seeking our help then?" Karlo asked.

Tranya Olan explained. "The seniority always preferred the protection of Mydreen mercenaries to protect themselves from the Vermeel or other bands of Mydreen raiders. With the long absence of the Vermeel and now the Mydreen's depletion, the Veil has been blanketed by the peace brought by your hand. Until now."

"They don't have a standing defense force?" I asked, already picturing a polity that preferred new shag carpeting in their offices over spending to maintain a homespun army.

"The seniority has never permitted a citizen army for fear of an armed populace. My family have been constabularies of the Veil for many generations. As debtors, they are prevented from election to the seniority, so their views that the constabulary is poorly equipped and too small are irrelevant."

There was a lot to dissect in that.

"I get it, Tranya Olan. They're left without choice but to pinch their noses and beg help."

"Though they ain't exactly begging," Dave put in.

Tranya Olan saddened. "Serians perceive an exalted status conferred by their wealth. It drives the arrogance of the Veil. When Keshin Tellest once explained how she navigated the Annamerian culture, she inadvertently revealed her pride in the deception and obtuseness permeating all interactions there. It is with shame I expose my people's ways to you."

"You're not your people," Dave said, beating me to it.

She smiled a smile she could not have known was a perfect copy of the Mona Lisa's. "Thank you, David Masamuni. I know I am seen by even my closest friends as secretive about my past, and you especially have been accepting and patient about my reluctance to speak of my adolescence in the Veil. Better than any explanation on my part, this experience will bring you understanding of how it is I came to serve the Guard of Mihdradahl."

05

From his self-sequester at the flitter's bow, Trayver Lomal scowled at the four of us. "We arrive. Have you informed them of the protocols, Tranya Olan? The seniority will rightly take insult if they are not observed."

"Tell him I got his protocols hanging," Dave said in USA English.

Tranya Olan used Mihdra to exclude her cousin. "Warlord, may I offer guidance as how to proceed?"

"I've been waiting for just that, Tranya Olan."

Her eyes twinkled. "Today, the obstinance I was taught in the Veil will be a gift returned in kind." She switched back to her birth tongue. "Respect will be given, elder cousin. And respect *will* be shown to the Warlord of Mihdradahl, or my counsel shall be to depart and allow the Veil to resume reliance on pride as its sole shield."

Trayver Lomal huffed and turned his back.

I gave her a wink. "That was almost diplomatic. Talis Darmon's rubbed off on you."

Dave beamed with pride. "She's the total package, Ben-dog. Brains, brawn, beauty, and bullshit."

Tranya Olan smirked. "Only one of those did I develop by association with you, David Masamuni."

I wasn't expecting to arrive at the grand entrance to their mystical city to find an ocean of banner-waving citizens, but this was underwhelming. We lowered over a desolate valley floor where a graded road vanished into a snaking canyon. Tranya Olan held up a fist to halt our descent.

"No, Trayver Lomal. This is the service entrance. Unacceptable. The Warlord of Mihdradahl will enter by the Platinum Bridge or not at all."

The dwarf sputtered as if he'd inhaled a June bug. "The Platinum Bridge you say! To be admitted into the Veil of Seriata is already the greatest of honors. It has been an age since the Platinum Bridge has welcomed any."

In Earth terms, an "age" referred to a period of a lengthy human life span, roughly the eighty to one hundred years which eventually became the unit of measure we called the century. Translated to Vistaran terms, an age represented about five centuries. In other words, Tranya Olan was insisting we make them roll out the red carpet in a manner fit for the history books.

She turned to me but spoke her native tongue. "We should return home, Warlord."

"Sounds good," I said, helicoptering a finger in a sign language even a feline-riding Martian miner could intuit.

He correctly sensed we weren't bluffing.

"Do not leave!" He voiced more objections, not quite resorting to beg, until our unanimous silence weakened his resolve. "On your behalf, I shall make the case for the welcome you request," he sighed out in defeat. I gave Dave the thumbs down, and we landed.

Tranya Olan instructed him one last time. "Elder cousin. This is not a negotiation. Tell the seniority."

Trayver Lomal huffed off and disappeared down the canyon road.

Karlo watched him go. "The Mydreen weren't as difficult to deal with."

"You got eyes on him?" I asked Garlak Ranz, captain of our ground force, still airborne with the rest of our sortie.

"Yes, Warlord. The trail is not lengthy. He passed into the mountain by a well-concealed entrance."

Much sooner than I expected, our emissary reappeared. Back on the flitter, his dejected manner gave off the stink of someone fresh from an ass-chewing.

"You know the way, Tranya Olan. We go." He turned to hide his sulk.

Dave set our course into the mountains and I opened an all-units channel.

"Garlak Ranz, drop foot patrols where you see fit. Tranya Olan says there's not much of an LZ, so it'll be just our party setting down and entering the city. CAP leader, stay on mission. We'll make contact every ten. No change to the five-point contingency plan. Out."

A twisting course through steep passes did not bring us to what I'd envisioned for the entrance to the realm of a people living in a fabulously rich mountain mine, and it sure wasn't constructed from any precious metal. A narrow stone bridge spanned the chasm between sheer mountain cliffs, and as unfriendly an ellipse to tread across as the St. Louis arch. The only available spot to put down was a confluence of goat trails that made a flat just before the arch. The bridge pierced the face of the opposite mountain, a rough overhang sheltering the entry somewhere deep within.

The road into the Veil was without curb or rail and hardly wide enough to allow a single file approach.

Dave said, "Must be something damn impressive on the other side for anyone go through the trouble to hike all the way up here to reach the front door. Still, pretty good engineering. Very defendable. Bet there's a thousand nasty arrow slits and murder holes waiting for anyone trying to leave a flaming bag of dog-doo on their front porch."

"Seems obvious where we land," I said as nonchalantly as I could muster. I leaned over the side to play crew chief as Dave set us down carefully on the narrow landing before the bridge, the only level ground. There was nothing to buttress a slide off into the rocky abyss.

Our guide was off and marching up the bridge. "This way." Before I could gulp, he passed over the apex and out of sight.

Okay. Truth time. Unless I'm flying, have a parachute on my back, or I'm climbing to reach some precipice because there's a good chance of shooting someone with my Mk 22, I avoid these kind of places like the plague—places where a fall could kill me.

Snubbing the service entrance suddenly seemed like bad manners on our part.

But nonetheless I set off after the bigoted dwarf.

"Ben don't like heights," Dave whispered to Tranya Olan.

"Blabbermouth. And, by the way, I was kidding about that," I lied. If Dave had a weakness I could lord over him, he had never admitted it nor had I found it.

I concentrated on the stone just in front of my feet and soon enough was secretly relieved to be descending the hump for the safety of the enclosure ahead. With plenty of Terra Firma—I mean, Vistara Firma—under my feet, I could face anything, including a pack of white apes.

Bringing up the rear, Karlo was stopped on the apex of the bridge. He arched backward to look high, then leaned over the edge to peer straight down. He would.

"This is more like it," he said with satisfaction. He often complained that Shansara was flat as Kansas. Karlo was one of those weirdos whose leisure time was spent climbing perilously high up a rock face, only to hammer a tent into its side and go to sleep hanging hundreds of feet above the bone-shattering death awaiting the failure of pitons possibly outsourced to Pakistani child labor.

Not me.

Trayver Lomal waited at the mouth of the mountain. "You bear arms! I trusted you to instruct that they be left behind, Tranya Olan!"

We'd all slung our K-specs before leaping off. "You know what to tell him," I said.

"The Warlord says you are welcome for the ride home. We depart." She spun on her heels and I followed her lead with butterfly wings flapping in my gut.

"Gaaah!" Trayver Lomal raged. He parted the drape from his face. "Come. The Superiority of Twenty await."

Amber stones in the walls awakened from slumber and defined an antechamber that barely fit the five of us. No obvious gateway to the interior of the mountain appeared. Trayver Lomal placed himself before a smooth cave wall, complaining under his breath as he did. "Ever the rude and brash child. You truly found your own amongst the boorish Mihdra." He cleared his throat and announced into the featureless rock face. "I serve at the pleasure of the Twenty."

Materializing from out of the stone stepped a man dressed in shimmering robes delicately woven from the threads of a silkworm that dined exclusively on platinum ore. His head was uncovered, his red beard and hair trimmed neat, and while he was taller than Trayver Lomal, he was nowhere as thick or muscular. I knew Dave and Karlo noted these small details as I did.

The frowning man castigated Trayver Lomal with contempt I heard even through decipher. "About time." He switched to Mihdra. "I am the secretary of the First Citizen. The Superiority of Twenty welcomes the Warlord of Mihdradahl."

The man's gaze rested blankly on Tranya Olan long enough to communicate he recognized but disregarded her.

He held out a small orb. "Follow Trayver Lomal and pass through. Do not be disturbed, there is no harm. Even the stone of the mountain serves the Twenty." My excellent ear for Mihdra meant his condescension burned my ass before the light speed of my decipher could translate into my brain's deep preference for English.

It was time to default to Warlord persona. I rose to my full height and expanded to superhero chest.

"We're familiar, thank you," I said dryly and with a slight sneer. It's a groove we all learn—how to broadcast the vibes of a military bearing that said, "What you're looking at is a veneer of civility. You don't want it to crack and release the savage beneath."

I followed Trayver Lomal through the permeable wall.

And gasped like a Victorian mother catching her daughter getting felt up in the parlor.

It was an underground world bathed in light radiating from a constellation of white diamonds. The cavernous sanctuary continued high, deep, and far. The platinum bridge was just that, a precious metal path spanning two sides of a grand mall. Tier after tier of promenades lined the depths and heights of the gap on both sides. Works of art were carved from the crystal formations of the walls and where they were not, vividly colored frescoes done in the style of the Baroque masters abounded.

It all spoke of an untold number of artisans toiling collective uncountable years, lifetimes spent dedicated to this creation.

Dave said, "You were wrong, Karlo. *This* is more like it, brah."

Shansara, a city more magnificent than any I'd ever imagined, suddenly seemed unremarkable. But even in its most desperate hours, Shansara had at least a faint pulse of life.

This city was a museum past closing time.

The heavenly luminosity shone down on barren galleries. Level upon level of the promenades skirting the vast cavern were without pedestrians. The spans of bridges joining side to side from high to low stood empty. The civil engineering was capable of accommodating the traffic of many thousands—but it was a ghost town.

"Is it usually so quiet?" I asked Tranya Olan.

She was troubled. "Never during the youth I spent in the Veil."

From the other side of the bridge came a pair of gray uniformed men with batons tucked in their sashes. They carried armfuls of the gauze-like garments Trayver Lomal wore. The secretary commanded them to halt. "There is no uncleanliness, constables. By order of the First Citizen, the gowns of purity are not necessary." He frowned at our white-clad companion. "You too, simpleton." Trayver Lomal reluctantly removed his garb as ordered, but stood by.

"Depart, I mean," the secretary said.

Trayver Lomal huffed off.

"The Twenty await." Mister Platinum Robes set off across the bridge of the same. He quickened his pace to prevent me assuming a place at his side, and I got the snub as intended. The secretary didn't invite my company for the stroll, didn't offer to act as tour guide, didn't ask about the wife and kids. Being declared acceptably "clean" yet not accorded the courtesy due any guest wasn't a mixed message. It was one clearly sent.

We need you, but we don't want you.

I waved Tranya Olan to fall in next to me.

"Uht-way ives-gay?" Pig Latin was the only language available to us in order to speak freely around our escort.

"As-ay I-ay old-tay ooh-yay. Ifficult-ay."

Dave was on my other side. "Otal-tay icks-day."

Karlo was usually pleased to be left to his own thoughts, and now was no different.

Before I could work out the pig Latin to say it wasn't just us, the secretary had been a jerk to Trayver Lomal too, we entered a room housing the conveyance system identical to the train car that took pilgrims to the White underworld. The secretary posed as if waiting on us to acknowledge its awesomeness.

"Remain at ease. This will conveniently carry us to the plaza of the seniority."

I used refined Mihdra. "Your artwork is splendid, but we have walk-through-walls and public transportation at home."

The secretary gave an irritable grunt and took a seat on the plush carriage. Twice now he'd failed to impress us country bumpkins with the mod-cons of the Veil.

We accelerated smoothly off into the tunnel, but without the accompaniment of flashing lights or theremin music like on our trip to discover the secrets of the Whites, fortunately. A comfortable and short ride later we stepped off into a receiving area even more opulent than we saw on the Platinum Bridge tour—which was saying something. Gargantuan doors done in precious metal reliefs depicting scenes from a hundred stories I didn't know parted open to reveal a long table. I didn't need to use all fingers and toes to count how many it seated there in wait.

Centermost in the highest backed chair to bring the total to twenty-one was the First Citizen.

The secretary announced us in reverse. "Warlord Benjamin Colt, you have the inestimable honor of being received by First Citizen Granday Fallis."

Had I just heard that right? This guy's mom named him Large Johnson? The snort I expected from Dave didn't come, but I knew it'd be the first thing out of his mouth when we were alone. Above the high collar of a garment beaded so densely with gems it could serve as armor, the clean-shaven First Citizen sat silent as the Sphinx, lips closed tight enough to repel a greased BB. Was he waiting for me to bow?

Hell would freeze first.

My irritation meter pegged. It was one thing to respect the traditions of another culture. It was another to drag me here to wait at his pleasure. Our time was being wasted. My wife and child waited. A kingdom needed its Warlord's protection. As a student of the Talis Darmon school of diplomacy, I'd learned it was not only okay, but sometimes necessary, to use a little Desert Storm shock and awe.

"I am dispatched by my queen to answer your call for aid. But there are matters of practicality. I am not a patient man. I need to hear it plainly and now, or I withdraw along with her offer of help. Why am I here?"

The First Citizen paused dramatically until in a voice so faint, I could barely hear him, said, "Show him."

A servant stepped forward presenting a pillow in both hands. On it was a small piece of dulled yellow metal, one I would recognize long after I forgot the faces of my parents.

It was the spent and burnished brass case of a 5.56 round.

I picked it up, feeling the familiar weight as I traced a finger over the straight and radiused portions of the object once so common a part of my daily life that it was easy to overlook for its complexity. Karlo and Dave moved close.

"Show it to us, Ben," Karlo said.

I turned the case base end up. There was the expected depression in the primer from a perfect firing pin strike, as was the stamping on the head. LC 22.

"Lake City ammunition plant," Dave said. "2022."

I expected to see the number 7323, that of our old A-team.

Karlo said, "This M855A1 didn't come from the ammo I made with Baby Blue. This came all the way from Earth."

✣ ✣ ✣

The now defunct subatomic matter mill had been essential to our victories on Mars. The brilliant engineers who pirated the alien tech to make an honest-to-god Star Trek replicator had dubbed it the Blue Fairy because it granted wishes. Dougie nicknamed the portable factory Baby Blue because of the Cherenkov radiation it produced while churning out product of every imaginable kind, and the name stuck. Bryant armed the Mydreen with M4s and ammo built by Baby Blue.

I searched my memory, but couldn't remember the headstamp from the ammo we brought to Mars. By Karlo's reaction, it meant he did. If this ammo didn't come to Mars on our C-17, then it was irrefutable evidence that the attack on the Veil had been done with weapons and ammo manufactured on Earth and brought here by someone other than us.

Dave's eyebrows shot up. "Whoa there, Karlo. I know where you're goin' with this, brah. No way."

I picked up for Dave. "No one else from Earth's on Vistara. It'd be impossible."

"We're holding proof it's not," Karlo said.

"You're positive about the year?" I asked.

"No," he said sheepishly.

I stopped losing more years off my life. "You're just having a pang of confidence because of what Doug said about the oddity of an IED on Vistara. Look, someone's simply got a battlefield-scavenged M4 with a mag of our old ammo that got lost by one of us early on. Shit happens.

I'm betting there's only one barely functional rifle with one half-full mag of ammo out there."

"Maybe," Karlo said with a lack of conviction.

I was adamant. "My explanation's more obvious, and it's the correct one, Karlo."

He accepted my logic with relief. "Of course you're right, Ben. I'll just feel better once I check the records."

"I don't remember the headstamps from what we brought from Earth either, Karlo," Dave said. "But if the log's still somewhere in our vault room under the palace, it'll check out. I'm certain, brah."

We'd been conferencing in English in front of the entire collection of Snow White's dwarves. "Okay, back to business," I said. Resuming in Mihdra, I addressed the First Citizen as I held up the case pinched between two fingers.

"We know what this is and where it came from."

"So I understand," said First Citizen John Holmes in the same imperious manner, speaking so quietly it strained the ear. It was then I saw that lost within the beadwork of his upper sleeve sat a decipher. A quick scan left and right and I failed to identify another. He noticed. "My secretary speaks Mihdra, as do I, but I alone wear the translation device. The seniority hears what I choose."

"How you govern doesn't concern the queen," I said. "If we're to help you in any way, I need to know what happened here."

The First Citizen raised his voice to be readily heard. "First, so that the terms are clear, what you hold in your hand is proof of Mihdradahl's culpability in the assault and pillaging committed against the Veil. Where normally we would negotiate a price with mercenaries, I demand your service against what is owed us in damages."

Dave didn't hold back. "That's some balls."

I agreed. "Because my interest in finding out who did this might serve my own kingdom, I won't fly off just yet and leave you to solve your own security problems. For the last time, what happened?"

The First Citizen spoke so all his fellow oligarchs could understand. "The Seniority grants you access to the Veil of Seriata. You will be escorted to where the crime occurred so you may see for yourselves."

Karlo spoke up. "Are you in need of medical assistance? We bring advanced healing technologies that may be of help."

For the first time, the leader of their ruling council showed a manner nearing appreciation. "It is welcome, but futile. The savages who penetrated our sanctuary murdered every Serian between them and their goal."

06

On the flats near what Tranya Olan derisively called the service entrance, we waited for the Black Bird. There was nothing more for me to do here. "Stay long enough to satisfy yourself that Garlak Ranz has a handle on things, Davey. Then leave him as much of a force as you see fit and send the rest back to the *Hope* before you come home. I'm releasing both flights of a black widow squadron for use as long as this emergency lasts, so don't be shy calling one for you and Tranya Olan."

"Roger-dodger, brah," Dave said. "Where you headed?"

"First to Filestra to catch up on progress with the investigation and to drop Karlo off to get back to ironing out the *Hope*'s many wrinkles. Then I'm flying to Shansara."

Karlo grimaced. "I can be useful here, Ben."

"It's back to the *Hope* for you, bro. We need you searching for the cure to what's plaguing her. What's going on here is small-picture. In case you've forgotten, you're a big-picture guy."

Karlo sank. "I understand, Ben." I knew I'd let the air out of his tires. This little trip gave him a taste of life as an operator again, and it was a flavor impossible not to crave more of.

Dave asked, "What about your pup? Not to mention, Sarkan Sell and Jodal Jark'll gripe about being left behind." The three of them were still sniffing around the crags and cracks of the Veil's hinterlands.

"Can't be helped," I said. "Apache's too big for the back of a black widow. Put the three of them on a slow boat to Shansara as soon as they're through here." After his first night crop-dusting our bedroom, my puppy would forgive me for leaving him behind. Jodal Jark and Sarkan Sell, not so easily. I'd have to make it up to them by keeping them glued to me for some time to come.

In flight I opened a cloud to Talis Darmon.

"Headed to Filestra then home in quick order. I should be there in time to feed Shara breakfast."

She beamed. "We look forward to the dawn. What news?"

"Where to start? We went ready to render military security assistance, but instead ended up playing detective. Sarkan Sell's convinced the Vermeel had some hand in the attack on the Veil, just like he's certain they did in Filestra." I told her about the only piece of hard evidence we had: the shell casing and the possibilities it suggested—both the obvious and the outlandish. She pounced on the latter with her logic.

"That is an interesting theory, though it seems inexplicable why Thulian soldiers suddenly thrust on Vistara would engage against us in such a way. It seems most probable that the Vermeel have armed themselves with remnants recovered from one of the numerous battlefields of Brandon Bryant's crusade. Hmm. I wonder, Benjamin Colt, is there not another possibility? Could it be we were deceived, and that the architect of the many campaigns to see us exterminated in fact *lives* and is waging a new war on us?"

Karlo was next to me in the cramped rear compartment. He leaned into the cloud and with the seriousness of a hanging judge, pronounced, "Queen Talis Darmon, it is with 100% certainty I attest that those were his remains you saw."

She chuckled. "I am relieved by the certainty with which you denounce my suggestion, Karlo Columbo. I accept your pronouncement as final that those foul scraps were vital remnants of the fouler Brandon Bryant. It was merely a logical avenue of consideration, given that his homicidal hatred combined with his record of injuries done to us made him the ultimate nexus of intent and ability."

The cabin tilted for me in a sudden wave of vertigo. The Black Bird hadn't taken a snap barrel roll. It was just me. What caused my world to spin was my realization that there was another player who fit Talis Darmon's description. Who unlike Brandon Bryant was alive and currently in location unknown. An enemy we'd built from scratch with our own hands.

Kleeve Hartus.

"That there is a connection between the incidents in Filestra and the Veil seems certain," Talis Darmon continued.

"I think so, too, sweetheart," I said, my equilibrium returning as I dismissed the possibility of the former First Shield being behind such villainy. "But as much as Sarkan Sell's ready to take his blood oath on it, our visit to the Veil has me less convinced it's the Vermeel."

Karlo jumped in. "What about the lack of physical evidence, Ben? It sure fits what Sarkan Sell says about the boogeyman reputation of the Pale."

She frowned at Karlo's slip into a vernacular with no word-for-word equivalent in Mihdra. He offered interpretation. "It means a killer with supernatural powers. Never seen. Leaves no footprints. Comes and goes like a ghost."

Talis Darmon cocked an eyebrow. "It is an emblematic description to fit the Vermeel. Their traceless predations were so vile that Mihdradahl and the Korund worked in concert to drive the savages from our lands. Even the Mydreen showed no mercy to our boogeymen."

She'd given me the springboard I needed to lay out my doubts. "Disguising an attacker's true numbers and even their identity is tactics, not boogeyman magic. I was raised on my Gramps's stories about Vietnam. They'd sweep a battlefield after a firefight and not find a single dead or wounded VC even though they were certain they'd dropped bodies by the score. It was demoralizing, and that's why they did it."

"Unconventional forces have used asymmetric tactics like that throughout history to thwart the advantages of a superior enemy," Karlo put in.

Talis Darmon absorbed the condensed lecture on the subject of war from the shadows. "If the Vermeel placed the explosive device in Filestra and also used Thulian weapons in the raid on Seriata, then they embraced *two* technologies previously unknown to them. That is a difficult hurdle to cross."

"Which is why I think if it is them, they're not alone," I said. "Tell her the rest, Karlo."

Karlo explained. "Talis Darmon, besides having access to the scene of the attack, I was also able to examine the bodies in their morgue. Of the twelve dead, four had throats cut in a manner Sarkan Sell says fits the Vermeel." He skipped the details, but the heads had been severed to leave them attached, hanging by a loose flap of neck skin—an M.O. known only to the Vermeel.

"The other eight were killed by gunfire." Now Karlo spared no detail. "Each of those were killed by a single shot to the brain. I have a lot of knowledge and experience in ballistics and mechanisms of wound damage. It's not only that the shots were made precisely, it's that they were also done from relatively long distances, from at least fifty yards or more."

I put a hand out to Karlo. Though it'd been a while since she'd practiced, by necessity Talis Darmon had become a student of marksmanship. I wanted to see if she understood the point without Karlo giving her the conclusion on a silver platter.

She did not disappoint.

"*That* was not a result produced by spraying and praying, as you so taught me the term."

"That's my girl," I said, proud as I could be. "It took Dave and I a while to catch up, but when Karlo pointed it out, there's no other way to see it. It also chopped the legs from under my wishful thinking that there's only one M4 with a few cartridges out there somewhere."

She'd been writing on a tablet which she now held up and read from. "Our evidence so far: the manner of the homicides in two separate locations, an uncollected shell casing, and the intuition of an experienced warrior of the Korund. What was stolen from the Serians?"

Karlo answered. "Nothing remarkable, which is to say, the very valuable products of their mines, but in small amounts. The other thing, though... The Serian's conceit would hardly permit them to admit it to us, but they had no explanation as to how the raiders gained entry into the sanctuary. The entrance gates are multilayered, and virtually invisible from the outside. They'd not been forcibly opened."

Talis Darmon's took on a curious quality that was almost childlike. "What was it like, husband?"

"The Veil of Seriata? Have you never been?"

She shook her head no. "To the best of my knowledge, no visitor in my lifetime has been admitted into their cloistered society. Tranya Olan is the sole person I know who has left their fold, but good manners have prevented me from questioning her about her birthplace. She has always seemed most reluctant to speak about her past there."

"She's ashamed of her people," I said. "She warned us they were difficult, but enduring their unpleasantness was worth it to get a look inside. All I can say is, wow! I've been in a lot of holes in the ground. Dark and smothering, all of them. Everywhere, the Veil was infused with the kind of light that made me think Tinkerbell and her fairies were going to buzz the air around us at any second."

Karlo agreed. "The highest art and architecture I've ever seen. It was amazing."

Talis Darmon wilted at being left out. "I have studied ancient renderings of the sanctuary, but they seemed too fantastic to believe as anything but a fantasy of the artist."

"There's nothing I know of to compare it to, sweetheart. It was incredible."

Sometimes, there was just no other option than to draw on a culture remembered only by four displaced Thulians. Karlo tapped into it. "It was a Fifth Avenue Christmas window display designed by Renaissance masters and built in Hollywood."

Her smile from imagining what we inadequately described faded. "And the First Citizen and his oligarchy? During my father's reign, I had the opportunity to review the trade contracts between our polities. I was glad for the attorneys to manage them. Negotiations required months and the cost of couriers was great, thanks to Serian insistence on sequestration from the rest of Vistara. Most tedious."

Recalling the First Citizen's demand wiped the canvas clean of my dreamy remembrances of the Veil's resplendence. "Is product liability law a thing here? Because quarantined in a fancy hole in the ground or not, they knew that shell casing came from a Thulian weapon. They're threatening to sue us!"

I was about to say it was as absurd as holding a baseball bat manufacturer liable because someone was beaten to death with a Louisville slugger, until I remembered that lawsuits just that ludicrous were brought all the time in the US of A. Maybe this was the proof there were other Thulians on Mars, only instead of gunfighters, they were trial attorneys.

"They are indeed a difficult people," she replied.

"But desperate enough to admit they need our help," Karlo said.

"And it's galling them," I added.

Talis Darmon sighed. "I am envious you witnessed such wonders for yourselves. Yet, I am more jealous of the insight you gained by personal interaction with the Serians. Strict isolationists who, despite themselves, invite us into their sanctuary. Even given the dire circumstances they find themselves in, it is a most unique relaxation of their code."

"What are you thinking, wife?" I knew she'd built a logic tree as solid and branched as the oldest oak.

"There are few facts and many contradictions. Hopefully, Zaylin Twee will discover more facts. As to the contradictions, it seems not only must we examine prejudices held about the primitive nature of the Vermeel, but something tells me that if I am to understand current events, I must also challenge premises I hold regarding the Serians."

✢ ✢ ✢

The pilot alerted that we approached Filestra. The two-day journey to the Veil by flitter had been reversed in thirty minutes by the black widow. It was the difference in travel by steam locomotive versus SR-71.

"Gotta sign off," I told her. "We're landing. I didn't give you the opportunity to catch me up on home."

"Worry not, Benjamin Colt. Your daughter is in perfect health, as am I. The council is... the details of our political climate can wait. Please be safe in your duties, husband, and return as soon as possible."

Mounted cavalry patrolled the sands around the grounded *Hope* and halted to look skyward. Many stood tall in stirrups and hailed us with arms stretched high. The sight of a black widow brought the same kind of response everywhere we flew. They're beautiful, but the sight of one sparked what I can only call patriotism.

Karlo looked out his own small window, pensively reflecting.

"The Black Birds are a symbol of pride in the kingdom," I told him. "They gave us our decisive victory over the Whites *and* Annameria. All thanks to you."

Whereas Cynar's insufferableness about his genius was partially an act, Karlo's humility was not. He squirmed with discomfort.

"Sorry, Karlo. Just didn't want the moment to pass without telling you how much we all appreciate you."

Now he winced. There was something deeper going on. I got distracted as we floated onto the hard deck without a bump.

"Reception committee's waiting." I moved to exit.

Karlo stayed seated. "Ben, hold up a minute."

I plopped back down, concerned. "What?"

"I have an ask of you. A big one. Put me back in the game."

I shouldn't have been surprised. We'd thrown crisis after crisis into Karlo's lap and time and again he'd come through. But whether it was the menial problems of the *Hope* that had finally worn him down or the accumulated stress he rightly carried from so many responsibilities, I understood. A vacation wasn't what he needed.

Man was the only creature who sought respite from one stressful activity by throwing himself into another.

"You need a break?"

He nodded. "I'm fried. I've admitted to myself I have to make a change. I know taking off the uniform's what I asked for..."

I headed him off before he took the dive to ask me. "Hey, no explanation necessary, Karlo. Soldiering's home. When you've been an operator as long as you have, you can't ever shake that first love. You want back, you're back."

Karlo's dark features grew darker as his speech fell heavy. "It's more than that, Ben. There's an emergency building. And I need to be on the front line of the coming war."

"War?" I said. The attack on Filestra was fresh in our experience, but —a war? Karlo saw my incredulity.

"It's just a hunch, Ben. But my intuition tells me Mihdradahl's survival is on the line."

On the spectrum of conflict and unrest, he saw us heading for World War II. I thought it was a Mars version of the 1970s and the likes of the Weather Underground or Black September. My Farmer's Almanac was saying plan for a rainy planting season while his was calling for nuclear winter and fallout shelters.

"Neither one of us are meteorologists so I'll just say, whatever's heading for us, we're lucky to have you back in uniform, brother." I pantomimed waving a magic wand. "Poof. As Warlord, I recall you to active duty. For the duration of the emergency or until you have a better offer."

He was visibly relieved. "Phew. Will Talis Darmon be okay with this?"

"Of course she will!" I fibbed. She'd come to depend on Karlo not only for his masterful organizing of the kingdom's sector of innovation and production, but as a sounding board for her plan to evolve the governance of Mihdradahl into something it had never known—a republicanism, still in the earliest stages of conception on a world that had never known the like.

"Thanks, Ben. Hope I'm wrong."

"Me too. Now, c'mon. Let's give the guys the good news."

"Along with the bad."

Standing alongside Khraal Kahlees and Dougie on the *Hope*'s top deck was Zaylin Twee. There were chest thumps at Karlo's return to trigger-puller, followed by a rundown about our trip to the Veil. I didn't expect to return to a major breakthrough having occurred in the investigation, and as breezily as I could, I teased the First Shield.

"Lay it on me, Zaylin Twee. Show me that smoking gun dangling upside down from the pencil sticking through the trigger guard. Who dunnit?"

She ignored my flippancy. "Without suspects to interrogate, investigations always progress slowly. But Wizard Supreme Cynar is at work with my best staff, and Douglas Knoblock's expertise has been invaluable. There *will* come a break in this case. Our doggedness is its guarantee."

Double-K bared tusks of approval. "You are most correct, First Shield. Tenacity is the quality of the victor."

Dougie scrunched his face. "We're plenty that, but we're behind on the score board. There's some bad actors out there and we still don't have a grip on 'em. Me-no-like-ee."

Throbbing lights pulsed on the wrists of both Zaylin Twee and Khraal Kahlees. Simultaneously, clouds erupted as I listened in stereo. Reporting to the heads of the army and police, I had a desert-clad captain in one ear and a red-cloaked Guard officer in the other.

"Thoria has been attacked, General," said the captain. "A sizeable explosion has occurred at a public event in the performance district. There are many dead and injured."

The Guardsman reported the same. "First Shield, Thoria has suffered an attack like that in Filestra. The situation is evolving but many are dead. I have ordered the city locked down."

"We're on our way," I said loudly to both. "Keep updates coming. We should be there in the hour." My friends eyed me. "All right, kids. Grab gear, be back in ten, or all you'll see is my vapor trail."

"Do not think to depart without me!" Double-K growled and dashed for the companionway to the lower decks.

Zaylin Twee had already sprinted off, taking my deadline at face value.

"I'm flying us," Doug said.

Karlo blew a raspberry. "Fat chance. Ben and I already have our kit in the Black Bird. You'll find me in the command pilot seat."

Dougie sprang off. "Back on the team for three minutes, and already busting stones." With one leap he was on the heels of Zaylin Twee and Khraal Kahlees to follow them to the bottom decks. Our superhuman abilities were always handy on Vistara. I had a flash of an idea.

"I'll be right back, too, Karlo."

He mocked me before stepping into the bullet-shaped aircraft. "You got nine minutes, Ben. An order's an order. No exceptions for rank."

"Glad you're feeling frisky, Karlo!" I yelled back. "We'll find out soon enough if ball-bustin's the only operator skill you've kept in shape."

We were skids up in eight. I let Dougie take the right seat and crammed with Double-K and Zaylin Twee into the back with all our war gear. Khraal Kahlees eyed the long case I cradled between my legs.

"What do you anticipate, Benjamin Colt?"

"You've said it before yourself, brother. Better to have and not need."

Zaylin Twee sat between us on the rear bulkhead folding jump seat, wrist cloud protruding from the mountain of gear packed around her while she received reports. I tuned out the grim scene unfolding to listen to Karlo and Dougie working together to navigate.

"Climb another ten thousand, Karlo. I'll spot with binos. We should be able to see reflections off the towers."

"Surely, at this time of day," Karlo said.

"And don't call me Shirley. Got ya, dude."

Khraal Kahlees's wrist pulsed. "General, an aerial patrol has sighted activity in the eastern desert."

"Hostile activity, Captain?" Double-K asked.

The Mihdra soldier gave a stumbling, discomfited answer. "Impossible to say, General. Movement by a small band on foot was sighted, then... lost."

"Seen by Red or Green?" Double-K asked. It was a fair question as Tarns did have the superior vision among our troops. Binoculars were a rare commodity, optics being one of the technologies that sorely lagged behind our many other advances.

"Both, General."

Double-K interrogated gruffly. "Then how is it that pursuit has not resulted in capture?"

I jumped in. "What did they see?"

The man snapped stiff. "Warlord, while observing from a fixed hover, a patrol detected movement on the far horizon. They called it in, and at the moment of their advance to investigate, they report witnessing no less than five figures vanish in rapid succession beneath the sands. I myself aided in the search. We found nothing. If not for the certainty of the soldiers, I would dismiss their report as a mirage."

"We'll be there within the hour. Have flitters waiting to take us there, Captain," I said. "We'll be joining the search. Out."

Khraal Kahlees seemed hesitant. "I have some sense of the Pale, Benjamin Colt, but with neither Sarkan Sell nor the war dog with us, I am a poor substitute for a tracker."

I had other plans. "I don't think sniffing grains of sand will be worthwhile. Nor trying to spot them by putting more eyes in the sky."

His tusked lower jaw thrust forward. "Is this why you retrieved the most prized courtesan of your personal harem?"

"Now, now, Double-K. I know how to share. If you didn't notice, I brought something along for you, too."

Zaylin Twee looked amused. "I would never take either of you as jealous competitors for the affections of a woman."

My green brother laughed. "I assure you, First Shield, unlike concubines, the affection returned by such beauties as these is genuine."

✠ ✠ ✠

Four hours later and sixty klicks east of Thoria, the sun was low and sinking lower by the minute, bringing welcome respite from the oven of the parched desert we watched over.

We left Zaylin Twee to manage the crisis response and flew off. Karlo and I paired up, and since Khraal Kahlees and Dougie enjoyed working together, I let them be a team. An entire company patrolled the air in narrow corridors, leaving wide patches of empty sky above the locations I'd hastily planned for the ground observation teams.

If there was a rat belly-crawling out there in the sands, I wanted him to have a place to run. Only seven of the teams had binoculars and night observation devices, and my Mk 22 and Double-K's M110 meant we were the only teams with weapons capable of both seeing *and* hitting at great distances.

Karlo lay prone beside me on the sandy bed between the smooth boulders we chose for our observation point. There were many of the formations in the desert, so odd and random in location they had to be natural rather than the remains of convenience store gas-and-go's along an ancient turnpike.

I faintly whispered, "Priority. Optics. And lots of them. Soon."

He whispered back so quietly, to anyone more than a foot away, it would pass for telepathy. "I got a guy on it. Several guys. It's a tall order."

Karlo changed the subject. "Dark soon." On a small tripod he used our only thermal binoculars. Thermals detect differentials in heat signatures and the desert had been the same as body temp since we'd laid out.

"You think there's any chance this'll pan out?" Karlo said.

I pursed my lips sideways in reply. It was for reasons more than the discipline of never leaving the optic. Even my sparing speech had fogged the lens of the scope on my Mk 22. It caught me by surprise. Apparently, there was enough water vapor in the air that as the temperature dropped, the humidity had moved up from perpetually zero to something.

Amazing.

"You got somewhere to be, Karlo?"

"Nope."

We didn't speak again for several hours and even then, spared only enough to communicate a pee break, performed by rolling to a side to fill a bottle. It's not glamorous work, remaining undetected. At all times you had to assume you were under the observation of an enemy as dedicated as you. The most masochistic monk would flail himself for the sin of envy at our ascetic discipline.

What fuels the motivation to endure such torment?

The reward of the hunter—meat in the freezer, so to speak.

We stayed like this through a long, cold night, surrendering turns off optics in shorter and shorter intervals as the burn in our fatiguing eyes built up faster and faster. Luckily, the shivering that soon set in had the effect of cooling my eyeballs. To ward off sleepiness, I pictured in my mind's eye the reticle coming to rest on all manner of things appearing in my field of view that begged to be shot.

But none did.

That special time came when the world through my PVS-27 enhanced into the brightest and clearest shades of black and green, signaling daylight was not far off. And when the final and deepest chill set in to mark the impending retreat of night, I looked forward to the reward of those first few hours of perfect warmth until the interminable heat of day returned to be suffered, begging the fall of night again.

My hasty plan to blanket the desert east of Thoria with a net of invisible eyes had been made with some rapidly set upon assumptions, calculated on my part with third grade mental math—the only kind I know. Combined with my oath to always trust the guy on the ground, I believed with conviction that a group of bipeds had been witnessed appearing from nowhere, only to vanish beneath the sands just as inexplicably.

But movement was movement and it was the first target indicator.

Everything I postulated about our enemy convinced me they were on foot, though no tracks had been discovered. There was fieldcraft to explain that. They couldn't be moving at a run—that made the fieldcraft next to impossible. Neither could they crawl. Not for such distances.

So at a pace of neither run nor crawl and lightly encumbered—moving cautiously and draped in whatever camouflage they used—I estimated their speed. With a need for frequent security halts, my guess at their maximum rate of movement was five kilometers an hour. If they were beating a retreating path for whatever base of operations they launched from, I was certain I'd placed us far ahead of their route. If they appeared again, one of our teams had an excellent chance of spotting them. Maybe of interdicting them.

Then I'd stop feeling like I was stuck in one of those stupid reality shows. The ones where the ghost hunters never found a ghost. Instead, we'd have a real phantasm sealed in a Tupperware bowl, or a bigfoot tied up in a burlap bag.

It. Would. Happen.

And of course, I wanted to be the one to pull the rubber mask off the Scooby-Doo villain.

With night over and a new day well underway, the silence of our wristlets meant no one had gotten lucky. The sun was at half-morning height and about to switch to bake mode. I was beginning to sweat. My back and ribs ached and it was a strain to breathe. And it was not even the end of the first twenty-four hours of what I'd budgeted for three days. I knew I could do it, and so could our troops.

It was Karlo I questioned had the stuff.

Karlo had once been the machine of machines on our A-team. And no matter how I loved and admired my brother, that was then, this was now. How I was running the routine on our OP wasn't meant as a test of fitness for his return to operator duty, but such were the circumstances. This was truly throwing him back in the deep end without him having swum a lap in a very long time. If he went for the edge of the pool, there'd be a conversation that despite his desire to be in uniform again, he wasn't fit enough to be back on the Olympic swim team with us.

I needn't have worried.

The sun was reaching zenith when I ended the vow of silence. "Pee break?" I said with a voice parched and lips dry and crusty. Neither of us had taken a sip in hours. His answer was evidence of equal dryness.

"You go. Everything's so numb I can't tell if my bladder's full or not. Maybe my kidneys have shut down. Means I can stay on glass longer."

It was good to have Karlo back.

A few hours later I was questioning everything about the iron maiden I'd consigned us to and my plan in general. We needed to hydrate, eat, and move. We needed to rotate for sleep breaks. It was only natural that as we fatigued our routine had to evolve to include those adjustments.

I'd pushed us hard—much harder than normal—for the first twenty-four hours of our observation. It may have been bad judgment on my part, but it was driven by the criticality of our reason for being here *and* by my cruel and ultimately unnecessary need to test Karlo's performance envelope. It was going to be another long night. Time to send Karlo off the OP and into the crag on the downslope behind us and let him snag some human time. Then I'd do the same.

Besides. I had a sneaking suspicion there was nobody to be found in all the nowhere and nothing we painstakingly gazed over. This was turning into a bust.

Just as my decision to ease our routine brought a little effervescence to my mood—ready to lay the gift on Karlo that his good showing meant he'd be the first to rest—a crazy vision appeared in the edge of my scope.

I squeezed both lids tight, took a deep breath, and opened them again, expecting the hallucination to be gone. I shifted my hips right to move my field of view in the opposite direction.

Center in my scope, what I saw extinguished all fatigue, discomfort, and irritability.

"Karlo. We got 'em."

"I see them, too! Two, three. Five of 'em." He was on thermal and at this distance, what he counted would appear only as ill-defined black smudges.

"Switch to the spotter," I said. Using my spotting scope he'd get a view nearly as good as I had through the optic on my Mk 22. I hit the button on my laser range finder, read the numbers, dialed the elevation, and got back on the scope. I zoomed to the highest magnification.

Five men stood out in the midst of desert nothingness. Risen like prairie dogs stretching from their hole, they'd abandoned the protection of the trench they low-crawled through. But I saw no trench or gulley or draw or dip or hole. The ground around them was as flat and smooth as a concrete shop floor.

Karlo read it as I did. "Four arms. Tarns. Wouldn't say they're bleached, but they're ashy looking. Maybe dusty. They're packing rifles of some kind."

I had no more to add, the flutter of rising mirage blurring greater detail. I moved the bolt handle up, then down, feeling the mechanism cock on the chambered round. It was a trick I learned a long time ago from a master sniper.

I was ready to send one, but just then, a pesky itch in my brain begged a scratch. And the guy next to me was the reason why. "Any question about ROE, Karlo?"

Karlo was the team's conscience, unafraid to pose the ethical question of whether we were right to take a life, regardless if anyone else had any doubt. It wasn't exactly like we'd caught these Tarns red-handed at anything except being in our sights. For crimes we only *thought* they'd committed, I was about to execute as many as I could. All without legal declaration, warrant, or hard proof whatsoever.

He hissed as loudly as an agitated cobra. "Hell no. Send it."

The mirage boiled straight up. There was no wind anywhere. I held left the correct amount to compensate for the right-hand spin of my bullet, breathed out so my chest rested empty, and the instant the hash mark I chose settled between the nipples of the centermost Tarn, between heartbeats I pressed the trigger.

The reticle lifted in recoil. I lost view of my magnified world for a millisecond until the scene in front of the many stacked black lines of laser etched grid returned to me. I found the trace of disturbed air trailing my bullet, watched it reach the apex, and continue along its descending path.

Impact.

The Tarn dropped like an anvil.

Some live to create art. Some live to critique it.

Of my own work, I am my biggest fan.

His buddies did the dance of *what the hell just happened?* I chambered the next round, chose a candidate with torso very much square to me, settled, and sent it. All of this I accomplished before the noise of the first shot could've traveled from my muzzle to reach their stubby ears. The fuzzy trail of air cut another perfect arc over the two-kilometer distance, and I greedily anticipated the pointed copper splash on flesh—

Just as every four-armed apparition vanished.

I don't mean they high-tailed it. I don't mean they splayed out prone. I mean they disappeared. Out of sight, gone-daddy-gone, splitsville.

Just. Like. That.

07

Where only a split second before a Tarn had stood, my bullet passed through empty space and disturbed a patch of sand a hundred meters beyond. My grasp on reality was challenged like that of a private-E-1 fresh out of basic stepping past the curtains of his first strip club.

It just hits different when you see it for yourself.

When you've been a day using voice so faint it wouldn't disturb a mouse nesting in your beard, my barely-above-a-whisper exclamation was like thunder in my head.

"Holy shit!"

Equally loud to me was Karlo's gasp, though like me, he used church-pew-level volume. "That's something new."

I remained locked through the scope on the body weaving left and right in the heat waves, as though he twitched with life, but didn't. I cursed as something pricked my sense of not-right, aimed, and fired. The trace passed within a millimeter of what I swore was a Tarn hand reaching up out of the ground. I knew I'd called it right when the arm snapped back into never-never land like a roller shade.

"Karlo! They're trying to recover their buddy! Get on your K-spec. I'll talk you on target!" I chambered another round and fired at the spot where'd the arm had sprung from. The trace dropped to that exact spot, and vanished without a splash. I don't know how I could've not seen the impact. I'd placed two more rounds on the sand near the body—this time dirt kicking up with my subsequent impacts—when Karlo told me ready.

"Send it."

The K-specs had only basic iron sights. At extended range the particle bursts of accelerated electrons sort of petered out. It wouldn't kill at this distance, but I wouldn't want to be hit by one. It would still make you feel like you'd touched your tongue to an electric fence, but all over. When we had a genuine optics operation going, pairing a piece of good glass with a more compact version of our K-maxes would mean that everyone would be world-class sniper. It would be as simple as aim dead-on, press the trigger, and whatever you could see would be toast.

Someday.

Karlo's first shot landed short and left by about two hundred meters, sending up a puff of red dust. Not bad. Three more shots and I had him talked onto a ten-meter area around our kill. "That's your sight picture. Send one every three to five seconds and spread it around closely as best you can. That'll discourage them from trying to make off with our prize. I'm calling for help."

I opened the cloud. "All stations, troops in contact. One enemy interdicted and presumed KIA. Requesting assistance to secure the objective."

Dougie was first to answer. "We're on our way." Khraal Kahlees had hold of Doug's wrist, pulling it close so that all I saw were frantic bowling ball–black eyes above a flat pug nose and a mouth of ivory teeth and tusks.

"No one has such perpetual good luck! You assigned yourself the best spot! Admit it, Benjamin Colt!"

Doug pulled his wrist away. "Be there ASAP, Ben. Pack up, Double-K, I'm calling our ride. Better luck next time, dude."

I kept the hand with my wristlet under the heel of the stock and narrated into it how it had all gone down, so everyone on the net knew what to look for. Karlo continued to pepper the area until his K-spec ran out of juice. Fortunately, the first combat aircar came into view just then and Karlo talked them in over the objective.

"We have the overwatch, Warlord," someone said from the hovering flitter, and for the first time in too long, I came off the gun and stood. My vision went dark at the edges as blood drained into my legs. Every joint screamed, every muscle ached, like getting out of bed after coming out of a coma.

The buzz in the air above grew louder as more flitters arrived. On the bow of the aircar making a beeline for us were Khraal Kahlees and Doug. Karlo did some slow air squats. "I gotta limber up in case Double-K's not over his sulk and we have to make a run for it."

I laughed, but we both knew what to expect. The flitter lowered and Doug piloted the nose around. On the bow, our Korundi brother beamed like headlights. Killing work done well brought out the best in him, no matter who'd done the deed. He vaulted over the side, landing on the boulder with a soft finesse, hands on his hips like he was claiming this land in the name of the queen.

"Our Warlord! Pride of Mihdradahl and the Korund! If not me, there is none I would rather see attain first kill. Allow me to bear your gear so that we may inspect your deadly handiwork with haste!"

He accepted my cased rifle with due care and after a short ride we stood on the sands a hundred meters from where the crumpled body lay. I held the troops back to prevent the site from being trampled, the pocked and scorched ground around the corpse looking as solid as the promise of death and taxes.

"At last we have a trophy," Double-K said with the same pride as my dad the first and every time I bagged a buck. I'll say this for my friend, he got over disappointment faster than anyone I'd ever known. Except for Dave, who seemed to never experience letdowns. Or the blues. Or doldrums. Or, for that matter, went the other way to have the yee-haws, the slap-happies, or the zoomies. Dave's name should've been Even Steven. I wished he were here, too, to share in the moment.

Khraal Kahlees's excitement was contagious, and my pulse quickened as we set off to collect the butcher's bill. I was proud. Not because my plan had worked. Not because I'd been the one to score the first victory in this new conflict. But because this was the beginning of a means to finish whatever sought to embroil us in yet another unwanted conflict.

This death meant peace was that much closer to returning.

We were almost there when Doug and Karlo both checked our advance, arms outstretched like parents restraining un-seatbelted children on a Buick's frictionless pleather bench seat.

Of course, they were right.

I cringed. "Sorry, guys. No excuse. Don't know what I was thinking. I wasn't," I admitted.

"S'okay, Ben-dog," Doug said. "Best let me."

"What transpires?" Double-K asked with unusual perplexity. "What is it not apparent to me?" Then realization struck. His anger returned. "Do you mean, you suspect another device for craven mass homicide? All to prevent us from claiming our kill? A mark of true savagery, indeed!"

Doug produced a coil of thick cord from a cargo pocket. "Best y'all move back a good distance."

I was very conflicted. Doug was too valuable. I considered hollering for the lieutenant to form a detail, but we'd never trained our troops for this. There'd been no need.

"Uh-uh. I know what'cher thinking there, Ben-dog," Dougie said. "It's gotta be done right and I'm the man for it."

I threw up my hands. "Say when, Engineer." I led us away, short one man, and told the troops what to expect and to pay attention. We watched as Doug crawled on hands and knees to the head of the corpse. On his belly he probed the sands beneath the body, then snaked a loop around the trunk. He reversed his trail while playing out the full length of cord, then assumed a rowing position.

"Everybody, cover," he yelled. "Here goes."

I was prone but lifted my chin and shielded my brow. Yeah, yeah, it was a classic case of do as I say not as I do, but I wasn't going to take my eyes off Doug for even a second.

Next to a white ape, Doug was likely the strongest two-legged critter on Vistara, and then only less by a fraction. I expected him to give a full body jerk on the line. Instead, with fists full of taut cord pulled to chest, he lay back smoothly, dragging the body over the sand the same small amount.

Nothing happened. Doug's forehead wrinkled with a look of, "How 'bout that?" He then bowed deeply over flexed thighs, gathered the slack line taut again, and with heels dug into the sand, exploded backward in a full force row like he meant to drown the other scullers in his waves.

The Tarn body launched off the sands toward Doug as if lifted off a carrier deck by steam catapult. The bed it had rested on erupted with a brilliant white flash. Like a Fourth of July sparkler, the air fizzled in a cascade of sparks, then cleared.

I sprang to my knees, cupping hands to mouth. "Dougie! You good?"

Doug stood and waved nonchalantly. "No school like the old school. That woulda crispy-crittered us for realsies, dudes."

Khraal Kahlees spewed venom. "I curse my ancestor's weakness for failing to exterminate all Vermeel!"

Doug chuckled to himself as he marched, slap-happy from the adrenaline buzz of his win. He towed the dead Tarn behind, effortlessly digging a furrow in the sand like a team of oxen pulling a plow through black topsoil. "You're not gonna believe this, dudes! It's a honkey."

"What Thulian babble does he spout?" Double-K asked as we broke into a trot to meet Doug halfway.

"Yeah, Ben, what's he mean?" Karlo parroted.

I thought it was obvious but then, unlike Karlo, I'd wasted my formative years watching reruns of '70s sitcoms. "He means it's a Pale, alright."

We met and Doug dropped the cord from over his shoulder to aim a knife hand back at the body. "Homeboy here's not Vermeel."

The body was unmistakably human.

The legs were a mess, scorched black as chicken skin left on a flaming grill. He wore a typical Tarn harness, but dangling from it at mid-rib level hung two limp arms fashioned from animal hide. My attention focused on the .30-caliber-sized hole I'd punched through the soft spot below the sternum. You may think me perverse, but it only made me curious what the exit wound on the back looked like.

"My man's Halloween costume sucks," Doug said. "It wouldn't fool anyone up close."

I flipped through the mental picture book of snapshots I'd taken of the kill zone. "I'm certain they were Tarns," I said, trying to convince myself they had been.

Khraal Kahlees pointed. "Benjamin Colt, he is the same shade of pale as when first ever I laid eyes on you. He is Thulian!"

Karlo squatted deep and stared without touching. The head was shaved smooth as was the jaw. The features were coarse, the nose crooked from having healed that way, a piece of an ear missing. He wouldn't have been a GQ cover boy. And no matter the angle from which I viewed the face, there was no characteristic that nailed his origin for me as being from a certain race of either world.

We left Karlo to continue his careful inspection of the body and moved to the blast scene. A rifle lay nearby. It was scorched, but the odd contours and lines were nothing like any fizzle gun produced in Mihdradahl. We cautiously tested the scene a step at a time and after not sinking into any quicksand, tromped and raked the top layers with our feet and hands. The ground was unremarkable and we uncovered no further clues.

Karlo walked up and I passed him the unusual weapon. He rolled it over and back several times. "Not ours. It looks Annamerian, but it's been modified for Tarn anthropometry. That doesn't make sense, though. No one hates Tarns more than the Annamese."

Doug's prior elation was gone. "Yeah, duder, but what I really want to know... did we just waste another expat from Earth? If so, who the hell is he and how'd he get here?"

Karlo squeezed his lips tight. "I can't tell. Yet."

"No," I said, dismissing the notion with a hard shake. "No way. There's another explanation. Let's get this body loaded up and get to work."

Three hours later, we got our big break. An aerial patrol found a hide site nestled beneath fiber-woven canopies in a shallow wind-cut canyon, one of among many similar channels in a large arroyo some distance away. With a slow sweep of his wrist, the sergeant showed me the site and surrounding terrain. I couldn't quite make out what all was beneath the camo screen, but something was moving.

"Per your orders, we have not entered the encampment, Warlord, but beneath the camouflage wait hobbled arkall and supplies."

I knew the reporting soldier. He was one of the original recruits who'd joined our reconstituted army, and posted back home in Thoria. Among those first enlistees had been infiltrators bent on killing the Thulians they associated with Bryant's rape of their city. This man and the rest of the Thorians had been a hard bunch to win over, but like many of his city, he served with honor and distinction against the greater enemy in Pyreenia.

Kezan Strahl had risen to platoon sergeant. Army life must've suited him.

"Warlord, the area surrounding the site is sanitized of any trace of their beasts or themselves. It was well done, but ten minutes' flight from here, a trail as obvious as the twin sisters above leads from the east. Orders, sir?"

Doug punched the air. "Yes! These chumps aren't ghosts. We got 'em now!"

Karlo was revved up, too. "They moved overland from another base of operations, then set up an ORP to launch a very long walk-in infiltration. They did it well, but that's as basic as it gets."

Khraal Kahlees practically roared, "The kill awaits, let us be off."

I thought for a minute. The guys shushed as they sensed I was working on something. "Sergeant Kezan Strahl, how many men do you have with you?"

"Two squads, Warlord."

Time was critical. If I were on the scene, I'd let the enemy patrol retrieve their mounts and hit them from high ground on their way out of that arroyo. But I wasn't there.

"Sergeant, are you ready to conduct an ambush?"

The man snapped tall. "Yes, Warlord."

Even Double-K nodded with approval as I gave the sergeant the concept of operation.

"I'm clearing the air corridors so we don't spook off your quarry. Send your own flitters away, lay-in an ambush, and personally make sure you've sanitized your AO cleaner than a barracks latrine before inspection. If you can, bag us some prisoners."

The sergeant hesitated, squinting the same way I did when I had a question of a superior. "Warlord, if circumstances do not permit and we must kill them to prevent their escape, is that a mission failure?"

I liked this kid even more. He was sharp. "No, Sergeant. I *want* a prisoner. I *require* you to prevent any of them from getting away."

Khraal Kahlees stepped close. "Sergeant, the Vermeel are a skillful enemy. It will necessitate absolute discipline and perfect fieldcraft to achieve success."

"You can rely on me, General Khraal Kahlees."

I had a good feeling. "Then I wish you successful hunting." I closed the cloud.

"That kid's riding high right now, Ben-dog," Doug said. "Nicely done."

Khraal Kahlees rested lower hands on weapons. "As you say, Benjamin Colt, eventually the training wheels must come off." It never ceased to amaze me how adroit Double-K was using our vernacular, especially since the closest he'd ever come to a bicycle was one of my unartistic stick drawings.

Karlo stayed quiet, more pensive even than usual. "You'd have run it differently, Karlo?" I asked.

He came back from wherever he'd drifted off. "Hmm? Oh, of course not, Ben. Time's critical and it's counterproductive for us to carry out every task if the goal is a fully functional army. The men are capable."

"What's on your mind then?"

He made a nasal grunt. "What's *not* on my mind, Ben? This is adding up to something more than just revenge attacks by some persecuted Tarn minority. But right this moment, it's evading me." He yawned. "Pro'ly not thinking too good 'cause I'm spent."

Dougie needled him. "Wishing you were back doing mad scientist stuff?"

"I got your wish right here, bro." Karlo gave a shake, blubbered his lips, and smacked his face lightly. "Sorry. Ready to keep on keeping on. What's next?"

Doug laughed. "My man! Chill, dog. So much time away may have you thinkin' you're the Lone Ranger of brain work, but in case you forgot how we do things on this team, Ben-dog's like a one-man division G-2 and CIA put together. We just gotta do our part while he figures this out."

Now it was my turn to yawn. "'Preciate the confidence, Dougie-Doug. If only."

"Brain work, indeed," Double-K said, putting his back to the late afternoon sun. He surveyed the eastern horizon, a seemingly endless view of nothing. "The Vermeel were long ago driven to take refuge in the depths of the Furrow. Even Mihdradahl's wastes are a paradise compared to the great mote. But the eastern lands? They are devoid of sustenance to provide for even the lowliest creature. I puzzle how it is that the winds push at our backs to seek the Vermeel in that desolation."

I have a lot in common with Double-K. The news the ambush nabbed us a prisoner had my Private First Class Hyde seething that it should've been *me* sweeping the kill zone with a Mk 48. But then my Sergeant Major Jekyll put my petty alter ego in its place, and by the time we landed at the ambush site, I was committed to doling out the praise that meant more to a soldier than any medal.

Sergeant Kezan Strahl stood tall with his men. I knew the look. They braced for an ass-chewing, dreading they had to tell me they'd dicked the dog.

"Warlord, we could not seal the kill zone. At least one, perhaps two, escaped in the manner you described, vanishing into the sands."

Karlo was already attending the unconscious Tarn prisoner. Dressings had been applied and he lay with all his limbs properly restrained. The two dead Tarn laid out side by side were obviously so, because they were missing major parts—just like their pack animals—chopped up by 7.62 and frag. An abundance of K-spec impacts everywhere told the tale.

I liked what I saw. A lot.

But by my count, the sergeant was right.

Someone had gotten away.

Which was a big "So what?"

It was time to lower these men off the hook they hung themselves on.

"This was an excellent example of combat leadership and tactical proficiency. Well done, everyone. Stand easy."

That cut the tension like a Damascus steel knife slicing the manila rope suspending a sandbag. I led and the rest of the gang followed, shaking everyone's hands, thumping shoulders, and laying on the praise. Double-K roared congratulations to each soldier.

"Blood does us proud. Honor to our regiment." He substituted regiment for clan in modification of the traditional Korund praise.

See, we were all meat eaters. And we were the fathers of sons who'd learned from us well. And when it comes to satisfying your urge to soldier, if you can't do it yourself, killing bad guys by proxy is a very close second. Even a ball-hog like Double-K had come around to the truth of what my gramps used to say.

The sun can't shine on the same gadron's ass every day.

With Karlo back, we tossed the site, examined the bodies, and found more of the odd looking fizzle guns among the slaughtered arkall, but found nothing out of the ordinary that looked to explain how the Pale were doing their undetected travel routine.

"It's just like Tremors, dudes," Doug said. "'Cept they *ride* the graboids."

I ignored Doug's attempt at intel analysis and said, "Sergeant Kezan Strahl, walk me through your ambush again."

"Yes, Warlord. I divided us to lay in from two sides, from there, and there." He pointed to the short canyon ridgelines separated by a gulley. It was a good seventy-five meters from the avenue of travel in and out of the hide site. It was a bit farther than you'd like for this kind of ambush, but the sergeant had done as I would have. Don't fight the terrain. Fight the enemy.

"We dropped from the aircars directly onto the lay-in. We moved with alacrity, but I took time to place items of brush and vegetation over our camouflage nets and permitted no one to disturb the ground in front of us. We did not have long of a wait.

"We did not see them appear, but activity within the cavern containing their pack animals told us they had arrived. They were efficient in breaking their encampment, but kept two alert warriors on security. We maintained strict discipline, and there were several times I thought they sensed our presence. I almost initiated the assault but patience persevered, and soon the column appeared on foot, leading their animals in single file.

"I tugged the line attached to my gunner's leg and he opened up with the 240. The rest of my men joined. The mix of K-spec and machine-gun fire was devastating, and there was no return fire. I continued to observe our effect and the enemy response. It was then I noted the odd shimmer on the sands and caught sight of a Tarn diving into a pool of haze. It was the first time I joined to fire my weapon, and I snapped a shot off after the escaping enemy. I could not determine where the Tarn went, and my shot had no obvious impact, which puzzled me. Seeing no effect, I threw a grenade and ordered others to do the same, and we sent many more for the spot."

"What was the effect of the grenades?" I asked.

"I'm uncertain, Warlord. As you can see." He gestured at the ground as he turned. "We shredded anything made of flesh, and the sands are disturbed everywhere. But I saw my first grenade drop from sight into the anomaly—and nothing happened."

The sergeant grimaced. "I apologize, Warlord. I am certain at least one or more of the infiltrators went into the conjured portal. My orders were to prevent their escape. I did not make the regiment proud."

This kid was genuinely concerned he'd let me down. My grin was so bright, it outshone the high sun.

"Nonsense. Perfect doesn't exist in combat, but you came as close as there is. You did great, son. And the kingdom's going to need you to do it again."

I left him to bask in my praise as he returned to his men, and pulled the guys close to me.

"That *was* a good job by Kezan Strahl," Doug said. "He's come a long way from being that sassy Thorian recruit."

"He should receive promotion to sub-lieutenant," Double-K said.

I'd considered it, but dismissed the idea. I wanted to check Karlo's acumen about the problem I'd been struggling with—our rank structure and promotion scheme.

"What say you, Karlo?"

Karlo pursed lips. "We can't keep bumping our best NCOs to O as the reward for being good combat leaders. We need a strong NCO corps as much as we need good officers."

"Bingo," I said.

"I disagree," Khraal Kahlees said. "There is no better way to select those best suited to lead than promoting those who have proven they can do themselves what they demand of subordinates."

I sighed. "Point taken."

The old system of how the officer corps were selected and trained had been closely linked to family position rather than by merit. It had produced an army full of aristocratic officers, of which some had been good, but of which many more simply reinforced the decline of the institution under Talis Darmon's father.

And we all knew how that worked out.

"Another item to be tabled for discussion until later."

I pointed up to the spot from where the sergeant described his view of the action. "What if they got lucky and did drop a frag into whatever magic hole the Pale vanished into? Could there be KIAs somewhere beneath our feet?"

Doug bounced his eyebrows. "I'm on it, Ben. The local Thorian guild of builders has excavators and dozers they use for clean up after one of the big sand storms. I'm giving them a contract. In the meantime until they get here, I'm putting a shovel in the hands of every other swinging Johnson not needed elsewhere. Before we're done, this place is gonna resemble one of those coal mines from your neck of the woods, Ben-dog."

Yeah... in my region they tunneled shafts instead of strip-mining, but I liked his plan, so I let it go.

"In case we hit pay dirt, I'll have Zaylin Twee peel off some of her investigators to help with evidence recovery. Choose a subordinate to run the show, Dougie. As soon as a second black widow gets here, we're all going back to the capital. *With* our prisoner."

Double-K's brow wrinkled as he ticked off items on fingers. "A detachment in the Veil of Seriata. The *Hope* remains in Filestra. Our expeditionary force further divides between there and Thoria. This is the front of the war. Should we not remain in the East to direct all efforts?"

I'd made my mind up. "Delegate. We'll direct from Shansara. Our responsibility for now is to step back from the tactical and strategize our response across the whole kingdom."

Karlo grunted. "This isn't going to stay contained to the frontier, is it?"

"We'd be a fool to plan that way," I said. "So unless our prisoner proves that this is nothing more than the work of a few albino anarchists, the whole kingdom's on terror watch."

✠ ✠ ✠

Talis Darmon smirked. "Boogeyman? Hardly."

"I agree, he's pretty pathetic looking," I said.

It wasn't possible for him to see us through the one-way glass of the interrogation room, but the Vermeel correctly sensed our presence, his black eyes fixed on where we stood. Whereas we used soft cord to bind prisoners in the field, our cops used cuffs little different from those I grew up with on TV. The prisoner sat with his upper limbs secured behind him, his less mobile lower arms manacled in front to allow him to reach his mouth with the water pouch he clasped, but ignored.

He was an anemic and cadaverous version of the hearty Tarns I knew, the faded green of a plant neglected by the friend who picked up your mail but forgot to water the fern. His skin stretched taut over stringy muscles and he wore abundant bandages on the many singes from near-misses by K-specs.

Since capture, the prisoner had stayed mute as if he didn't have a tongue, which Karlo checked and said he did. Whether the Vermeel couldn't understand or was simply acting the part of POW, we didn't yet know. My bet was both. Holding out a silver bracelet, Zaylin Twee approached the Vermeel.

"No harm will come to you," she said in soothing Mihdra. The prisoner stiffened but didn't show fear or twist away as she closed the hinge of the decipher band above an available bicep. It shrank and conformed into the crease between shoulder and arm.

"This will give you the ability to understand and answer our questions."

I remembered my first experience of decipher magic. It was unsettling at first, the comprehension of words foreign to the ear but spoken in translation by your own internal voice. But it was also enticing. Perhaps enough to coax him to speak. Zaylin Twee took a seat at the table.

"By order of Queen Talis Darmon, you are held for crimes committed against the Kingdom of Mihdradahl. With unprovoked aggression you have murdered our citizens. But in our system of governance, you have rights, and it is our way to make sure you understand those guarantees. You will be treated without deprivation. You will not be harmed. If you choose not to speak, you will not be tortured. You will have proper representation to advise you of our law and to explain your side of events when tried for your crimes. Do you understand?"

The Vermeel gave no indication he did or didn't.

Formalities over, Zaylin Twee began what I anticipated would be a series of masterful psychological ploys to leverage an admission, and offered another carrot before showing him the stick.

"I know what you are thinking. If the fires do not await you, nor fear of having your skin peeled away, for what reason should you speak? I will tell you. Because in exchange for cooperation—if it be sufficient to please the queen—she may free you as a reward for your assistance."

Khraal Kahlees growled at my side. "The First Shield wastes time by enticement of the queen's mercy. What she stipulates shall *not* be done is in fact the way to timely success. With proper torture there is no loss of face for a Mydreen to surrender information—as long as one limb has been severed or more than half of the skin has been sufficiently charred. Or, for example, consider the Yellows. Even less need be done to them before the threshold is reached for them to satisfy honor and surrender their obligation to resist. It would be no different for primitives like the Pale."

"What about Korundi?" Doug teased.

Double-K snorted. "No Korundi would capitulate to such minor discomfort, but my examples hold true for those honorless cultures."

Dave groaned in our ears. "Yeah, yeah, Double-K, you're always making those noises. But you took an oath that your prisoner torturing days were finished. You won't break it, so why pretend, brah?"

"True, David Masamuni," Double-K said. "But cannot a comrade share nostalgia for the old ways? As you say, don't judge me."

"It's okay, my friend," Karlo said. "I knew you were just walking down memory lane."

Double-K clucked. "Thank you, Karlo Columbo. I truly appreciate that you are again in the profession of arms. It is good to have the support of a true teammate, more so than—" Double-K jabbed two right thumbs toward Dave.

Doug grasped the shoulder-pad muscles aside Karlo's thick neck and gave him a playful shake. "Man, it's great to have the band back together."

I felt the same high of combat success, but enough was enough. "Shh! Do I have to play squad leader the rest of my life? Good Lord! Shut it!"

Our antics had not distracted Talis Darmon. Her eyes had never ceased their dissection of the face the color of spoiled meat. The first

Vermeel any of us had ever seen had me considering that any dogma painting the Pale as nothing but primitive savages was legitimate. Whereas a killer might be remorseless, it was more like our prisoner were an animal, blissfully unaware an ethic against slaughtering civilians even existed. Like one who acted on the natural instinct that made a lion guiltless for sinking fangs into a tiny deer.

Zaylin Twee continued with her persuasion.

"Nothing to say? Very well. You will be taken to the healer for another treatment then returned to confinement. As you await our next meeting, reflect on this: your sunless cell could well be your home for the span of a very, very long life spent in our care."

The prisoner did not so much as blink.

"I believe you understand me and choose to remain mute. You may think silence is honorable but consider—for the mass murders perpetrated in Thoria and Filestra, the queen has no choice but to declare war on the Vermeel. A vast military campaign is already underway to punish your kind, wherever they may be. If you remain silent, your hands will be stained by the blood of the many innocent women and hatchlings of your people, killed in a war to secure the safety of our citizens. Instead, provide knowledge to prevent further acts of aggression against us and you will save countless lives, Red and Pale."

Eyelids widened to reveal glimmering black pools suddenly alive with intelligence. His gravelly speech reached my ears and my brain understood the strange Vermeel tongue from first clicks, hisses, and whistles.

"Do you truly believe threats against the People or promises of kind treatment will pry open my maw?"

His vocabulary was well-constructed and not the stuff of the primitive I expected.

The First Shield continued. "If there are other targets, you must tell me now before the consequences to your people become grave beyond your imagining."

The Vermeel gagged a laugh. "The People embrace death as the price for justly punishing our Red oppressor. About which, you unwittingly bring me joyous news of my comrade's success in Filestra! Power to the people!"

Zaylin Twee shook her head disapprovingly. "A people as intelligent as yourselves must know this will end badly. War as you cannot imagine looms. If not with consideration for your comrades, what of the cost to the women and hatchlings?"

Now he bared his tusks in pleasure. "I will never betray the People. I will tell you nothing. Though we take bloody revenge on you, you brag of your laws and despise of torture, as if it were virtue! It is because your decadence has turned your stomach sour for doing what is necessary. Your weak and sick culture disgusts me. It is *your* hands that will be coated in the blood of your women and hatchlings. When next you visit my cell, it will not stink of fear, but the sweetness of joy when I hear you cry in true grief. Take me away."

"This is no dumb animal!" Khraal Kahlees declared.

"He's been highly indoctrinated," Karlo said with analytical awe.

I stayed quiet as something new developed on the other side of the glass. It was a Zaylin Twee I'd never seen before. Her sly smile showed the teeth of a fox and her words dripped the sweet sap a carnivorous flower used to trap prey. A shiver ran down the back of my neck at her resemblance to Hannibal Lecter describing a savory meal.

"Crude pain can loosen a tongue, but it is not for lack of stomach that we do not torture our prisoners. There are far better methods. You boast of your people's willingness to sacrifice their lives in this cause, but in my experience, it is easy to make such offerings in the abstract.

"We have forgotten much about the Vermeel, so I beg ask of you, what happens to the clan of a traitor? Because, I not only know who you are—Peritar the Finder of the Black Tusk clan—I know where you nest."

Thick saliva drizzled off tusks askance in shock. If the decipher had failed to surprised him, the revelation that his name and clan were known jolted him like Ben Franklin holding the kite string.

Zaylin Twee was pleased by his reaction.

"I will direct my spies to let it be known that *your* family hatched a traitor who revealed all to the Red enemy. When all of your line has been torn to pieces, will you still so fervently boast of the nobility of total sacrifice in your cause against us?"

The Pale dropped the hydration pouch he'd been ignoring. "How... how could you know these things?"

The First Shield rose and went for the door. "I know much more, Peritar. Think on what I have said until we speak again." While the prisoner was escorted away, staggering and dazed, Zaylin Twee joined us. Dave was the first to demonstrate a respect he typically reserved for the aftermath left by JDAMs and MOABs.

"Daaaaamn. Someone knows how to play hardball."

Zaylin Twee smirked. "Thanks to Master Sarkan Sell. He alone knew the Vermeel carry with them the miniscule piece of the birth shell on which is inscribed their tribal identity. It is sewn into the belt of their harness. Otherwise, even had we found it, we would not have recognized its importance. It is the necessary token of admission into their afterlife, lest they be turned away by their ancestors as unknown. With that knowledge and thanks to the queen's brilliant research to reacquaint with the characters of their language, we are no longer without the keys to understanding our enemy."

"I did little more than direct the staff of the library," Talis Darmon said, deflecting credit. "It was once partially analyzed, but interest in the field was abandoned long ago. Once I understood the essence of their symbology, loading a decipher to translate their language was the simplest of tasks."

The First Shield bowed. "Nonetheless, Queen, the synergy of tactical and academic efforts has produced a pivotal advancement in our battle."

Khraal Kahlees was chagrined. "If we know the location of the prisoner's clan, why were we not informed? I would already have assembled an incursion force and struck before the enemy learns we have made interdiction of the attackers!"

Doug rolled his eyes. "He don't know that *we* don't know where his homeboys chill, Double-K. Zaylin Twee was psyching him out, duder. It was beautiful, First Shield."

Double-K pulled his chin back as if a jab had landed. "You do not have spies among the Vermeel, First Shield?"

Zaylin Twee let him down with a kind smile. "Not yet."

"Torture does not require so many layers of chicanery. It is so much more honest." The green giant made a favorite lament. "How have I fallen into such low company?"

"I'm almost afraid to ask what's next up in your interrogation," I said. "You just threatened him with what's tantamount to the murder of his entire family."

Zaylin Twee was circumspect. "It will depend on the subject's remaining resistance, Warlord. I anticipate he will bargain with information. They will be lies, of course. But simply advancing our process to that of a two-way exchange, even one fraught with falsehoods, will produce opportunities for deconstruction and reconstruction of a narrative."

Grinning, Doug said, "Yeah, I learned that one when I was still in middle school. If the cops nab you and you say the drugs in your front pocket aren't yours because these aren't your pants you're wearing, they still already got you to admit the drugs are *drugs*—right? Busted! Then they work on you from that angle. This is so much cooler than tactical questioning on the battlefield. It's like NYPD Blue or something!"

Now it was Karlo's turn to make a favorite lament. "Oh, Dougie, what the hell kind of childhood did you have, anyway?"

The First Shield appraised Doug; I just wasn't sure if it was a look of morbid curiosity or the pragmatic appreciation for the once misguided youth who turned from crime to become a force for great good.

"If it interests you, Douglas Knoblock, and your duties as a general do not prevent it, you would be welcome to join the interrogation team. I will alert you when I think the time has come that you could be helpful."

Doug beamed. "Thanks, Zaylin Twee. I'd really like that."

"Ah, boy," Dave groaned. "Just what the world needs. From criminal to Green Beret to homicide cop. What happens when that gets old, Dougie? What's next for you then? Rock n' roll hit man for hire?"

Doug shot Dave the one-finger salute. "Right here, bro. This is for you."

In the way I knew too well, Talis Darmon made ready for an accelerated exit. "Thank you, First Shield. My compliments to your Guardians for their excellent work. Come, Warlord. Let us depart before this all too brief moment of hope for salvation of the kingdom smothers beneath a landslide of puerile antics."

Everyone bowed as Talis Darmon turned to leave. I caught nervous glances from my chastised brothers, but waved their concerns away and said, "See you later, boys."

I trotted to catch up to my wife who when I reached her side said only, "I shall never understand."

08

"The council chamber is too stifling and oppressive an atmosphere for my mood, Benjamin Colt. Can we not conduct affairs in setting more conducive to free exchange with our dearest?"

Relaxed from a long tub soak, she seemed over her vexation at how the boys conducted themselves around her. She sat at her dressing table, brushing her thick locks in front of the mirror. I never tired of the views.

"You mean, have everyone over for a party?" I asked. "*Everyone?*"

In the Venn diagram of all the factions sitting on the council, at the center would be a damn small group that met the definition of "dearest."

She chuckled. "You understand me perfectly, husband. I mean to exclude the larger council from this gathering. There is much to be examined. Despite my distaste for the manner in which you and your brethren conduct your dialectics, your results are unimpeachable.

I wish an environment to solicit insights from those we most value, with food, drink, and fraternity invited in the comforts of our home."

"Careful," I teased. "You're just getting over your latest irritation at the boys. If you're really hoping they'll feel comfortable enough to hang loose, you have to be prepared for what comes along with that."

I'd given up trying to make her understand how it was practically a love language when one of us accused another of being the product of incest.

"They've fought for us above, below, and beyond, wife. And they'll do it all again tomorrow without even having to be asked. That's how much they love us. And above all, they *respect* you. I've told you, it's nothing to be offended by."

"I truly understand that, Benjamin Colt. I do. I am regretful of my frequent umbrages. I, too, am a product of my environment."

"You're an aristocrat and a scholar. And we're all—not. It's as much a man/woman difference as it is a soldier/civilian kind of dichotomy, honey. I'll ask the guys to be on their best behavior, but I promise it won't be necessary."

"Do not, Benjamin Colt. I want none of our friends to feel as though they must tread daintily in our home. It would be at cross purposes for what I desire." She sighed. "It is just so difficult to understand the process whereby a great mind prefaces a rational, intelligent criticism by first making an accusation that the opponent has mated with his own mother."

She listed more of the examples that perplexed her.

"Douglas Knoblock often says to Karlo Columbo, 'it must hurt to be that stupid.' I cannot countenance those as the words of a friend, much less to one so clearly brilliant as our lead innovator. It makes no sense. And I have heard David Masamuni tell Khraal Kahlees that he should, 'apologize to the Air Wizards for wasting the oxygen they make.' And I have even overheard Khraal Kahlees tell you, 'the best part of your egg dried on the outside.'"

She shook the jibes and the associated imagery away.

"No matter. I insist on complete informality at this gathering and I will not spoil the atmosphere with signs of displeasure, regardless of what is said. I promise."

"Fair 'nuff," I said, though I still had my doubts. She noticed my apprehension and renewed her resolve.

"You will see, Benjamin Colt. As I delve into the ideals of republicanism, I have examined my attitudes about royal privilege. I take my oath before you." She placed both hands over her bosom. "I am accepting of your process, no matter how unfathomable to me it seems to make dining recommendations to a trusted comrade of a psycho-sexual cannibalistic nature. I shall absolutely deafen myself to that which I normally perceive as improper decorum."

"Okay, okay, I'm convinced."

But I was still going to tell the guys to chill.

"Also, I wish to extend our inner circle. My aim is to use the occasion to combine purposes. I speak specifically of Douglas Knoblock's companions. There is no time like the present."

Our life together was pretty much a non-stop roller coaster ride of screaming dives into the pits of hell followed by rocket rides shooting us high to pierce the clouds of heaven. Down, up, and back down—again and again. And through it all, our friends held on tight with us for the ride. And until Filestra, we'd been on a long run of level track, enjoying a smooth peace. But my wife and I had failed to do as we'd sworn to each other so many times while holding our little Shara together in the dark—to gather closely and as often as we could with those who'd done so much for us.

Time just seems to get away.

Paradoxically so on Vistara, where a lifetime is many times that of what we were once bound to as Earthlings. Ahead of us were lifespans perhaps many hundreds of years.

I often caught myself inhaling the scent of Vistaran malaise like a sweet secondhand smoke, tempting me to adopt a two -pack-a-day habit myself. There was no hurry, because there was time for everything. On Vistara, the sands were never going to run out of the hourglass. Our lives would not burn away in the fire of time as it did on Earth.

So I was glad that Talis Darmon was making the move to carpe that diem and show our friends how much we appreciated them. But I had another concern, born of experience.

"Aren't you worried with everything that's going on right now that a private shindig might burn the butts of all the fancy pants when they hear they weren't invited?"

I guess I deserved the eye roll. "You prematurely lapse into Thulian crudeness, but you are most wise in judging the tender sensibilities of the council. I shall leave no time for the fermenting of any jealousy on their part. We will hold a similar event the very next night to rain our adoration on them. First, we make an effort to cherish our friends. Second, we shall perform our royal duties to maintain the favor of the aristocracy."

Such was the privilege that came with being queen that by the next night, things were ready as though it'd been planned for months.

The lower chambers of our comfortable apartments were designed for just such a use, though were rarely ever employed so. We may not be the Veil of Seriata, but unlike the cold resplendence I experienced there, our showcase of Mihdradahl's culture exuded not only grandness, but warmth and welcome.

Tables of food and wine beckoned. Couches and cushions woven in the finest patterns promised comfort for all. The masterworks of Mihdra artisans filled our home and complemented the beauty and genius of the hostess, our queen. She toted a joyfully gurgling Shara while mingling with our friends, and for the first time in a long time, I reflected on the astronomical collision of circumstances that had brought me to this time and place.

If Dave's true name was Even Steven, mine was Luckiest SOB Alive.

I dragged Apache away before his lack of manners became an issue and left him outside with Sarkan Sell and Jodal Jark, just in time to meet a grinning Doug with three shy women huddling close to him as they reached the doors. As instructed, they were the last on the list to arrive.

"Look who's here," I said, as I pushed them through the foyer to a waiting Talis Darmon who passed me a fussy Shara. She moved to greet the last arrivals—as she intended—before an audience my wife rightly called our dearest.

"Oh, my friends! My heart is so very full to have you here." The three women dipped as one in formal courtesy, returned in equal depth by my wife. She moved to embrace the nearest, the tiny red head. "Bandra Lang, are you well? Your shoulder is as flawless as the rest of your enviable complexion. Does it pain you in any way, dear lady?"

Bandra Lang grew timid, then her eyes became puffy and she sniffed. "No, Queen, I thank you for your concern. I enjoy perfect health."

Talis Darmon cupped her face. "How I hope that is true, my brave friend. I worried so!"

Doug threw a massive arm around Bandra Lang's shoulders and grinned. "I'm supervising her therapy, Talis Darmon. She's already exercising again, thanks to your healer."

Talis Darmon greeted the dark Faahl Saleen and lavender-haired Selvin Wharran with the same embrace, affection, and concern. The first time the three reclusive women visited our home, Talis Darmon had been in the grips of an insidious strife that strangled her reason and compassion and would soon have ended her life, had we not discovered the disease and almost too late, the cure.

And in the throes of her psychologic infirmity, she'd mistreated Doug's loves. And though readily forgiven for that which she was not responsible, Talis Darmon sought to make amends almost immediately after her return to full faculties. She made a public declaration of friendship by including the women in as many public events as possible —signaling to all that the Thorian ladies had her confidence—but what bringing to court may have done for the confidence of someone bred in Shansara or Clymaira, only served to discomfit the Thorian ladies.

To top it off, ringside seats at ground zero in Filestra had hardly turned into the bonding experience Talis Darmon intended.

Now, the women laughed, blushed, and blossomed. Talis Darmon had at last coaxed them from their demure states. And the only magic my sorceress used was being her genuine self. The self she wanted to be all the time. The self she couldn't be if she were to be first and always the regent of a kingdom.

Doug's eyes sparkled as he mouthed silently to me, "Thank you, brother."

I winked and gave him my widest, stupidest grin, the lump in my throat so big no words could pass it. I'm just like that.

When my homie's hearts are full, mine is too.

As many as had ever been together with us in the great room lounged, each and every one a proven friend. It was another stop and smell the roses moment.

Khraal Kahlees sat in a massive chair meant especially for a Tarn's comfort, with his daughter Beraal beside him rather than at his feet in the normal custom of the Korund. Dave and Tranya Olan shared a cushion and next to them in conversation were Keshin Tellest, Shasa Karin, and their former boss in the Guard, Zaylin Twee.

Karlo and Doug were in discussion, the three Thorian women taking turns cuddling Shara as they pelted Talis Darmon with questions about motherhood. Perrin Halser had the gaunt and weary look of one still in the process of physical recovery, and shared the air with Cynar and his companion Dureen Zell.

Cynar was the oldest of all, perhaps the oldest man on all of Vistara, yet this evening he seemed to me more vital and less unhinged than ever. If the mists of time had shown me a future depicting this Cynar—leading a normal life and with a girlfriend—I'd have smashed the mirror right then and there for being the disinformation tool of some insidious enemy.

I carried a fussy Shara to bed and she fell into an instant slumber. I was already eager for her next awakening and the glorious sensation of brushing the tip of my nose back and forth over her soft cheeks like a paintbrush.

I returned to find conversation had at last turned to current events.

"That explosion was *not* a chemical one," Doug was saying. "I just don't know how they got a stone to discharge like that. Red stones are perfect for cutting charges. Safe as can be. They burn. If there's a way to make them go high-order, I haven't figured it out."

Karlo said, "And white stones potentiate chemical explosives, like the ones in our mortar rounds. By themselves, they're pretty benign."

Dave joined in. "Even the Yellows had to make their bombs out of good ol' fashioned nitrates. So the Vermeel know what the rest of the world doesn't—how to make energy stones go kerblooie."

"You talking about the IEDs?" I said as I plopped down next to my wife.

Doug nodded. "Yup. I've tested every type of stone and their combinations, trying to develop a substitute for C-4 and I've yet to come close."

Cynar said, "Not *every* stone have you experimented with, Douglas Knoblock. A stone that harnesses the tenth ray but able to discharge at the speed of light to release its rays while also capturing the natural adjacent rays, such a lattice may exist. I say, events have proven it does."

For reasons not yet apparent, Cynar rose, disregarding the plate balanced on his lap as morsels bounced onto the carpet, to Dureen Zell's embarrassed complaints. It was the kind of opportunity Apache lived for. Too bad he was outside. Cynar surrendered his plate to her.

"Moreso, it must have an arrangement like this." He hiked his robes up and crouched into a deep squat. Folding himself then shooting his arms through crossed legs, he placed his palms on the carpet and lifted himself off the floor in a yoga-like balance.

Dougie snorted. "Dude! No one wants to see *your* stones. Keep them ornaments in the attic until after Thanksgiving, dog."

The first test of my wife's oath had arrived. She scrunched her eyelids, but said nothing.

"Please bleach my eyes, babe," Dave muttered to Tranya Olan, who put a finger to her lips.

Cynar held the pose. "Picture each of my limbs as an axis for repeating layers. I have not encountered such a stone myself, but the signature I gathered is evidence it *must* exist."

He unwound and tugged his robes into place before relaxing back into a seated position. He popped a confection into his mouth from the plate Dureen Zell held out, chewed noisily, and gulped before issuing a triumphant, "Hehehe."

Whether Cynar was pleased by his deduction or his demonstration, I was just relieved he'd not paralyzed himself pantomiming the chemistry of the stone he postulated. For all his effort, I wasn't any better enlightened.

"Speaking of evidence," I said. "What about the excavation of the ambush site?"

"I was waiting to tell you," Doug said. "I got the call earlier. About ten meters down, they found a blood trail. No bodies so far, but the dig goes on."

Double-K grinned devilishly as only a Tarn can, his tusks thrust forward as if to gore an invisible challenger. "Victory is at hand. I never doubted. For when this tribe of warriors joins together in effort, the very pillars of this world tremble at our might."

My friend spoke truth. The universe that conspired to kill us on a regular basis was about to fail again. Because we were together. Flushing emerald with pride, Beraal linked an arm through her father's and the glow filled us all with a contentment as warm as a campfire on a chilly night.

For everyone but Karlo. The gears in his head turned beneath a cocked eyebrow as he hummed the sustained note that was the polite warning he was about to spoil the mood.

Dave confronted Karlo's plunder of our brief serenity. "Way to read the room, brah. Can't let us have a moment. So, spill. Whatcha got?"

"We need to shift our focus. If the Vermeel have a secret mine where they dig the stone Cynar says must exist, locating it becomes the priority. We need to build detectors and dedicate every asset to the search. We cover every square inch of desert until we find it. We cut off the source, we cut off their ability to harm us."

Khraal Kahlees frowned. "Do not be fooled by the unexpected quality of intellect the prisoner demonstrates, Karlo Columbo. The Vermeel are neither miners nor engineers. I suspect the Annamese are behind them. If we are to search anywhere, we should look to the south."

Cynar frowned. "I am sorry to tell you it is not possible to detect such a stone unless actively emitting, else deposits of stones could be discovered with ease anywhere, Karlo Columbo."

Perrin Halser raised a finger. "I have supervised the kingdom's sourcing and assaying of stones for many years. Whatever the source of these unique stones, it is wholly unknown to me."

Dave grunted. "How about we focus on how they're moving underground? If it's the walk-through-walls kind of thing, there's got to be a way to futz with it. Some kind of electric fence we could use as a border wall or something?"

We'd first experienced the technology infiltrating through the subterranean lair of the local Water Priest whose duty station lay beneath the Fountains of Persidia—when Shansara had been an enemy-held city. The hidden entrance to the Platinum Bridge and the Veil utilized the same kind of magic.

Cynar shook his head, but not in the exasperatedly rabid way he so often did when correcting a misunderstanding of something he considered self-evident to any and everyone.

"The transmuting of solid into something temporarily shifted from cohesion may seem like a similar phenomenon, David Masamuni, but it is entirely different. The portals themselves are impregnated with crystals that resonate the fourth ray. The surrounding framework holds stones producing the seventh ray. The key activates the rays into a reinforcing harmony, permitting the solid barrier to lose cohesion. It is a dual-encoded process."

Karlo nodded like he got it. "Passage through the portals is possible because they're part of a dependent, not an independent system, like what this other technology must use."

Cynar smiled at Karlo's intuition, though it wasn't clear to me—or anyone else except the smiling Perrin Halser—what that meant. The scraggly bearded millegenarian continued. "It is not control of the fourth and seventh rays alone. To manifest the effect as the Vermeel seem to be doing, it requires a means novel to me."

"Any chance it's actually sorcery?" I said.

"None," Cynar declared, but we'd all looked to Talis Darmon. She smiled.

"Our wizard is peerless in his understanding of things. He is correct; it is no form of sorcery. It must be science." Her praise restored another hundred years of Cynar's already improved vitality. Dureen Zell stroked her man's back and he did not shy away.

Cynar had disproven my belief that you can't teach an old wizard new tricks.

Khraal Kahlees's snort was equally firm. "The Vermeel have neither sorcery nor science. Karlo Columbo, tell us of the human found conspiring with the Pale. This must be the source of the technology enabling their militancy. Is he another Thulian arrival, bringing transformation to disrupt Vistara?"

Talis Darmon and I already knew the answer so as Karlo explained, she whispered in my ear. "Did you caution your brothers to restrain their jocular profanity? They speak to each other respectfully and with collegial spirit."

I shook my head. "I didn't say a word to them about it. You wanted the boys to be themselves, here they are." I actually hadn't. Her eyebrows arched pleasantly high. I tuned in to Karlo again.

"The dead man wasn't circumcised," Karlo said, "which doesn't necessarily mean much. He had no appendix, and no surgical scar. The absence of an appendix is the norm for Vistarans. It's an anatomical rarity on Earth, I don't remember the incidence, but it could be the case here. However, the superficial layer of his skin was definitely bleached by some process. The physicians couldn't say anything definite about the deeper pigments—whether they mean a red or yellow complexion. As far as stature and features, it's hard to classify those traits to any one particular race as well. One thing for sure, he'd lived a rough life. He carried a lot of old scars from lacerations knitted by healing stone rather than joined together by suture—another check mark on the local-boy side of the column. Put it all together, our best forensic evidence points to him being Vistaran."

Zaylin Twee said, "We are examining all records. If ever arrested or if he was in fact at one time a soldier serving in the kingdom, we will discover his identity. If he is Annamerian..." She let it hang. "We will not be able to do so."

I knew who could tell us. "Is our pasty prisoner any closer to going back on his word to starve our ears of his speech?"

Zaylin Twee was philosophic. "Not as yet, Benjamin Colt, but have hope. Given time, many a mute suspect has miraculously developed the powers of speech. We are in the earliest stages of our work."

Double-K frowned. "The human pretending to be a Pale may be of our world, but it is difficult to believe a soldier serving Mihdradahl—even one highly treasonous—would conspire with the Vermeel against his own. This again implicates the Yellow. The Annamese may despise all Tarn regardless of tribe, but if it suits their purpose, nothing is beneath them. Their liberation from the oppression of their matriarchal despotism does not diminish the resentment they hold from defeat at our hands. It is for these reasons I believe this man most likely to be Annamerian."

Zaylin Twee shrugged. "His identity remains a mystery."

Dave abandoned his relaxed speech and spoke as he did when engaged in official duties. "For everything we don't know, there's just as much that we do. We finally have proof the Vermeel aren't figments of our imagination. We've got their M.O., and the whole army is running interdiction to head off the next attack. Our people are good at what they do. They're going to intercept the next one of these infiltration teams, and the next after that. With each one we'll have more intel and soon enough, we'll have a full picture painted. Those are our knowns, and they more than balance the unknowns."

Talis Darmon smiled approvingly. "Here, here, David Masamuni. That is a perfect assessment and one you shall present to the council tomorrow. Our security is already much improved and the kingdom is well on its way to return to tranquility. Well done, all."

We joined her to raise glasses, except Karlo, who produced a scroll. "Before we relax, I have something else. I thought we might look at this again. It's been a while." He adjusted the open scroll and projected an image for us all to see.

My pulse went thready.

It was from the 3-D navigational system of the commandeered White ship.

We witnessed the virtual globe for only a short time during a hectic and uncertain time of crisis—while piloting a captured ship and plotting how we would reclaim the queen's seat on the throne. In the chaotic and desperate atmosphere of that spherical cabin, the hologram challenged what we thought we knew about our world.

Represented in colorful reliefs, we'd seen mountains and gorges, fruited plains and bodies of water shining clear as diamonds, and as shocking—scattered sparsely around the sphere at vast distances from our scorched and dehydrated Mihdradahl—were clusters of what had to be cities. Whether they were ancient ruins or civilizations living as we did in isolation, no scholar could say.

We still had the captured ship, but not the global mapping system. During Karlo's attempts to help Cynar reverse engineer the Whites' technology, the console containing the nav system wiped itself clean as a chalkboard before Friday's dismissal bell.

"I had more images of the entire nav system on my iPad," Karlo said as we stared at the floating projection. "But like a lot of the data we've tried to transfer to memory crystals, it scrambled into junk."

"Have all your tablets and laptops crapped out like the rest of ours?" Doug asked.

Karlo nodded. "Yup. Mine are dead and useless, too."

Not one of our computers from Earth still worked, and a lot more than just the Whites' map had been lost. Doug sighed as he remembered.

"I never got Ben's playlist copied before it stopped working. Damn shame."

"I still kick myself for losing that map," Karlo said.

"It was not to be, Karlo Columbo," Perrin Halser comforted him. "The destruction of the navigation system was automated and not the result of carelessness on your part. Of that, hold no doubt."

Cynar cackled. "Hehehe. Instead, my gifted Thulian friend, take heart that the Whites had not means to foil us from obtaining all other manner of secrets from their ship. Hehehe."

Cynar was referring to the ray-killing beam that we used to drop the Annamese super-destroyers.

I returned my attention to the image above us. Roughly a quarter of Vistara's northern hemisphere was represented in the spatial view, centered more or less on our own neighborhood, with Shansara in the lower portion. Crossing the equator at the bottom of the screen was the fantastically deep, wide, and long gash running northeast to southwest called the Furrow of the Creator's Hand. The massive canyon was a natural geographical barrier between us and the Annamese to our south. The walled capital city of the former Annamerian Kingdom was cut off at the lower border of the image.

North of Mihdradahl spanned the Korund Mountain Range, nearly as long east to west as was the Furrow far to its south. At the north pole lay the Sharpa Mountains, beneath which had concealed the hiding place where the evil Whites carried out their parasitism for centuries. The left edge of the image extended little beyond our westernmost city of Pyreenia, but to the right, the screen held the eastern curvature of the globe.

Beyond Thoria lay the great featureless expanse of the desolation Khraal Kahlees proclaimed as too cruel for even the Vermeel. But far beyond that, half a world away, a pointed skyline of a range of white-capped mountains lifted from the curvature of the horizon. A central plain of green lay beneath. And in the confluence where flat green plains blended into the steepening terrain of the western slopes, spread a white stain. And within it, straight lines, right angles, and smooth radiuses; the telltale marks of builders.

It was the sprawl of a massive civilization.

With astonishment, the lavender-haired Selvin Wharran said, "Xanalar."

Faahl Saleen and Bandra Lang echoed agreement in whispered gasps. "It must be." "It must."

"What's that you say, babes?" Doug asked.

Talis Darmon was intrigued. "Xanalar. I hear it in the voice of my mother, for it has been since she spoke the fable to me as a child that I have heard the name."

"I recall as well," Beraal said. "The epic of Xanalar is not known in the Korund. I was as enchanted as the hatchling I held on my lap whilst your mother entertained us with the epic."

Talis Darmon closed her eyes.

"Pleasured lands of perfumed scents fragranced by the blooms of trees
That touch the sky and tease a rest sublime beneath their care.
Rivers gold in sunlight fair cause thirst to slake by vision there
And honey sweet and rich dark meat do fill the hunger bare.

Dulcimer notes carry
Fill the very air we breathe
With kisses soft as mother's love
Bring rapture so contentedly.

Xanalar, home Xanalar
Crib and comfort properly
Doth bathe and blanket
Suckle, nurture
Leave no appetite for mortal poetry

Oh harmony of air and land and sea
Inland sea
Where beckons alabaster skin
And lips of red to melt for me and thee,
Only thee."

The three ladies each added a piece of the tale, speaking with the same dreamy quality Talis Darmon used while lost in recollection.

"Two young lovers escaped their disapproving families to be together."

"They flew away through tallest forests of crystal towers on a steed lighter than air."

"It was a giant creature who once delved the oceans but learned instead how to swim through the sky."

"Where water showers down from boughs of soft ether floating high above, and lush growth covers the ground in a velvet blanket," Beraal finished.

Dave whispered to Tranya Olan, "I didn't savvy a word of that poem, but it made me horny."

Her reply was an ice bath. "I am deafened to anything but more of the epic of Xanalar."

Wheels spun at high rev in my head as I stared at the map, and the energy in the room told me I was not alone. Was the civilization teased by the map the same from which the fable of Xanalar arose, or perhaps right now, persisted?

Of the Seven Ancient Wonders of Earth, only the Great Pyramid of Giza stood as testament to being more than myth. The rest left virtually no trace that they actually ever existed. Was the map enticing us with a wonder to surpass the Hanging Gardens of Babylon and all the other ancient mysteries of Earth?

I knew how often Vistaran legend had turned out to be fact.

Dave shrugged. "It's fun to think about, I s'pose."

As if reading my mind, Karlo said, "Remember, what we're seeing is a representation. It isn't overhead imagery like a satellite photo. If you look closely at our own cities, they're not accurate. What we're looking at may have turned to dust ages ago."

"So what makes you bring this up, Karlo?" I didn't permit him time to answer my rhetorical. "This isn't about trying to tease us back into our plans for exploring Vistara. You're bringing it up because you think there's a chance *that's* got something to do with our latest crisis."

Karlo grimaced. "It seems farfetched, I know. But everything seems to point east. The Vermeel have been out of the picture for so long, who really knows where and what they've been up to? And when I consider we have a *new* enemy using *new* technologies, it bears consideration there's a new source to our troubles."

Dougie frowned. "Still don't explain how they got M4s or who's trained them to use them."

Double-K slid his jaw and tusks side to side in rumination. "You suggest we seek not an old foe, but one wholly unknown to us. It is an intriguing premise, Karlo Columbo."

"Dude!" Doug exclaimed. "And they come here all the way from La-La Land just to F with us? How come?"

Karlo opened his mouth, but nothing came out. He slumped. "Yeah. It sounds even stupider out loud. Which is why we do things this way. Sorry, everyone. Disregard."

Dougie was quick to come back. "Not so fast there, bro-man. I wasn't dissing your hypotheticals, I was trolling for Ben-dog or Davey-Dave to jump in." He grew deadly serious. "See, you weren't under the Sharpa Mountains with us, Karlo. You didn't see what we did."

Dave nodded. "Dougie's dead-nuts-on. We don't talk about it, but we haven't forgotten. There was more than one branch of the River Blix for floating gondolas of merry pilgrims north to spend an eternity with the Whites. Lashura was a liar through and through, but when she said they drew from more than just Mihdradahl—once we saw those other streams of mercury that off-ramped to their reception hall—I knew she was telling the truth."

"Doug and Dave are right," I said. "The mystery city on the map seems like a good candidate for being one of those sources."

Dougie was anxious to say more. "Dude, I don't know about you, but sometimes I dream about what we saw down there, especially all the religious kind of stuff on the walls and that big Mount Rushmore sculpture. It was easy to pick out the Tarns, but some looked, I dunno, not like us or them, know what I mean?"

Dave frowned. "Ben, d'you remember that day Kleeve Hartus took us to the Hah Shur to see Marviel Lanconin and the others be whisked away on the railway north? It wasn't Xanalar, but I remember he named some other place that supposedly sent pilgrims north."

I was trying to remember when Talis Darmon said, "Xanalar is mentioned in the texts, as are Turmalia, and others."

Zaylin Twee said softly, "The texts remain, but there are no priests to question on the matter."

What lay at the other end of the rivers were on the lengthy list of things I intended to investigate someday, things we'd encountered above, below, and beyond Vistara. But they'd all become like the hamburger buried at the bottom of the chest freezer. We had an auto-delivery of fresh-ground problems piling up on the reg, so I almost never thought about thawing out the old stuff.

Speaking as though he'd made up his mind, Dave said, "A lot of our strategic planning's been overcome by events, but eventually we were going to do long-range recons. Let's take a black widow for a sightseeing trip east. We call the mission Flight Marco Polo, 'cause just like him, there's no other way to discover what's there except to go."

Doug grinned. "Or we can be Columbus and call whatever place we find Xanalar, even if there's someone there to tell us we're wrong."

Talis Darmon's eyes were on me. Me, myself, and I controlled the black widows.

"I have both squadrons spun-up to support our current security needs."

Before I could explain the math behind my decisions of how I apportioned the strategic craft to help the interdiction efforts while keeping a healthy reserve on standby to run us around like our own private fleet of supersonic Concorde jets, Talis Darmon said, "Cannot one craft be spared for a mission to evaluate the distant region? How much time could be required?"

I'd worked it out. "It's not the distance. It's that navigation's going to be like flying to the moon without so much as a slide rule. But my concern isn't about being short one bird for a limited time. It's the same argument we've had about what unintended consequences our exploration might bring."

Karlo explained for the benefit of the others listening. "If detected, a high-altitude reconnaissance could be interpreted as a hostile act. Maybe it precipitates a response we're not prepared to deal with, especially amidst the new crisis we have going on."

Dave used the terminology we'd swiped straight from *Star Trek*.

"We don't know how First Contact's going to go."

I said, "That's why our exploration plan's linked with our diplomatic outreach also having a big stick to carry behind its back. That's what the *Hope of Vistara* is supposed to be."

Aloud, Khraal Kahlees mulled it over. "Alerting an unknown polity of our presence may be unwise at this time."

"Perhaps it is prudent to table the idea of a reconnaissance for now?" Talis Darmon said.

"I didn't say that," I replied. "When we offer hands of friendship to whoever else may be on the planet, I want the *Hope* ready. But there *is* a need to take at least a look in the far east. So, how about after the council meeting tomorrow, we draw up an operations order for a covert reconnaissance of Xanalar?"

Talis Darmon was pleased. "Agreed. Karlo Columbo, I am glad a subject so long dormant was brought again to our attention. I think you correct in estimating it germane to the current situation."

Karlo closed the image, and Talis Darmon switched courses.

"Wizard Cynar, you have said many interesting things when discussing your investigations into the unknown methods employed by this new enemy, but one in particular I found compelling—that the rays to produce such effects must come from stones of rare quality."

Cynar bowed from his reclining position. "Yes, Queen Talis Darmon, I believe that to be the most likely explanation. What, may I ask, intrigues you?"

She fixed on the man next to him. "Perrin Halser, you have been minister of production and master of the Golden Hub since before my father was king. Is a source for such rarity truly unknown to you?"

"It is, Queen."

Talis Darmon clucked. "Does it not seem obvious what the source of such rare elements must be? It lies not in the far eastern lands of a poem, but one much closer. In a polity that insulates itself from Vistara in a gilded cage. The Veil of Seriata."

My jaw dropped like the bucket on a front-end loader. The boys shared equally stupid looks of epiphany. The Serians' claim they didn't know why they'd been attacked or what had been stolen was conspicuous for its unbelievability. It suddenly fit as part of the bigger lie to hide something from us.

Tsking, Talis Darmon gave the women a significant glance. "Do not be distressed at the men's ineptitude, gentle ladies. I have learned a great deal from these warriors. But I never let myself forget that at the core of their being, their thoughts are primarily on what they can eat, fornicate, or kill."

She turned her eyes to the men. "That is why you missed the obvious, dickheads."

A deadened vacuum took over like we were in an anechoic chamber. Did I hear her right? No man twitched so much as a muscle. My vocal cords froze like I'd imbibed liquid nitrogen. I wished the proverbial pin would drop just to prove I hadn't gone deaf as well as paralyzed.

Doug's Adam's apple bobbed as he gulped.

Scrunching her elegant brow, Talis Darmon said, "Husband, is that not the appropriate insult? Dickhead? Perhaps, it would have had been better to have accused cranial-rectal impaction?"

Dave sputtered his drink then pounded his chest. "Is she busting balls?"

Talis Darmon sat tall and showed her pearly whites. "I am!"

Doug exploded. "Look at her! She's proud. Oh. My. God!" He broke into his best Monty Python voice. "I am the queen! And my royal decree is that you—are all—dickheads!"

Dave fell over laughing, splinting his stomach with both arms. "Bwahahaha! She thought telling us we had our heads up our asses woulda been better! Take me now, I'm done!"

Khraal Kahlees hooted in the Tarn manner, gagging as if choking on a chicken bone. Tears ran down our faces, breaths grew strained as if we ran through sand carrying sixty-pound rucks.

It took minutes to recover until those of us so struck wiped at our red eyes. The women laughed because we were laughing, but theirs was a polite and sympathetic display compared to ours.

"Have I proven adaptable to your methods, gentlemen?" Talis Darmon said, pleased with herself.

I kissed her. "You have, sweetheart."

Dave sat up and sighed loudly, placing an arm around his girlfriend. "Holy-guacamole, I needed that, brah. Talis Darmon caught me da kine flat footed." He broke into the chuckles again and dragged a sleeve across his eyes.

With playful disdain, Tranya Olan shook her head. "The longer I am with you, David Masamuni, the less I understand you and your friends."

We said goodnight, laughter, tears, and fatigued abs the farewell gift, with a morning council awaiting some of us unfortunates. Zaylin Twee tarried, nearly the last to depart, leaving her with just us, Beraal, and Double-K. Her smile faded as she bowed, indicating a purpose. "There is something I wished to speak of. It should not wait until tomorrow, but I did not think it appropriate for the group."

Talis Darmon held on to my waist as a readmitted Apache nearly toppled us over with his rubbing. "Please speak, trusted friend."

Zaylin Twee took a deep breath. "I was present to hear Shaera Kōall carry your message of solace to the people of Filestra. At first, I thought I perhaps misinterpreted her meaning."

The blonde aristocrat had spread the queen's message across Filestra, then went on to Thoria. She was due back soon from Clymaira. Zaylin Twee was greatly discomfited as she explained.

"When I heard her speak again in Thoria, her militancy was much refined; blatant, even. It was then I knew there had been no misunderstanding on my part."

My lingering humor was gone. "What did she say, First Shield?"

"The homicide attacks are but a symptom of a pervasive rot. Pyreenia isolates herself further from the kingdom due to the influence of a flourishing fringe religion. Our own traditions have been attacked and undermined.

"She places blame for all on the queen's move to dissolve the regency."

09

Talis Darmon hadn't been the slightest bit perturbed by Zaylin Twee's report and after checking on the baby, immediately fell asleep. Not me. I lay in a burning bed as I wrote and rewrote the script I'd read from when I dressed down the two-faced opportunist on her return from a campaign to undermine my wife.

I must have grumbled words from the scene I rehearsed, because my wife stirred and placed a hand over mine.

"You would not fret over combat, husband. I do not over politics. Leave your anger. She is no cause to poison yourself." She patted my arm and rolled over and soon resumed her gentle snore.

I eventually found sleep, but not before picturing giving Shaera Kōall the old heave-ho into the Furrow. I woke with the bitterness gone, the smiles of my wife and daughter melting me again into the mold of a better man. I promised to remember the division of labor. Talis Darmon would handle the newly revealed duchess of demagoguery. Applied mayhem was my job.

Next to dad, it was the best job in the world.

I milled around and greeted the multitudes of arriving functionaries while playing the game I called council-room-blending-101. Shaera Kōall had reset my attitude regarding the elite back to baseline—distrust and disrespect—so I had to work extra hard to maintain my plastered-on smile.

Karlo no longer had to attend council, and Doug avoided this room like a tuberculosis ward. My smile muscles were fatiguing until at last, Double-K arrived, providing plausible deniability for my departure from a group discussing the latest fashion in capes. We spoke in low tones as though we engaged in state secrets.

"Where's Davey-Dave? Hungover?"

"David Masamuni has asked me to present his report to the council. He is deeply engaged in other matters, Warlord."

"Whazzup?"

"He sends apologies. He has been meeting with the pilots since before sunrise, planning Flight Marco Polo."

Dave had come to think of himself as a jet-jockey. Air planning was the difference between success and disaster in most special operations, and he'd assigned himself the role of S-3 Air.

"I get it. He wants to have the recon plan ready so we can launch ASAP. Okay, the queen won't mind. But, maybe play it cool and let me tackle any questions?"

"It is you I should remind to chill, brother. Look."

The pink and platinum woman was here, draped in clingy silken gold that shimmered as she moved. In a room full of peacocks, she stood out irritably like harsh flashing neon. I was suddenly reminded of something a friend who'd served in the Pentagon once shared. I asked him what he got out of his two years in Washington and like a priest naming heresy, said, "I learned the true definition of politics. Deception of the masses for personal gain. That's all it is, and that's all it's ever been."

He soon left the army and moved to the remote wilderness of Alaska. Maybe he's still there.

I reconsidered the merits of taking this schemer for that one-way flitter ride to the Grand Canyon.

I'd never do that! But just like Double-K's nostalgia for torture, I could fantasize about such an expedient solution.

Shaera Kōall caught me staring and gave me one of those slit-eyed mean girl smiles that said, "I know you know what I'm up to, but what are you going to do about it?"

What would become of the kingdom if Talis Darmon did eventually step aside and people like Shaera Kōall ended up running things? I already knew. Energy stones and flying cars, super strength and ray guns, four-armed greenies and eight-legged critters—all of them be damned—it'd be no different here than the world I came from.

I suddenly remembered Dave's take on democracy as being the worst form of government, right after all the others. "We're doing just fine with Talis Darmon," he'd said. I suddenly wished I could go back in time a year and tell younger me to leave that faded copy of the Declaration of Independence in my rucksack to mildew away into pulp.

"Benjamin Colt," Double-K pulled me from my dark thoughts. "I have more important news to bring you. Warmaster Garlak Ranz has just made communication. A message from the seniority of twenty was sent him this very morning. The Veil expelled the security force without explanation. It is demanded that all our forces depart at once. Garlak Ranz reports the Veil is sealed and refuses to answer any hails at her doors."

"Oh, boy. Tell Garlak Ranz to stay on site and continue security operations. What are the Serians going to do about it? Throw sticks and rocks at us? C'mon, that's the chime to take seats."

Reports were made by the various departments on the council and Talis Darmon finished by giving her own. I was a little bit surprised that she revealed to the functionaries most everything we'd discussed last night in our small group. Almost everything. She skipped something significant and went on to brief her plan.

"As you see, questions remain regarding the attack on the Serian sanctuary and its potential relation to the attacks we subsequently suffered. The situation demands an expediency best accomplished by the regent herself. Therefore, the Warlord travels with me today to the Veil of Seriata."

A minister interjected. "The Serians are no threat to us, Queen. It is the Yellows who demand scrutiny. It is more critical to determine if *they* are complicit in the attacks on our people. They are an infinitely more potent threat!"

Talis Darmon answered calmly. "As I discussed, the possibility of Annamerian involvement is also under investigation. I plan to visit our trade partners in the south soon enough, but first, we go to the Veil. From there I will then visit Filestra, Thoria, and Clymaira to cement the bricks of comfort Shaera Kōall so ably laid on my behalf."

She gave blondie a sweet smile but yellow flames flickered in her eyes. Shaera Kōall's rosy-pink complexion blanched nearly to that of our new pale enemy. Seeing her message had been received, the queen indicated Perrin Halser.

"With his return to robust health, Perrin Halser will resume duties as chancellor and act in my authority during our brief absence from Shansara."

Another minister spoke out. "Is the Warlord not returning to lead the battle in the eastern desert? It was by his hand that we delivered vengeance to the savages!"

I spoke for the first time in the meeting. "I appreciate the compliment, but from top to bottom, our soldiers and Guardsmen are capable and competent. They have my complete confidence."

"As you say, Warlord," the minister said, not totally convinced of his safety unless I were heading back to the desert with a gun in my hand. I wasn't mad he'd voiced misgivings about the queen's allocation of my time. It's nice to have a cheering section, I guess.

A different minister, a woman, spoke out. "Queen, does it not demonstrate a certain desperation to go to the First Citizen and his seniority? We have the position of power. They should be coming to us. To whom else can they turn for protection?"

A man across the table came to the queen's defense. "Minister, you read too little into the queen's strategy. She will no doubt use our blanket of protection as leverage to gain trade concessions from the Serians as has never before been possible. They extort a ransom from us with each shipment of stones. Her royal personage alone will serve to enfeeble the proud dwarves. Not to mention, when she then entreats with them, she will wield her great skill like a comely blade of sharpest edge. It is a masterful plan, Queen, and a propitious time to make such a daring maneuver."

It was bit too much kiss-ass for my liking, but even if he was way off base, his answer satisfied the councilwoman, who let the issue pass. Another functionary stood, his manner irritable and speech aggressive.

"Such a strategy will work against the ridiculous Serians, and it is past time we bring them to heel. But the Annamese? A royal visit is not the tack I would recommend against *them*. If we even *suspect* their complicity in this assault on our peace, then we should levy threats, and do it now. Issue a decree that if their involvement is discovered, we would halt all trade with them. Just the threat alone would do as much to stop any secret plotting on their part and do it rapidly—that is how much they are dependent on us."

It was the minister of trade. He was *that* guy. You know, the one who always had a question. The one who loved the sound of his own voice.

He was the second lieutenant of a grunt's nightmares. I let a groan slip, but recovered adequate will to restrain myself from saying, "Buddy, whenever you speak, it just makes me feel tired all over."

Our chancellor leaned forward with an eager look. "May I address the minister of trade, Queen?" Unlike me, Perrin Halser was energized by Second Lieutenant Sir Dufus, still standing to hold discussion open regarding his foreign policy recommendation.

Talis Darmon gave Perrin Halser a relieved smile. The brilliant engineer and all-around capable genius was Karlo's older brother from another mother. This would be good.

"Sir, we depend on Annameria at least as much as she depends on us."

The trade minister huffed. "Whatever do you mean, Perrin Halser? I sit on the agriculture board in addition to overseeing trade. We export to Annameria protein of the highest quality because they cannot match what we produce. They would starve without us."

Perrin Halser was a patient teacher. "True, sir, our methods produce livestock with a per pound density of nutrition that is much higher than Annamese agricultural methods. However, we import a vastly greater tonnage of meat from them. Their cuisine prefers the richness of our product and they use it in small quantities in their dishes. The Mihdra cuisine prefers a large quantity of meat, and how we prepare it makes the richness of the meat not as important to our consumers."

The minister completely missed the point and fell back on the oldest form of aristocratic privilege—ridicule. "I did not know such an accomplished engineer was also a chef, Perrin Halser. Enlighten me then, kitchen master."

Perrin Halser remained kindly as he did.

"It is the high quality of our meats that make them our number one food export. By weight, we import four times as much of the lower quality Annamese meats as what we send them. Equivalent in value, but not equal in tonnage. Should we do as you suggest and cease our exports, we could not increase production enough to offset the difference and satisfy our home market. You could say, we are the number one exporter of meats because we are the number one importer of meats, and vice versa."

The queen gave a polite smile. "Thus, threatening the Annamerians with a trade embargo would harm us more than them, Minister."

The minister's face turned fire-engine red and he plopped down. Yet, he gave no acknowledgement of the unassailability of Perrin Halser's economics lesson. The exchange told me—and anyone else paying attention—that our minister of trade was as qualified to oversee policy as an Amish toddler was to run a nuclear reactor.

But as I watched him turn to speak to the assistant hurriedly taking his dictation, I knew no such realization had come. I had no doubt, not five minutes after this meeting broke up, his assistant would have a petition ready bearing the minister's idiotic strategy, and he'd make the rounds to garner enough support to bring the matter up again for a vote at the next council.

There's just no explaining the free market to a person who thinks the world works in ways it doesn't, much less to someone married to the premise he can exercise control over something he doesn't understand. Trying to control consumer tastes was about as useful as trying to train a housecat to read. By the time you were done, kitty cat would do everything *but* look at the book.

A new woman rose to speak. "If I may address this body? I begin by saying I know I am not alone in admiration and gratitude toward the Warlord and all our forces for their daring in addressing this emergency."

The usual round of polite agreements went around the table, and I wondered where this was going. In this room, compliments were bait for a trap.

"I wish to preface by begging you to forgive my words if at first what I suggest seems crude. I bring this question forward out of a pragmatic love for our kingdom. The question I pose is simply this: could it be that a new enemy is actually just what the kingdom needs at this time?"

I nearly swallowed my tongue. Was cluelessness a virtue? Because here was another elite proudly waving the banner of cognitive dissonance. I could not wait to hear where the primrose path she cut was leading, intrigued how she thought to convince the rest of us to traipse alongside her.

Apparently, Talis Darmon was just as curious. She gave a friendly nod for the councilwoman to continue.

"As Perrin Halser states, trade is strong. Productivity is at a high. Our wealth increases. It is unquestionably a new age. If the wars were not responsible, they have at the very least been the authority from which our prosperity has flowered anew. Could it be that this new emergency, no matter how unwanted, may actually have the effect of extending this boom of vitality?"

Talis Darmon's father, King Osric Darmon, was advised by a council that refused to defend the kingdom's interests, even when his own daughter's life was at stake. When Talis Darmon took the throne, the remnants of her father's council were still around, unrepentant and just as impotent in the face of the threats continuing to bear down on us. With Talis Darmon behind me, I took the bull by the horns and led our army to victory after victory, dragging the aristocracy kicking and screaming all the way. But what this councilwoman was suggesting was quite a departure from the old orthodoxy.

She was saying war is good, gimme more.

It truly was a new era for the council.

My wife again remained silent, but I knew what no one else did. On the outside was a beauty and elegance unmatched in any part of the universe. On the inside—she was a streetfighter. Her lack of reaction was a feint. She was dropping her lead hand to give her opponent an opening, ready to exploit the invited lunge, and her silence was the irresistible lure.

Shaera Kōall took the bait.

The blonde woman rose majestically, sweeping gossamer sleeves aside in dramatic fashion to reveal bare rose petal shoulders. The current speaker surrendered the floor to Shaera Kōall with a bow.

"I thank my friend for speaking with candor. She accurately states what many of us believe. Who could with honesty say they wish the recent wars had not been fought? That our kingdom today is not more prosperous as a result? The ethos this council once swore by—that at all costs war must be avoided because of its terribleness—became a paradox they refused to acknowledge despite the result they saw revealed. While we remember them fondly, I must admit I am glad they have departed from influence."

Heads bobbed around the table and Shaera Kōall flushed with their support. Now she was the color of the red roses in Granny's flower bed, the ones I learned to trim to the ground when the leaves got spots. It was the only way to get rid of the disease without getting scratched.

"The ruling class were slow to learn the Warlord's lessons. But we have been educated. We have no excuse for repeating past mistakes." She became apologetic and switched to plea mode.

"No sane person would wish for us to be enveloped by another cataclysmic struggle, but we find ourselves once more in circumstances not of our choosing. We have not sought conflict but instead have been provoked. Viciously attacked. Our way of life literally threatened with destruction."

She spread her arms wide in supplication.

"If we address this challenge with the same determination, how will we not prosper in the end? How will we not be richer, more secure, and happier?"

"Here, here," echoed loudly around the table. I glanced sideways at my wife. Her eyes smiled even if her mouth did not. Somewhere in the deepest well of her patience, her right cross was cocked and waiting, ready to deliver the knockout blow. Shaera Kōall pressed what she thought was her advantage, her final impassioned call to action raising goosebumps on my arms and sending a shiver down the back of my neck.

"We should be bold in our response. We should not stop at simply blanketing the deserts with our army to purge the sands of the enemies hiding beneath them. If there is suspicion the neighboring polities support those harming us, then—in the name of our own security—we should act. We should seize the Veil. We should dominate Annameria. Our army is peerless and we have the ability.

"It is with this in mind that I ask for the council's unanimous call to petition our queen—unleash the might of our kingdom against all our enemies! Let the righteous and terrible hand of our Warlord lead us to victory!"

Thunderous applause broke out. A fever gripped the room. I had a vison of brown shirts in perfect rank and file saluting a small man on a podium.

I'd underestimated Shaera Kōall.

This was no petty politician.

This was a tyrant in the making.

Talis Darmon's smile said her time to unleash had at last arrived. I was heady with anticipation at her knockout punch to come.

All took seats and waited with eyes on the queen.

"I named the Warlord second only to me in responsibility and authority for all matters existential to the kingdom. More so, Benjamin Colt was confirmed by the Warlord Jawn Kurz himself, who blessed him as the sole person ever worthy to inherit his mantle."

I heard the pfft of someone's disbelief but didn't see who'd done the deed. Khraal Kahlees revved a growl.

"I. Was. There."

There was a loud gulp, maybe from the doubter.

"As was I," Cynar said in shrill pitch, as tinny high as Double-K's defense was rumbling bass. "And my science means there is no more reliable observer to confirm the truth of what was witnessed that day."

Time was when Double-K would've threatened to pull a sassy aristocrat's lungs out through their mouth and Cynar would've sputtered insult after insult, then rhetorically questioning why he wasted his last bit of life energy explaining himself to minds incapable of understanding.

While I was impressed how they'd both matured, I also wondered why the queen had brought up my pedigree.

"Thank you, gentleman," she said in manner to restrain our friends further. "I was reminding this body of the Warlord's unique status before Benjamin Colt himself addresses this petition for war."

Her fight strategy all along was—*me*?

Thanks a lot for the heads-up, honey.

Now all eyes were on yours truly. No one wanted to see me pull a rabbit out of my hat more than I did. Khraal Kahlees crossed arms and bowed, as did Beraal. Perrin Halser dipped his head, as did Zaylin Twee. Talis Darmon looked at me with love in her eyes.

"Don't bungle it," Cynar mumbled.

I took a deep breath. I did not mean to be condescending. But with heat at my brow and sorrow in my chest—equal parts angered and saddened—I began the chastisement of a father disappointed at his wayward children. Though they were not the words I'd composed last night, a new script was ready in my mouth as if I had.

"War made the state, so the state made war."

I paused before continuing my sermon.

"And the state was strengthened by it. With war came peace and security. With war came strength and greater social interdependence. Came a rising material status for the citizen. All of them were gifts from the god of war."

No longer the avatar for some wise sage who proved to everyone he knew all the questions and their answers, I directed my next to one person.

"Shaera Kōall, each and every time I prosecuted total war, it was because no other choice existed."

For someone who sought attention, she didn't seem to enjoy having mine.

"You talk about having learned my lesson, but you've taken the wrong one. War is not the means to great advance. The regeneration of our society comes not because of war, but because Mihdra everywhere want a future of life, not death.

"There is no one who believes more than I do in the necessity of total war. To not wage total war when required is immoral. It is a betrayal of the most basic oath of one who serves his people."

The great gathering table vibrated as I dropped my fist.

"But total war is necessary *only* when it is necessary. Seeking out or prolonging warfare for the purpose of economic and political gain is *exactly* what every foot soldier suspects as the true purpose behind those who send him to fight.

"I am a son of two worlds. Worlds that have much in common. But it is only evident to me at this very instant—on the world I will die to defend—that politicians are the same everywhere.

"This is why soldiers of both worlds are just in their suspicion of those who send them."

A lot of necks bent down just then, but there were as many who placed their gaze on me, the most important being my friends. Both told me I'd done well. It was time to finish.

"This kingdom will not wage war for political purposes, nor declare any form of war on anyone not deserving. There are many tools for constructing our security. Have faith they are all being utilized at this very moment."

Applause, some raucous, some reserved, broke out. There was only one person neither demonstrating support nor concealing their regret. As the claps faded, Shaera Kōall selected glibness as the shield against the cannonball I'd broadsided her with.

"Of course, Warlord! Of course we defer to your judgment how best to treat these existential matters. I was perhaps too strong in how I chose to show my support. I did not mean to recommend strategy."

She quickly recomposed her motion.

"Whatever the Warlord's decision as to how to prosecute this war—be it to root out and exterminate the vermin in the desert or be it to prosecute action against the Veil and Annameria—I move we register unanimous support, here and now. Who will second the motion?" She smiled sweetly and folded her hands.

My wife answered in equally sugary tones.

"Unnecessary, Shaera Kōall, but your regent appreciates the formal gesture. The council is dismissed."

The meeting broke up, leaving us alone with our friends.

"I detest this chamber," Double-K said. "But long would I regret my absence from today's events. *That one*, she is dangerous."

With narrowed eyes, Zaylin Twee followed the blonde mane departing the hall. "She is a poison flower."

I snorted at my wife. "Thanks, honeybunch. 'Preciate advance notice on the speech. What if you'd bet on the wrong arkall?"

She blew me off. "You needed no such preparation, Warlord, and your skills as a rider have proven adequate."

Beraal took up for the queen. "How many times must it be demonstrated, Benjamin Colt? Talis Darmon always knows best."

My wife giggled. "Thank you, dear Beraal, but it is more than that. It *was* Jawn Kurz who confirmed Benjamin Colt's position. And my husband has never failed to prove the ancient spirit correct."

I shrugged it off. "Thanks for being a fan. Autographed photos are ten bucks. By the way, I noticed you chose to keep our plan to recon Xanalar from the council."

"Correct, husband. Because I suspected such sentiments as these were becoming prevalent in the nobility. Revealing there may be a burgeoning kingdom to the east—one perhaps rich and potentially involved in our current troubles—would have only led to a louder rattling of sabers. You have silenced that."

Double-K chuckled. "I take leave to join the others in the planning of the reconnaissance. It shall be most gratifying to taste the jealousy of our brothers when I tell them what they missed. It was well said, Benjamin Colt."

Talis Darmon laid a hand on my arm. "Have you decided who will travel with us, husband? It is time we make for the Serian sanctuary."

I tilted my forehead at her. "Are you *sure* this is the best time for this? Who knows what shenanigans Shaera Kōall will get up to if she thinks you're not watching? When the cat's away, the mice will play."

My wife rolled her beautiful eyes. "Enough Thulian wisdom, husband. This is exactly the best time. Beraal has obtained reports of Shaera Kōall's remarks from many witnesses. She is instituting an information campaign to discredit our ambitious young friend. With little persuasion on the Dosenie's part, public orators around the capital discuss Shaera Kōall's diatribe. Even this morning she was being insinuated as disloyal. She is exposed. And with the council chastened by your ethical discourse, they will distance themselves from her. Perrin Halser is recovered and here to act as my able deputy. With your brothers and First Shield Zaylin Twee at his flanks, there could be no better time to be away from Shansara. I was truthful when I said this matter demanded an expediency which only I can provide."

I relinquished. "Yes, Queen."

"Come, Warlord. We leave internal politics behind for a new diplomatic joust and while so doing, permit me the selfish opportunity to satisfy an old curiosity. Let us depart at once. The fabled majesty of the Veil awaits."

10

Karlo and I flew while Tranya Olan sat with Talis Darmon discussing the First Citizen and his oligarchs. We'd just leveled out from a climb so high, it seemed like the next stop was the edge of space when Karlo said, "That must've been something, Ben. Sorry I wasn't there. But we did finish the reconnaissance plan."

"Good. But, are you really sorry you were doing that instead of sitting in another council meeting?"

"Nope!" Karlo fired back like a howitzer. "I got the lowdown. Double-K did a good job paraphrasing you. Or should I say, paraphrasing you paraphrasing Charles Tilley. Perfect reference at the perfect time, brother."

Karlo used the name like I knew it well. It was as foreign to my ear as any classical composition was to Dougie.

"Who?" I said.

Karlo winced. "Sorry, Ben. There's me being a jerk again. It's just, the lecture you gave the council, you know? War-making by the state as a form of organized crime. You must've read that paper at some point, even if you don't remember it. I thought about it a lot those last few years on Earth. Tilley referenced European history, but it captured our own time very well."

There'd been a moment when I'd wondered if the words I'd come up with hadn't been fed to me by the spirit of Jawn Kurz. Turns out, the only magic was that of a crappy memory; I was just plagiarizing from my subconscious without realizing it.

I've always loved history, read a lot, but hardly more than the broad strokes stuck with me for long. I'd often feel confident I understood the when and where of who did what and why like a good CONOP, until I tried to run through it a week later and my memory did its broken coffee maker routine. Rather than have dark gold in my coffee cup to savor, the facts leaked out on the kitchen counter, and all I had to show for the effort were the wet grounds on the filter.

Unlike me, what was in Karlo's brain was sealed tight and fresh like ambrosia salad in Tupperware. Karlo was the closest thing to an encyclopedia of Earth knowledge we were ever going to have.

"I have a thumb drive full of stuff and I bet that Tilley paper's in there," Karlo said before sighing deeply. "I should've gotten everything transferred to scroll before all our stuff finally died. Freaking software updates."

"Here's your retirement project," I said. "Write a history of Earth. It'll be a best seller."

I wasn't joking, but as I thought about how I'd likened the politicians of my two worlds, I had a funny idea. "Or better yet, you should do a Nostradamus routine—make a bunch of predictions for Vistara based on Earth history. Nostra-Karlo. Everyone'll be amazed. They don't know it'll be because we've already seen this movie."

Karlo snorted. "Quatrains of vague predictions that could apply to nearly anything is definitely not my style, Ben. But your first idea's a good one. But we should collaborate. You're a better read student of history than I am."

"Pfft. I can't keep straight which came first, the fall of Constantinople that ended the Byzantine Empire or the Ottoman Siege of Vienna that was turned back by the Polish Hussars."

Karlo set me right. "Ah. That's some great history, but that particular siege of Vienna happened about two hundred years *after* the Ottomans took Constantinople. There were many previous attempts. And you should know, they didn't call themselves Byzantines. They called themselves Romans."

"See what I mean?" I said. "I'm always mixing things up because the same people do the same things over and over so many times."

"Don't sell yourself short, Ben. Your interest's always been modern military history. And you have a real grasp of historical trends and how they repeat, and that's what's important."

I suddenly realized that the women's chatting had ceased for some time.

"I am curious, gentlemen," Talis Darmon said from behind us. "You both speak of events in Earth's history as recurring in cycles. Was there a defined pattern to repeating societal trends in your history?"

"I was always taught there was," I said. I may not have Karlo's memory, but for any deep thought that fit on a bumper sticker, I was solid. Especially the ones the instructors at the Special Warfare Center used as the lead PowerPoint slide to set the tone for a particular block of instruction. I gave her one that applied—one I remembered from my first day of the Operations and Intelligence course.

"We look to the past to predict the future because, there's nowhere else to look."

Talis Darmon made a pleasing sound. "It is an aphorism of our world as well," she said. "Though in my experience, one held in regard only when historical evidence supports a proposal, and disregarded whenever it is pointed out that something has been tried before and failed."

I snorted. "You're validating my unified field theory about politicians, Talis Darmon."

"What is the sequence to the repeating cycles of Earth history?" she asked.

I scoffed. "She's talking to you, Karlo, because I don't know."

Karlo frowned as he thought. "Well, the rise and fall of civilizations were often analogized by the seasons."

Puzzled, Talis Darmon said, "Hmmm. Remind me as to the manifestations of the equinoxes on Thulia."

"Four," I began, describing them from a youth in Appalachia where seasons were full and a real wardrobe was necessary, not like the Florida panhandle where winter was a couple of weeks of morning frost. In seasonless Mihdradahl, it was pretty much the same weight of flimsy garments all year long.

"I see," Talis Darmon said, engaged. "So the patterns of history were compared to a birth in the spring, the steady growth during a summer, then the harvest and reaping of riches in the fall, followed by the inevitable decay and death of winter—only to repeat again."

"As usual, sweetheart, right on the mark. Why do you ask?"

"Merely more of my personal curiosity. I formulated a similar theory regarding repeating trends in our history from as far back as the first kingdoms of Oceania. My book on the subject was well regarded."

"You wrote a book?" I asked, not knowing.

Tranya Olan's voice dripped exasperation. "Benjamin Colt, when her family ascended to the regency, the queen was already a well-recognized scholar. She was famed as the youngest to ever achieve full membership in the academy. How is it you do not know your wife has authored many tomes?"

"Well, she doesn't know I have a first place trophy from the 325th infantry regiment's floor buffer races."

I have more than one superpower. I could *hear* their eyes rolling. "Seriously, of course that doesn't surprise me. I'd love for you to tell us all about your theory."

"As would I, Talis Darmon," Karlo said earnestly.

"When we have the time, I would be pleased. But I return to present matters. The First Citizen."

"He makes me fond for the dragon lady," I said. "Guy thinks his shit don't stink. What's your game plan?"

"Tranya Olan and I have been discussing that very thing. The values of our societies are at odds. Mihdra seek compromise whenever possible. We prefer forthrightness and open statements of goals. Serian diplomacy is adversarial, more akin to financial competition. They value secrecy and view transparency as a weakness to exploit."

"Sounds just like the Annamese," I said.

"In respect to a cultural principle that insists on total self-interest above all other considerations, they are indeed similar. Neither acknowledge that reaching a mutual benefit between parties is a desirable goal in business and diplomacy."

"Where does that leave us?" I asked. "Do we have to do what that dipshit on the council recommended and threaten to leave them high and dry without protection unless they come clean about what really happened?"

"That is a tactic, but one I prefer not to use as an opening move."

I hmphed. "I wouldn't say it to anyone else, but lord poopy-pants on your council wasn't 100% wrong about our big stick reputation. We had to bomb Annameria back to the Stone Age and promise to do it again if they didn't treat us the same way they expected to be treated."

"I know you jest, husband. Though Annameria was a perpetual source of anxiety, we actually had quite equitable trade with them even before the war. And as you have so recently pointed out, we brought total war to the Annamese because they abandoned the hypothetical to become an actual threat. The Serians are no threat. They have information we want. And as opposed to the Annamese, they can be embarrassed. The only tool to shame the Annamese into compliance was military defeat."

"How will you make the Serians lose face?"

"Irrefutable proof would be lovely. As we lack that, I plan to follow the example set by Zaylin Twee during her masterful manipulation of our Vermeel prisoner."

"You're going to bluff them?" I said.

"We know enough to at least implicate them in the role of accomplice. I will imply we have the evidence. It is no crime to deceive a deceiver."

My pleasure at hearing her paraphrase a quotation that had such profound significance for the both of us was interrupted by the engine's hum ceasing.

After a slight pause, the lack of propulsion destabilized our bullet-shaped aircraft and our tail shimmied like a hooked fish pulled onto lake ice. Our nose took a dip and a knot of dread tied itself in my stomach as I pictured us going into a flat spin. Gravity's pull reversed and the tightness in my gut floated higher into my throat.

"Take the yoke, Ben," Karlo said calmly and pulled a checklist from next to his seat and read aloud while I fought to keep us level. There are relatively few crystals on the control console of a Black Bird, darn near as few as on a flitter. Most were cold.

I fought the stiff yoke to pull our nose up. In everyone's jump school class, there was always that one paratrooper who'd ask how much time you had if the main canopy failed and you had to activate the reserve parachute before hitting the ground.

The answer was, of course, the rest of your life.

The stubby wings of the Black Bird provided next to nothing for lift, but we had good altitude. I could still see the curvature of the horizon. The rest of my life until we figured this out was a lot longer than under a malfunctioning T-11 parachute. Especially because I thought I knew why we'd lost power.

"I know what this is, Karlo."

Karlo didn't hear me over his own voice as he read the list again and retried a sequence to bring life back to the cold control stones. The ladies made uncomfortable noises as the plane shook. I tried again for Karlo's attention.

"I've been in this situation. We got hit by a ray-killer. Means we didn't wipe out all the Whites. They're back. But we can beat this. All we have to do is get out of the track of the beam, the effect'll stop, and we'll get power back. It's our best shot. We should dive."

Karlo put the checklist away. "We should, Ben, but not for the reasons you think." He placed hands on the yoke. "With me. Nose down. Now."

The atmosphere of Vistara is thin, even at low altitude. Up here, there were few aerodynamic forces working for our good. What little air there was buffeted our course and knocked us violently in multiple planes at once. The bird responded slowly as we tried to aim our bullet-shaped nose straight down. Slowly, our precession and yaw settled and we regained some stability. Loose items floated around the cabin as we achieved negative G—freefall. A place I felt at home.

But the distance above the ground that I'd taken as a positive just a minute ago was becoming a rapidly diminishing commodity.

"Try to light her again, Karlo," I said.

"I will, Ben, but it won't work." Karlo repeated the sequence, and like he'd sworn, none of the dead indicator stones woke up.

I wasn't a real pilot. I knew that for certain. Because I'd seen the documentaries and heard the voices—the voices that survived on the flight recorders, telling the story of the last minutes of their lives. Those voices were cool and collected—all the way until the moment the recording stopped—until their owners disintegrated into atoms along with the thousands of pounds of aluminum around them.

My voice wasn't like theirs. It was high as a castrated twelve-year-old soprano.

"Why'd you say that, Karlo? Why won't it work?"

"I know why we haven't been able to fix the *Hope,* Ben. We missed the obvious."

"How does that help us now?" I squeaked.

The square of a square function that was acceleration by gravity meant the ground was coming at us faster and faster, causing parts of my anatomy to pucker while others loosened. "Shouldn't we pull up? Try for a glide?"

"Everyone, brace," Karlo said. "This is gonna be bad."

Karlo did something to the control panel and everything happened at once, leaving no time for goodbyes, prayers, or curses. My spine pressed against the front of my chest and my brains pushed my eyeballs from behind to bulge from the sockets. I entered a long train tunnel and my vision went dim.

The last thing I saw before I went black?

Starburst trails in the sands left by desert rats fleeing in all directions from the spot we aimed to dig our grave.

The Black Bird floated in a frozen hover a few feet above the sands, as perfect as if it'd just come from detailing and a wax job to wait the photo shoot for the cover of hypersonic flyers monthly. I pulled the groggy women out and was heading back for Karlo when he appeared in the door.

"Grab weapons, Karlo. If they're coming to check on the results, we're gonna spoil their day."

He hopped urgently onto the sands, arching his back like a cat and, also like one, making the hairball retching sound.

"Sorry, Ben," he wiped his mouth and spit. "There's no ground assault coming our way, I'd bet our lives. Let me check on the women."

When I returned with all our kit, both women were sitting up and sipping water. I had a comm open to the operations center and as I explained we'd been downed by a ray-killer, a half a dozen heads popped into the cloud. Doug eased the ops duty officer out of the way.

"WHA'PEN?" he blurted. "Dude, where'd the whites of your eyes go? They look like red velvet cake."

"Later, Dougie. We're grounded, we're alive. Launch CSAR. We're expecting trouble."

Khraal Kahlees flared. "It is the work of the Whites! They have survived and retaliate! The queen announced her travel plans only to the council. They are in collusion! I shall have them all arrested. First, I bring relief. Then, we return to skin the aristocrats alive!"

Karlo was beside me. "Hold up! Do *not* put a single Black Bird up. Everyone, calm down. Ben, I didn't get a chance to explain. It wasn't the Whites and it wasn't a ray-killer."

"Sure it was!" I said with all the incredulity I could muster.

"No, Ben. For one, not all the stones lost charge."

I thought back. It was true. There'd been indicator stones for airspeed and artificial horizon still functioning.

Karlo held up a second finger. "And another thing, we still had some flight control."

Talis Darmon was beside us, the white of her eyes also crimson from tender capillaries burst by the rapid deceleration. "Tell us, Karlo Columbo, what has happened? What we do next demands careful consideration."

A dry wind picked up and scraped my eyes like coarse grit sandpaper across a dry piece of wood.

"Get Cynar and Perrin Halser linked in, please," Karlo said before continuing. "We missed the obvious. All the failures on the *Hope*—we thought they were systems integration problems, that there was interference between them. We've never had so many complex systems operating in conjunction and in such close proximity. Some produced rays that caused constructive interference patterns with other systems, some caused destructive interference patterns. We shielded, removed shielding, separated components and stations, brought others closer, added more stones, removed stones, changed stones—we tried everything."

Karlo dropped his bombshell. "But we've never looked at the stones themselves."

Perrin Halser was there. "Not true. Stones are sampled and tested before they are released from the central receiving facility."

Karlo said, "Yes, but not every stone is tested, just samples from each lot. We bench test them before we install them, but even then, it's just a check for the appropriate charge of ray. Our demand for stones went up a thousand percent when we started construction on the *Hope,* correct, Perrin Halser?"

"Yes, Karlo Columbo. It required much negotiation. The Serians increased production and fulfilled the demand, though they nearly scalped us in the process."

Karlo said, "Did we increase the staff for quality control to keep pace with the new demand?"

Perrin Halser frowned. "I ordered an increase in the number of engineers working on just that. It was a routine matter. I do not recall ever receiving a hold on any product due to failure in testing."

Karlo gritted teeth. "That's a red flag in and of itself. We pushed for components in numbers and at a rate never before seen and unintentionally created an atmosphere where meeting demand became job one. We may have set the very conditions that caused us to miss something so basic. But I have a much deeper suspicion."

Cynar was there. "I, too, intuit a profoundly disturbing doubt. There is something occurring here that we have not known to look for. Again!"

"Like what?" I said, truly puzzled.

Cynar's bushy gray eyebrows narrowed. "Until now I have been blind to the possibility. But what if the stones received from the Serian mines are not of poor quality? What if they have been tampered with? Engineered to fail?"

Grimacing in disgust, Karlo agreed. "Cynar, that's exactly what I think. We've been dependent on one source for a strategic material, and they've sabotaged us."

Perrin Halser was skeptical. "Is such a thing possible, Wizard Supreme? You yourself have described the complexity of the stones. Science has not been able to duplicate their structure to reliably synthesize even the simple amber stones we use for lighting."

With his fists balled tight, Cynar said, "It does not mean that it has not been done, only that how it was done is unknown to us." He'd been deceived in a matter of science. There was no more personal form of attack against him. "Come, Perrin Halser, we must hasten to my workshop. It is time to investigate."

"Stand fast, everyone," I said. "Karlo, are you saying that our Black Bird fell out of the sky because it was powered by stones with a ticking time bomb built into them?"

"That's what I'm saying."

My eyes felt like his looked. "Why the hell d'you make us dive?"

"Blackbirds have a glide ratio of nothing to nothing and nose down is the only way to stabilize a bullet when it's lost velocity. We were on our way to a flat spin or even a tumble. We'd never have recovered. I had to build a kinetic charge in the safety system in case the repulsor stones were as faulty as the propulsion stones. We'll never know if they would've worked on their own, but I couldn't risk it. It was our only chance to make sure they were at full charge. Sorry about the whiplash."

I gave a benediction as sincere as if I wore the pointy pope hat. "All your sins are forgiven."

Talis Darmon held her hands over her heart and bowed. "We owe you our lives, Karlo Columbo."

Tranya Olan searched the cloud. "Where is David Masamuni? Is he not in the operations center?"

Doug's face pained like he had a kidney stone. "He took a Black Bird with Turv Densman for a co-pilot and headed for Xanalar before you guys even left. We've been trying since you called.

"We can't reach Flight Marco Polo."

✢ ✢ ✢

Talis Darmon stroked the small head in her lap. "Do not worry, Tranya Olan."

I'd seen Tranya Olan kill men many times her size, but cry? Our friend's eyes misted only one time before, when she'd agreed to use her own trauma as a bridge to a Talis Darmon succumbing to a call by the Great Forlorn to end her life.

Karlo was deep in a wrist cloud conference, walking engineers and technicians through the process to determine which, if any, Black Birds had stones installed from older and presumably safe batches sent from the Veil. Perrin Halser and Cynar were trying to identify if we even *had* any stores of the most powerful 9th ray stones remaining from before the arrival of the possibly sabotaged lots. They'd found very small stores of older lots of the less powerful stones used to power our aircars, but it would take time to get those into circulation where they were needed most. In the meantime, all Black Birds were grounded and all flitters restricted to emergency use and low-level flight.

We were going to be stuck for a while.

Tranya Olan sobbed into Talis Darmon's lap. "I have been a poor companion. David Masamuni has showered me with unconditional affection and acceptance. Me. The coldest and most selfish person above Vistara." She broke into sobs again.

My building dread at having to eat my words before the council when I declared war on the Veil suddenly seemed unimportant, and I knelt to offer my comfort as well.

"Tranya Olan, I'm not worried. You know Dave. When we least expect it, there he'll be, wearing a big dumb grin, puzzled why we'd even be concerned about him."

She looked at me, choking on swallowed tears. "This is quite different, Benjamin Colt, and you know it to be so. If his conveyance suffered the same failure as ours, even my invincible Thulian warrior-prince is but a fragile and small thing compared to the mightiest of Vistara's forces. If I have forever failed in bravery to shed stubbornness and reveal how much I need him, how much I value him, I shall never forgive myself." Her face fell to her hands and her body shook as Talis Darmon stroked her back.

I'd never heard Tranya Olan use so many words, much less ones filled with so much emotion. My heart hurt for her and I tried again.

"He already knows that, Tranya Olan. I'm his closest friend on two worlds and beyond. He's never, ever been happier than since you came into his life. I would never lie to you about this; he knows how you feel."

She dried her eyes against a bare arm and calmed. "How can you be so certain he is unharmed, Benjamin Colt?"

"The ops center had a routine contact from him an hour ago, and they were flying fine. He's just out of communication range. Not even Cynar knows what the max range is for our wristlets. Under the Sharpa Mountains, we couldn't make commo. Halfway around Vistara, Dave and Turv Densman surely hit the limit. Losing communication was part of the mission plan. They anticipated it. That's all this is."

Tranya Olan's momentary respite from worry crashed again. "If it is not that? If their propulsion has failed? Would they have remedy without the help of Karlo Columbo?" The tears streamed down her face.

Karlo appeared. "I just confirmed Dave's bird has the least number of hours of any in the fleet. So even if their stones are faulty, they have a good chance of getting through this entire flight before they malfunction. Ops will be back in contact and warn them to ground before there's any chance of that. I'm certain."

Talis Darmon smiled. "See, my friend? The brightest and most experienced minds in all the kingdom know these things as true. Trust their counsel."

Tranya Olan wiped her face dry and steadied herself with a deep breath. "Of course. Please, forgive my..."

I stopped her midsentence. "You know what Dave would say?"

Tranya Olan's eyes shot up at a diagonal and stayed there as she searched her brain for the right Dave-ism. I beat her to it.

"Worry in one hand and shit in the other, see which one does you more good in a gunfight."

Even Talis Darmon couldn't suppress a smile, though a conservative one. Tranya Olan stood and brushed herself off. "I shall erect a shelter and start a meal, then we begin watch shifts for the queen's security."

"Yes, ma'am." I saluted.

When she was out of earshot, I asked Karlo, "Is that true about Dave's bird?"

Karlo's guilty face admitted the lie. "I wish it were."

✠ ✠ ✠

After splitting a ration, we reclined beneath the shade of a tarp spread from a stubby wing while Karlo poured over the scroll of the Black Bird maintenance log. Tranya Olan paced a perimeter, and I made zero attempt to dissuade her by pointing out it was a useless expenditure of effort and energy. I understood.

When the world weakens you, put on the armor of your instinct to be who you are.

On the last hourly check with Shansara, Doug told us a mission from Filestra was headed to retrieve us. It would take them days to reach us by flitters limited to safe speed and altitude, prepared to lose power at any second. Our best minds were working the problem hard, just as Talis Darmon was, lost to her own thoughts as she strategized.

Me? I tried to sleep. My wife's repeated sighs kept me from dozing.

"What is it, sweetheart?"

She squeezed handfuls of sand tightly before allowing them to drain from her grasp. "I consider many potential courses of action. All of them fraught with consequences I cannot predict."

I laid my head back, closed my eyes, and mumbled, "Vague intelligence is worse than no intelligence." The comment just popped into my head and was meant to be apropos of nothing. But it irritated her.

"Do *you* think there is explanation other than the Serians have acted to harm us in a vastly insidious way?"

I realized my error. "I apologize. I just mean, it's time to take a break. I'm anxious to take definitive action, too. And we will. But we need more information."

She softened. "I apologize as well. You are correct. But these sands are a bed of nails and every part of me aches, my kingdom is in peril, and I am helpless to act."

I'd had a sergeant major who was famous for doling out advice on all subjects tactical and not. One day I passed him, sounding off with a strong, "Airborne, Sergeant Major," to receive the appropriate reply of, "All the way."

But instead of continuing past, he halted smartly.

I froze, expecting the inevitable correction for some infraction of my uniform, but instead he said, "PFC Colt, the secret to a long and successful marriage is, if you don't know what else to do, rub her neck." He just as inexplicably resumed course, leaving me puzzled but amused.

He was famous for randomly spouting advice like that to any Joe Snuffy he crossed paths with. That, and knife handing some stupid paratrooper for walking on the grass, chewing his ass until there was nothing left for a fourth point of contact in a parachute landing fall. But what made us all hold him in a twisted kind of awe... he was infamous for showing up drunk at random hours to try and catch the charge of quarters sleeping on duty.

If a guy got caught, we knew it because the next day the dozing paratrooper would be walking a circuit around the battalion area wearing a truck tire around his neck like a horse collar.

But if he snuck up on you and you were sharp an STRAC...

When it happened to me, in the darkest and quietest hours, when sleep pulled on eyelids like forty-five-pound plates, I was not found wanting. I popped sharply to parade rest as if I'd had prior intel the sergeant major was in the area. And what happened next—it was an induction into the secret society others had spoken of.

Smaj pulled up a chair and with a voice barreling across the cinder block barracks like his private Carnegie Hall, I became the audience for his one-man show.

He told me stories about combat and garrison life; being the first on his squad to get a knife kill, blinding North Koreans across the DMZ with a laser target designator, a game of chicken to see who was the last to take cover after firing a 40-mm round straight up, and many more stories of mayhem and young paratrooper idiocy, until passing out on the cot in the back room. It was a rule that you used a broom handle to poke him awake in the morning.

He always came up swinging.

I learned a lot from that guy.

I moved to massage Talis Darmon's shoulders and neck. After working the muscles until they finally surrendered tension like a garden hose in the sun, I moved to her calves and feet. It was then another anxiety-relieving therapy came to mind.

"You promised to tell us about the cycles of Vistaran history. Feel like doing it now?"

Karlo put down the scroll. "I haven't forgotten either, Talis Darmon. And chances are you can present your thesis without interruption." He indicated the level nothingness beyond the shade of our tarp. Tranya Olan halted her pacing circuit and I gestured her over to sit, which she reluctantly did.

"Then I refuse to disappoint, especially if you continue to rub my feet, husband. I shall endeavor to make it as entertaining as I know how, but be warned—it is a topic of interest to only two groups: scholars of the arcane and insomniacs."

Her humor had returned and I thanked that sergeant major for sharing his wide spectrum of worldly knowledge, no matter how surreal and psychotic some of it had been.

She cleared her throat.

"There are four social moods to describe each period I call a transfiguration. And within a transfiguration exist four generations with four distinct personality archetypes: the Prophet, the Nomad, the Hero, and the Artist."

She continued to define her terms.

"A transfiguration is a social period dominated by a mood, one characterized by an overall inclination or tendency. I name the four transfiguration periods as Exalted, Awakening, Unraveling, and Crisis.

"These periods closely correspond to a division each of roughly one hundred years, where the same mood persists to dominate the attitudes and events within the society. Each of the four personality types demonstrates typical characteristics that remain consistent within that archetype; their respective dominance and influence likewise change through the course of each period. The predominance of that influence defines the overall societal mood of that transfiguration."

Karlo squinted and raised a finger. "An Earth generation is about twenty-five years, which is about a quarter of a lifespan, which is how a century of one hundred years came to be accepted as a significant measure. For the purposes of your theory, is one hundred years chosen because it represents one-fourth of a lifespan?"

She smiled. "Yes! Life is commonly much longer, but the patterns fit that periodicity."

Karlo nodded. "Four becomes almost a supreme constant. Four generations composed of four archetypes, interacting with each other during a societal period of a hundred years, repeating in four patterns of distinct inclinations. Fascinating."

Talis Darmon clapped hands like a gleeful schoolgirl and even squealed. "Karlo Columbo! You are truly a prodigy at whatever field you set your mind to! Not the most brilliant in the academy understood this so rapidly!"

I wasn't lost. Because to be lost, it's first necessary to have known where you were at the beginning. Tranya Olan gave me the sideways glance that told me we were in the same boat, but I needed to take a stab at it to let my wife know I was trying.

"What about the archetypes? How do they go? I mean, we know who the heroes are," I said while indicating our circle, trying to sound clever and funny.

She was a kind professor. "You are not incorrect that the appellation of hero fits those who are intuitive and powerful. I, however, am not of the hero archetype. It is difficult to judge oneself, but I believe history will name me a Prophet, as I may likely be characterized as a visionary. One who was moralizing and often unyielding. One who was judgmental and resolute."

I opened my mouth to protest that those characteristics weren't expansive enough. They didn't include her warmth, sympathy, or humanity, but Karlo cut me off.

"You are of an early mid-life generation, is that so, Talis Darmon?"

She agreed. "We are often called the Sufferers. It is a slightly derisive title, referring to a tendency to suffer the imaginary turmoil caused by access to so many comfortable options. My father the king was of the Hearth generation, characterized by contentedness and the shunning of challenge and change over preference for safety and constancy."

"Is there another generation between you and your father's?"

"Two, in fact."

I never knew how old her father was, but I roughed a guess this meant he'd been at least three hundred years older than Talis Darmon. Had my father-in-law not been killed by his own son—my brother-in-law, whom Talis Darmon turned into a sieve—what would that've made the king? Five hundred years old?

It was staggering to think about. I was just over the hump of thirty. For some reason, a young and wrinkle-free face popped into mind.

"What about Shaera Kōall?" I said. "What's she? Is there a scumbag generation or a shitbag archetype?"

Talis Darmon chuckled as she drew her feet from my lap to sit cross-legged.

"She is of the generation behind mine, one not yet fully established in trait to be named. I have decided to call them the Lost generation, come to age in a time of uncertainty. And by archetype she is, I believe, a Nomad. Nomads are characterized by their pragmatism. Alienated. Abandoned. Practical and effective yet often desperate and reckless."

Tranya Olan spoke for the first time. "Queen, what of these periods? Exalted, Awakening, Unraveling, and Crisis?" She repeated them perfectly from memory, bringing another smile to Talis Darmon's face and dropping me to last place in this episode of *Jeopardy*. "Surely, we sit in the time of crisis?"

Now Talis Darmon's smile faded.

"No. Not by any measure. If we are to go by the order of transfigurations, we are only mid-unraveling. The period of crisis is yet to arrive."

A period was one hundred years. And by Talis Darmon's prediction, we had not yet even commenced the beginning of the tumult of a century distinguished by dilemma and disaster. It made me wonder.

What the hell did a real crisis look like if that wasn't what we'd been living through?

There was no chill wind to blame for my shiver.

We'd been stuck in silence for some time when Talis Darmon spoke with circumspect concern. "In a time of crisis, those who rise to power are generally of the Nomad archetype. Like Shaera Kōall."

Apparently, the young aristocrat haunted Talis Darmon as well.

Something new popped up from my repository of bumper sticker knowledge and I recited in English as if reading it off the once popular meme burned into my brain.

"Weak men create hard times.
Hard times create strong men.
Strong men create good times.
Good times create weak men."

Her eyebrows lifted, Talis Darmon exclaimed, "Impressive! Forgive me, husband, I have never discounted your brilliance but, I did not know you composed such poetry. So perfectly your stanzas follow the rule of four to illustrate the essence of the cyclic pattern to societal evolutions."

I'd rarely seen her marvel at anything less supernatural than meeting her two-thousand-years-dead relative, a predecessor queen of ancient Mihdradahl. I was quick to prevent her from crediting me with a brilliance not mine.

"It's not my work, sweetheart. It comes from a land far away."

"America?"

"Facebook."

Such was her love of scholarship that she flushed with almost the same stimulation from—you know—*that* kind of thing. "I cannot express my delight. It is a beautiful encapsulation. Such wonderful simplicity, yet it contains the essence of a subject I have dissected finitely.

It will feature prominently in the updated version of my book when I include the fascinating patterns from your world." She was quick to add, "I shall make just translation and of course, credit Professor Face Book of Thulia."

"He'd like that," I said.

It seemed a minor cruelty to let her unknowingly bear the brunt of a joke meant to be between me and Karlo. Fun is something you have right now, not save for later.

He shook his head disapprovingly.

Our wristlets buzzed.

"Hey there, homies." It was Doug. "Good news, bad news. Good news, we've got a Black Bird screaming your way. Keep those wristlets fired up to help with a triangulation. Set a fire, get the signal mirrors out —anything you can do to mark your location."

The second part to what should have completed his hackneyed preamble, didn't come.

"Out with it, Dougie, what's the bad news. Is it... Dave?"

"Sorry! No, Ben. I guess no news is good news there. But there's more than one bit of bad news. First shitty thing, the Black Bird I sent your way, Cynar used the last clean stones he's found to refit it. Every other stone in the inventory is compromised."

"What's the other?"

Khraal Kahlees was there with tusks flaring. "Curse the Vermeel and curse the Serians as well to damnation in the void! Clymaira has been struck, Warlord, and we remain impotent, separated from any means to render additional aid."

11

Warmaster Garlak Ranz was on the ground with a platoon to guide us down to a landing in a deep valley west of the service entrance to the Veil. I halted Talis Darmon as she moved to step down from the Black Bird.

"Hey! Back you go. We discussed this. No ifs, ands, or buts. You don't get to see the Veil on this trip. And if they piss me off any more than they already have, there's a strong chance that you never will, because I'm liable to drop their mountain on top of them and finish by salting the ground before we leave."

The unyielding quality she described as emblematic of a visionary was front and center. "That was not *discussed* during your plan, Warlord. *You* issued a decree that I would return to Shansara. Your queen never indicated agreement."

I thought she'd been unusually quiet as we sped to the Veil. She'd been refining a different plan than the penetration and seizure Karlo and I planned as we packed up the campsite. I grasped her waist gently and brought her down from the black widow and into my embrace. "No, wife. It won't be safe and there's nothing I can do to make it safe for you. Please go back to Shansara. The kingdom's future depends on your guiding hand. Division of labor, remember?"

I held her at eye level and she wrapped her arms around my neck. "Husband, you know it is no selfish desire that drives me to remain. I only wish to see this resolved."

I lapsed into hillbilly. "Garlak Ranz says they've locked their doors and turned off the lights and are playin' no one's home. I'm about to serve a no-knock warrant on 'em and with only three platoons, I'm short on the ass I need to shut down their meth factory without too much of a dust-up."

I got the look. "What does it say about me that I understood everything you just said, Benjamin Colt? You have reduced me to your level of loutish vulgarian."

I set her down like a fine -glass figurine returned to its display cabinet, and she responded with equal tenderness.

"Allow me to at least try, Benjamin Colt. Under a banner of diplomacy you shall announce me at their entrance, just as we had planned. If they do not respond, there is nothing more to do. With conscience clean can you then proceed with just aggression."

Her gentleness commanded obedience. I almost agreed, but then my steel returned.

"No. Knowing what we do now, we're anticipating all kinds of deadly surprises. Heck, who knows what would've happened had we arrived safe and sound? The Black Bird conking out and sparking Karlo to figure it all out spoiled their secret. It may have ended up saving our lives."

She was genuinely shocked. "They would not dare harm my person! It would lead to a retaliatory act of war and their complete destruction!"

"I think they've secretly declared war on us," I said. "And as far as I'm concerned, barricading themselves in is as good as an admission of guilt."

Talis Darmon considered. “They act erratically and irrationally. I would know why. What do you say?” She turned to Karlo and Tranya Olan close by.

Karlo was quick. “Your safety is paramount, Talis Darmon. For the good of the kingdom, you must return to Shansara.”

We all looked to Tranya Olan. “I no longer know the Veil, queen. They are strangers to me more than ever. I think the First Citizen truly capable of treacheries we cannot conceive.”

When I moved to lift her back into the Black Bird, she didn’t resist. “Fly the queen safely home. Go directly to the palace.”

“At once, Warlord,” the pilot said.

“Sweetheart, promise me you won’t order him to detour to Clymaira or anywhere else. Shara needs you home, too.”

It was an unguarded moment. My wife’s control slipped and a dark aura draped her in the shadow of our impending separation. “Her name is Tashara Colt,” she said with a sniffle. My little girl’s golden hair and sweet smile wrapped my heart.

“It is, wife. Promise me.”

“I do promise.”

I watched until the Black Bird burst into lightning speed to chase the setting sun, then shook Karlo’s rough hand. “Luck, bro.”

He pumped mine and said the same, then hopped onto a flitter and was off.

The vertical terrain leading to the Platinum Bridge was currently seeded with an assault element and Karlo was electrified to take the challenge of fighting through an entrance as high as a door set into the peak of Mount Everest. With luck, entering the mouth of the monster by the Platinum Bridge would only be a day on the climbing wall for Karlo and his boys, because I planned on reaming the beast from its waste ejection port up to its heart before it could belch any foulness their way.

I aimed a knife hand at Tranya Olan. "*You* stay in the rear with the gear in the ORP until I bring you up. Your work starts when kinetics are over, not before. Yes?"

This time she saluted. "I am no argumentative aristocrat. I serve, Warlord."

She was indeed a soldier.

It's not for reasons of supernatural strength that I bounded effortlessly with Garlak Ranz and the men up zig-zagging paths through narrow jagged passes so typical of the Korund. Blood pumping leg muscles against the weight of the kit draped on you, rifle in hand—it's a feeling of imperviousness like no other. We came out onto a slope overlooking the sandy bed below the service entrance to the Veil, the veritable tunnels underneath Disneyland where the ugly happened to keep main street glamorous.

The patrol led us perfectly to a spot with a vantage down the trail and a view of the last bend leading to the hidden entrance. Our trade barges delivered a hold's worth of goods onto those sands, receiving in return a small pallet brought down that inconspicuous trail, no different from any other minor draw among the thousands in the mountain foothills. I'd seen the service entrance from this side of the mountain, or rather, *where* it was. The actual entry point was truly indistinguishable from the rest of the terrain. And I'd seen it from the other side. From the cavernous chamber where the stones were packaged and stores received, a winding tunnel coursed back and forth like a snake, one way then the other to the exit.

We'd paced it out during our examination of the crime scene. The shipping and receiving cavern was 150 meters from side to side. Every centimeter of its floor was exposed beneath a dome that served as the central spoke of a wheel. Carpal tunnel syndrome awaited the OSHA inspector's wrist who'd be writing the C&D tags for all the precarious platform lifts serving the bird's nests spread across the cavern walls. Each balcony serviced a tunnel bored into the mountain, each leading to mines deep and ancient.

Reverse slopes, literal high ground on all sides, and a killing floor broken up by nothing more substantial for cover than stacks of crates; when we examined the scene, I evaluated it as ground for a gunfight the same way I did every place, including my own bathroom. And I'd made myself a promise to never attack the Veil through the service entrance.

At least, not without using every bit of evil at my disposal.

Through a gap between the jagged monoliths concealing our rally point I could make out the team on top another rock-capped spur. They aimed a long tube at the featureless breach point, hidden from my line of sight down the end of the short canyon. The rocket launcher wasn't a Javelin, or a Karl Gustaf. What Karlo invented was deserving of a name as cool Goose, but even Dave had given up after many tries. "Sometimes, brah, insisting on originality and fallin' short just makes everyone wish you'd stuck with a classic."

So, Goose it was.

Teams checked-in ready. I was about to stab a finger toward the position with the Goose as my cue for Garlak Ranz to start the fireworks, when a human face painted in desert camo broke in over the cloud on the warmaster's wrist.

"Warmaster, we have civilians exiting the mountain. Twenty to thirty, carrying belongings. Men, women, children."

Sarkan Sell had located several of the Serians' all but invisible entrances during the time spent combing the mountains for sign of the Vermeel. Two-man teams watched them from concealment.

"Refugees!" Garlak Ranz exclaimed. "Your contingency order was well anticipated, Warlord."

"This isn't a siege," I said. "We aren't trying to starve them into submission. Let's see if more come out."

During our visit to the Veil, even Tranya Olan had been puzzled at the extent to which concourses were empty and streets deserted. The Serians may be snobs and germophobes, but my intuition was there was another reason; they'd been ordered to stay in. And what I'd hoped—that something just like this would happen—was telling me I was right to think the Serians were not in complete lockstep with the First Citizen.

Here were folks voting with their feet. They wanted no part of the hardcore mosh pit we were bringing to their polka party.

The sergeant spun to answer an unseen voice, and blurted a command. "Nail his ass!"

I called a hold on the assault and we waited. The sergeant's painted face reappeared. "Warmaster, one of those gray-costumed constables popped out and shot at the civilians. Right in their backs, he did! We dropped him, but not before he killed some."

Garlak Ranz replied. "Protect the civilians, Sergeant."

The sergeant wrinkled his brow. "Warmaster, one the refugees approaches at a run. I recognize him. It is that bearded character ever at odds with Tranya Olan."

"I want to speak to that man," I said. A minute later, the sergeant was back in the cloud and next to him, Trayver Lomal. This was going to make for awkward comms. I pulled up Tranya Olan in my cloud and held it in front of Garlak Ranz's wrist and then told her, "Ask him what's happening."

The tattooed fire plug launched into explanation before translation came his way.

"The first citizen has gone mad with power. The seniority is fractured and many have been arrested for suggesting he is leading us on a path to ignominy. Arms have been issued to the constabulary, and they use them against the people. A gathering of concerned and fearful folk was decried as a violent danger and were savagely cut down. People are herded against their will into the mines to be sealed there, supposedly for their own safety."

He painted a grim picture inside the mountain.

"Tell him we're here to help," I said to Tranya Olan. "And tell him when this is over, I expect him to be of use."

She translated rapidly. Trayver Lomal's face was uncovered. His bushy red beard and thick braids hid his expressive features like a mask. But those eyes. The ice-blue eyes set deep beneath the thick brow were lanterns in the dark. He grasped the sergeant's wrist and brought it close to his face. The revulsion that gripped him by proximity to a non-Serian was gone.

"Had I only known."

"Let's rock," I said, shifting to the command cloud. "This is the Warlord. Standby to execute." I gave Garlak Ranz the nod to light the candle. I don't have a Tarn's eyesight, but even I could see the sparkle from the tip of the warhead in the fading light as the gunner exposed himself just before launching.

The penetrator rounds were tipped with what Karlo declared the hardest substance on Earth or Mars. As much as the large crystal resembled a diamond porcupine, Karlo said it was tougher and more impregnable than either. Behind it was a package of chemical explosive potentiated by stones that made for a bunker buster so devastating, the Pentagon would've bestowed us riches to make Raytheon green with envy.

A flash, a boom, and a cloud of material raised so massive, it always made me wonder if it wasn't really some micro-scale nuclear fission that powered the destruction. Only the gunners could see if their missile had succeeded. I silently prayed that the Goose team had taken cover—lest shards of stone spall slice them to bloody bits of meat—when the flash of a second missile trail shot from the top of the spur. A smaller cloud rained up, the boom of this second explosion sounding different to my ear—more focused, as if through a megaphone. I imagined the second warhead detonating deeper into the mountain, and from Garlak Ranz's wrist came the sweet words.

"Positive breach."

I brought my own wrist up. "Assault, assault, assault."

We were running.

The tunnel was exposed and desert-clad men and Tarns disappeared ahead of me like Jonah into the whale. Screams from the dark reached my ears followed by a whooshing sound I couldn't place. I vaulted over and around the destruction of the mountain face. Someone shouted from the depths.

"Flaming liquid pours from the walls!"

Two soldiers dragged another backward by the shoulders, his body consumed by fire. Another rushed ahead and tossed a grenade deep into the tunnel as he yelled warning, and all of us dropped. Soldiers scooped sand from the floor onto the burning trooper, whose twitches and screams ceased, leaving him lying in the way, violet and yellow flames dancing over him as his flesh charred and shrank to the crackling sound a plastic bag made when thrown on a fire.

I crushed together with the throng moving around both sides of the immolated soldier, glad to be past the dead man. Someone had thrown amber stones ahead to light the way and burning globs of fire dribbled along the walls. Their trails led up to apertures on each side of the tunnel.

"Burn those out," a voice said ahead, aiming his own K-spec and firing at one. Beams joined his and rock shattered and rained.

"Again," came the order and beams shot out.

The same trooper tapped another man and a Tarn. "You and you. With me. Rest of you, hold."

The three soldiers moved on line, slowly, carefully, mindfully inspecting the surfaces ahead of them as they advanced to the first bend. One of them short-stocked the butt of his K-spec over shoulder and back—the release signal to go with him—and the three exploded together around the bend. In a second, the Tarn returned and pumped a fist from a lower arm and we all broke into a run down the long tunnel, the fear of being coated by sticky flaming juice forgotten.

A halt of dense men acted like a traffic pileup. From around the bend, noises of grating metal and anguished cries. The wall of men moved backward and I was forced back with it. K-spec flashes reflected off the stone walls from around the bend, but they were out-going, not incoming. It was from troops holding the angle, firing at whatever lay hidden from my sight.

"Pull them out," someone said.

An angry voice replied, "NO! Keep firing. And anyway, they're dead."

I'd had enough.

"Make a hole!"

I pushed, shoved, and pried my way to the front where a pair of troopers hugged the inner radius of the turn, one kneeling, the other standing above him, both firing into the tunnel ahead. No fire returned. I slid over to risk a look. On the ground not far down the next passage, three lay dead. Obviously dead. They were pegged to the ground, dozens of shafts of thin crystal rods piercing their bodies like papier-mâché, them and the floor around them pincushioned with bolts that must've come from above.

Down the corridor was another bend and after that, a last turn where the tunnel would open into the chamber—the loading docks of the Veil. Garlak Ranz was there with me.

"What manner of cowardly deterrent is this?"

I pulled him back. "Order up thumper."

"Yes, Warlord." He dropped back to pass the order on and I started to prepare. I unstrapped my K-spec and handed it to a trooper. "Hang on to this for me. I'll want it back."

I had my 203 on my back and I moved it front. I checked the tube. A 40-mm HE sat in the pipe. Garlak Ranz was there with a pair of soldiers in tow sharing the carrying of a pole across their shoulders. Dangling from the middle of it was a Sputnik-looking thing. Spherical, yet quite pointy in places.

"Set it down," I said.

"Warlord, what do you propose?"

My plan had as many holes as a slice of Swiss cheese. There were other ways to do this, but I couldn't think of any just then.

"Pull everyone back, Warmaster."

Garlak Ranz sucked air through tusks. "No, Benjamin Colt! I have been at your side before when you set on reckless course to bring about a quick end. As I once pled of you, we will find another way!"

"Worked out fine that time, didn't it?"

Garlak Ranz growled. "Does the lair of a soul-eater await ahead?"

"They're gonna wish it was something pleasant like that. Now, get everyone back."

"Very well." The Tarn I'd given his first taste of Earth-type combat and whom I'd watched advance to lead instructor and field officer gave a vicious growl to announce his coming order. "Fall back. With me. To the entrance. Fall back."

I was alone.

I hefted the thumper with both arms, fingers threaded between spikes, and held it against my chest. It was more awkward than heavy, and some of the pointy protrusions found a resting place on top of my mags. Not bad.

I eased around the corner. The dead troopers lay about ten meters ahead, fixed to the ground like an insect collection to a display board. Their payback was coming. I took a deep breath. If Indiana Jones could do it, I sure as hell could.

I backed up, and charged. Just short of the bodies, I launched up and ahead in a shallow trajectory, landed, and sprang again. A symphony of whizzing hummingbirds sheered at my heels. I sprang again, bringing my knees in front of me, intending to land feet first against the wall of the bend ahead. I'd touch the wall, do a Jackie Chan, and change direction, landing on my feet and looking cool, just far enough into the next bend to be out of the path of any more of the Lucite arrows loaded into the ceiling.

I don't know how to do a Jackie Chan.

I crashed ass-end into the wall and fell upside down onto my head. I cringed as I waited for a crystal bolt to shoot straight down into my proffered buttocks and tender bits pointed at the ceiling, and when it didn't, rolled over and made a desperate and clumsy hop to land across the finish line just around the last bend.

I arrived in one piece and set the thumper down.

The corridor was only a few meters long. The grand chamber's wide opening was still a narrow slit from this acute angle of view. Whoever was on the other side of this would be waiting to blast whatever moved into view, like a city boy on his first deer hunt. Only I wasn't a skunk, dog, cow, horse, or goat.

I was prime game.

I slid over just enough to make sure I had the space, then took a single step as I aimed and pressed the trigger.

Bloop. Pause. Ker-blooey.

I'd already dropped another 40 mike-mike HE in the tube, stepped out and sent another, and another. I fumbled the 203 on my back and hefted the thumper. I was about to pop out when fizzle gun fire from inside the dome splashed around the portal. I grumbled as I wrapped the thumper in one arm, pressing it against the wall with my chest, and fumbled for a frag with the other hand. I thumbed the safety clip and actually pulled the pin with my teeth—a first ever.

I sidled over to the end of the wall and flipped the grenade into the room. I hoped the layout of the floor had stayed the way I remembered and there'd not been a rearrangement made after inspection by the home office. By the time the grenade detonated deep in the space, I'd located the two red stones in the widest space between spikes, pressed them both, and sprang into the opening.

The central path between stacks of crates and materials remained. I hadn't bowled since I was in grade school and used the same technique I did then. Between my legs and with both hands I rolled the thumper away, sending it with enough English to curve a spot I pretended was about midway down the lane. There was an intersecting path marking it as a wonderful central location. Maybe it mattered, maybe not, but I tried for it anyway.

Fizzle fire gave me a jolt, and I fell back. Near miss. I scrambled. I was on my feet.

I was hauling ass.

Without having to heft a thing the size and shape of a WW2 underwater mine, I turned the bend to the gauntlet of crystal darts and poured it on. The air behind me swished with the flight from an ample reserve of more of the screaming missiles, piercing into the sand behind me like lawn darts.

This time I did something not even old Jackie could've pulled off.

I went up the wall at a dead run, and stayed there like a stock car on a high bank as I rounded the bend. Here and there tiny dribs of fire trickled down the walls of the home stretch, and I course corrected for the ground at an uninterrupted dead-ass run, in sight of the rubble strewn path indicating the exit.

"Coming through!" I tried to yell, but couldn't.

It was a different sensation than drowning. Instantly, the air sucked from my lungs, then a wind with the force of a hurricane hit me in the face and I reversed directions as if a giant finger had flicked me on the chest. I crashed and rolled as my lungs were pulled out of my mouth. I went dark for a second, then gasped, alert. The wind was gone. The first breath was thin. The next after that, denser. With the next, my lungs filled to the base and the starved asphyxiation feeling was gone.

Garlak Ranz was there with a skad of desert-clad troops, a dozen hands lifting me to my feet.

"Warlord, are you injured? A wind such as I have never felt was sucked into the tunnel! Like the bellows drawing on my clan's forge!"

I coughed. "Tell me about it. Let's go."

Reversing course yet again, around the bend every square foot of the corridor was peppered uniformly across its floor with corn rows of glass arrows. How could there be any more left?

"I think it's safe," I said. Garlak Ranz grasped the drag handle on my armor as I stepped off, snatching me to a dead stop.

"Not this time, Benjamin Colt."

A pair of Tarns hefted the deck plate of a flitter overhead and set off. They reached the end of the corridor without triggering any response, threw the makeshift shield aside, and drew swords. Garlak Ranz roared and drew his own and tore off to inspire the charge. With so many amped up troops blasting off with him, I'd have had to batter some aside to reach the front. I followed the herd at a trot, arriving around the last turn to see the tail of our stampede pour into the cavern.

When I arrived, troops were spread far into the room, weapons aimed high, covering all arcs high and low, forward and reverse. There was no firing, but even had there been, my attention was commanded by what lay at the center of the floor. The thumper was there, resting perfectly in the four-way intersection of the two aisles—not like the work of a PBA tour champion, but with the perfection of a pool table trick shot master.

The thumper had expanded into a sphere so large, an entire squad could not have grasped hands and surrounded it. The sphere's surface was smooth as glass.

How much atmosphere had it sucked away in that instant? I had no idea. But gray uniformed snipers with cyanotic faces hung from bird's nests, their tongues blue and limp, and more lay in gasping death over the barricaded passage blocking the way out.

"Will the entirety of the Veil be so, Warlord?" someone asked.

Karlo said it wasn't so much that the thumper sucked up oxygen, but that the suction caused the tiny grape clusters of the lung alveoli to collapse, never to open again. "I don't think so. The doors past there are pretty stout."

I pulled up the cloud. "We're in."

Karlo had a watch cap on and in the background a field of dazzling stars was interrupted by the outlines of black mountain peaks. "How bad?" he asked.

I told him about the traps and how the constabulary murdered escaping citizens. "Any refugees come across the Platinum Bridge?"

"Negative."

"Hmm. They got it barricaded, too. Sit tight. I won't send your element in unless we hit real resistance, or until we open the gate from the inside and invite you to stroll in."

"If you say, Ben. Don't be shy. I've got Cynar's slim-jim. He says it'll dematerialize that door permanently."

"I won't be shy. If I call you, it'll be because we need you, and there's no other choice but to have you fight that fight. It's a worse way in than this was."

"I've got the ROV. We'll send the thumper in first if we have to."

"It works, man. I can tell you that!"

"You used a thumper?" The spot between Karlo's eyes wrinkled. "How'd you emplace it? We've got the only mule with us."

"I'll explain later."

"Tell me this—if Dave were here, would he threaten to whip your ass?"

"Of course he would," I said with a heavy heart. "Out."

My warmaster was back. "We hold the outer way, Warlord."

"Good." I held a finger up to him to hold him in place while I pictured Tranya Olan. Her face appeared above my wrist.

"Did you pick up Trayver Lomal?"

"Yes, Benjamin Colt."

"An escort will be waiting outside the service entrance to bring you both into our lines. It's time to put him to work."

✠ ✠ ✠

We didn't have enough of a force to leave behind anywhere to hold ground. We had to keep moving. There were no more medieval surprises along our paths. At major thoroughfares and intersections we hit blocking points, easily defeated by superior tactics and firepower, and we leveled constables without losing another single troop. Tranya Olan said the constabulary totaled less than a hundred, and it could be that some had shed the gray to hide with their families.

The smart ones, that is.

It took a half a day to travel the route, clearing along the way, until we arrived at the grand mall. In very little time we eliminated the few constabularies holding the Platinum Bridge. With Karlo's element joining, we rested, refit, and considered our options. The Veil was a honeycomb of thin crevices and massive caverns, deep tunnels and vaulted halls, and it was much too large for our assault force of a hundred to scour, much less control.

I had a good idea where I thought First Citizen Biggus Dickus would be.

"Is there a way into the plaza of the seniority without having to take that train ride? I'm betting that tunnel's booby-trapped like the service entrance."

Trayver Lomal had been brought forward and stood with me, Karlo, Garlak Ranz, and the platoon commanders. Tranya Olan translated for the metallic-tattooed dwarf, who frowned. "What do you intend for the First Citizen and his Seniority?"

"Oh, I have intents. Plural. A prison cell is my first preference, only because I want answers. But I'll accept his head in a basket if that's the choice he leaves me. If you can answer my questions, it'll save us the trouble of nabbing him, and I'll gladly just proceed to snuff him out."

"What answers do you seek?" He seemed motivated to help.

"The Vermeel are waging a war on us using types of stones not known to exist, swimming through the ground in a way no one can explain and laying explosive stone charges beneath our cities. Mihdradahl's entire infrastructure has been poisoned with sabotaged stones. Everything points to the Veil as the source for these calamities. And the First Citizen's so much as admitted it by barricading in when we've come with questions. What's behind all this nonsense?"

Trayver Lomal squinted. "Poisoned stones? Stones to allow passage beneath the surface? Stones that explode? No such stones exist. Long have I mined. I am afraid you must trouble yourselves to question the seniority, but there is no... no..."

His eyes went wide, and he stuttered to a halt.

Tranya Olan prodded him. "Elder cousin, if you know something, you must tell the Warlord."

"I am but the arm of their will! I am not privy to the inner workings or decisions of the seniority. But... "

A longer pause followed, and he seemed to relent.

"We were told it was a new system for accountancy. There is a place where all products of the mines are first diverted. None are allowed inside."

The line work tattoos of gold and silver covering forearms as thick as my thighs rippled like sunlight on rapids as Trayver Lomal clenched his fists over and over. "The First Citizen is under an influence. The system came hence with the arrival of a strange visitor."

"What visitor?" I said, curiosity meter pegged.

"I saw him but once. I was charged with bringing him unseen into the Veil. He was cloaked and did not did not speak. Though foreign, he was not ill appearing nor ignoble in manner. I did not see his face, but he was not man nor Tarn, but somewhere in between in stature. Secretly he arrived and secretly he departed. But it was afterward that all else evolved."

"Like what?" Karlo asked.

"Fey the First Citizen became... erratic. Always, he had the support of the seniority, but soon he began treating them with contempt, and no longer courted their approval in council, acting more so a king. I believe now it was under the influence of the visitor that change came. To what end, I cannot say."

Karlo caught my eye. "We've run into possession before. Do you think?" He knew I knew what he very conspicuously refrained from naming.

"Nope. Talis Darmon would've known. It's not the fur-squid god. It's something else." I addressed Trayver Lomal. "Where will he be?"

"In his bed with wine in hand. The Seat of the Excellency is reached only by the carriage system, as is the private plaza of the seniority's residences. Between them is a passage. But I know ways unknown. Tunnels long forgotten." Karlo handed him a scroll and the dwarf sketched a map, elaborate and detailed, as I would expect from a man who bored through granite for a living.

"I am guide as no other, but I ask of you—there are those held in the mines by the constabulary with orders to do what I dread imagine. I beg your help. Free them."

I considered. "First I need you to take us to where the First Citizen is likely hiding out."

Tranya OIan spoke before she translated my words. "I do not know these tunnels to the meeting place of the seniority, but the mines I know well. Warlord, would you not consider dividing into two missions? I can serve as guide."

I checked Karlo, who nodded.

"All right. Warmaster, choose a platoon and a leader for the mission. Tranya Olan is detached to them as civilian scout, translator, and adviser. Release them to depart when they're ready."

He brought his upper fist to his chest. "Yes, Warlord."

I caught her arm before she left. "Stay out of the gunplay."

Did she learn her "butter wouldn't melt in her mouth" look from me?

"You know me, Warlord."

"I do. A gazraal can't change its spots."

Her eyes glazed in a thousand-yard stare. "That was most similar to one of his." Her focus returned. "But I promise, Warlord. And if opportunity presents to use negotiation to bring reason to the constabulary, I am best suited to do so. They are my clan. Or were." She set off.

"There goes our translator," Karlo said. "Trayver Lomal won't be able to understand a thing we say."

At hearing his name, the dwarf flared.

"Speak you not my name with foreign words of mockery! I may know not your tongue, but I know the tone of insult when I hear it!"

Karlo held up his hands. "Easy now, easy. Sheesh."

Trayver Lomal folded his arms over a chest so broad, he could barely clasp his own wrists. "I was born with a pick in hand and weaned on stone. Carried loads greater than a sōkoon can bear and hammered until the burn of my body stoked the forge of my soul. Keep up if you can, Mihdra, because I lead us far and fast, through passages known only to delvers of old."

The fireplug marched off without looking back to see if we followed, and vanished around the bend of the concourse.

"Shit. Warmaster, get us moving before we lose him," I said, then mumbled to myself, "I see where Tranya Olan gets it."

12

"Where's the ROV?"

Karlo had a cloud open and a slate on his lap, monitoring the mule as it advanced through the rail tunnel. "There's light ahead. We're near the plaza. If they have any nasty deterrents waiting, you'd think they'd kick in pretty—"

Liquid fire poured from the walls. I called the Serians some choice names.

"Will the mule keep going?" I asked.

Karlo was unconcerned. "A little napalm won't hurt it much."

I released the team to move up the tunnel and start clearing the carriage tramway of those fire spigots and any more traps sprung by the mule. And if anyone tried to escape down the railway, they'd be running straight into the waiting arms of our blockers.

But that way in to the seniority's place of business was plan B.

"Assault elements respond ready," I ordered.

Three ready checks came back over my wrist.

"Execute."

Using the chart Trayver Lomal had drawn, we'd made ourselves understood, pointing and pantomiming, him guessing what we tried to communicate. He finally grew exasperated.

"I have explained to you as best I can. At those locations the shafts course nearest the Seat of the Excellency and the seniority. With a dozen of my kin, we could tunnel passages to enter in a manner so rapid, you would marvel. None of you appear capable of assisting me in the task, so by myself, it would require hours. This unused tunnel leads to the least difficult location to do so. It will place us onto the arrival area outside the hall of the seniority."

Karlo pointed to one of the boundaries again and pantomimed, infuriating Trayver Lomal.

"Cease with the absurd gestures and mouth noises!" He threw his hands apart fingers splayed, his cheeks puffing out a sudden breath to mimic back our same gesture.

"It is no clearer to me however many times this act is repeated! It means nothing to me!"

He didn't get it then, but he was about to.

The WHUMP and tremor from three distinctly different forces vibrated the rough stone walls around us, arriving in intervals several seconds apart in a one-two-three cadence. Where Trayver Lomal indicated was the thickest barrier of stone between the old tunnel and the space beyond, the Goose got a workout. At another, a shape charge. The last, just around the bend of the roughly excavated passage we huddled in, a purely stone-powered cutting-charge. Though ours was last to detonate in the breaching series, our close standoff distance from the charge meant we'd be first through the breach and onto the objective.

As much as I wanted to be up front, I used restraint and held back. How would I feel if some general pushed his way to the front of the stack? Okay, I wasn't some paunchy, old guy has-been operator, but I did have the job of one.

There was a time for the Warlord to lead from the front. It was not every time, all the time.

Just as Trayver Lomal had sketched, the tram station floor lay about two meters below the breach. Troops spilled through the rupture onto the grand entrance outside the council room of the seniority. At my turn I leaped down onto the polished mosaic floor, now strewn with jeweled rubble and chunks of the frescoed walls we'd blown out. There were many Gray constables doing good imitations of corpses. From breaches in two other demolished walls poured more troops in mottled red and brown uniforms, moving with controlled violence and explosive force.

My heart soared like the eagle at the sight.

An entry team was testing the massive embossed doors and behind them a breach team was readying a door charge.

"YAAAAH!"

A red-bearded maniac blasted past me, feet pounding the floor with the menacing sound Grandad's prize bull made when he chased me through the pasture. Unlike me and that bull, Trayver Lomal's quarry didn't have a head start. He hefted a gargantuan tool; part-hammer, part-pick. Where he'd picked it up, I hadn't seen. Elbows high, he cocked rearward as he hurtled at the shut portals.

"Don't shoot him!" I screamed, fearful the entry team would think the coming hammer swing was meant for them. They saw, understood, and acted as one, diving away from the doors. The miner reached the end of his run, swinging the broad hammer into the center joint of the two panels. The hammer rebounded like it was made of rubber and I felt a sympathetic tearing in my own rotator cuffs.

Not a mark had been left on the doors.

"Yaaaah!" The mighty dwarf recoiled and swung again, and again, and again. His last blow was too much for any material less dense than the core of the mountain itself. The doors shattered like a cookie sheet of room temperature peanut brittle.

Trayver Lomal barreled in.

Karlo sprang with me to launch after him. Our unfair advantage meant we were first to land together on the other side of the wrecked doors. Expecting gray uniforms and fizzle fire, instead there was only the huge table and its many chairs, empty of their oligarchs. We arrived in time to see Trayver Lomal disappear through an exit at the far end of the table.

For a guy built like a bulldog and twice as ugly, he moved quick.

I directed troops to clear the portal at the opposite end of the council table, thereby exhausting the last bit of knowledge I had of the layout to the chambers of the seniority. I followed Karlo after the dwarf, the footfalls of troops close behind us.

Through empty rooms I sped, just on Karlo's tail, until we came to a winding staircase. Karlo and I effortlessly bounded a dozen steps a time up the circular stairs, leaving our men far behind us by the time we reached the landing.

The FOOSH of fizzle fire greeted us from an open door. Karlo and I came on line, M4s up and ready to fire, and slid towards the opening. The dwarf was a half-step into the room, all but blocked the threshold. We poured in to either side of him, his hammer held high by one arm, the other dangling limply at his side.

I cleared my corner and swung center to a pair of constables, their fizzle fire scorching the air around me. How bad did you have to be to miss with a fizzle gun at 25 meters? I'd just sent a pair at the first and was transitioning to the other to run a box drill and give him a couple before I shifted up to the head, then transitioned back to my first target to put one in his brain box, when the second man dropped. Karlo'd started the same from his side of the room, and we'd overlapped effort.

Exposed now was a platinum-robed man with a neat-trimmed beard, arms held out to ward off harm. It was the First Citizen's secretary.

"KILL ME NOT! I am unarmed. I surrender!"

Before I knew what was happening, my view of the secretary was replaced by the massive miner's tool spinning end-over-end. The pick struck Platinum Robes in the chest, lifted him off his feet, and drove him against a tapestry depicting bathing maidens, where he stuck.

Trayver Lomal roared, "Depart from sight yourself! ASS!"

"Coming in!" a voice called from outside.

"Come in!" Karlo yelled back. Panting troopers flowed in and through, taking over.

Trayver Lomal massaged his limp arm, flexing the fingers of the dangling hand. "A minor slap. Worse from bar wenches have I had."

I pointed at the crucified secretary and put on the same face I used when Apache took a dump inside the house. "Hey, what the hell? We needed that guy!"

Trayver Lomal scowled back. "Bottle your babble, unclean rube. I know your complaint even without comprehension of your boorish speech. That sot deserved to taste the steel of a delver!" He rose on tippy-toes to reach his crooked nose up to my face, close enough I could smell what he had for breakfast. "And *you* do not order me here. Not in the Veil!"

His eyes were wild. He was on his way to a frenzy. Such was the way sometimes when the trapdoor holding back the murderer in us all opened. And what poured out of Trayver Lomal was a long-held resentment stoking the passion for more murder.

There was only one way I knew to reach him.

I snatched his harness at the chest and with one hand, hefted him aloft high above me. He grasped my wrist with both hands, his dead arm finding power again. The crush of his grip was fierce and if I relaxed my own, he'd bow my forearm bones together and they'd splinter like dry pine.

"Naughty-naughty," I said. I pumped my arm like one of those As Seen on TV shake-weights. With legs flailing and squat head bobbling like one of those desktop miniatures, his grip relaxed to something closer to that of a guy simply trying to hang on for dear life. I stopped rattling his cage before he spewed all over me like a nauseous toddler.

My action had been violent, now my voice was calm and soothing.

"Buddy, we've all been there. But you gotta chill."

He nodded as if he comprehended hillbilly like he grew up in the holler next to mine. I set him down softly and released my grip.

"Sorcery!" he exclaimed under his breath. "The rumors do not bear full measure of your strength!"

Message. Received.

"Now that you understand who I am, how about we go find Granday Fallis?"

"The First Citizen?" Trayver Lomal said with a bit of lilt. "Yes. Of course. Let us go. I know where he is to be found. Come."

He was out the door before I could get him to say where.

"That guy's exhausting," I said to Karlo. "Let's go."

My brother seated a fresh mag, gave it a firm pull, and deposited the removed mag in his dump pouch. He felt the bolt and closed the dustcover over the ejection port without looking, all while shaking his head in pity.

"Why'd I think this was the break I needed from the workbench?"

We followed the miner through a maze of passages until we came out onto the grand plaza that held the private residences of the seniority. The rest of the assault force had already seized the sanctuary, and the search for the First Citizen was underway.

At one end was a tram platform where a long ornate carriage was docked. The rectangular open court was lined by zero lot-line mansions, each fronted by short walls protecting narrow lawns of fine cropped turf and beds of pale flowering plants. I'd not seen green space since Annameria. Apparently, the white-diamond light from the crystalline icicles that dangled like ceiling rafters could nourish plant life. Our underground farms were lit amber, not pale, and I wondered what besides ornamentals could grow by the light of the stalactites.

"Less is more" was not a thing anywhere in the Veil, but in the private sanctuary of the sitting oligarchs, more was not enough. It was dense with masterpieces.

Sculptures of past prominent Serians stood in the court, each seeming to be minutely larger in scale than any other—a game of one-upmanship for posterity—until all were left behind in the competition by the monument of a figure mounted on a jewel bedazzled sōkoon.

The subject atop the animal balanced a pick over one shoulder, the other arm outstretched with palm holding high a gem the size of a state fair pumpkin—an actual jewel, not crystal chiseled to appear as if it were one.

Trayver Lomal scowled at the face of the rider. It was one I'd seen before. "He has laid not tool to stone in his life," the dwarf spat. "Nor have these others."

Dominating the opposite end of the plaza sat the winner of *Homes of the Rich and Shameless* of the Veil's Beverly Hills. I didn't need the Zillow app to label the grandest of all the mansions as the addy of the First Citizen.

Trayver Lomal trailed behind, seemingly a little wary of coming within arm's reach of me. We passed teams working efficiently to enter and clear the residences—ornate doors were demolished, flowers tramped, tapestries ripped from windows.

"This is a well-oiled machine," Karlo said, correctly interpreting my own thoughts about the working troops we passed on our way to the end of the plaza. "What else do you notice about this company, Ben?"

Our platoons were still largely segregated into Mihdra and Tarn. This company came from our expeditionary unit on the *Hope.* Even there, that nominal organization continued. What Karlo was trying to get me to take notice of: as combat taskings evolved on this operation, there was a seamless integration of both races working together as one team.

"I notice a lot, Karlo. And I'm glad for it. Because until we're no longer effectively cut off from each other—for what may be a very, very long time—we have no choice but to restructure into independent combat teams. If this is any indication of how they're going to perform, then I say, we can pull it off."

But as we arrived at the largest mansion, it seemed there was a stall in the action. I understood why. Though the landscaping invited the way to an entrance, there was none. Nor were there balconies or terraces like the other homes had.

Garlak Ranz and an entire platoon searched for a way in.

"Desist the search for the entry," the warmaster said. "We have wasted enough time." A Goose gunner and his assistant appeared and correctly anticipating what was about to come, the troops pulled back.

"HOLD, Warmaster!" Karlo yelled. He had his daypack off and fished in the main compartment, producing a gizmo I'd never seen. It was a cross between a fidget spinner and a snow globe. He started it up. The spiral curlicue at the top of the orb turned and flashed. Satisfied, Karlo held it out, his other hand maintaining a firing grip on his carbine.

"I've got Cynar's universal remote. If there's a hidden portal, this should do the trick."

Sure enough, as he neared the building, the reliefs came alive. A bookend pair of three-tailed anteaters with ears like bats and stubby T-Rex arms stretched and threw their heads back as if to roar. The gizmo atop the globe spun faster in time as the lights flashed brighter. The section of wall bearing the carved creatures vanished.

The way in was clear.

Karlo stood aside and replaced the tool in his daypack as troops streamed in two-by-two like they were loading onto Noah's ark. Karlo and I weaved our way through the mansion, past rooms held at doorways by a trooper in visual contact with another posted in the next doorway. An amber gem lay on the floor outside each threshold, indicating the room had been cleared.

Without being asked, Trayver Lomal said, "Surely there is some den stuffed with riches where he thinks himself immunized from harm." We came into a ballroom with a staircase Ellie May Clampett wouldn't have been out of place gliding down.

On the landing above appeared Garlak Ranz.

"Up here, Warlord."

Through a sitting room we passed a trooper casually guarding a pair of plainly dressed young servant women holding each other in fright. Garlak Ranz waved us to follow him through a bed chamber the size of a basketball court and stepped through an ornate arch.

"Welp," I said. "I gotta give credit where credit's due. He called it."

With more guns on him than Saddam coming out of his spider hole, rested the First Citizen of the Veil of Seriata. Far from disheveled, he lay in a precious metal tub footed its length by pairs of seven-toed feet, immersed in a viscous slurry of small red gems. He scowled and squirmed, causing the overfilled tub to slop waterfalls of the gems over the brim to bounce onto the tiled floor like gravel shed from the bed of a dump truck on the highway.

Trayver Lomal gave an insolent laugh. "I imagined much, but profligacy such as this! Never."

Granday Fallis glared at the dwarf, his discomfort at having so many guns pointed at him sublimating as fast as dry ice turned to mist, and issued an angered accusation. "Delver. Peasant. Debtor. I should have left you in the pits."

I shifted weight to the balls of my feet, ready to tackle the dwarf before his massive fingers could pop bathing beauty's head off, but for once, Trayver Lomal used his words.

"I *am* a delver. Of the oldest line of delvers. The delvers who grind, excoriate, and wrest all wealth from the mountain, exchanging our sweat, skin, and blood to spin the threads that weave the Veil. Masons build. Smiths fashion. Artists flatter. Lenders extort. But delvers! All Serians ride atop the broad shoulders of us miners."

The First Citizen snorted. "Delvers. Pah! You are all alike. I elevated you, Trayver Lomal, and in repayment, you bring contamination into the heart of the Veil, to the very nursery of our people's flower."

Trayver Lomal roared, "And what does that make those whom you *murdered*? Weeds in your garden? Your primacy is at an end. My only shame is it required the intrusion of filthy outsiders to bring you down. It should have been the hands of delvers who cast the Superiority into the bowels of Vistara."

Then Trayver Lomal sobbed, managing to choke out, "Why have you done this, Granday Fallis? And what blade yet waits in the dark to be slipped between the ribs of our backs?"

Granday Fallis was taken aback, brows raising high. "I have done nothing amiss. You may have fooled these begrimed intruders to assist you in overthrowing the rightful government, but it is you who have been fooled. *They* are the ones responsible for what disruptions have occurred in the Veil, not I."

Rolling his eyes, Karlo said, "Admit nothing. Deny everything. Make counteraccusations."

It was as though the First Citizen had learned it from the E-4 Mafia. Granday Fallis had his decipher on and understood Karlo.

"I am the head of state. I need explain nothing. I expelled all Mihdra. You have no right to be here, nor to question me. Begone, filth. I will say no more."

I gave Garlak Ranz the high sign. Before the First Citizen could say shit like he had a mouth full of it, he was out of the tub, bound, and hooded. Someone came out of the bed chambers with a robe. A Tarn on one side and a human on the other, the soldiers perp-walked Granday Fallis away. Gems freed from folds and dark places shed from beneath his robe to tink and dance on the floor as he departed.

"He goes back to Shansara," I said. "We're not even screwing around with him. Talis Darmon can zap him with one of her auras the second his ass hits an interrogation room chair." I reached Tranya Olan in the cloud and gave her the news.

"We've captured Granday Fallis."

"That is welcome news, Warlord. We have accepted the surrender of one group of constables and freed those they held in the mines. However, another band is proving less reasonable. The capture of their leader may encourage the process. Regardless, we are soon to end the stalemate."

"Good job. Finish translating and get transport and meet us at the Platinum Bridge. We have other matters to attend to. Out."

With a look of revolt as sour as that he'd previously reserved for us unclean Mihdra, Trayver Lomal examined the opulence around us and shook his head in disgust. "The labors of my fathers! Used to tile the toilet room of our oppressor!"

"Oppressor?" I whispered to Karlo. "Sounds like the talk of a Vermeel we know."

"Hard to blame him," Karlo said. "The system here's held people down for a long time. DOL, baby."

DOL was the Special Forces motto. De Oppresso Liber. To free from oppression.

"DOL's right," I agreed, then sighed. "So, we got that going for us. But the Pale are still hitting us and we don't know how. All our best technology's sabotaged. We've heard nothing from Dave. And Trayver Lomal's saying there's yet another new boogeyman working somewhere behind the scenes we have to track down. What've I left out?"

"Only that we're going to crush this," Karlo said. He got Trayver Lomal's attention and spoke in a pretty good approximation of the Serian language. Leave it to Karlo to have already memorized key phrases in a language he'd been exposed to for all of a hundred words. Our reluctant guide was surprised.

"Go to the Platinum Bridge, you say?"

Karlo nodded and we let Trayver Lomal take us to the tram carriage and soon enough, we were back where the Platinum bridge joined the gap of the deep canyon mall. Only now, Serians stole cautious glances at us from the concourses and terraces above and below. Our friendly waves caused them to recoil away.

"Ben. Check it." Karlo pointed down. On the floor of the canyon, a tiny train of pale sōkoon ambled nose to tail, each bearing multiple riders with many more walking on foot.

Trayver Lomal said, "Sōkoon carry the eldest. The seniority's edict to sequester in the mines spared not even those unable to walk. Those with secret spaces—as most delvers have in their domiciles—hid in their homes. I wonder how many without met their deaths, trying to escape as I instructed my neighbors to do. I have not said so, but if not for you, we would have been slaughtered or returned to the mines to await an unknown fate."

He slammed his fist into his palm. "The Grays must be held accountable. Disarmed, nothing will save the constabulary from the just revenge of delvers everywhere."

Tranya Olan joined us just then. "They shall be held to account, elder cousin. All are in custody."

"Let's get this show on the road," I said. With a little tweaking we had split clouds open with Talis Darmon and Beraal in one, Double-K and Doug in the other, and the First Shield in the last. I gave the rundown, ending with the capture of the head of the seniority and the release of the hostage citizenry.

The queen blew a breath of relief. "Excellent. We have news as well, Warlord. General Douglas Knoblock, would you please?"

Dougie grinned. "We got it, boys."

"Got what?" I said, playing along.

"The Vermeel gizmo. The excavation team found it just a little while ago, about a klick from the ambush site and about ten meters down. They kept following the blood trails until they hit gold. There were two croaked Vermeel in a kind of a chamber, one of them wearing a chest plate with some funky stones in it. That's how far they made it before they bled out."

Karlo jumped. "That's great. Where is it?"

"It remains in Thoria," Double-K said.

Karlo was excited. "If you send the Black Bird to retrieve it on the way to picking us up, Cynar and I will start pulling it apart the moment we get it to the lab."

"Hold that thought," I said. "Let's finish settling the status of the Veil."

Talis Darmon shook her head in agreement. "Yes. I did not suspect such despotism ruled the Veil. It was a thing well done, Warlord. Hmm. And by your appearance, something tells me I have heard but cursory details of your part in the operation."

My appearance? I knew I was grimy, sweaty, and filthy, but that was normal. Karlo grabbed my shoulder to point out where a large rent ran down the uniform sleeve. I guess one of the crystal bolts had come closer than I thought. It had felt a little drafty on my triceps.

The queen continued without questioning me further, but I knew when I got home I'd hear more about it. "And you are correct, Benjamin Colt. The First Citizen and I should have a face-to-face meeting as soon as can be arranged."

"I'll be bringing him," I said. "With your agreement, Talis Darmon, this is my plan... Karlo, as much as you want to be there to help, if we're going to put you to work as an engineer, right here is where you're needed. You're the man to investigate what's going on with the stone processing. Find out what and how the stones have been tinkered with, and get the Serians back on track to shipping good stones to Shansara ASAP. I know it's not the job you want, but it's the job you've got."

He made a face like he had gas pains. "Yes, Ben. Can do."

I switched to the diminutive woman next to him. "Tranya Olan, you're staying, too. With the queen's permission, the regency is appointing you governor of the occupation. Warmaster Garlak Ranz remains in command of the military task force, subordinate to the governor."

Talis Darmon nodded. "I concur. Beraal drafts the royal appointment as we speak. Tranya Olan, you hereby carry the authority of your regent. I commission you to restore order, investigate crimes of bad faith committed by the oligarchs against the people of the Veil, and to be just in the application of our laws."

Tranya Olan bowed deeply. "Yes, Queen Talis Darmon."

Zaylin Twee spoke up in the cloud. "Queen? If I may offer advice? This is a military occupation, but the army is ill prepared for all necessary tasks. I would send a detachment of Guardians to maintain civil order and assist in the investigation, but as that is not possible, I can assign advisors to offer advice remotely."

"Accepted, First Shield," the queen said.

"Good," I said. "Gents, get that Black Bird prepped, but don't launch before we have a chance to review any urgent needs and get you a list. Sending us a decipher for Trayver Lomal is one item. Good to go?"

"Roger, Ben-dog," Doug said.

Tranya Olan had been translating for Trayver Lomal, who showed interest at the prospect of having a decipher. I slumped a bit, dreading how to put into words my next thought.

All I came up with was, "Dave?"

Dougie shook his head. "Nada. When you get home, I'd like permission to turn the Black Bird around and send it out to do a search."

I didn't want to say no—not in front of Tranya Olan—but I couldn't say yes. We had one Black Bird. One. And until we had more, our sole functioning hypersonic craft was needed to join together the disparate parts of the kingdom, a need more critical than allowing it to search for a grain of sand lost in a billion trillion grains of sand over thousands of square miles of empty desert.

Even if that one grain of sand was my best friend. And Dave would've been the first to agree. So I told a lesser lie.

"We'll figure it out when I get there. Out."

I moved off by myself for a private conversation with my wife.

"We have time to speak alone, sweetheart. Is everything else okay?"

"Tashara Colt misses her father."

"I miss her back. I'll be home tonight. Anything else?"

"Small but interesting developments."

"Such as?"

"In Clymaira, an unexpected source of help has appeared to render aid and provide solace to the people. Kleeve Hartus."

I gulped.

Partly by intent and partly by circumstance, the whereabouts of the former First Shield of Mihdradahl had become unknown. At once I was flooded with the many labels I'd stamped on the memory files of the different Kleeve Hartuses I'd known. Loyal friend. Brilliant tactician. Stalwart lawman. Brave warrior. Religious fanatic. Ritual murderer. There were others that came to mind, but they were the brands I reserved for myself and my wife to describe our own part in his fall from grace. They all boiled down to one that fit best.

Machiavellian strategist.

Talis Darmon continued. "A small core of followers of the Well of Tears from Pyreenia have been in Clymaira for some time. Apparently, Kleeve Hartus has been among them. As it is his home, it was suspected he would be among them, but until the terror attack, his presence was not confirmed."

"What's he been doing?"

"As I said, he and his fellow monks offer support as they can, rendering aid and organizing relief without evidence of subversion or fomenting of religious strife. You would be the first to admit Kleeve Hartus was peerless in a task such as managing civil emergencies. Reports are that he and his group have worked tirelessly."

I tried to imagine Kleeve Hartus with a shaved head—or worse, one of those reverse cereal bowl-type cuts—dressed like a Franciscan friar or however the adherents to the old Pyreenian faith showed their gang colors.

"Meaning, Zaylin Twee knows he's in Clymaira?" As Guardians, they'd been the closest of comrades. As lovers, they'd been bound by intimacy at all levels.

"She does," my wife confirmed. "She has not shared with me feelings, other than embarrassment at the intelligence failure of her Guardians in regards to his whereabouts."

"We pretty much told her to be hands off concerning Kleeve Hartus."

"Just so. You of all people understand what it is to bear a sense of duty and responsibility for even those things beyond your control."

"I don't like it," I said. "It may be a coincidence that he and his cult buddies just happened to be in Clymaira when it got hit, but I don't think he's there simply to go door-to-door asking folks if they've considered Desudun Cahlair for their savior. He's there to cause trouble for us."

My wife's beautiful face fell. "Discussion of the seasons on Thulia brings to mind one of your aphorisms, Benjamin Colt. When it rains, it pours. But I think the Vistaran version more appropriate.

"Annoys the grain of sand, chafes by pinch, flays by storm."

13

It was a perfect morning in Shansara, which is to say, it was a morning like every morning. For all the strife in the kingdom, the city was alive and bustling. More babies than I'd ever seen were carried in arms or pushed in prams. Children too young for school accompanied mothers shopping. Traveling to and fro around us at their own pace and purpose, the streets teamed with citizens at their business.

Gossamer cloth of every color and simple jewelry worn in bands or curls wrapped around bodies and limbs the color of deep red adobe. Everywhere else, exposed bare skin radiated the warmth and health of a sun unimpeded by clouds. The same rays reflected off iridescent towers joined by walks seemingly suspended without support against gravity. We were nearing the Fountains of Persidia, splashes and fine mist heard and tasted before they could be seen.

If it was a choice between the Veil and Shansara—687 out of 687 days a year—I'd take Shansara, every time.

It was easy to feel safe, content, and carefree here. I breathed it in, promising to preserve and protect this place that nurtured such wellbeing, and returned to caution. But of what I was most cautious against was not a drift into complacency.

It was the ashen Tarn ahead of me on the street.

Sarkan Sell and Jodal Jark kept pace with me a few steps behind the Vermeel prisoner. Alongside were his escorts Zaylin Twee and Doug. Apache, we had to leave at home. His obedience only went so far when it came to being in the vicinity of our prisoner—and prisoner he was—though he was being treated like a visiting dignitary.

The Vermeel was not bound. Dressed in garb to resemble the average Korundi—loin cloth, leather arm bracers, and harness—though he was pale, his color brought no undue attention from those about their business. Peritar the Finder had filled out a little. His skin did not sag so loosely, his wrinkles smoothed some. This was his first trip to this part of the city and the fountains, and I heard him suck a breath as we rounded into view of the rain.

"Do you care to go closer?" Zaylin Twee inquired. Even for Korundi, the first sight of so much water was startling. For a Vermeel, it might spark hydrophobia.

Peritar grunted. He was not one for verbosity, not unless making vitriolic political critiques of our kingdom.

"Come on," Doug said, veering our group toward the showering fountain encircled by monuments. A pair of mothers laughed nervously while attending closely to the small children wading in the basin. There was a time the Fountains of Persidia were held in almost sacred reverence, one of the very few places in the kingdom where water was allowed to form such a massive pool in the open air. Not that water wasn't still a precious commodity; it was. But with our atmosphere improved and more water flowing than ever, the fearful veneration of scarcity the monument was meant to inspire, had relaxed.

No Shansaran—no matter how conservative—should be able to hold back the kind of smile I wore at the sight of beautiful children splashing in the fountain. Not after what we'd been through, not after how far we'd come.

And what the heck was a fountain for if not for kids to splash around in?

Peritar scoffed. "Here is enough water to sustain for a thousand days my entire clan. But in your care, it is given to the people as a toy. Decadence!"

"Water's life, just like air," Doug said. He dipped hands into the pool and touched the bottom. "Come on. It's okay. Have you ever felt water covering your skin?"

Peritar had at first refused the water pouches given him in his cell. But it wasn't long before the Guards noticed they came back empty, until he was consuming one with each meal, another thing he'd taken to—eating three times a day whatever was offered.

Zaylin Twee joined Doug to wet her own hands, then making show to press them to her cheeks. "Appreciating the creation around us brings us closer to the one who made us all."

At this, Peritar seemed to soften. "The true People are made in the image of the great creator, and for his People he created all." I could hear the big P in people.

Sarkan Sell moved to the fountain. Rather than reveal his loathing of the Pale, the old man fully embraced the role of eldest warrior and wisest of strategists. He reveled in the game to coerce our enemy into revealing himself.

"In craft holding a dozen warriors have I floated on underground rivers. I have trod those same waters even up to my chest. It is as unnatural to Korundi as it would be to Vermeel. But as we have accustomed to flying, we have accepted water as something to master, no matter how disconcerting." He knelt and stuck a single lower finger into the pool.

"Is a terror of the desert such as you fearful to touch more than drops to tongue?"

Sarkan Sell could've taught at the JFK Special Warfare Center.

Peritar bristled at the challenge and cautiously approached the fountain. The toddlers were still splashing around on the other side. Whether it was the tiny humans' disregard for the danger or Sarkan Sell's manipulative ball-busting persuasion, the Vermeel knelt. One finger, two, then both lower hands, then up to his elbows all four arms were plunged in the pool.

Doug sat on the rim next to a Peritar exploring and experiencing sensations he'd most likely never had. "Not so bad, huh?"

The Vermeel withdrew and stood, seemingly unmoved by the immersive encounter, ready to be guided elsewhere.

"Let us continue our journey," Zaylin Twee said.

Peritar the Finder of the Black Tusk clan stood fast and snarled, and I put a hand on my pistol.

"I know what you attempt, Mihdra. You mean to weaken me. To twist me and tempt me with the softness of your society. But what I see is nothing but lies. You exploit many so few can live in abundance. Wealth is your master, as is comfort. It is your enslavement."

"Then come see some more of how all us slaves live, dude," Doug said. "Would ya rather sit in your cell?"

Peritar capitulated. "I would not."

I knew where we were going. Not far away was an open-air food market. It was considered quaint and an anachronism in the capital, but a cherished one. Vendor stalls cooked all sorts of delicacies, even many favored by the Korundi, whose tastes and diets were not entirely the same as humans'. During the day it was a common spot to find off-duty soldiers. At night, well—if the guy thought a fountain was decadent, I didn't see us taking Peritar to the red-light district.

We strolled among the varieties of foods grown in our underground farms and things we traded for with the Annamese. As we passed one of the roast godahl stalls, I couldn't help but notice Peritar sniff. "Why don't you get us a table, guys?" I said to my Tarn companions.

In exchange for a coin bearing my wife's likeness and a few minutes later, a server was placing plates in front of us. The guys and I came here once in a while. While they said the human cook at this stall was the best, they always griped it wasn't authentic Korund godahl. As long as I was paying, they still snarfed it down like it was their Grandma's recipe.

Sarkan Sell noticed Peritar's hesitation to pick up the charred limb in front of him. "It may be different from what you are accustomed to, Peritar the Finder, but it is not rancid. Join."

Bones shattered under Peritar's ravenous chomping; sharp splinters along with meat and marrow escaped around tusks at high velocity. Even a Mydreen would've felt revulsion at the Vermeel's table comportment and felt forced to shield his plate. When the blackened leg had been devoured, he ran his tongue over the greasy shrapnel on his hands and arms, and for a second, I thought Zaylin Twee across from him was in danger of getting licked to recover more of the bits he'd lost.

It was on the stroll back to jail that Zaylin Twee worked him.

"May I ask a question, Peritar the Finder?"

The Vermeel was back to grunting.

"We have shown you much. There is much more I would show you, but all will display the same openness and freedom of our society. There is no hunger or thirst. There is exchange by mutual agreement and without violence. None are abused, maltreated, or exploited in the manner I believe would fit any definition of the term you so frequently use—oppressed."

Peritar was gruff. "What is your question of me?"

"What is it you find so profoundly corrupt about our way of life?"

He wasted no time. "It appalls: the waste. The lack of direction. Even before we were introduced to the great ideal, the People worked together for one purpose. The tribe is the People and the People serve the tribe. Here, I see no unity, no common goal, no subservience to a greater good. Only selfishness. It is wrong. It must be eliminated for the benefit of all."

I'd heard it, too. It was masterful on her part; the first solid reveal she'd manipulated from him. Before I could make the interrogative, Zaylin Twee did. "What is this 'great ideal' you speak of?"

Peritar growled condescendingly. "A collectivist state controlled by the will of the People, of course."

I'd been chewing a small cube picked from the bowl resting on our lunch table. At Peritar's revelation, I inhaled it down the wrong pipe. I strained to get enough air *in* so I could get the words *out*, and squeaked, "C-commies"—cough, cough—"space commies."

The confused look on Doug's face would've been funny, save the fact I was in the throes of asphyxiation. Distracted by my bizarre declaration, Doug didn't notice my predicament. "What the heck are you talking about, dude? Commies from space?"

It wasn't exactly what I meant and tried again to explain. Cough, wheeze, cough. Then—nothing.

The unflavored animal gristle assumed a consistency similar to gum after you chewed it a while, and my million-dollar idea was to make it sweet. My innovation would wipe out the rest of the chewing gum market overnight, and it'd buy me and Talis Darmon a mansion overlooking the Furrow. That would never happen now. Because while I struggled to tell my friends I'd been wrong—that here was proof that whoever was working to disrupt our society had indeed come from Earth—I successfully sucked the moist, firm cube of mouth cleanser the rest of the way down my trachea for the grand prize.

A complete airway obstruction.

My hands clutched my throat as I realized—here at last, came my demise. It had been promised many times by many enemies. In her last minutes Lashura, the queen of the Whites, had taunted me that the Mists of Time had shown her my end. Was this what she'd seen? Me exiting by the most banal and pedestrian of mechanisms possible? Contrary to popular belief, there are no good ways to die. Only worse ways. And before the animalistic panic of oxygen starvation took over completely, I realized that mine was about to be the worst possible death of all.

Because of all the forces the universe set against me, it was communism that was about to claim final victory over the Warlord of Mars.

"I know what is required!" Jodal Jark exclaimed. "A hatch mate of my brood was often in this predicament. He frequently choked on large bones while eating in haste. I saved his life many a time, though later was forced to kill him over a matter of honor." He began his first aid, or should I say, assault. He pummeled the space between my shoulder blades like a four-fisted power hammer.

I don't know which was worse, choking to death or the Tarn version of the Heimlich maneuver.

Jodal Jark spun me around. "Now I must reach down his gullet!"

"Move it, Ranger," Dougie said, pushing Jodal Jark away. "The N stands for knowledge. A solid A for the effort though, homie." He bear-hugged me from behind and rapid-fire pumped his balled fist upward into my gut, lifting me off my feet with each thrust. On the fourth, the offending homicide implement shot like a cannonball from my mouth to bounce off Peritar's chest, causing him as little reaction as a windowpane to the dead-end flight of a sparrow.

I sucked in a huge breath.

"I was wrong." I hacked a final violent cough. "That guy I shot disguised as a Vermeel—he's from Earth!"

Doug gawked. "Holy shit, duder! Could it really be?"

I pointed at the Vermeel. "Peritar, who laid that great idea on you about a collectivist state?"

My question bounced off him like the piece of gum I'd spat. Zaylin Twee's raised eyebrow said she was less concerned for my welfare and more grateful I'd ceased the interruption of her work. She cleared her throat gently.

"Peritar the Finder, in you I have met a being of intelligence and learning. I do not know the full accounting of past injustices done to your people. I was not there. I can understand a hatred for us. But surely you must see—those on whom you make war are beings like yourselves, people who simply wish to live their lives. They do so at no one else's expense. You do not live without in the desert because they have more. So I must ask, does what you see jibe with what you have been told of us?"

Peritar seemed about to speak, then changed his mind. "I wish to return to my confinement now."

It was a quiet return walk to the headquarters of the Guard. When Peritar was taken away, Zaylin Twee turned and placed a hand on my arm, showing concern for the first time. "Benjamin Colt, are you quite alright? I fail in understanding of what surprised you to the verge of near death."

My swallowing muscles burned and I was sore everywhere. "I'm fine, thanks, but as for what made me forget how to chew gum and walk at the same time, well, that's going to require a bit of an explanation." Just then I was interrupted by the buzzing of my wristlet. Beraal's face appeared.

"Benjamin Colt, the queen asks you to witness her interrogation of the Serian prisoner."

Talis Darmon was supposed to have a minor council scheduled for this morning. "Did you know she was here?" I asked Zaylin Twee.

"I knew only she hoped to start her questioning of the First Citizen sometime later today, Warlord."

"We're just downstairs. Be right there," I said. We entered the observation area to find Beraal standing with Shasa Karin and Keshin Tellest, all staring through the large pane of one-way glass. On the same side of the table as my wife was an investigator, and across from them sat Granday Fallis. Beads of sweat ran from his scalp, his jail garment saturated like a cheap paper towel sopped with water from a backed-up toilet.

"Beraal," I whispered. "Why wasn't I informed?"

She replied in equally reverent tones. "The queen did not desire you disturbed, Benjamin Colt. You were engaged with the First Shield in an important task. A last-minute change occurred in her schedule. Talis Darmon was most clear that we must each move with alacrity and exercise all skills to treat our many current dilemmas. Do not you usually make quip of, 'divide and conquer,' brother?"

"Yeah, but I wanted to be there for this."

My adopted sister jutted a curled tusk my way. "You are here now, Benjamin Colt."

I reminded myself you always had to pick your battles with a Tarn. "Ay yi yi! Fill me in on what I've missed."

"Shh. Precious little. Behold."

Talis Darmon extended her hands across the table and a ball of yellow light glowed between her palms. "Granday Fallis, do not look away. Open your eyes and see the light of truth and allow it to bathe you in its purity."

The Serian did open his eyes. But rather than assume the mesmerized look I expected, he bore down, more sweat beading on his forehead, and found strength to shut his eyes tightly again. Talis Darmon began a chant in a language not even my decipher could render and her aura grew fiery red. Still the Serian resisted.

"Who has influenced you? Who has tempted you? What has been promised you in exchange for your misdeeds?" She fired more questions at the First Citizen, yet his lips remained as sealed as his eyes. The aura vanished and she withdrew hands to her lap. The Serian collapsed.

"Take him away, investigator."

Guards appeared and stood the First Citizen. Exhausted yet with a defiant smile, he was escorted off. Talis Darmon joined us outside.

"Benjamin Colt, I am glad you were here to witness. Was success with the Vermeel wrought from today's efforts?"

"I was about to ask you the same. I think we made a little headway. The First Shield's strategy is whittling away at the Vermeel's reluctance to speak. What'd you get out of him?" I thumbed in the direction of the interrogation room.

She sighed. "Nothing. It has been the better part of two hours the investigator and I have questioned Granday Fallis. Thrice have I resorted to sorcery and thrice have I failed to weaken his resolve to withhold inner thoughts from me."

"His resistance is remarkable, Talis Darmon," Beraal said, impressed. "I have never witnessed like."

I had to ask. "Now that you have him in front of you, did you sense anything—dark?"

She shook her head slowly and definitively. "No, husband. His resistance does not stem from that manner of evil. He is not possessed. Instead, I sense the deepest commitment. Were it other, I would swear its essence was altruistic service to someone or something. Instead, I gather it stems from an all-encompassing sort of... greed."

"Could it be the dwarves are immune to your sorcery?" I wondered.

"No, Benjamin Colt," she said with equal assuredness.

Doug's brow furrowed. "Are you going to take another run at him soon, Talis Darmon? It looked like you had him on the ropes at the end there."

She looked troubled. "The thought is morally repellent, Douglas Knoblock. Even in defense of our people, it would be no different from applying any other common torture."

I was conflicted with feelings of disappointment and pride. "I'd expect you to say nothing different, sweetheart. But what about the Vermeel? He knows who the humans working with the Pale are, and it's become more vital than ever we find out." I told her what I thought.

She scrunched her face. "I do not understand the connection you have made with Earth."

"Nor I, Benjamin Colt," Zaylin Twee said.

"Okay, it's like this," I began. "Even allowing for the inexactness of how things are translated by the deciphers, there's just been something from the get-go about Peritar's language that's struck us as very, very reminiscent of an ideology from Earth."

Doug was nodding. "All his talk about oppressors and exploitation. It's like he graduated from Patrice Lumumba University in Moscow."

All of the women frowned.

I tried to form a brief explanation. "It was a place where an enemy schooled people in their ideology and returned them to their own country to indoctrinate and organize others against us."

Doug mumbled, "Or UC Berkley, I guess."

Talis Darmon understood. "And you believe the Vermeel's most recent revelation is indicative of the presence of such foes here on Vistara? From your Earth?"

I shrugged. "If you zapped Peritar, we could find out pretty quickly."

With lips pursed, Zaylin Twee hummed disagreement. "I do not wish to impede progress in achieving a complete picture of our enemy,

Warlord, but I have *extreme* reservations regarding that course of action. While the queen could most assuredly wrest knowledge from Peritar, he is highly intelligent. Such an assault would erase what sympathetic connection I have formed with him. It would most certainly render him unwilling to engage in further discourse, whence he otherwise may become inclined to speak without coercion. I believe it would be counterproductive to our efforts to gain insight into our enemy. I think we may be near a true breakthrough with him. He may even be converted into an ally, useful in some way difficult to predict."

I blew out a breath. She was right, but... as I pictured the morning my family was whisked away, covered in red ichor, I spoke harsher than I intended.

"We're running out of time, Zaylin Twee. The next attack could come at any time."

"Husband," Talis Darmon said like she tip-toed into a minefield. "I must make something clear. I have used my unique application of Sylah sorcery only when there seemed little other choice. When I questioned the conspirator who nearly succeeded in your murder, it was an imperative. When I used this skill today, it was for the same reason. But much as you renounce unjust warfare, I decry frivolous reliance on my skill. I would die for the taint of a regent who abuses her uncommon gifts to commit an assault on civil liberties."

Hesitantly, Zaylin Twee said, "Warlord, I have an alternative to suggest. I am largely convinced by Karlo Columbo and our experts that the Vermeel imposter is of Vistaran origin. Our best efforts so far have failed to identify him. If that were achieved, I believe it would quell worries there is an otherworldly conspiracy at play, yes?"

Even Shasa Karin and Keshin Tellest nodded in sympathetic agreement.

Talis Darmon was eager. "What is your suggestion, First Shield?"

Now Zaylin Twee spoke with the greatest reserve. "The Guard has diminished in capability in some ways since... since... *he* was lost to us."

I'm glad I wasn't chewing any gum.

"You gotta be kidding! You want to bring Kleeve Hartus in on this? No freaking way!"

Zaylin Twee was quick to allay my concerns. "Not in the way you may be thinking, Warlord. I do not petition for dispensation to return him to service in the Guard. But, please consider—Kleeve Hartus was chosen as the hand of the queen's law for many good reasons, some of which may not have been fully appreciated. There has never been a Guard in our history with such an eye, such a memory, such a recognition for human foibles. At times, many of us thought him a sorcerer. It is one of the many reasons he was elevated to his position in Clymaira at such a young age, and no coincidence his talents were recognized by you. He was as much a prodigy in the Guard as the queen was at the academy."

"What're you recommending?" I said, curious.

"I do not know if he would agree to supply us aid, but I believe it is worth trying. If he fails or if he refuses, then, what must be done must be done to protect the kingdom. I would then be the first to beg the queen to use her skills to wrest any and all information from Peritar."

I met my wife's gaze. "What do you think?"

"Yes," she said firmly. "Zaylin Twee, what plan have you in mind?"

The First Shield responded by raising her wristlet. "Captain of the Guard Hyalan Reece."

The man in gold armor and red cape saluted fist to chest. "At your service, First Shield."

"Do you know the current location of Kleeve Hartus?"

The Guard commander of Clymaira's eyes widened. "He can be located, First Shield."

"My assignment to you is this: find him. Tell him that Zaylin Twee wishes to speak to him. Not the First Shield of Mihdradahl. Zaylin Twee. Persuade him; do not command him. Plead with him if you must that it is of urgent need I speak with him. Can I trust you with this mission?"

The Guard commander did not salute stiffly, instead he relaxed into the familiarity of some unspoken confidence between them. "I understand, Zaylin Twee. He was once a great inspiration to me. Perhaps he will remember the spirit of what we once shared and will hear me out. I can but try."

"Thank you, trusted friend." She extinguished the cloud. "This may produce rapid results. I would ask us to repair to my offices, at least for a time, in case our reach returns with fruit grasped in hand. We can refresh ourselves as we wait."

I sent Jodal Jark and Sarkan Sell to take Apache off the house staff's hands while the rest of us went to Zaylin Twee's offices. We had just taken our first sips of the bitter tea when her wristlet buzzed.

His head was not shaved and he did not wear a heavy brown robe. His clothes were the modest, somber color and concealing length preferred in Pyreenia. The face that was once handsome and noble had become angular and stern beneath the curls of hair longer than he'd worn beneath the golden helm of the Guard. He did not yet see anyone but the woman in front of him.

"I have answered your plea, Zaylin Twee. I am gladdened that you appear well, though I warn you against becoming snared by the trap of false pride at your high office, my own grievous sin that I would see you avoid at the cost of your eternal soul. Why have you called? Is it to seek the way to be redeemed from your failings? None are without, I can assure you. The difference is in so knowing. Only by following her example are we cleansed."

The fervor he'd once had for justice had found a new devotion. I knew this had to be hard for her, but Zaylin Twee proceeded with resolution.

"No, Kleeve Hartus. I beg your assistance in a matter regarding our carnal world and not one spiritual in nature in the least."

I stepped closer to the cloud, joined by Talis Darmon, and announced us. "Hello, Kleeve Hartus."

His face grew dark like a storm cloud and he released his fury. "I should have known. The ruler placed by heredity rather than grace and her chief blasphemer." He spat. "Would that I never saw you again."

Zaylin Twee folded hands. "Please, Kleeve Hartus. I did not beseech your presence for purpose of spite or remonstration. Your good deeds in Clymaira have eased great suffering and speak to your compassion. Please, allow me to make of you my full plea."

With eyes closed, Kleeve Hartus breathed deeply, then mumbled something I couldn't hear. I thought it some sort of prayer. He opened his eyes.

"I falter in the example of Desudun Cahlair. I will not air grievances no matter how righteous, nor will I ask for any forgiveness. I shall only say, mistakes were made."

Talis Darmon repeated the words softly as a kind of admission of her own. "Mistakes were made."

Kleeve Hartus shrugged. "Make of me your request. I promise nothing."

We'd agreed what we would reveal and what we would not, and Zaylin Twee carefully narrated events, ending with our perplexity regarding the human man found assisting the Vermeel terrorists.

"And you seek my help in determining the identity of this man?"

Zaylin Twee nodded. "I ask you to exercise an expertise we lack, Kleeve Hartus."

He scowled again. "Know this! If I agree to aid you, it is with the understanding it is not for the regent of Mihdradahl that I would do this. I hold not in my heart any sense of selfless duty to the kingdom. My duty is to mercy for all living things. It is by the example of Desudun Cahlair that it would be done, to prevent loss of further innocent life. And..." He paused. "There would be a price."

I couldn't imagine what he wanted.

"What is that price?" Talis Darmon demanded, all contrition gone.

Kleeve Hartus smiled smugly. "A royal pardon."

"For what could you desire my pardon?" Talis Darmon asked. "When I was rescued from the false White custodians of the underworld, I forgave you of your betrayal in front of the entire kingdom, and took your renewed oath. You departed of your own accord. Is it that for which you seek pardon? Deserting your duty?"

I knew what she wanted him to admit.

Kleeve Hartus narrowed his eyes. "I ask for a blanket pardon. I desire to move throughout the kingdom without fear that I will be persecuted with accusation for some act from a time before my conversion."

I had to say it. "Do you mean, royal forgiveness for skinning all those priests alive?"

Kleeve Hartus was cold as the Sharpa Mountains. "As you well should remember, Benjamin Colt, I know the law like no other. I admit nothing. You have heard my request."

"Given," the queen spit with finality. "It is being drafted as we speak. Here. Beraal has drawn up the official scroll and with all to witness, I bear upon it my signature and seal. It is done."

Beraal held the document in front of the cloud for Kleeve Hartus to read. He seemed satisfied.

"Then command your servant to permit me access to the resources of the Guard, and I shall do this for you—if it is a thing that can be done. Do you have the likeness?"

Zaylin Twee manipulated the cloud and the autopsy pics of the dead human appeared. Kleeve Hartus manipulated the images in the wristlet cloud of the Guard commander. His dark face lightened with a slight smile, and for a moment it reminded me of the man I'd called brother. Then came the laugh. It was a cruel laugh such as I'd never heard from the Kleeve Hartus I once thought I knew so well.

"Truly, you do not know from whence this man comes? Oh! How bountiful is the grace of Desudun Cahlair!" He laughed a forced and derisive laugh.

"Who is it?" I wanted to know then and there.

"Allow me time, and the knowledge of this man's lineage traced to before the fall shall be delivered to you." He vanished from sight. Zaylin Twee and the Guard commander exchanged a few short words and the cloud extinguished.

"Well, that wasn't the least bit creepy," Doug said, then rubbed the goosebumps on his huge forearms. "Brr. What do you suppose he's so shickled titless about? Not to mention, all that crazy talk about Desi-doom Cold-pair." He purposely mispronounced the name.

Talis Darmon hugged herself as if chilled. "I, too, am left at unease, husband. What do you imagine ignited such ugly passion in him?"

"Dunno," I said. "Whatever it is, I just hope he tells us soon."

14

We enjoyed a quiet dinner at home, Beraal back to fussing over each like she was nanny over us all. Afterward we relaxed, and I sat on the carpet and gave all my attention to Shara as she showed off her latest accomplishment, crawling between me, her mother, and Beraal, looking for approval whenever she successfully reached a destination. She giggled wildly every time I made a peek-a-boo and I wished she'd stay this age forever.

My wristlet buzzed and Karlo appeared.

"Sorry to bug you during family time, Ben," he said.

"You're family, Karlo. I told you to buzz in when you had something. Do you?"

"I want to bring Cynar in on this. Just a sec." The floating cloud split and next to one of the handsomest faces, one of the homeliest appeared in my living room.

"Ben, are you up to speed on the general sitrep here in the Veil?" Karlo asked.

"Yeah. Tranya Olan updated us a bit ago. Sounds like a post-earthquake mood. The ground's not shaking any longer, but there's lots of big cracks and fear. The seniority are locked up and things are as stable as they can be at this stage."

"That's my take, Ben. She's doing a great job. I've been down in the mines, and Cynar and I've been communicating. Hate to say it, but it *is* another good news/bad news thing."

"I'd expect nothing less. Lay it on me."

Cynar made his gummy grin. "I was correct."

Of course that would be the first thing he said. He held between thumb and forefinger a black stone dissimilar in color and shape from any I'd ever seen. It had large and small facets that made for an irregular shape that nonetheless gave it an appearance of symmetric asymmetry. "This is what enables the sustained effect for travel through solid matter. Stones holding the seventh and ninth rays in the breastplate link to this one and control the effect. It is the brilliant achievement of some great mind."

"Great news!" I pumped a fist. "Have you tried it out?"

Cynar recoiled. "No, you dunce!" Perrin Halser crowded in to view beside Cynar to explain.

"We considered it, Warlord, but if we failed in correctly operating the device, it would be lost to us again."

Talis Darmon said, "And it would be at the loss of lives myself and the entire kingdom would mourn with agony, dear friends."

Perrin Halser bowed. "Thank you, Queen. But there is something else Cynar the Magnificent has deduced."

The old wizard cackled. "I have named this the fifteenth ray. Fifteen, because it is an ill number for those who believe such superstition."

"Why's that?" I asked.

"Because any exposed to the rays of this combined field will certainly sustain severe damage by its use. Cumulative, irreparable, deadly. I must do further testing to determine the mathematics of it, but continued and prolonged use of this device is slow suicide for those who travel in its field."

Karlo spoke. "The black stones came from the Veil, Ben. Now that Trayver Lomal's found his bearings, he's admitted it to me. They're super rare and when one's discovered, it's treated like a secret. But like a lot of the stuff they mine, the Serians aren't big on the technical applications. Cynar explained to Trayver Lomal how the black stones are being used, and it was just a big puzzlement to him. Do you see where I'm going with this?"

I thought I did. "It wasn't the Serians who supplied the Vermeel with the tech to travel through solid matter, and we still don't know who did."

"Bingo, Ben. Except I have an intuition it's the same people who gave the Serians the tech to sabotage the stones by loading a virus into them; or at least, that's my analogy. I can't really say how it's done. It's going to take Cynar and Perrin Halser to work out. It's happening in that new secret step in the process that Trayver Lomal admitted."

"He took you to the room?"

Karlo nodded. "Thank Cynar for his slim-jim. The workshop was protected behind another encoded entrance. Not even Trayver Lomal knows who was working in there to tweak all the stones, but there're a dozen stations that seem to have been performing the functions. It would've required a large staff."

I made the natural deduction. "Which means sooner rather than later, someone in the Veil who took part's going to talk."

Karlo shrugged. "That's the hope."

"What about the high-order explosive stones?"

"Can't say because we still don't have an example of one to show Trayver Lomal. There are other rare stones he'll admit to, but the Veil is currently cleaned out of all of them. The other possibility—I'll wager these devices transmute stones to alter their lattice so they can become explosive. I'm the first to admit I'm in way over my head here, Ben. This is *not* my area of expertise."

"Understood, Karlo. But you've still done a helluva job."

"Thanks, Ben. Some answers, more questions, but it does feel like progress."

I'd been waiting for the other shoe to drop. "None of that was the bad news, though, was it? I gave you two big jobs. Don't drag it out, man. What's the situation with getting new, clean stones?"

Karlo winced. "You guessed it, Ben; not good. Everything currently in the warehouses is undoubtedly tainted. By order of the Seniority, mining's been dialed back for some time. I see it as more evidence they not only meant to sabotage us, but to create a supply chain problem to prevent us from recovering once we found out about the sabotage. Any luck getting Granday Fallis to spill?"

Talis Darmon answered. "He is silent as the mountains he resided beneath."

Karlo continued. "Trayver Lomal says getting people back to work's no problem, but it's going to be a trickle of stones at first. Even the more common ray-holding stones don't exist in abundance. It takes months for the labor force to gather the shipments we expect."

The weight of Vistara pressed down on my wife's shoulders. "So, enfeebled we must remain for the foreseeable future."

Perrin Halser spoke up. "Queen, there is an alternative. Annameria. They produce stones—not of the highest quality on the whole, and they demanded a dear price—and at one time we acquired a portion of our needs from their empire. I believe with our current relationship, we could make acquisition from their stores until the Veil is able to produce at capacity."

Shara squealed in delight. Holding on to the couch she had risen by herself to stand. She raised her hands and looked to see if she had our attention when she promptly plopped on to her diapered rear end, and burst into tears.

Beraal scooped her up and made soothing noises. "Time for bed, little one."

"We shall be along shortly," Talis Darmon said before returning to Perrin Halser. "Will you send appropriate request to the Annamese in my name? There is no need for committees or debates involving those not versed in these matters. I trust you above all to manage this issue."

"I shall do so at once, Queen."

"Is there anything else?" she asked. I knew she wanted to bring things to a close and return to family time so we could tuck our daughter into bed together.

"Perrin Halser," I said. "Tell the Annamese I'm coming. I'll be there tomorrow morning."

Talis Darmon was rattled. "The urgency is great, but why must it be you? You've hardly just returned!"

Without answering her I continued. "I'll check in with you in the morning. Thank you all for your tireless work for the kingdom. We're grateful as always. G'night." The three men looked embarrassed for me as the cloud vanished.

"Oh! Benjamin Colt! Why, why, why?"

"I'm sorry, love. It really has to be me. We need stones and we need them immediately. And just in case our only Black Bird is running on crappy stones, too, I'm the only one here who knows how to recover it from a failure. I *can't* send someone else. I just can't."

She slumped. "I suppose. But your poor eyes are only just recovered!" She'd gotten into a healing bed on her return. I'd gotten a quick treatment yesterday, but Karlo and Tranya Olan still had eyes like crazed zombies.

"It'll be okay. A quick zip over the Furrow and back, then another family evening tomorrow. Promise."

She sighed. "Such things you cannot promise, though as always, as they are made, I know you truly mean them. Very well. I leave you to make arrangements, but please come to our rooms as soon as you are able."

"I won't be a minute, sweetheart." I brought my wristlet up. "Dougie. Me and you. Road trip. Tomorrow morn."

I'd caught Dougie working out, covered in sweat and holding a jump rope. "Sure thing, homie. Double-K not coming along?"

"Not on this one. Someone needs to be large and in charge around here."

Dougie laughed. "He is that. He's been out with the battalions every day. Back to sword fighting and cavalry charges. Where we goin'?"

"Aetheria."

"Groovy. What up in the Yellow Kingdom, bro?"

"We gotta see a man about some stones."

* * *

We headed out mid-morn. Despite assurances the Black Bird's power source checked out, I was apprehensive. Funny how nearly crashing a plane nose-first leaves a bit of lingering dread. We wore our repulsor harnesses, but they amounted to a hole in a bucket. The chance that we could escape the aircraft if it went into an uncontrollable spin were slim to none.

It was sometime in the first few days of military freefall school when we got the lecture about all the great ways you could die. The statistics for civilian skydivers said you were more likely to be killed on the drive to the airfield than you were on a jump, but there were some notable exceptions. There were several incidents where whole planes full of jumpers—with the jump door wide open—had all perished when the plane lost controlled flight. The centrifugal forces involved were such that not even with parachutes in place and door wide open were jumpers able to exit the compartment of an aircraft spinning and tumbling towards the ground.

Oh well.

"'Preciate you comin' along, Dougie-Doug," I said once we leveled off, the sun barely risen.

"No sweat, amigo. 'Sides, who else knows Annameria and the Annamese like I do?"

I felt a pang. "Just Dave."

His name hung in the air. "I feel shitty, Doug. It's on me. I'm the one's ordered us to abandon him. I'm the guy saying a Black Bird's more important than lives."

Doug's deep voice dropped even lower. "Stop right there, bro. It is what it is and ain't no two ways about it, it's the right call. And what's at stake's more than just Dave and Turv Densman's lives. We are in deep doo-doo and this bird's all we got to keep us in the race to beat these bastards. And don't forget, there's a SAR running for them out of Thoria as we speak."

We'd sent two flitters with a skeleton crew to search the flight path, but even if their stones didn't conk out, in days of travel they could only have covered an hour's worth of flight by the Black Bird once it had crossed our eastern borders. We'd had commo checks from Dave long after that.

"I know," I said with no real belief in the rightness of my call. "But if our roles were reversed, I think Dave would be tearing up the skies looking for me."

"Duder, we score enough stones to charge up even one more Black Bird, we turn that bad-boy loose soon as we get back. Right?"

"Goddamn right," I said. "That. Is. The. Plan."

I looked down into the Furrow. The undulating sands of its basin ran like the smooth contours of a giant brain laid out for a thousand miles in all directions. The Vermeel once roamed the Furrow. Driven from Mihdradahl and pursued to near total genocide by the Yellows, the Annamese had even created a race of Amazon giantesses, bred with an insatiable hatred for all Tarn—among other nasty proclivities.

Where were the Vermeel to be found now?

The course to Aetheria was well known. Markers sat on the lip of our side of the Furrow, pointing the way. Ignoring the danger, we goosed the Black Bird's stones for all she was worth and in less than a couple of hours, the shine of the Annamese capital drew us to Aetheria like moths.

"They know we're coming for brunch, right?" Dougie asked as we slowed and dropped toward the great walled harbor, long dry as the rest of the Furrow.

"Eidolon Sah's expecting us."

"That guy." Doug shook his head. He didn't need to say more.

"Yeah, I know, Dougie. But you send the pitcher you got to the mound."

"Roger that, dude. Let's set her down."

One of our massive trade barges sat in the harbor, put on hold until the issue of the stones could be resolved. I hoped the crew was getting better treatment in the capital than we'd received on our first visit to Aetheria.

The tops of the walls separating the old harbor from the rest of the city were absent any of the spear-wielding soldiers I'd expected to see in an unbroken ring of human battlements. Our arrival and landing brought very little notice, and the portcullis to the first ring of the city was open. A pair of disinterested watchmen leaned against the tunnel walls. They waved us through and at the other end of the short tunnel another pair of watchmen manned a simple drop barrier.

We wore only pistols. I'd half expected a hassle about bearing arms, but the guards gave as little notice to our sidearms as they had us, waving us through with little interest.

Doug hmphed. "Guess stomping their asses into the dirt left a lasting impression, huh?"

"Ah, I'm sure word got sent to expect us. And after all, this *is* a state visit by the number two of Mihdradahl." Outside the walls of the port, the streets were empty. Refuse sat in piles. There were no pedestrians and no sleds. The odor of human waste reached my nose. It was a big departure from the Aetheria I remembered.

"No palanquin to tote us? No parade?" Doug said. "What gives?"

"Let's hoof it," I said. "I know the way. I'd kinda like to check out the general vibe."

"I'm down," Doug said.

The farther we got from the ghost town of the port, signs of life picked up. We made polite nods and waves to Annamese in the streets. Some ignored us. Many spoke to each other in hushed tones. Some retreated behind doors and closed shop windows as we passed. No one looked happy to see us.

"Never were the friendliest bunch," Doug said. "That ain't changed."

Coming into view was the top of the wall of the next encirclement partitioning the city. "This way to the next tunnel," I said. We turned the corner only to plow into several children with dirty faces and ragged clothes.

"Spare a coin?" a little girl said.

Her friends moved closer and held out their hands as well. "Coins? Coins?"

"Let me see what I've got," I said. I knew they couldn't understand me, but I made a show of putting a hand into my front pocket. I produced a coin. Before I could hand it over, the girl snatched it. A dozen more young urchins appeared, then a dozen more. I hadn't even seen where they'd come from.

"Coins! Coins!" they demanded. Tiny hands patted my pockets front, back, and everywhere.

"Whaddaheck?" Dougie exclaimed. "Hands off my pistol, kid!"

All of a sudden, my arms and legs were anchored with street urchins. There must've been a half-dozen hanging on each arm and leg. The tiny girl climbed up my uniform like a cargo net. Holding a sharpened stick in a reverse grip, she menaced it at my face with a stabbing motion.

"I kill you! I kill you! Give me coins!"

I spun. I kicked. I flailed and shook. Urchins flung in all directions with more running to take their place.

"Whaddawedo?" I yelled as I brushed away tiny grips and dodged sharpened sticks and broken bottles wrapped in leather cord.

"What the hell do you think?" Doug yelled back. "RUN!"

Doug sprang off, an orphan clinging to his back and choking him. I was on Doug's tail too, leaping as high and far as I could. Doug landed, flipped forward at the waist, and his passenger toppled over Doug's head and onto the paving stones. The urchin thudded on the pavement. I winced, thinking the boy might be seriously hurt, just when he took off like a jackrabbit in heat. I quickly patted myself for wounds. My chest and cargo pockets had been torn away and hung loose from my uniform like floppy elephant ears.

"Don't stop!" Doug yelled, his only warning before leaping again. The sound of a mob of furious munchkins roared behind me like a rising tsunami and without looking back, I kicked it into high gear. I caught up to Doug and together we bounded, ran, bounded, then ran some more. The tunnel gate through the next wall was in sight. We arrived out of breath in front of a pair of green uniformed soldiers manning the drop bar blocking the path through the tunnel.

Both busted out laughing.

"Do you see this?" the one said to his buddy as he pointed at us.

"Total rubes!" the other said.

They continued to guffaw as if we were the funniest thing they'd ever seen. I looked behind in a panic, expecting to see the charge of the light brigade of street urchins rounding the corner at any second. The bar lifted and the soldiers waved us through, still laughing.

"Go on, go on, get out of here."

"Reds!" exclaimed his buddy. "How stupid can you be?"

We eased cautiously out the tunnel and into the bright daylight, not sure what to expect. The foot traffic seemed calm. A sled floated by carrying a well-dressed couple, and I noticed that unlike the outer ring near the port, the streets were free of the odor of sewage.

Doug panted and wiped his forehead.

"Say what you will, dawg, but this kinda shit *never* went on when the dragon lady was in charge!"

We eventually ended up at the innermost circle in what had been the Serene Sanctuary of the Supreme Magnate, her courtiers, and the most important functionaries of the empire. We'd bombed most of it as the first move in our war for regime change and thanks to the black widows, decapitated their whole government before they even knew we were coming.

It was nowhere near as grand as the former palace grounds, but the governance was clean and without sign of the devastation we'd wreaked.

The Annamese were efficient folk.

Eidolon Sah sat waiting atop a red cushioned chair reminiscent of the Supreme Magnate's throne—gold and entwined with dragon-like creatures—save it put him at eye-level with me, instead of at a height that required a contortion artist's neck flexibility to view. This was something of an improvement. Seated next to him on a slightly lower level was our ambassador, Tomellan Cart.

The recently installed Most Benevolent Protector of Annameria had always been a man of two faces. He greeted us with the one that said no one he deemed a spy was listening.

"Well, if it isn't the Warlord. Hey, Dougie! How's tricks? Let's start the party!"

He'd gotten fat. He looked us up and down.

"What happened to you two? You look like dookie."

Eidolon Sah's Mihdra was textbook perfect before, but after spending time in Mihdradahl as a sort of hostage, he'd perfected the idiomatic parts of the Red language through study spent in the bars and brothels of Shansara.

"*What happened*?" I shot back at him. "Gee, Eidolon Sah, I guess you could say we got the genuine Aetheria experience."

He gritted his teeth and ducked down. "Ooh! Sorry about that. Yeah, they tell me things can be a little rough around the docks."

I was coming hat in hand, but I got a little hot.

"What's going on, Eidolon Sah? Parts of the city are filthy, there's been a breakdown of civil order, people look hungry—you swore to bring change for the better after we got rid of the Supreme Magnate!"

Eidolon Sah took offense. "Whoa, whoa, whoa, hold up right there, buddy. You said you're gonna do *me* like you did *her* if I made to carry on around here like it was the same ol', same ol'. Now, you're bitching 'cause I'm staying hands off and letting the proles do their own thing? I swear, there's just no pleasing some people!"

Our ambassador cringed. "Warlord, as I have communicated with the queen, the protectorate's development into a free society is an evolving process. For example," he cleared his throat in an obsequious way, "reminding the head of state not to refer to the citizens entrusted in his care as 'proles.'"

Eidolon Sah threw up his hands. "What do you want from me, Tom-Tom? By any name you got, a stupid peasant's a stupid peasant. Tell you what. Benjamin Colt, Douglas Knoblock—let me make things up to you after your rough landing in Aetheria. Whaddya say we move somewhere more comfortable and toast this reunion properly!"

I took a cleansing breath. "Thank you, Eidolon Sah, but I'm here on an urgent matter."

"So I understand." He leaned over to the ambassador. "Did I ever tell you how grateful I am to this guy, Tom-Tom? He bombed this place FLAT. Blew my crazy ex-wife to tiny bits right along with all the junior consorts—any one of which would've sold me out for a plucky tune and a bowl of soup—not to mention, took care of her entire secret police. Until he showed up, my days in Annameria were numbered."

I knew Ambassador Tomellan Cart back when he was a vice-minister of trade. He wasn't a bad guy, for one of the nobility. I felt a little sorry for him having to tolerate Eidolon Sah's buffoonery, but not too sorry. He'd trash-talked me in my early days as Warlord. But he was never part of the conspiracy that nearly succeeded in making me permanently MIA. As much as I'd like to see Eidolon Sah put a few drinks down and get even surlier with the ambassador, we had real business.

"Eidolon Sah, I have a favor to ask."

"For you, Warlord? Anything. You're the best friend I've ever had, you unstoppable murder machine, you! I hear you're experiencing some supply chain problems."

"Stones," I said succinctly, trying to move things along.

"You need stones? Why didn't you say so? Mine's yours. *I* got stones, *you* got stones. Whatever you need. In fact, call it a gift."

The ambassador cringed again. "Of course, Eidolon Sah, the kingdom of Mihdradahl must *pay* the protectorate. The resources of Annameria are not your personal property to make gift of to our government."

Eidolon Sah winked at me. "This guy, am I right?" He laughed, then leaned forward and kinked a finger to draw me close. In hushed tones he said, "Err, is it *a lot* of stones you're needing, Benjamin Colt? I do have mouths to feed around here. Plus, there's malcontents on the payroll I need to keep happy so they don't get bright ideas about doing *you know what* to *you know who*." He drew a finger across his own throat.

I wasn't about to confide in him everything that was going on, but I had to tell him something.

"There's a problem with the Veil of Seriata. We're working it out—peacefully—but we find ourselves in need of a short-term solution."

Eidolon Sah winked and tented his fingers. "So your man said in the message. I sent for our guy in charge of the mines a while ago. We'll get this ball rolling soon as he shows. Ah! Here he is now." Eidolon Sah sat tall and switched to High Annamese. "Goh-fahl Zin, what has kept you? I call you to an important meeting and you act as if Annameria bears no cost for the hours you wastefully burn in her service."

"Apologies, Most Benevolent Protector." The man remained bowed.

Eidolon Sah whispered to me, "I know what you're thinking. Hey, I tried it different, I really did. To be the big chief around here, you gotta always keep these guys on their toes. Snap at 'em and just as quickly forgive 'em, then all they remember is you didn't actually dig fangs into them. I tell you, our whole culture's based on lessons taken from desert jackals."

He switched back to the formal language of the Supreme Magnate's court.

"Goh-fahl Zin, think nothing of it. It has provided welcome opportunity for the esteemed partners from Mihdradahl to enjoy the hospitality of our great culture. Please, proceed with your report."

Rather than act relieved, the man turned absolutely pallid. "Most Benevolent Protector, there was a problem."

"What problem is that, able director of the protectorate's strategic mines?"

"Most Benevolent Protector, the message sent to my office is in Mihdra. No one can read it."

Eidolon Sah groaned, then spoke to me in more low-Mihdra.

"He's an idiot. I had to promote from within, you know? You may have done Annameria a solid by ridding us of my ex-wife, but you also killed nearly all our competent people. And this guy obviously wasn't one of the *good* survivors."

Ambassador Tomellan Cart cleared his throat. "I would be most pleased to assist, Goh-fahl Zin. Please permit me to make the proper translation."

Eidolon Sah snorted. "Pass the scroll to me, Director." Then to the ambassador he said, "Your high-Annamese still ain't that great, Tom-Tom. Only the revered ancestors know what the heck your translation might say. Could be telling this dummy you need guano and he's so stupid he wouldn't double-check before they shoveled your boat full to the top deck with shit." He cackled at his own joke like the desert jackal he'd maligned.

I didn't believe Cynar and Eidolon Sah had ever met. But I was sure, within minutes they'd become either mortal enemies or best friends.

Eidolon Sah ran a stylus over the scroll, double-checked it, then handed it back to Goh-fahl Zin.

"I am confident you will make careful review, able Director. Please take adequate time to consider as we discuss other matters. Kind guests, please accompany me." He stood. "We might as well get comfortable. Dumbass will probably still have to get someone to read it to him."

It was a nice spread. We ate. Our host was a little put off that we stuck to water, but it didn't prevent him from drinking several goblets of the good stuff. A serving girl in a short silk skirt such as I'd never seen in Annameria refilled his cup as he nudged the ambassador. "Tom-Tom, you know Dougie here has *three* wives? How's it going by the way, Doug? Everything blissful under your roof? I don't know how you do it, I swear. 'Cause I can't get to sleep without having at least FOUR to cuddle up to!" He roared at his own joke.

Doug laughed politely. "You are something else, Eidolon Sah."

"I learned it from you, DUDE!" The Most Benevolent Protector howled again. "Ah, here's shit-for-brains now." He smoothed his jacket. "Able Director, do you have a report for us?"

The director bowed and handed the scroll to the Most Benevolent Protector. Eidolon Sah picked up a stylus and started tallying. "That's some shopping list. Hmm. Handling fee. Scarcity fee. Express service fee. Additional 4% for the new port improvement tax. Here you go, Warlord." He held the scroll out.

My eyes popped out of my head.

"You're asking for as much agriculture as we produce in a year! And in exchange for only about a quarter of what we're requesting in stones!"

Eidolon Sah took a sip from his goblet, then sniffed. "You got someone else lined up for a bid, maybe?"

My vision turned red, my ears boiled, and my hand found a grip on my pistol. Eidolon Sah held hands up defensively as though they might stop the lasers shooting from my eyes or the bullets I wanted to send his way.

"Hey, hey, hey! We're all friends here! I'm just throwing out the first round of numbers, okay? I got the supply, you got the demand, right? I'm still trying to get the hang of this free market thing. Don't get all regime-changey on me."

I was still tongue-tied when Doug stepped in. "Eidolon Sah! Dude? C'mon. Homies don't treat homies like this. Get real, bro. We've done right by you. Don't start jerking our chain now."

With a flit of his wrist he copied from some courtesan, Eidolon Sah giggled. "I can't play games with this guy, I love him so much. Okay, let me see what I can do."

The scroll traveled back and forth between us a dozen times more until there was no room left for another line of corrected figures. I remembered the last figures from Seriata, and we'd arrived at a number slightly below them. Yes, I was told the Annamese stones were of lower quality than what we'd been getting from the Veil—until they started sabotaging them, that is—but I didn't want to stick the knife in too deep. Saving face was important here, and if I hurt Eidolon Sah too badly in the deal, it might come back to haunt us later.

"The Kingdom of Mihdradahl will accept this figure, Eidolon Sah."

A wide grin of relief broke out on his face as it did the director of strategic mines when he was handed the scroll. I gave Eidolon Sah another scroll I was carrying.

"Please have these items placed immediately in our black widow in the harbor. Deliver the rest of the order as soon as possible to our trade barge. When the captain's confident the new stones will let him fly to Mihdradahl safely, the regular schedule for trade can resume."

Eidolon Sah raised an eyebrow at me. "So, we're just supposed to take credit for all this? There's an additional fee if this is on credit."

I yelled. "Just get me the stones so we can get out of here, Eidolon Sah!"

He handed the scroll to the director. "Able Director, please have these items delivered at once to the royal yacht of the Mihdra. Our valued allies must return hastily across the Furrow so their voyage is blessed by the divine sunlight over Annameria."

The man bowed. "At once, Most Benevolent Protector."

Eidolon Sah rolled his eyes. "Fair warning, better check that load against the invoice. Literacy ain't what it used to be around here. I'll get you boys a lift to the port. Let's do it again when you got more time so we can do the town together. Thanks for doing business. My best to the queen. Now, I gotta see a man about an arkall. C'mon, Tom-Tom."

The ambassador caught my eye, shook his head, and followed the Most Benevolent Protector, each of his arms around the shoulders of a serving girl.

Doug watched him go. "How long you think he lasts, bro?"

"Not much longer," I said with exhaustion. I felt about as tired as if I'd just finished the murder marathon of Aetheria for a second time. "I simply cannot *wait* to get home and tell Talis Darmon that on top of everything else, we've got problems again in Annameria, too."

15

I placed a small box directly in the hands of the techs at the hanger and received assurances a black widow would be up-checked and ready to go by tomorrow morning. Dave's flight plan had already been burned into the brains of a pair of our best pilots, both of whom had been frothing at the mouths to get airborne ever since Dave went past his planned contact window.

Most of our pilots had come from the Guard. They'd been the source of our best flyers, experienced from running the flitter patrols that once protected the kingdom's borders from Mydreen raiding parties. Many chose to sign on to the army, the best of them becoming Black Bird hotrodders. To a man, they were meat eaters, gunfighters, and steely-eyed missile men.

Dougie gave them permission to go for it as soon as the techs sealed the access panels.

"Don't be heroes," I said. "We only received enough ninth ray stones to power up this one Black Bird, and it may be weeks before we get more. You have seventy-two hours, then I want you back, understood?"

I received fist to chest salutes and returned it with the same solemnity.

"We will not fail, Warlord."

"We will bring General David Masamuni and Pilot Turv Densman home."

These guys were the real deal. It went without saying by any of us that we hoped beyond hope they'd be bringing them home alive.

"Bring yourselves back," Doug said, shook their hands and we were off. He strolled with me to our flitters. It looked like I'd make good on my promise to be home by dinner—not a first, but not exactly the norm either—when my wristlet buzzed. Zaylin Twee's calls always put a little pucker into me, and seeing Double-K with her didn't diminish the feeling.

"Warlord, we have report from Kleeve Hartus," she said.

"And?"

"It is a thing best discussed in person, Benjamin Colt," he said.

"See you at my place." I signed off. "Hey, if you gotta get home, Dougie, it's cool. I'll get you up to speed later."

"You kidding, dawg? Just try and keep me away."

I blew raspberries on Shara's soft tummy to squeals of a delight I shared, then bounced her on my knee until the First Shield and Khraal Kahlees arrived. One of the housestaff ladies took Shara to the kitchens and when we were alone with Talis Darmon, Zaylin Twee began.

"Kleeve Hartus would not make his report without Benjamin Colt present. I conferred with Captain of the Guard Hyalan Reece, but whatever Kleeve Hartus has determined about the identity of the terrorist, he holds secret."

"You ready to get this show on the road?" I asked my wife.

"Indeed," she said and took her seat next to me on the couch. The rest pulled up chairs and Zaylin Twee opened a link to the captain of the Clymaira Guard. After a brief wait, Kleeve Hartus appeared, face dour but eyes amused.

"I see you have collected the gallery of rogues, Zaylin Twee. Are the Thulians David Masamuni and Karlo Columbo no longer a part of your inner circle, or have they been banished over some disagreement?"

Double-K growled. "Show respect, Kleeve Hartus. You injure none but yourself by your impertinence."

Kleeve Hartus scowled, then squeezed his eyelids tightly shut, mumbling another one of his prayers or mantras or twelve-steps or whatever he needed to remind himself to stay on the straight and narrow path of his conversion. His eyes opened, the bitterness gone for the moment. "Shall I reveal my findings?"

Talis Darmon said, "Was your task completed successfully, Kleeve Hartus?"

He suppressed a smirk. "It was."

The cloud showed the autopsy photo of the scarred man. Next to it, a clean photo of another man appeared. This one had a head full of black hair in the short, tight curls of a beauty shop permanent. The nose was not crooked. The ears were not as low. The brow ridge was much less defined.

But they were the same man.

"I recognized the pattern of surgical changes applied to the unknown subject almost immediately. Had I examined the body, it would have been even more readily apparent. Did your experts fail to notice the evidence of surgical cosmesis?"

I answered. "They did."

A patronizing smile swept over Kleeve Hartus's face.

"What pattern of changes do you refer to, Kleeve Hartus?" Talis Darmon asked.

He ignored her. "Douglas Knoblock, do you not recognize this man?"

Shaking his head, Doug stared, then leaned forward with renewed focus. Just as suddenly, he snapped stiff.

"Hey. Hey! HEY! I know that geezer! He's a thug from one of the Thorian crime syndicates!"

Kleeve Hartus sniffed. "The man's name was Karsan Most. A Thorian. The picture is of him as a young offender. The Blood Stones, the Sons of the Gazraal, the Hammerskins—many resort to changing their appearance when they become known to the Guard. As they were performed by a single practitioner relied on by all the gangs for his work, there was a common pattern to the look produced by the cosmetic procedures."

"How'd you know him, Doug?" I asked, already suspecting his answer.

"I didn't know-know him," he said. "There was this group of hard pipe-hitters from the gangs. After we took over the city, the big man from one of the syndicates tried to stand up to us. Marky-Mark opened him like a fish in front of his gang, cut his face off, then fed it to the gadrons. The rest of them got in line quick. When I saw him, he was a little worse for wear than he looks in that mugshot; he'd picked up the broken nose. Later on it was this guy and some others who I'd see running around with Marky like a personal bodyguard for him and... Bryant."

"Brandon Bryant!" Talis Darmon spat with more venom than I'd ever heard her use.

Kleeve Hartus was aglow with schadenfreude, his voice accusatory.

"The Thulians are the destroyers of both Vistara and themselves. Your new affliction is but another ailment spread here by the disease of your alien hearts. This is the lesson you must take, Benjamin Colt, and until you repent and seek forgiveness by the example of Desudun Cahlair, all are doomed."

After an awkward silence, Zaylin Twee took charge. "Kleeve Hartus, is there additional crucial information you might share?"

He dismissed her coolly. "I have fulfilled my obligation."

"You have, Kleeve Hartus, and with my gratitude," the First Shield said softly. "But if there were anything else you might offer as insight, it would aid us in protecting innocent lives."

At that, his brow smoothed. "There is an investigation file," he admitted. "Incomplete. I named it Heradoltus, after the ancient seeker of truth. In the first days after Shansara's liberation, we attempted to identify those in the army and Guard who had been complicit with Prince Carolinus Darmon's evil. We knew that after we liberated Shansara, many survived and subsequently escaped to Pyreenia to rejoin the Thulians. Very few were I ever able to name, such was the chaos at the time. Our difficulties in identifying and discerning disloyal from loyal, willing conspirator from those who realized too late they had been duped..."

He grew mournful.

"I still see the mass graves of those executed by Carolinus Darmon during his last days on the throne. They were filled with red and gold cloaks. We failed to give names to so many, many of them, so brutally had they been treated."

He returned to Zaylin Twee's gaze.

"The spirit of Desudun Cahlair tells me there are men once twisted by the Thulians who have seen the error in their ways, and work to bring retribution to a Kingdom warped by Brandon Bryant and Benjamin Colt, and all his compatriots dead and yet living. They seek to remove the curse the Thulians have brought to our home."

Casting an imperious look, Talis Darmon said, "So long as you do not act to aid their cause, Kleeve Hartus. My pardon will not forgive *that*."

The once noble lawman was defiant. "I did not say they were just in the eyes of Desudun Cahlair! And I have taken an oath to never raise my hand to another again. I have kept my end of the bargain. I now return to my holy mission. I will not say fare well, as it is a sin to lie. Instead, I pray for your eternal souls to come to the light."

The cloud closed.

Beraal laid a hand on Khraal Kahlees's arm. "Father, could this be true?"

Double-K jutted his tusks side to side. "Perhaps our enemies in the ranks of Mihdradahl's traitors did not escape to Pyreenia. Mayhap they took refuge elsewhere and wage senseless retribution against us now, joined by our ancient enemy, the Vermeel."

"What do you think, Benjamin Colt?" my wife asked.

Kleeve Hartus had answered a critical question for me, even if he raised others. "I think, this is evidence enough to quit worrying about a secret wave of Marxist terrorists from Earth come to disrupt things. Doug, you were up close and personal with the corpse. Did that guy's appearance really not spark any kind of recall?"

Doug fretted. "Bro, you remember. Things were kinda fuzzy for me back in Thoria. You were in a dungeon. Then we thought you were dead. Dave, Karlo, and Matty split and left me behind. Bryant, Marky, and Chuck were running all over the kingdom building their army. I... I checked out."

Regret washed over me. "Sorry, Doug. I didn't mean to rehash those days."

Doug gave me one of his forgiving smiles. "It's cool, Ben. I just mean, no, it never, ever occurred to me who the dead guy was. But it makes sense. Now we know where they got M4s and who trained them."

I sighed. "But it still doesn't answer why they're hooked up with the Vermeel or who supplied them with the tech to walk through solid matter."

Zaylin Twee said, "Warlord, I believe we are near a breakthrough with Peritar the Finder. When our latest revelations are shared with him, he may at last speak candidly."

"Then I guess we'll see you in the morning for another stroll around the city," I said.

After seeing everyone out, I returned to find my wife deep in thought. Before I could ask, she looked up at me. "Kleeve Hartus said he named the investigation to identify those who'd done the will of my brother after the truth-seeker, Heradoltus."

"Is there a significance to that?" I asked, knowing that's why she'd brought it up.

"Heradoltus was a skeptic. He was known as a great philosopher, concerned with objective truth. Among other things, he did not believe in the underworld. To that end, he took a shovel and dug a deep hole, sworn to accept whatever evidence came before him."

"What happened?"

"The hole collapsed on top of him, and there he was buried."

"Not much of an engineer. Shoulda asked Doug to do it for him."

There was no eye roll. "It is meant as an instructive fable."

"Do you think the irony of that was lost on Kleeve Hartus today?"

She stood. "This is what I believe: while Kleeve Hartus served as a tool for my revenge against the priests, I may have been mistaken that he suffered punishment enough for his zeal and betrayal. And to our potential regret, I have restored his freedom to roam the kingdom."

Despite everything, I still held pity for him. "He's suffered your punishment and more. You saw him when he talked about the mass graves."

She shrugged, and turned toward the kitchen.

"We have all suffered. Now, come, and leave all other matters behind. Our family dinner hour awaits."

It was dark and I was up early, tip-toeing out of our bedroom to join Doug and Double-K for a PT session. Then I was due at a staff meeting to get caught up on all operations, make sure the search and rescue for Dave was underway, followed by a meetup with the First Shield to try once again to peel back more of Peritar's shell. I'd almost made it through the bedroom door when my wristlet buzzed. Had I ever actually said I missed cell phones? Talis Darmon's wristlet came alive as well and she snapped upright.

Double-K was in the ops center. "Warlord, anomalies are sighted within Shansara. The enemy have arrived!"

The queen's wrist cloud held Zaylin Twee, telling her the same.

The houseguard were there with Beraal, Keshin Tellest, and Shasa Karin, a shield-bearing legion to protect my wife and child as they marched them away. We'd decide that airborne was the safest place should this emergency ever come to pass. With my family safe, I had no other concern than going on the hunt. I had my kit and weapons and with Jodal Jark, Sarkan Sell, and Apache, we ran.

We arrived on the landing deck outside our apartments as the flitter carrying my family to safety lifted. Doug stood behind the console of a gunship lowering to take the place of the departed craft. We dove in before he'd touched down and in seconds were in the air over Shansara, the luminous towers shifting from nighttime to day colors as we sped by.

Information filtered to me through Double-K in the ops center. “Patrols in the southeast suburbs saw the anomaly appear briefly, identified a peeper, then it disappeared.”

The infiltrators were already in the city. We’d completely failed to intercept them before they could do harm. My stomach clenched as I relayed the obvious.

“It’s too late to call for a city-wide evacuation.” If we did, it would simply mass people together, making even denser targets for the attackers. A stay-at-home order to keep people off the streets was the best we could do.

“We have initiated the shelter-in-place for all citizens, Warlord,” Double-K said. “Security forces are at 100% mobilization in all sectors.”

For the moment, there was nothing to do but circle high over the royal palace and government center. We’d reckoned their navigation was imperfect, and they had to come up for visual waypoints every so often; maybe they did it to breathe as well. The sun was rising and movement on the streets by Guard and soldier—searching, observing, turning citizens back into their homes to remain in place—was all we saw.

“Peeper spotted!” a voice said in the ops center cloud. “In the Golden Hub, near the Towers of the Twin Sisters. A trooper got a shot off, but no effect.” The pair of spires named for our moons were some of the tallest buildings in Shansara. A very reliable landmark for navigating the city.

Cynar’s voice came over the ops center cloud. “I am able to detect the rays of their device in use. I am attempting to track them. Wait for my efforts to... there! Allow me a moment.”

“Where the heck’s Cynar?” Doug asked. “Is he airborne?”

There were many flitters at many altitudes all around the city. Some stationary, some like ours, making orbits. I raised my binos and searched the airspace near the Towers of the Twin Sisters. Squinting, I could make out his crazy white head and beard between the desert uniforms crowding the deck of a flitter weaving a lazy course back and forth.

Someone in the ops center said, "General Khraal Kahlees, the wizard sends this. Observe."

Our cloud of the ops center room split and an overhead map of the city appeared beside us. A red line traced from the southeastern suburbs to the Towers of the Twins Sisters. Another line took a new course from there, extending only a few millimeters, curved and indeterminate as to its direction.

"They are beneath us!" Cynar said with excitement.

I got on the net. "Cynar! What can you do about it?"

There was anguish in his answer. "Spit?"

I seethed, not at him, but at our predicament. "What do you see from your vantage, Cynar? What stands out?" I tried to pull from memory what landmarks could be seen from ground-level in the neighborhood of the towers.

"There are a multitude of spires and bridges across the skyline, Benjamin Colt! Their course is not yet predicted, though it moves in a general northwesterly direction. We must give it time to develop."

I checked the map. The air factory was one of the tallest structures and visible from most anywhere in the city, but lay in the distant east, so it seemed that was safe. The red line advanced over the map as I watched. It seemed the infiltrators found the going easy and had picked up their pace to a run.

It seemed clear where their course projected.

"They're headed toward the palace," I blurted.

Cynar spoke, "The palace stands higher than government chambers, but the most distinctive is the roof of the Spectral Hall. Yet, observe! The course aims west and wide of the governance."

I checked the map again before bringing my binos up. In a conspicuous gap in the skyline, rays of the morning sun caught the rising mist.

"They're headed for the Fountains of Persidia!" I exclaimed.

Khraal Kahlees's face appeared in every cloud. "All unit commanders, the enemy's course has been determined. Destination is the Fountain of Persidia."

"Let's go," I hollered, but Doug already had us pointed at the fountains and kicked us into full speed.

Standing on the nose, my eyes watered as I fought not to blink, the wide plaza and the mists rising above it locked in my sight. We arrived to find only a pair of young Red troopers there on the ground. They'd most likely patrolled the paths between the many monuments all night, bored and counting down the minutes until their reliefs came. They raced around the fountain to meet us at our LZ.

We landed on the earthen rise overlooking the fountains. It was covered by an artificial layer of crimson turf meant to simulate the ancient grasses whose short blades once covered the plains of southern Mihdradahl. We were out and spreading over the vista and picnic areas. The massive statues of mythical figures ringing the plaza and fountain served to block swathes of our views and by natural extension, our lines of fire. The fountain's cascades, splashes, and bubbles irritated my ear, obscuring any sound that might indicate the arrival of the interlopers. The air was a haze of mist.

"This is no good, Ben," Dougie yelled. "We got height, but everything else sucks. I'm going down to eye level and taking those troopers with me."

"I'll join," I said.

"No, dawg. Blast distance, yo. Stay here, or better yet, have one of the overwatch flitters come take you up and work from there." Three combat aircars had been hovering low around the plaza, K-max gunners aimed on the park.

"No thanks," I said. Apache was next to me, eyes fixed on the fountains, sniffing the air intently.

"We will join below, Warlord," Sarkan Sell said. "It is an enormous area to cover."

I growled. Our armored vehicles were still en route. "As soon as the Kardans arrive, everyone, get cover inside one and use the firing ports. If they don't come up for a spot check and we miss them, we're all too close if this is where they mean to cook off their bomb."

Cynar's voice came from my wrist. "Warlord, the infiltrators approach."

I made a quick diversion to check my wrist. The red line on the map had grown at an incredible rate, far faster than I'd anticipated. They must be moving at a dead run. The line stopped growing. I stood erect and scanned the scene, my M4 up and ready.

A K-spec buzz rang out and I dodged to see around the statue of a four-headed lion. Through the mists was a wavy distortion in the pavement and a Pale sprang out, followed by another, both firing fizzle guns wildly in all directions. Something about how they moved—their actions, their appearances—struck me as odd, even before they fell to the multiple blasts of K-spec fire from Doug and his troopers. I fired into the patch of shimmer still active across the stone pavement, expecting yet more Pales to appear, and was joined by massive fire from the K-maxes hovering above.

Things happened in a blur.

First the shimmer vanished. Then there was a brief, calm pause. Wristlets remained silent; only the burbling of the fountains filled the air. Two bleached Tarn bodies lay in the plaza.

"EVERYONE, BACK," I yelled, and dropped.

The explosion was a replay of Filestra. Yellow light blazed and a dull sizzle danced over my skin. The concussion came, followed by the earthquake and a rain of stone. Something large and heavy landed on the back of my helmet, and the world winked out.

I was being pulled roughly by the drag handle of my armor. The artificial turf where I'd lain was deflating like a soufflé pulled too soon from the oven. The entire hillside was becoming a sinkhole. The ground rumbled angrily and the colossal statues around the plaza toppled over and disappeared.

My travel ceased and I was dropped, the back of my head stinging sore as my helmet bounced on the hard ground. Apache whined and snuffled as he licked my face. I sputtered his drool and mine and sat up. I was wet everywhere. A warm kind of wet. I panicked and began running hands over my body, expecting to see them red with my own blood. Instead, they came away clear. It was water I was drenched with.

The berm I'd been on was gone and in its place, springs bubbled from the ground. Below that hilltop had been the chamber that led to the vast underground waterworks of Shansara. I'd been there several times, each of them memorable for their own reasons.

Air cars filled the sky above me. A face leaned over the side of the one lowering and his words pelted me before the face came into focus.

"You dunce! Why would you place yourself in such proximity! You are an *idiot*!"

Hands pulled me onto the flitter and Apache leaped on the deck beside me. My bell had been rung, but the high-pitched tone was going away and my vision sharpened.

"I'm fine, Cynar! What about everyone else?"

The pilot drifted us over the plaza. The large crater that had been the fountain plaza was filling with turbulent waters, swirling higher. Doug waved wildly atop the short wall at the edge of the promenade, still solid and standing, the two troopers beside him. On the same wall opposite the plaza signaled Sarkan Sell and Jodal Jark.

Of us all, I'd taken the brunt of the beating.

Cynar assessed the scene below. "The detonation occurred deep beneath the fountain, Benjamin Colt. The cavern and passages, the viaducts and water chambers, all served to tamp the explosion and limit the destructive effect above the surface. But the damage to the sacred waterworks—it is massive."

There'd been a lone water priest manning the works in the traditional hermitage of the guild, refusing to abandon his solitary existence as Cynar had done.

"What about Lemuel the Novice?" I asked.

Cynar shook his head. "I have tried to raise him to no avail. Perhaps he lives."

Wading into the muddy slurry were Doug and the two troopers. They formed a chain to anchor Doug, chest deep in the swirling waters. Floating in the rolling eddy currents were two Pale bodies. He fished out the floating corpses and aimed them one at a time with a push toward the shallows. Working together they corralled the bobbing bodies and crawled from the roiling water for the shallows. The waters spread, lapping at the low wall that bordered the plaza, the basin of a new, greatly larger pool.

"What a mess," I exclaimed, master of the understatement. There was much about what I'd witnessed that I didn't understand, but undeniable was the evidence that our nemesis could reach us anywhere.

Where and how to strike back at them?

The loose jigsaw pieces I had to assemble into a plan didn't come with a picture on the box.

16

Doug threatened to body-slam me onto Cynar's healing bed if I continued to protest.

"Stop being an ass, Benjamin Colt," Cynar said. "Your dim brain cannot stand to lose a single synapse more, lest you become the drooling idiot we all know you to be. Lie still, dunce!"

I'd spoken to Khraal Kahlees and then Talis Darmon on the ride to Cynar's lab and gotten reassurance that everyone but me and possibly Lemuel the Younger were fine. Apache was his usual self, drooling and wagging a stubby tail and rump so large, it rocked Sarkan Sell and Jodal Jark beside him.

Apparently I'd been laid low by a big-ass chunk of something that thumped my helmeted head. Probably the explosion had knocked a head off one of the enormous statues. Whatever it was, it struck me hard, leaving me in this bed to be "nursed" by a crazy old man. I surrendered to his care. I bathed in the warm yellow light and drifted into a meditative sleep, the conversations going on just outside the healing field lost to me.

I awoke feeling better.

"Let's go to the ops center," I said on rising.

"Home for you, Ben-dog," Doug said.

"Bullshit. Ops center, Doug. That's an order, bro."

"All right, all right, but you better call Talis Darmon. She gave me strict orders and if I'm gonna disobey the queen, you have to take the ass -chewing for me, duder."

I did as my friend suggested, and my wife gave me marching orders. "I wish to view the devastation immediately. Douglas Knoblock, bring the Warlord and retrieve me from the palace." Before I could say anything, the cloud closed.

"You heard her, bro-man," Doug said.

"I shall accompany you," Cynar said. "There is much only I am able to determine regarding the fountains and the works beneath. The minister in charge of the city distribution from whence the waters arise is an appointed moron."

We picked up my wife and her crew minus Beraal, who would keep Shara glued to herself until one of us returned. We returned to the scene and took a high orbit over the crater that had been the Fountains of Persidia.

The water level had fallen and its surface was not as turbulent.

A protective cordon had formed and buildings surrounding the plaza were being evacuated as a precaution. Not even Cynar yet knew if the waters escaping the massive underground works would erode the underpinnings of the nearby towers.

"Not a remnant do I see," Talis Darmon said with deep sadness. "It was created at the founding of Shansara as a monument to life. During our fall, it served as the reminder of what once was and the promise of what could be again."

Her anger rose. "I credit our enemy for knowing exactly where to attack us to sap our reserve of perseverance. To demoralize us. But they have made a critical mistake. This will only unite us to drive to dust the forces who wish us ill." She snapped to face me. "What is the Warlord's action to be now?"

The memory of an accusation she once threw in my face returned.

"Zaylin Twee," I said into my wrist. "Have the prisoner Peritar escorted to the Fountains of Persidia. I'm going to question him myself."

"I am coordinating efforts as we speak, Warlord," she replied, evidently over the city in her airborne command flitter. "I shall have him brought immediately and join you there."

Talis Darmon was quizzical. "Are you intending for me to influence the prisoner with my skill?"

"No," I said, and offered nothing more.

"Very well," she said brusquely. She was angry, as was I. Even Apache sensed the ill vibes at our exchange and he slunk down.

She wasn't blaming me for what had happened, I knew that. She carried the kingdom and I carried her. Together, we wanted this crisis over. But right now, somewhere in her, she expected me to do better.

We landed and soon a Guard flitter joined us on the street nearby. I'd told Doug what I wanted, and he departed to join Zaylin Twee and take our Vermeel prisoner for a closer view of the devastation. Everyone unloaded, save my wife and me.

Talis Darmon came close. "Benjamin Colt." She was apologetic. "Forgive my earlier manner. I am relieved you are well, upset that you again were at the center of the maelstrom, distraught that my kingdom continues to be endangered."

I took her offered hand. Her eyes twinkled for a moment, then looked past me at Doug and Zaylin Twee as they ushered Peritar nearer the destruction that consumed the plaza.

"What is it you hope to accomplish by showing the terrorist what his comrades have wrought? Is it not a reward?"

"I think the First Shield's correct that we're near a breakthrough. I have an intuition this might push him to make a decision." I turned to her bodyguards. "Ladies, protect the Queen. I'll signal if I think it's safe for me to bring the prisoner to her. Apache, stay. Sarkan Sell, Cynar—with me."

Talis Darmon didn't seem pleased, but she didn't object. "Very well, Warlord. I shall observe from here."

Peritar's face was always as emotive as a stone and was no different after viewing the wreckage. But standing between Doug and Zaylin Twee, I thought he looked smaller.

"Unlike the day we brought you here, there were no children playing in the fountain when your comrades destroyed it," I said as I came to a halt in front of him.

As usual, he said nothing but whereas he usually met my eyes, this time, he did not.

"Peritar," I began, "I don't know the exact circumstances, but this is what I think happened to bring us together. Your people were met by a group of Mihdra who were once engaged against us in our civil war—a war they lost, by the way—and they tapped into your grievances and influenced you with an ideology meant to divide the world into oppressors and oppressed."

He listened, but gave nothing.

"The Reds who taught you this and got your people to join them to wage war on us, they were trained by people from my world. Men who were masters of chaos. These renegade Mihdra appealed to your desire for vengeance and convinced you it's in your best interest to harm us, and that any means you use are justified because of what's been done to you in the past.

"But I'm telling you, they've only exploited you. They're using you as tools to achieve their own purposes against us."

The ideology Peritar had been fed was old. It was one of envy. The principles of class warfare promoted by its inventor fell on such deaf ears in his own country—and the rest of industrialized Europe—that the ideas only found traction among the disaffected of a backwards country mired in the greatest disproportions of wealth and education. And so it remained until that ideology eroded into the minds of morally deficient malcontents of more advanced societies, perverted and subverted by systematic programs of insidious counter-culture education.

Sensing Peritar was inching toward the edge of a break, Sarkan Sell spoke his part.

"Tarn and Mihdra engaged in a long campaign against the Vermeel. History may be written by the victors, but the atrocities and predation by your people on ours was such that it demanded generations of warfare to protect our nesting grounds. Even the Mydreen had some sense of boundaries in what they considered acceptable in their raids and extortions. The Vermeel had none."

Peritar remained unmoved.

I made my next move. "What did your Red comrades tell you would be the end result of your attacks against us?"

Finally, Peritar spoke. "They said it was the only way to achieve a return of the People to our homeland."

"Your people want to return to the deserts of Mihdradahl?"

Peritar was quick. "No. We were driven from Mihdradahl long, long ago. The Furrow became our home, and a sheltering land it was, rich in bounty. There it was the Yellows who pursued us relentlessly. They bred a foul form of Yellow as large as a Tarn, and unleashed their creatures to hunt us to extinction. We had no choice but to move farther and farther into the lands of the rising sun, barren though they be."

If the floor of the Furrow had been a land of plenty for the Vermeel, how bad did the far eastern deserts have to be?

"You wish to return to the Furrow?" I asked.

Now Peritar stood proud. "First, we will exact our price from the Mihdra and gain access to the sweet sands of the Furrow. Then, as we have the Reds, we wage like war against the Yellows, until all are forced to accept our return to the abundance that rightfully belongs to the People. It was made for us and promised to us by the creator. So it is written, so all know to be true."

Zaylin Twee said, "Peritar, the Mihdra bear no grudge against your people, nor do we desire to harm your kind. The Yellows no longer have their exterminator class. They have been destroyed by the Warlord. The ruler of the Yellows is our ally. Without need of threat, nor coercion through violence, nor any price exacted upon us by shed of our blood, such a return to the Furrow could be obtained for your people—by treaty and oath."

I said, "My queen will make it so, Peritar. In exchange for a permanent peace, the People could return to the Furrow. Mihdradahl will do everything in its power to assist the Vermeel, to share our wealth with the People."

Doug said, "Peritar, there's water in the Furrow. I've seen it—a lake forming out of the sands at the southern end. If it was a good place for your people before, it must be even more so now. Queen Talis Darmon's the most just and wise ruler that's ever been. She'll want to see your people returned to their rightful home."

Peritar bared his tusks. "I have no reason to trust you."

Cynar stepped forward. "Peritar, there is more to consider. Come."

The deck of a Guard flitter was bare save for two bodies beneath covers.

Gesturing at the bodies, Cynar said, "The device you use to plunge through Vistara—it is killing you all. With each use, it damages you. Look upon them and tell me if you do not see the evidence of rot in your comrades."

The sheet was removed and Peritar gazed on the bodies. "They are from an operative cell from another clan, ancient Red. I cannot identify them for you."

The wizard took no offense at being called ancient. "I do not ask that. I wish you to look closely."

Peritar squinted. I also saw that in many places the contours of their skins were misshapen, like wet clay smeared beneath the potter's fingers. The faces were subtly contorted as well, their mouths and eyes drooped on one side like melted candle wax.

Cynar said, "What is apparent on the outside will be reflected in their brains and viscera. The rays of this device are responsible for this harm, and will do so to any who continue to travel by that method."

Peritar raged. "Lies! Our Red comrades walk the path with us! They toil and fight alongside the People. If what you say were true, it would kill them as you claim it does us. Why would they subject themselves to such a terrible fate? I reject your ridiculous attempts to turn me against those who opened our eyes to the truth!"

I confronted him with the obvious. "Unless they didn't know either. Peritar, where did your Red comrades obtain the device? Because knowledge of it does not exist anywhere in Mihdradahl."

I didn't expect him to reply, but the seeds of doubt we'd sown were sprouting results.

The pale Tarn frowned. "I do not know. Only that it was provided by those who seek to help us in destroying the ruling classes and bring justice to the oppressed."

I believed him truthful. I thought I knew where the device came from, but there were many more dots to connect before I had the picture. "Were you with the group that attacked the Veil of Seriata?"

He didn't deny it. "The cadre of Red comrades chose us, the Black Tusk clan, to join them in the righteous mission against those who plunder the mountains in avarice. They too tried to exterminate the People. The oppressors of the Veil made puppets of the Mydreen and the Korundi and even the Reds to wield the sword against us."

"Why did you raid the Veil?"

"To obtain more of the black stones. They were needed for our campaign of justice."

There were more gaps, but I was pretty sure Peritar wasn't the one to fill them in for me.

The queen and her entourage—including Apache held at the collar by Jodal Jark—had been shadowing us. With them now was Khraal Kahlees. He must've arrived while I engaged with Peritar. Together they moved for us with the queen leading in bold haste, much to the consternation of her retinue.

"I have heard all," Talis Darmon announced. "Peritar the Finder, I offer pardon for your crimes. I would release you to return to your people and carry the solemn promise of the Queen of Mihdradahl. In exchange for peace, I will see the Vermeel restored to the Furrow of the Creator's Hand."

I tried to remain nonplussed, but gritted my teeth. She'd abruptly sprung an offer premature to my own. Just as a Tarn was gonna Tarn, the queen was gonna queen.

Peritar was flat, sober, and undaunted by the queen's regal presence or her proposal. "I am Black Tusk Clan. The People are many clans. The elders of the Black Tusk would hear me, but none other."

I took over again. "Peritar, we'll speak soon." I motioned two of Zaylin Twee's Guard to take Peritar to their flitter.

I moved to squelch the irritation building in Talis Darmon's face. "I'm pleased Peritar got the offer directly from you, but there are some nuances I have yet to work out with Peritar before I'm ready to proceed."

She frowned, and I moved closer to whisper.

"We're close, Talis Darmon, and getting closer. I feel the urgency, too. I'm itching to get out of Shansara and move to the next phase of this operation."

"Leave Shansara?" my wife said loudly, anger in her voice and concern on her face.

"Everyone, bring it in," I said. Instead of answering her, I had Karlo in the cloud and quickly brought him up to speed before introducing the new items for our entire group.

"There's no doubt in my military mind that Bryant orchestrated this whole thing," I pronounced. "He trained the cadre that Peritar calls the Red comrades. Bryant gave them a crash course in how to implement a Vermeel insurgency and loosed them on us. I don't know if it started while he was in Pyreenia—before Chuck got possessed by the Harridans and Anso-Kylon and that whole mess—or if he did it once he got established in Annameria. Either way, I *know* that's what went down."

Karlo was rarely shocked, not even while piloting a Black Bird that lost flight, but he was shocked now. "Bryant's truly the gift that keeps on giving."

Talis Darmon said, "He was a marvel of evil."

Khraal Kahlees seethed. "Would that I had removed his stones and fed them to him."

I went on. "And Bryant could hardly have found a better population to exploit than the Vermeel. For this purpose they were an even better find than the Mydreen."

Doug squinted. "If he did it when he was in Annameria, might explain where the walk-through-rock tech came from."

"Not a chance," Karlo replied. "If the Annamese had something like that, they'd have used it a dozen times over to infiltrate Shansara, and done it without any compunction about what the process did to the people using it."

"Exactly," I said. "Which leads me to my next. I think Bryant's Red A-team had another source of help. Karlo, tell us what you've found digging through the records in Seriata."

Karlo nodded. "You were spot on, Ben. The records indicate the Serians have been engaged in trade with customers besides just us. Particularly, the Annamese."

Talis Darmon pursed her lips. "It is not surprising the Annamese also purchase critical stones from the Serians."

"No, ma'am," Karlo said. "Annameria's been shipping stones *to* the Veil. In turn, the Veil's been passing those stones off on us as though they'd come from their own mines, and making a bundle. A shipment arrived in the Veil from Annameria not three months ago."

Now it was the queen's turn to be shocked. "How long has this arrangement existed between the Veil and Annameria?"

"Since long before you took the throne, Talis Darmon. And there's more. It looks like the Annamese have also been trading our agriculture to the Veil. I'm pretty good with figures, but I'm no accountant. I don't know how they did it, but it looks like they received nearly double the value from the Serians for the same commodities we traded to the Annamese."

My ears burned. "I oughta kill Eidolon Sah."

Double-K snorted. "Forgive any impudence on my part, Benjamin Colt, but was it not *you* who complained to me how the nobles lack in understanding of the free market economy? I am no apologist for the Yellows, but how does this differ?"

He had me there.

"What else, Karlo?"

"Besides the transactions with us and the Annamese, there are two additional customer codes recording regular trades with parties unknown."

Talis Darmon tapped her lips with an index finger. "That the Annamese trade secretly with the Serians should not surprise me. But that there exist *two* other entities who deal covertly with the dwarves? *That* is wholly unexpected."

"Well, ours was only one of three silver rivers beneath the Sharpa," Doug reminded us.

I redirected the conversation. "How's stone production coming, Karlo?"

"Trayver Lomal's running his people hard, but they're enthusiastic about their work. Stores are building up, including trickles of the strategically critical categories."

Not that I expected different, but Karlo had performed flawlessly. "Strong work. Mission accomplished. I want you headed to Filestra to start refitting the *Hope*. Getting her ready for war sits next in our work priorities."

Rather than the snappy salute or "affirmative" I expected, Karlo's furrowed brow told me he disagreed. "You don't need me for that, Ben. I've identified what the issue is. The technicians on the *Hope* can handle the changeover."

His expression was sour, so I stayed silent and gave him his say.

"Ben, I made a command decision out here without consulting you. I hope I haven't betrayed your trust, but here it is. I've already been sending stones to Filestra with the order to refit the *Hope*. I've also collected as many critical stones as are ready, and I want you to send the Black Bird to come retrieve them. Along with me. You need me there with you and the team."

I may be Warlord, but I've never, ever forgotten how a Special Forces operator worked. Independently, making the best decision possible, ready to stand tall and take the heat if he was wrong.

He wasn't wrong.

"Okay, Karlo. Come home. Let's see this to the end together."

A weight came off him. "Thank you, Ben. Anything to pass on to Tranya Olan?"

The queen said, "Please tell the governor I shall be in touch later."

"Yes, Queen Talis Darmon." Karlo closed the cloud.

I had only inklings about my next course of action. Using the steps of a logical method I'd learned from Talis Darmon, I set the conditions, analyzed the facts, and made a decision.

"First Shield, I understand Granday Fallis continues his recalcitrance."

"Yes, Warlord. His resistance is almost admirable," she confirmed.

"You've won me over to the idea that a good stroll can be a productive setting for an interrogation. I'd like to try something similar. Will you return Peritar and have the First Citizen placed in an interview room? I'll be right over, along with Doug and Khraal Kahlees."

"At once, Benjamin Colt." The First Shield took her leave.

Talis Darmon frowned. "Why do you precisely exclude mention of myself in your instructions to the First Shield?"

I pulled her aside and took her hand. "I have a feeling, my princess, that before they've even stepped in the ring together, that Cynar and the minister of works will require a referee."

It'd been a long time since I'd used the pet name. It worked. She softened and chuckled at my prediction.

"You are correct, husband. I must provide the direction for our efforts as well as bring comfort and assurance to the kingdom and, as you say, take the role of referee. I shall see you at home later, but I fear it will be a brief dinner together as a family. The needs of the kingdom are many today. I depart."

If she'd suspected I had other reasons for sending her and the rest away, they remained obscured to her.

As intended.

Double-K questioned me from the other side of the console as Doug flew us to the Guard HQ.

"Benjamin Colt, it is implied that the First Citizen does not possess even a fraction of the conscience of our savage Pale. Do you believe viewing the devastation will hold sway over him as well?"

I'd meditated deeply on that very thing.

"I'm almost certain it will not."

Granday Fallis was seated alone in the interview room. He looked relaxed, collected, and more than just free of anxiety; he seemed self-assured, as if the machinery of his oligarchy were just outside, waiting at his beck and call.

But I believed it was more than resistance mentality that comforted him. There was another reason he seemed unconcerned by the prospect of being our permanent guest.

"Shall we, Zaylin Twee?"

"Of course, Warlord. Is it truly your intention to escort the prisoner through the city? If so, I prefer to have security posted along any route you plan."

"Not necessary, First Shield. We're amply capable of preventing the prisoner's elopement."

Double-K cracked knuckles on both sets of hands.

Zaylin Twee looked as though she suspected something was amiss, but didn't say so. "Of course, Benjamin Colt. May I accompany you?"

I sighed. The unintended consequence to my plan was right in front of me. "Yes, my friend. I hope you'll always be at my side."

I opened the door to the interrogation room and stepped in, beaming like the sunflower my granny always told me I resembled when I was leaving for a hunt.

"Hello, Granday Fallis. I thought it might be a nice change of pace to get some fresh air. May I show you the grandeur of our capital. Have you ever been? I mean, before we brought you here in chains?"

The First Citizen gave my invitation the consideration a king showed a cockroach.

"You have somewhere else to be?" I sprinkled it on like cinnamon.

He stood, so I took it I had his interest. Then, he spit on the floor. He spoke the first words I'd heard him utter since his arrest.

"I will view your slum."

"Excellent. Walk with me."

I'd made up my mind. Or rather, he'd made it for me.

I turned right and Zaylin Twee started to protest, but I waved her off. I knew where I was going. It was a place I'd been many times. Kleeve Hartus and I would stand alone on the roof of the Guard headquarters at night, admiring Shansara's skyline, bathed in the lights of stars and moons.

During rare moments together when no exigent threats demanded our attention, we'd reflected on the astronomically fantastic events that had brought us together in time and place.

Those had been moments I treasured with a man I greatly respected.

Zaylin Twee whispered behind me. "Douglas Knoblock, do you know what the Warlord intends?"

Once again, my secret superpower permitted me to visualize one of Doug's shrugs of innocent cluelessness, sincere and truthful. He didn't know, because I didn't know. I wasn't entirely sure what I would do, only that Granday Fallis knew where the hidden treasure was buried, and I wanted it.

I pushed open the portal and allowed the First Citizen to step onto the flat roof of the headquarters. This was one of the few structures outside the factories and workshops of the Golden Hub that didn't rise in a spiral or sharp peak; government architecture at its utilitarian best.

The seductive allure and air of mystery cast over Shansara past sunset was not present in the rooftop view baked in the bright light of late midday. The sharp detail of our city invited examination as things were, not the imaginings her face at night enticed.

And it was time for clarity.

The activity over the scene of this morning's attack remained, flitters circling and dust hanging over the devastation like a cloud. Nearby, the plaza of the governance and the hall of the spectral throne stood out. Elsewhere, the hurtling towers and skybridges in their many varieties shamed any other possible conception of what constituted beauty.

"The Veil of Seriata has a magnificence all its own," I said, gesturing at the view. "Queen Talis Darmon's jealous that she's not been afforded the honor of visiting your legendary domain. But as I hope you can see, we're lacking neither in beauty nor in abundant riches, just like your home."

The short man sneered as though I'd said something ridiculous.

"So that just makes me wonder—" Before he could so much as gasp, I spun him upside down and took him by a single ankle and extended him upside down over ten stories of nothing. "What could they offer you that we couldn't?"

He screamed. He sputtered in a babble of barely comprehensible Serian and Mihdra, arms flailing as he did.

Behind me, my friends exclaimed.

Zaylin Twee pleaded. "No! Warlord, you must not! This is improper!"

Dougie blurted a favorite Dave-ism. "Holy Guacamole!"

And Khraal Kahlees just laughed. He guffawed through tusks as he slapped at his sides.

Granday Fallis's screams petered out. Tiny onlookers below pointed up at the unusual sight, and he whimpered like a beaten dog. I took that as a sign. Time for the First Citizen to receive the instruction I'd given to foes much greater.

"I am Warlord of Mihdradahl. I hold supreme power in all matters existential to my queen's kingdom. If I suspect a threat is posed by Serians concealing secret abilities, then it's my prerogative to test for any powers that could pose a danger to us. So, besides a resistance to sorcery, can you also fly, dwarf?"

Granday Fallis started screaming again, shrill and terrified. Goodness, holding his ankle by one hand as he wriggled was tiring. I switched hands and grasped the other ankle, lifting him higher to face me, albeit upside-down.

"WHAT DID THEY OFFER YOU?"

The man impervious to Talis Darmon's sorcery could not resist mine.

"A place among them! Riches! A new home! A life of splendor above ground! They said they would protect me."

"*Who* offered you?"

The translation wasn't perfect, but three times he blurted their name in a recognizable enough way. "The Xanalara! The Xanalara! The Xanalara!"

From the moment I decided to question the First Citizen, my mind swam with possibilities. Truth be told, I had no clear idea what I would do to encourage a confession from the Serian until I was doing it. I deposited him gently on the roof, then snatched him to his feet and held him as his knees buckled. I emphasized each syllable.

"You will not like what I do next if you do not answer every question I put to you, fully and without reservation. DO YOU UNDERSTAND?"

He nodded like a jack hammer. I released him and he collapsed into a fetal position. A pair of Guardsmen appeared and carried him away. Both shot me cautious looks as they hurried past.

Khraal Kahlees had driving hands on his knees, sky hands on his head, still convulsing in laughter. Doug's mouth hung open in astonishment. "Dude! I'd never have believed it if I hadn't seen it for myself. Holy friggin' shades of LA Confidential!"

Double-K wiped his drooling tusks. "What is that you speak of, Douglas Knoblock? Is that another of the stories from your Thulian entertainment scrolls? I truly wish I could view them, clansman. Your retelling is done with such flair, I can only imagine how satisfying the originals must be!"

Dougie laughed. "Well, you ain't gotta see that one, Double-K. Ben-dog just out-Russell-Crowe'd the hell out of that one."

I shook my head. "Never saw it."

Dougie seemed surprised. "Really? You just came up with that on your own? Sick, dude!"

After today's attack, I was feeling impotent and small. I was failing in my sacred duty to protect my queen's kingdom. Once in a moment of desperation, Talis Darmon had accused me of not being up to the task of bearing the mantle of Warlord. Later, she apologized many times over for flaying my pride, but it prompted me to ask a deep question of myself.

What did it mean to be Warlord?

It had sent me on a search to discover all I could about the first and only other man to bear the title, the Warlord Jawn Kurz. In the history mirrors I saw him. A warrior's warrior. A leader. A demi-god. Against innumerable foes he led the charge. Fearless and deadly. Always victorious.

Then, I met him. Or rather, he reached out to me. I still don't understand how it happened, but it did. There'd been times since that I'd called to him, hoping he'd speak to me. To guide me or command me. To tell me what he would do. As we flew here, I asked him that same question.

But I received no answer.

All I knew was, I was failing. I'd been acting as a soldier. Not as a Warlord.

"I guess, Dougie, it wasn't an original idea," I said. "I kinda remembered a Schwarzenegger movie where he did something like that."

Dougie snapped his fingers as he made the connection, then shot me with his finger gun. "Classic, dude. It sure got Large Johnson to sing like a canary."

Zaylin Twee had not moved. It was without prompting that she usually anticipated her role in a situation and moved to recommend an action. Conspicuously, she said nothing, so I did.

"First Shield, I think your investigators will find the prisoner better conditioned to cooperate. I recommend you capitalize on his reformed attitude. If he should falter, inform me at once. I'm only too happy to assist."

She wasn't angry, but neither was she at peace with my methods. Her eyes seemed to hold me in uncertain appraisal. All nuclear bombs had fallout, and this was my radioactive waste to clean up.

"Zaylin Twee, I'm truly regretful if this changes the way you see me. It wasn't my intention to deceive you or abuse your trust. It was simply a thing that had to be done. I am the Warlord."

Her eyes were a jury with a verdict.

"The Warlord Benjamin Colt. Savior of the kingdom. Victorious above and beneath Vistara and in realms unvisited by mortal man. Compared to him, what is the law?"

She left us beneath the harsh rays of a sun that exposed us to the reality that, like my queen's kingdom, we stood alone.

Doug tried to console me. "Ah, she'll get over it, dude. Deep down, Zaylin Twee understands. She's had to do some rough stuff in her career."

She had. But always at the orders of those appointed above her, not as the chief protector of the law of our land. Being the apex of the pyramid meant you rested on layers upon layers of a thousand solid blocks. But it's only when you're at the tip that you truly understand the pyramid is actually inverted, and it's on your point that you balance all that weight.

Khraal Kahlees recovered from his mirth. "When this land is restored, the First Shield will remember it was *you* who did all to save the kingdom. None other. Her law is for those who deserve it. The lawless deserve only death. And it is time we bring it to them. What are your orders, Benjamin Colt?"

It was simple. "First," I said, "we stop the Vermeel."

"Then?" Doug coaxed.

They already knew. They simply wanted to savor the words I would speak.

"Then, brothers, it's on to Xanalar."

17

We crammed ourselves into a pair of Black Birds only just restored—Karlo, Doug, Jodal Jark, and Peritar in one; myself, Khraal Kahlees, Sarkan Sell, and the gear in the other. We took a single pilot for each to return our precious capability to the capital and await further orders. We were loaded and about to lift for Thoria when we got the news. On their return to Shansara and crossing that very moment into wristlink contact range, the mission to search for Flight Marco Polo called in their report.

After diligent and exhaustive efforts, Xanalar had been found.

Along a mountain range as mighty as the Korund and under cover of a moonless night, they located the slopes and plains covered in the twinkling lights of a great civilization, as yet all but unknown except by fable. While the high-altitude flyover yielded limited information, it was enough.

The pilots mapped the celestial course that would lead back to the mysterious people Granday Fallis implicated as the cause of our current troubles. Then they began the next search. Over and again, in patterns that crossed the desolate lands between our domains they flew, at high and low altitudes, ready to ground and investigate—a crash site, a message trod in the sand, a signal mirror flash—anything.

"We have yet to locate trace of Flight Marco Polo," the lead pilot said with heaviness. "We searched an area above the northeast breaks of the Furrow—where the terrain lends itself particularly difficult to visual discernment—and a violent sandstorm kicked up and forced us to higher altitudes. We would have continued, but so near the seventy-two-hour limit of our mission parameters, I chose to return us to communications range. But I speak for us both, Warlord—we are fit and prepared to continue the search."

Perhaps Dave and his co-pilot, Turv Densman, had done as Karlo and I had managed, and brought themselves down safely. Perhaps the sabotaged stones had done their insidious work over Xanalar. Perhaps the two of them weren't dying of thirst in the desert right now, but were instead sitting in a prison cell. In my wildest hopes, they lay poolside at some Xanalar resort and were being treated like kings.

Or perhaps, no amount of searching over the vast uncharted nothing would ever yield results.

"No," I said. "You've performed a highly difficult and dangerous task and have done so with skill and honor. Return to base."

The co-pilot spoke up. "Then we seek permission to send further sorties, Warlord. We've barely begun to search. We now have navigation charts reliable enough to avoid unintended penetration into any potential domain of observation and control by this unknown polity. We agree it can be done with minimal risk of compromise."

Like these warriors, I wasn't yet ready to declare Dave's rescue hopeless.

"Permission granted. The commander's intent remains the same; we proceed on the assumption our boys are trying to survive in the wasteland. Set a limit of advance so we don't encroach on Xanalar territory. We're not prepared for that meeting. If our men are in Xanalar, there's nothing we can do about it just yet. Once we launch from Thoria for our own mission, I'm returning both of these Black Birds to your control. Plan the sorties, brief the crews, and stand yourselves down until you've had proper refit. Job well done."

"Thank you, Warlord," the pilots said in unison, saluting from behind their yokes before signing off.

Khraal Kahlees pondered aloud. "It will be a difficult campaign on Xanalar, so distant is the nest of this new enemy. But surely, their isolation also serves to lull them into a false sense of security. It is in that ignorance they shall be crushed by the stone giant they have awakened from slumber."

"Why they strike at us is surely a mystery," Sarkan Sell said. "Only a fool would attack an enemy they have no estimation of."

I said nothing.

The why behind Xanalar's desire to harm us would have to come later. So would what punishment I would craft to fit their transgression. I wasted no time fretting over it now.

There was a lesson I'd mastered, courtesy of my attendance at many long and difficult schools of training. Each demanded a slog of endless challenges that lasted weeks or months—and in the case of the Q course, a period measured in nearly two years of daily challenges—until you crossed a finish line so distant, it couldn't be seen until you stood on that the very last hill.

The lesson I learned was this: when a slew of difficult tasks lies ahead, the secret was don't try to do everything.

Just do the *next* thing.

"The next thing's to find the Vermeel," I said, sharing my thoughts aloud.

"And either they end their campaign of evil..." Sarkan Sell started.

"Or *they* are ended," Double-K replied.

✤ ✤ ✤

Peritar hadn't been disturbed by the close confines of the Black Bird cabin, which seemed to fit what I pictured about the Vermeel; hovelling together in cramped caves or holes dug in the ground to hide from their enemies.

But flying on an open-deck flitter was another matter. He sweated acridly and panted like a cat in the car on its way to the vet. Worse was that he couldn't easily relate the terrain passing below to how he knew to navigate on the sands. Finding the elders of the Black Tusk Clan was sure to be a grind. We aimed for the direction of the rising sun and trusted we'd find a way to accomplish our task.

It was the case back on Earth that initial contact with a guerilla force was most often made by our friends at Christians In Action. The particular branch of that organization responsible for that kind of work was filled with folks recruited from the ranks of Special Forces.

I'd only been on my first A-Team a short while when the world fell apart and we ended up on Mars, but it was a thing well understood by all in SF that accidental collisions with members of our tribe in the employ of the clandestine service were possible, if not likely. You could unexpectedly run into an old teammate in virtually any operational setting, ranging from backwater locations that shouldn't exist in the modern world, all the way up to the most cosmopolitan and bustling cities conceivable.

They could appear to be a vagabond, a professional businessman, a researcher, and speaking the native language or one of many European languages used in diplomacy and trade. And when you did run into them, a nod or a wink was all you'd get. More likely, you'd receive no recognition at all.

And you needed to let that chance coincidence of meeting pass without reunion.

But just maybe, that guy was *your* guy. You'd never know his real name, and if an older operator on the team did, he wouldn't say. This was the guy who provided the knapsack stuffed with $100 bills to buy mercenary soldiers and agents for your intel net. This was the guy to arrange your safehouses and the semitruck that would smuggle you across a border.

And this was the guy in contact with the underground that the people he worked for had been supporting for decades. And he arranged the sit-down for you to meet the resistance and start the process where'd you'd take that bunch of freedom fighters into action.

Those guys were indispensable. But we didn't have that guy.

We had me.

And we had a Vermeel communist revolutionary of questionable loyalty who right now seemed of little use as he puked over the railing. Fortunately, the farther the spires of Thoria retreated on the tail of our flitter, the quicker Peritar found his sea legs, regained his bearings, and became talkative.

"Nothing escapes the far-reaching eye of the People," Peritar bragged as he directed our flight. "Footfall on sand makes vibrations far felt. The newest hatchling knows to taste the wind for scent. It is impossible for an enemy to appear at our nest without being long revealed to us."

"And if they do detect anyone?" Doug asked.

Peritar was prideful. "Silent death. Or, the People take course that cannot be followed, leaving no trace."

Double-K was dubious. "The greatly perfected skill of the Pale to run and hide did nothing to fend off the many armies set against you." Double-K was not entirely on board with my plan. His recommendation was we use Peritar to locate the Vermeel, then carpet-bomb the deserts on a scale grander than we'd bombed Aetheria. Though he'd never heard of Curtis LeMay, in him he would've met his biggest fan.

Karlo nudged Double-K like he was the dinner date who'd dropped an F-bomb in front of her parents and priest. Unfazed, Khraal Kahlees made one of his trademark scoffs. "I have stated my preference in this matter."

"How do we meet the elders?" I asked.

"First, I must be admitted to the den." Peritar agreed to locate the elders of his clan, and to make a fair case for them to speak with me. But he warned there could be many possible outcomes, including what would happen if it were another clan we came across first.

"Many of the traditional ways remain. Others are relinquished since the clans united in common struggle against the oppressor. The elders of one of the other clans may first require a test of worthiness before hearing me. If there is a claim of a blood feud, they will cleave all our necks to wander the hunting lands, forever lost and confused, with eyes fixed on our chests."

"So that's why they leave the heads attached by a flap of skin," Doug mused.

Double-K gave a rich laugh. "Let them try."

Peritar continued. "If it is the Black Tusk clan we find, they will take me to the elders, or as we now call them, the People's Committee. Though we have adopted many new ways to bring about a people's paradise, my clan will not reject such basic courtesy. What is unchanged is that the Black Tusk revere loyalty."

Khraal Kahlees scoffed at Peritar's mention of loyalty, but kept further skepticism to himself.

"What drove the clans to unite?" I asked. Peritar had described a very fractious relationship between the many clans of the Vermeel. It was tribalism at its most severe.

"It was by the message of the Red comrades the clans made move to cooperate."

At last, we'd reached a point where he might open up about the Mihdra cadre who carried out Bryant's plan to wage an insurgency against us. "Tell me about them," I said.

Peritar thought. "They said they were New Men, not like other Mihdra. They were the first men I have known, so I cannot judge."

When he revealed no more, I prodded to keep him talking. "What do you know about the Mihdra we killed from your cell?"

"Comrade Seven?" Peritar began, but stopped and suddenly seemed unsure. I noticed something odd. He'd said "Seven" in pretty good Mihdra.

"What is it?" I asked, referring to his uncertainty.

"It is only at this moment something has occurred to me. By the decipher I now understand his Mihdra name represents a number in your language. So all the Red Comrades were called."

Bryant's use of basic security measures to obscure the identities of his operators was evident.

"How many were there?" I asked.

"Eight in all," Peritar said. He appeared troubled. "There is something I do not understand. As I now consider, the Red Comrades are named One through Seven, but their leader is not named as they are. He is named Comrade Zero."

Karlo was there to help. "Ben, many ancient numbering systems didn't contain a placeholder for zero. I think the Vermeel don't have the concept in their mathematics."

Peritar stared at us blankly. Double-K's snort was adequate to say he was further proven right regarding his estimation of the Vermeel.

"How were things organized?"

He explained that two cells were built and trained from the Black Tusk, followed by the Sharp Claws. The two cells of the Black Tusk were sent out for their first operation against the Veil with Comrade

Zero along. They later divided to hit Filestra and Thoria while Comrade Zero returned to the Vermeel with the spoils taken from the Serians. We destroyed Peritar's cell on its move to return home.

"Who hit Shansara?"

"Sharp Claws. For reasons of security we do not know the tasks assigned to the other cells but though distorted, I recognized them as Sharp Claws. It puzzled me there were only two, but I suspect the rest continued west to your most distant city."

"I bet none of them made it to Pyreenia," Karlo said. "Given how badly the two in Shansara looked."

"If the device is cooking them, maybe it's a self-limiting problem," Doug said.

"What about the other clans?" I asked.

"Cells were being trained from their ranks, but were not yet ready when we departed," Peritar admitted.

He was in one of his talkative moods, so I probed for more.

"Tell me about Comrade Zero."

He was pensive for a moment. "I now believe he was eldest among them; he was grown largest. The other cadre were strong in conviction of the teachings they shared with us, but Comrade Zero always presented with greatest wisdom. All the cadre treated him as senior, therefore we did as well."

As we flew ever eastward following Peritar's navigation, we all took turns behind the controls and spending time with him. Except of course, Double-K. Sometimes Peritar seemed trusting and freely answered questions about his people; at other times, his mouth stayed sealed. Of us, he had few questions.

"I do not trust him," Double-K said to me as we watched him converse with Karlo, who seemed to be forming the best connection.

"He definitely keeps his own counsel," I agreed. "But he's proving to be very, very intelligent. Doesn't it change your mind about the Vermeel?"

"Pfft," my Tarn brother spat. "Do not forget Wizard Cynar's criticisms of those who base opinions on limited examples."

The sun grew hotter and the nights more chill. As was so often the case, terrain that seemed largely flat from higher altitude, at lower elevation revealed dips, channels, and furrows; hills, rises, and plains; rocky masses lightly disguised beneath shallow sands, their wind-eroded crests breaching the desert like a smooth glacier floating at sea and hinting of great mass beneath. After two days of flight, Peritar indicated that if he was to locate his people, we needed to go to ground.

In a depression we concealed the flitter. "Should we put on our funky get-ups?" Doug asked. With Peritar's help, we'd constructed costumes like that worn by the Red Comrade we'd killed.

"It will not yet be helpful," Peritar said.

"Nor will they be. Ridiculous and pointless," Double-K pronounced for at least the tenth time.

"We're trusting you, Peritar," I said and with rucks stuffed, we set off. Despite Double-K's contempt, even he stayed close to learn how Peritar used his senses to navigate our way. To Jodal Jark's pleasure, it was Sarkan Sell's turn to be mocked for his lack of desert acumen.

At a halt at the end of the first day on the march I tried to nail Peritar down for clues as to how I would proceed when we finally found his people.

"How did the Red's first make contact with your people, Peritar?"

"The Reds rode mounts into the range of the Black Tusk," he said. "We observed them for many days, until finally they were too close to ignore. We surrounded them and though well-armed, they abandoned ill intent and to our surprise, knew our language; not well, but enough.

They brought scrolls bearing many messages written in the symbols of the People. And they brought gifts."

"What gifts?" Doug asked. "Guns?"

"Later they shared the weapons carried by their arkall," Peritar said. "The first gift was the one best received: an arkall skin brimming with the heads of many Yellows. After that gift of friendship, the elders were well disposed to hear their petition."

Khraal Kahlees griped, "Had we known earlier, that could have been arranged."

"Where d'ya s'pose they got so many Yellow heads?" Doug asked.

I'd had a lot of thinking time as I marched, and Brandon Bryant occupied much of it. "I'm positive the Yellow Roamak had plenty to spare. I think it's another indication Bryant developed this plan in Annameria, funded and supported by his girlfriend, the head of the secret police. They undoubtedly had good intelligence on the Vermeel."

Earth's most totalitarian dictatorships would've been green with envy and jealous admiration for the apparatus that maintained the power of the Annamese state. By comparison, the Stasi and KGB were girl scouts.

"That's not only plausible," Karlo said, "I think it's a lock. After Bryant's Genghis Khan attempt failed, he decided his next weapon against us was to pull a Che Guevara. He trained a cadre in the essentials of unconventional warfare, taught them the political indoctrination methods that would inspire the Vermeel to fight, and sent them off to make contact and build an insurgency against us."

Doug snorted. "But just like Che, Bryant got the dirt nap, yo. Chief may've been brilliant, but he couldn't outsmart Ben. And he ain't gonna do it from beyond the grave, neither. We finish this, we never have to think about that asshole again."

If Doug was wrong, I couldn't imagine how.

But unspoken by us were many things. The renegade Mihdra that Bryant took with him to Aetheria, unquestionably they had to have been highly motivated. To undertake a mission to bring the Vermeel to war with us—those of us who wore the Green Beret knew it was a lengthy, arduous, and dangerous undertaking. How had Bryant inspired such devotion from them? We knew for certain at least one of the Red comrades had been a career criminal, a subculture not generally known for committing to such disciplined and unrewarding work as unconventional warfare.

Who were the soldiers of the Red cadre? Before I could try another line of questioning, Peritar rose from his squat on the sands.

"We are being observed."

The waves of the desertscape were broken up only by the rare outcrop of the oddly piled boulders that I likened to lighthouses on the shore. Even rarer were the narrow valleys that might have been the remnants of an ancient riverbed or more likely, accidental formations left by the cataclysmic storms known to flay the skin off any creature caught in the sandblast.

"Where?" I asked without moving.

Peritar indicated with a thrust of his jaw. "In front of me. Cast your vision far."

The sharp-eyed Jodal Jark said, "I see nothing." If he didn't see anything, I had no chance.

Karlo tossed me his thermals. Two black shapes burned hot at the limit of its range.

"They're about two thousand meters away, lying on that saddle between the two dunes," I said before passing the device to Double-K.

With the binos held to his eyes, he said, "I believe they use a concealing cover." He passed them to Doug.

"They can't hide from this," Dougie said.

"Nor from my senses," Peritar said. "I will go to meet. If I am successful, I will return for you."

"How long do you expect us to wait, Pale?" Khraal Kahlees asked accusingly.

"When I see you again, it will be known." I'd returned to him his knife chipped from some sort of flint, and off he marched with nothing else.

I said, "Let's set a perimeter and be prepared to wait." With naked eyes I watched Peritar's progress. After a few hundred meters, I lost him. His smooth travel combined with his natural coloration allowed him to blend like a deer with the browns of an autumnal forest. I took the thermals again. When these eventually died, they would be sorely missed. Three white-hot Tarn stood out against the light charcoal background.

Double-K said, "Benjamin Colt, does Peritar suspect we monitor his speech through his decipher?" We had a backdoor to Peritar's decipher that broadcast to our wrist links. We'd be able to eavesdrop on whatever happened.

"Let's find out," I said, activating my wristlet. Peritar arrived on the saddle where the two Vermeel had raised to stand. Without speaking, the three of them vanished behind the dunes.

"Huh," Doug said with the sense of confusion I felt. "No hail or passcode or so much as a, 'where you been, dude?'"

Voices coated with poison malice came from my wristlet.

"Peritar the Finder! In the company of Mihdra! You lead them to our nest! Traitor!"

Another accusation came. "You betray the cause, Comrade Peritar! You know the price for collaboration!"

The sounds of a scuffle broke out.

"Shit!" Doug said, putting his ruck on. "We gotta go!"

We were geared up and moving. We hadn't gone far when Karlo had the thermals up and said, "On the saddle again. It must be Peritar. He's waving sky hands like everything's okay."

The sands were firm and we picked the pace up to a trot. We found Peritar standing over a bound and bloodied Vermeel. Laying on the backside of the slope was the other Pale, blood leaking from multiple deep punctures and slashes that the sands sucked like a sponge. The head was all but lopped off save the flap of skin attaching it to the body at the front of the neck.

"Peritar's a badass," Doug said under his breath.

"Are they Black Tusk?" I asked. They'd recognized him by name in their accusations of collaboration with their enemy.

Peritar scowled. "I concede they are. Their absence of courtesy enrages me. Had they been Sharp Claws or Blood Slaked or Silent Foot, I would expect no different. But Black Tusk acting as executioners before judgment of the elders? This irks me."

Karlo frowned. "Is that why you didn't want us to wear the disguises just yet? Was this part of a plan to test them?"

Peritar gave no reply.

"So I take it we expect a fight waiting for us?" I said.

"It will be so," Peritar confirmed my fear. "These were sentries of the outer range. The inner range and the den of the elders will still be many days' travel. The clan has moved since I departed, which is why I spared this one to hasten finding the nest. I am as anxious to speak to the elders as they should be to listen. Stand!" Peritar ordered the bound Pale. "You are defeated."

The prisoner's head dropped to his chest. "I do not wish to wander lost in the afterlife with eyes cast forever on the sands."

"Then show proper manners."

We marched steadily north, following our captive's directions. It was later that day Peritar suddenly jerked the leash around his prisoner's neck. With irritation he said, "This hatchling thinks I do not know we near the inner range of the clan. Wait here. I shall return quickly."

We spread into a close perimeter, ready for anything as Peritar led his prisoner off behind a dune. As I suspected, he soon returned alone.

"I have the spoor. Do not fear, he will not soon be found."

Before we could question his actions, he squatted beside me.

"I have thought on this, Mihdra. I am committed to the struggle of the People. But this rejection of clan law, it is intolerable. I do not fully trust you, but I trust what I have seen for myself of the might of your kingdom. The People are few. Despite the pleasure of vengeance, the Red comrades have brought much ill to us with their teachings. I ask a final time. How do I know that your queen's promise is recorded with blood?"

There was some cultural significance there, but I didn't know the proper response. All I could do was give it my best. "My queen's promise to you is like the sun, certain and eternal. I wouldn't be here if we didn't mean everything we said."

Peritar seemed to have made a decision. "I do not wish to bring further death to my people, but if the elders will not listen, then some must die lest all be sacrificed. I will lead the People home and back to our true way."

This was a startling admission. He'd made some grand determination about the future of the Vermeel.

"What's your plan, Peritar?"

"We near the inner range of the Black Tusk. It will now serve for you take to your disguises. Once I have learned the location of the den of the elders, we must then travel beneath the sands by the light of the path."

Khraal Kahlees's growl carried across the sands, but it was Karlo who beat him to the drop to shoot the hole in Peritar's plan. "I know we brought the device along just in case, but it causes cellular damage! Ben, you're not seriously considering this, are you?"

Doug turned his head from the stock of his K-spec. "Dude! Check me. We had this kid straight outta RASP. First weekend in the platoon, on a dare, he drinks as many energy drinks as he can, as fast as he can. He'd just finished number thirty-one when he passed out. The medic did CPR on him for, like, twenty minutes, but he never came back. DRT."

Karlo aimed his voice toward Doug. "Huh? What's that kid dropping dead right there from a lethal dose of caffeine got to do with anything?"

Doug turned fully to find the very puzzled Karlo. "You're smart, dude, don't you get it? That gung-ho Ranger did us a huge solid. He proved the limit's thirty-one. All we gotta do's not hit the limit. Like, we don't even have to drink thirty. We only drink, I dunno, one or two cans. Maybe a six-pack at the most. See what I mean?"

Jodal Jark was enthusiastic. "I volunteer to walk beneath the surface!"

"As do I," Sarkan Sell joined.

Karlo groaned. "We don't know the exposure limit and Cynar said the effect was cumulative."

Peritar said, "I have traveled often by the light."

Doug grinned. "See? And Peritar's fine. Quit worrying, dude."

Double-K grunted. "We do this. I will not have it said a Korundi would fail in daring compared to a Vermeel savage."

Dougie sniggered in Karlo's direction. "Missin' your laboratory now, dude?"

Karlo sighed. "I drank a bunch of energy drinks once during a rough week of finals. *Mi sono cagato sotto*. Never again." I couldn't remember the last time he spoke in Italian. Even Peritar's decipher must've picked up the translation, because he barked a rough Tarn chuckle with the rest of us, the first I'd ever heard from him.

Karlo rose from prone and started digging in his ruck. "Maybe this won't be any worse than shitting my pants. What do you say, Ben?"

I remembered the half-melted faces of the dead Pale. But I also remembered the bodies of the bloody civilians we'd carried off the plaza so long ago in Filestra. "We're all volunteers. We do this for the ones that weren't."

18

Wearing Vermeel loin cloths and harnesses bearing the extra pair of limp arms, we were a bunch of 4th graders dressed for Trick-or-Treat as Tarn corpses. We passed the stone over each other's skin wherever we couldn't reach ourselves, and our deeply tanned color faded to a sickly gray under the cosmetic rays.

"You look terrible, dude," Doug said, passing the tool back to me. It looked like a deodorant roller but instead of a ball at the end, it had a white stone.

"That's the idea, isn't it?" I said.

Khraal Kahlees snorted. "You fool no one. But neither do we Korundi. None are as emaciated as a Pale. Not even Peritar is the desiccated desert dweller he once was."

Peritar took no offense. "The disguise is meant only to confuse the eye of the oppressor that the Red Comrades are of the People. To the common folk you will be recognized as part of an operative cell of the People's Committee. The elders demand all in the kraals to provide us support, and to leave us unquestioned as we perform the People's business. You will allow me to do all the talking but should you be hailed, say only this—"

We listened carefully to the difficult Vermeel words as the decipher translated.

"Power to the People."

He had us all repeat the phrase, correcting us each time until he said, "That is at least as good as the Red comrades have mastered. It will suffice. As for the Korundi..." Peritar sniffed. "Best to remain mute."

We set off in a single file march as instructed. We took a winding course over sands Peritar instinctively judged as suitably firm so as to leave little evidence of our passing. Jodal Jark was tail-man and behind him he dragged a construction of woven branches that raked and obscured our tracks. Peritar found suitable vegetation outside Thoria, stating it was similar enough to the rare brush found in his desserts to suffice, and with skillful hands fashioned the rake. The Pale bushcraft was supporting his claims that the Vermeel could move through the deserts without trace.

The sun was scorching. I'd made a long trek of survival through the Korund Mountains with little water, but though I steadily drained the canteens in my ruck, my thirst never left.

Doug broke me from the trance of my droning march.

"Dudes, be cool."

Staring at us from a shoal of rock on the side of a dune were the first Vermeel we'd seen; two adults and two small children. All saluted with a single clenched fist overhead and Peritar returned same. We marched past and when I looked back, the family had vanished.

"Guess we fooled 'em," Doug said.

"They are simple and understand nothing of political theory," Peritar said. "They do not question what the elders tell them."

"How much farther?" I asked him.

"We march till dusk. Then we will encounter the first kraals of the clan."

Near sunset we came to a channel-like gorge. After days in the sterile desert, the faint scent of arkall hit my nose like ammonia salts. Peritar halted us. "The villagers know we pass near and our coming will have been seen. It would be abnormal to not seek clan hospitality. Remember your words and use them if you must, otherwise remain withdrawn as if weary from a long campaign."

He led us down the tiers of a stone path worn by countless eons of steps and into the ravine. Beneath overhangs and tucked into the many fissures were tents, animals, and Vermeel. From above, the narrow chasm and what lay in its base would be all but impossible to see. We returned the salute many times until we reached the center of the village where a small group of Pale awaited our arrival. A male half the height of our guide was first to speak with the eagerness of youthful curiosity.

"Comrades, are you returned from the struggle? What news of the blows against our oppressor? We hear of troubles."

An elderly and haggard female stepped forward and croaked. "Mannerless hatchling! Offer our comrades the hospitality of the clan and question them nothing." She shooed him away and as we followed Peritar to squat in a close circle beneath the shelter of a ledge, several young women appeared bearing plates and small cups. I took mine and croaked out my best, "Power to the people," to Peritar's grimace. Karlo accepted his and in the coarse language said, "I thank you for this sustenance." The young woman folded all hands over her chest and bowed as she backed away, smiling as she said, "The Red comrade is welcome." She tittered as she joined her friends.

"Listen how that Mihdra has learned our speech so well. Their affection for us is true."

The old woman was nodding with similar approval as she squatted beside us. Peritar shot Karlo a friendly grunt. The time he'd spent with Peritar on the journey here had apparently not been wasted. Karlo was always a wonder.

The rest of us huddled over our plates with heads bowed like the weary travelers Peritar wanted us to play. The water smelled and tasted foul, as did the dried mystery meat, but I worked at them both with the necessity required to not raise suspicion. The old woman spoke.

"For having come far, you are all fat and wet."

Next to me Sarkan Sell slowly placed a hand on his K-spec. We were about to be busted.

Peritar grunted. "We carried away many riches of the Mihdra but our arkall were killed. We gorged to lighten our load as we made the long march home."

The old women grunted. "That was great wisdom."

Peritar masterfully turned the conversation. "What trouble does that hatchling speak of?"

Our hostess obediently replied, "We met Blood Slaked on route to these grounds. They told rumor that the struggle fails."

Peritar was cautious. "The struggle does not fail. The Black Tooth have struck well in the heart of the oppressor. What nonsense did the Blood Slaked say that gave doubt?"

The old woman made a humming sound of hesitation before she said, "A cell of the Blood Slaked was found dead in the deserts, murdered. They suspect the Sharp Claws and Silent Foot are not loyal to the cause and still carry blood feud."

Peritar made a similar sound before answering. "This is disturbing," is all he said.

"Will you take refuge?" the crone asked.

"We must depart. The committee of elder comrades summons."

She made signs in the sand and spoke noises the decipher didn't translate and when she was through, Peritar erased the symbols with a hand swipe. Without saying anything, he rose and we followed. Not until we'd marched out of the gorge and were far along did he halt.

"You all did well enough and gave no suspicion for us to be interrogated. I received the location of the elder den. You did particularly well, Karlo the Inquisitive."

Dougie grinned. "That's our name for him, too."

"What do you make of what she said about a cell being killed?" I asked.

He paused before answering. "A blood feud it could have been. Not all have put aside the old ways." He stood. "A runner departed as soon as we appeared to carry word of our arrival. We must march hard to arrive before dawn when the message will be given. It is unlikely we will be approached on our way, but if we are, be prepared to follow my lead. Silent death must be dealt to any who recognize me. And we need no prisoners."

Peritar placed his hand on his knife.

Karlo could hold back his distaste for barbarity no longer. "Did you have to kill that kid?"

Peritar misunderstood. "Have no cause for concern, Karlo the Inquisitive. I sent him to the hunting grounds intact. But I cannot yet say the manner in which I will send any other to the next life if necessary. What of you, Korundi? Do you have any such qualms?"

The full spread of Double-K's tusks reflected the light of the moons overhead.

"You have proven a worthy guide, Peritar the Finder, but don't press your luck with me."

✠ ✠ ✠

I checked my chrono. The moons had set and it was the darkest it had yet been on our movement, but we had only a brief time before the sunrise tease of Begin Morning Nautical Twilight would be upon us.

Motioning us near, Peritar whispered, "Beyond that rise will be the mountain beneath the sands where the kraal of the elder den will be found. It is time."

He removed the chest plate from the sack on his back and donned it.

My heart pounded in my chest and I gulped. I was not alone. Excitement and trepidation became the cold scents exuded from the pores of everyone around me. Since no one else asked the obvious, I did. "What do we do?"

His tusks thrusted ahead with pride, Peritar said, "Are you frightened, Mihdra? Do you soil yourselves, Korundi? Simply be as you have, hatchlings trailing a mother, and follow me!"

He used four hands to touch the gems on the front of the plate. They glowed with dull multicolored lights but at the center, the black gem shone the brightest. It took on a dark foreboding color that spoke of voids and emptiness, absence and dark power, sucking the light of the other gems into it. An oval shimmer roughly several meters long appeared on the ground and as if it opened to a waiting staircase, Peritar descended through the event horizon and disappeared.

"Me next!" Doug said in a hush that poorly contained his enthusiasm, and stepped after him.

"I follow," said Sarkan Sell, drawing sword and knife.

"Oh, boy," Karlo said, and went next. I tapped Jodal Jark, who placed a toe into the shimmer as though he tested the springtime waters of a swimming pool. Finding the temperature acceptable, he went for it.

Double-K placed a hand on my shoulder. "If the Pale means to betray us, this is his moment for calumny."

"If it is, it is." I drew my pistol and stepped in.

I passed through layers of spun angel hair; light and fluffy was the feel on my skin before I found myself in a dark chamber beside my friends.

Double-K appeared behind me, a pistol in one lower hand, a dagger in the other.

"Sorcery!" Double-K exclaimed as he examined the space.

"Check it out," Doug said with his head craned back. The rippling ceiling was a window smeared in Vaseline through which the stars of a blurry night sky shimmered. The device Peritar wore provided the only other illumination. The chamber we stood in was of uncertain dimensions, its limits ill-defined by the effect that rendered the solid irrelevant.

"We have not far to travel," Peritar said, pointing the way. He adjusted the gems on the chest plate and the space around us changed shape. The edges of the distortion shifted closer, menacing with unknown consequences. "Move to stand behind me," Peritar said but even before he did, we were already hustling like recruits trying to avoid the wrath of their drill sergeant, packing ourselves nuts to butts at his back.

Peritar gave as human a groan as I'd ever heard. "You need not behave like scuttling vereen."

Dougie's enthusiasm had dimmed. "This *is* like a rat hole though, dude."

Karlo sounded like a movie mafioso. "Hey Peritar, not for nuttin', but how 'bout a little bit more explaining what's goin' down before you spring sumtin' on us, huh?" We were being treated to the full gamut of Karlo's diverse background.

Our guide was stymied. "I comprehend none of your words."

Sarkan Sell was the voice of calm persuasion. "Friend Peritar, the task is urgent, but it is necessary for its success that we are instructed. As the Red comrades first taught you, so must you teach us."

"I couldn't have said it better myself," I mumbled in his ear.

"Observe," Peritar said, touching the distortion beside him. His hand pressed against the blur without effect. "The light of the path is shaped to allow me to lead. Do not fear, there is ample room for you behind me."

Our chamber had taken on a shape that tapered on the ends of its long axis, like a blunted cigar. We relaxed and spread apart.

"How do you know what direction to go?" Doug asked.

"I have sighted the Clumsy Thief." He indicated the stars above. "We will move deeper and lose sight of the sky, but do not worry. None of the True People lose their way once a path is set."

Peritar checked the night sky a last time and set off. The moonroof of our limousine closed off until disconcertedly, all that remained was the dark glow from Peritar's chest against the distortion of the field allowing our passage through solid matter. I fought the feeling of suffocation and instead counted. Whenever I reached eighty-eight of my own steps, Peritar said something to himself and I realized just as I was, he was keeping a pace count in whatever units the Vermeel used for distance.

We kept a steady measure for what I estimated was about a thousand meters from our starting point when we slowed with a resistance that felt like wading into the surf through hip-deep water.

"We pass into the mountain beneath the sand," he said. "We are slowed but were it only one or two of us, we could run through the mountain if needed. The light of the path has power beyond legend, but even it has limitations."

"You know where we're going?" Doug asked.

"There are as many like this as there are stars. Within will be many kraal and also the den of the elders, but I have never been within this haven. Come."

We'd proceeded only a little farther when at the tip of our advance, an amber light appeared. Through the distortion filtered the familiar glow of amber stones. We'd reached a cave formation. I sucked a breath as a Vermeel passed in front of us, seemingly oblivious to our presence.

"Do not be overly vigilant just yet," Peritar reassured. "Though we see, they neither see nor hear us. I must move nearer for observation. Now, you must be the stealthy hunter and make no noise." He inched closer and the distortion spread, letting more light in. When the event horizon was as wide as Peritar's shoulders, he stuck his head slowly through the glass waves and carefully evaluated the other side before withdrawing. He retreated, the distortion sealed, and our chamber darkened again.

"Soon I will have the den of the elders located."

He took a course of ninety-degree turns and several times more we brushed against the walls of subterranean caverns and amber light seeped into our bubble. Peritar adjusted our course at each encounter, until once more he cautiously widened the event horizon and probed into the chamber beyond. He retreated from this one and turned to us with purpose.

"I scent the morning brew. The elders will be gathering. From below we will appear in their midst. I must be the last to surface to hold the portal open. If we are to surprise and overwhelm them, this must be done well and quickly."

"It is *your* time to relinquish any fear, Pale," Double-K said as he drew weapons again.

Peritar showed his teeth and tusks. "Kill only if given no choice, Korundi! I desire to set upon them with surprise like sudden gale. Then I will command their ears to listen."

"We understand," I said.

"Then we go," Peritar agreed. We took another series of jags and through familiarity gained by on-the-job experience, I sensed us take a descending course. "Observe," Peritar commanded. Above, amber light seeped over us through a tiny opening. Peritar worked the stones on his chest and the aperture grew incrementally wider, then stopped. "We have not pierced the surface, but may view what lies above." The ceiling of the adjacent chamber was high, but vanished for a moment beneath a shadow. Someone had walked directly over our position without effect.

"We shall appear in the middle of the council gathering. There will be elders and first sons in attendance. Abuse them no more than necessary. I do not know which among them are beyond redemption. Gather and be ready!"

With Peritar at our center, we joined in a circle facing out, all of us staring high. "Follow me," I said and before anyone could object at my usual insistence to lead, the event horizon drew near. I sprang up through the shimmer and re-entered the solid world. I was joined by my team and just as instantaneously came the reaction of the Vermeel.

What else would one expect?

Directly in front of me a seated Pale rose, drawing a pair of daggers. He was larger than Peritar and thick with sinew. I snapped a fist square into his snout, toppling him backward over the low stool. From beside the one I'd just sent reeling raised a younger pair, the one to my left bringing up one of the odd fizzle guns. I grasped the gun with both hands and spun and threw him over my head to crash into the other Tarn. I took the rifle and buttstroked each on the head.

Karlo threw a Pale lengthwise through the air to crash into several young warriors. A grinning Doug hefted a pair high in each hand and clanked their heads together, casting their limp bodies away with flair.

My Korundi were peerless fighters but didn't possess our supernatural abilities, and had to deal one-on-one with each Pale adversary they met. After a small amount of assistance by us to send the last Pales careening into the rock walls, the active resistance was over. We all had K-specs off our backs and with the exit and stunned Vermeel covered, Peritar spoke.

"Submit, Black Tusk! Elders and sons! Submit to Peritar the Finder or journey to the eternal hunting grounds!"

The large Pale I'd pasted on the nose pushed with all his hands to sit up, blood streaming down his chin. "Comrade Peritar! Is this your challenge for leadership of the clan? You know the People's committee outlawed those traditions. Why am I not surprised! Comrade Zero warned us of your defection."

Peritar aimed his dagger point at the Vermeel. "Defection? I have struck deep blows against the oppressor in his nest! I have fought and sacrificed in the cause while you remained in safety. Why was I was met by Black Tusk executioners?"

The Vermeel wiped dark blood from his lips. "You attack us with Korundi and Mihdra disguised as an operative cell, so do not pretend you are not a traitor to the state!"

Baring his teeth and tusks, Peritar said, "That is why you are named Kernmaal the Wisest. Nothing escapes your perception. But what is this accusation from Comrade Zero? Speak!"

The Pale answered. "A week ago a cell of the Blood Slaked was found wiped out not far beyond the range of their outer kraal. Before that, a cell of the Sharp Claws was found dead. A blood feud was considered, but Comrade Zero believes there is a Mihdra force operating within our territories, and that a traitor is responsible. It seems he is correct!"

Peritar scooped a long flint dagger off the floor and tossed it to the elder. "Enough! Fight standing or die on your knees!"

Before I could stop them, it was on! The Vermeel caught the blade midair and launched at Peritar.

And just as quickly, it was over.

Peritar buried his blade into one side of the elder's neck, the point protruding out the other. Kernmaal's resistance ceased. Holding the comrade leader upright by his harness, Peritar turned his blade and sawed as the older Pale gurgled and twitched. I pictured the anatomy as Peritar adeptly probed with the edge of his knife. More rapidly than I expected, he found the soft space between vertebra and finished the cut, flipping the head forward onto the chest. The geyser of blood continued and he let the body drop.

Turning to his audience, Peritar said, "Meet the same fate or return to embrace the ways of the Black Tusk. What is your response, Elder Dulak?" He pointed his knife at a kneeling Pale.

"We will hear you, Comrade."

Peritar snarled at the title. "Enough of that. Listen with ears of wisdom and I shall tell you why we must abandon the teachings of the Red Comrades. They have deceived us. I have seen the Mihdra. Their realm is great, their numbers uncountable. All we have accomplished is to reawaken their hatred for us. If we continue in this struggle, the People will vanish forever beneath the sands. Thus I bring news that there is another way."

Peritar told the hostile elders a compact version of events, ending with the promise to be returned to the Furrow.

A free-for-all of shouting broke out.

One elder roared, "How can you ignore the history of the People's exploitation at the hands of the oppressor? That much at least the Red Comrades spoke in truth."

"I say you have betrayed the People!" another shouted. "Comrade Zero is wise in the ways of political warfare. The struggle will be long but we will be victorious."

A more reasonable voice came in. "Even if the Red comrades are but the expelled defeated who seek revenge on the new Mihdra Kingdom, why should we trust the promise of a different group of Mihdra?"

Peritar tried again, this time almost pleading. "We have little choice. This I know to be true: the Mydreen have been wiped away by the Mihdra. Even the Yellows have they vanquished and their race of exterminators obliterated. All was done under the hand of this Mihdra, their Warlord. The People have never had an enemy so cruel and capable as he."

I was about to speak when Double-K stepped forward, at his full height and blazing with a fierce speech that though unintelligible to them, it silenced the room.

"Hiding in your mountains beneath the sand, destruction will loom above you day and night for an eternity." Peritar translated Khraal Kahlees's words. "I have no love for your kind, but for their sake, heed what Peritar the Finder tells you. If you offer this Warlord no choice, he *will* see the Vermeel vanish into the memory of the desert."

One of the eldest sons leaped to his feet. Jodal Jark and Sarkan Sell aimed K-specs at him but it seemed Peritar's seething words were what brought him to a halt.

"Your father proved he was not the wisest after all, Grandesh. Do not follow in his steps."

The young Vermeel raged. I recognized him as the one I'd taken the rifle from. "If not by the sorcery device of our Red Comrades, this little Mihdra could not have bested me or my father."

"Perish, if you so choose," Peritar said. He turned to me. "There is no choice, Mihdra."

I'd grown irritable and was in no mood to draw this out. So before every member of my team could inevitably object and offer to take the challenge themselves, I tossed Doug my K-spec and jumped.

My opponent was already moving at me like a Mack truck, upper hands reaching to trap me, lowers balled into pummeling fists. The Mydreen fought similarly, as did the Korundi. I had ample counters against such a simple, overcommitted attack. But of the many schools of martial talent I'd trained in over the years, I tapped into none of them. Because I'd already decided this wasn't an opportunity to win respect from the Black Tusk elders through a demonstration of noble restraint.

My blow landed first, freezing his advance like liquid nitrogen. His sternum split beneath my fist with a loud crack. I thrust knife fingers into the fracture, then pulled the rib cage apart with both hands to the sounds of splintering ribs and the wet sounds of blood and viscera.

Wide-eyed, he fell to his knees. The crush of my open palms met his skull between them and the thick Tarn skull cracked like a melon. For what was truly the first time, I'd held back nothing. But even I was a little surprised by the results.

It was an attentive group of Pale that stared at me. It was time to be the Warlord.

"I *will* see the People exterminated," I said. "But that is not what I desire."

Even my own crew seemed to snap to.

"So listen up."

19

Welp. No doubt about it. My methodology wouldn't have found approval among the ranks of the diplomats in the US State Department. But as a means to persuade the Vermeel away from their path as Marxist terrorists, my Warlord approach was showing merits.

"Dude, that was unreal!" Doug whispered as the bodies were removed.

Double-K was likewise affected. "Impressive, clansman. Thulians are peerless in strength, but I have not witnessed the like from you before."

I shrugged. "I just sorta went for it." Accepting my explanation, they joined me to settle into the circle to begin our conference with the Pales, who were now attentive.

A gentle hand on my back drew my attention to Karlo kneeling beside me. I prepared for the lecture to come, his perturbed look surely the result of my wanton violence, until he said, "Ben, how do you feel?"

There was deep concern on his face, so much so that I took a second and self-assessed.

"Worn, same as I know we all are. Otherwise, I feel good. You?"

"Yeah, good. Let me see your hands."

Karlo probed the bones of my knuckles and wrists. I felt no pain. His brow furrowed and he took a seat. Whatever troubled my buddy the verifiable genius, he kept it to himself. Over the next several hours the elders listened to Peritar's tale and his impressions from his many hours spent in Shansara with Doug and Zaylin Twee. His assessment of us was interesting.

"It is not as we were told. The Mihdra live differently than we do, but they do not oppress the masses. Even if they are consumed by material wealth rather than equality ensured by the state, they do not do evil to each other."

He finally ended by saying, "We can hurt them, but we cannot win against them. If we continue the struggle as taught to us by the Red Comrades, they will destroy us. If we abandon our fight, we shall have the Mihdra's assistance in returning to the Furrow."

The elders shifted in their seats as if anxious. If I were any judge, the prospect of returning to the Furrow seemed to entice them—as Peritar said it would—but a reluctance prevented any of them from speaking. This was the downside to my Kung-Fu diplomacy; they were intimidated that if they said something displeasing, I'd give them the same as I'd given their friends.

I said, "Have no fear to speak your mind. Peritar can tell you; our society protects the right of the individual to voice their opinion. It is our tradition."

Still, none spoke.

Peritar answered for them. "Obedience to the needs of the clan is *our* tradition, which means obedience to the elders. But it has become that the State determines the needs of the People. As I have said, the development of a political conscience has transcended our traditions with the result you see before you: here the elders sit, mute and infirm." He spat, but the gathered Pale did nothing to prove him wrong by speaking.

Doug smacked his forehead. "Ask 'em this: what the heck did the Red Comrades say to these guys that convinced them to abandon everything they've been raised to believe?"

Peritar repeated Doug's question, pointing to the Black Tusk I'd made eldest of the elders. Dulak threw all his palms open.

"Kernmaal was strongly convinced. When I saw the others were, too, I could not speak against, lest I be given the wanderer's death."

"I was never convinced," denied another. "The rest of you voiced such passion for the new ideals, I dared not be singled out for my opposition."

The dominoes toppled as one Pale after another renounced commitment or credence to the cause they'd participated in. I know next to nothing about human psychology, much less the Vermeel mind, but what I heard struck me as emblematic of a behavior that had brought the ruin of societies throughout history.

Double-K scowled. "Even the Mydreen despised the Vermeel for their barbarous incivility, but hearing for myself the pusillanimous nature of their leaders, I know why they were so easily manipulated. Did Brandon Bryant have knowledge of this, or was it serendipitous that the Vermeel proved so pliable?"

"Bryant always was lucky," I said. "And he was good."

Dougie smirked. "Not good enough."

Pensive, Karlo said, "Ben's not only better, he's luckier than Bryant. Capturing Peritar's the proof. Listen."

While we bantered, Peritar had been speaking. "I am now prime elder. If you are not ready to return to tradition and accept that, then continue to believe that I am but one among equals in service to the People. Either way, I move that we show hospitality to the Mihdra and let them take respite among our clan. Are there any opposed? Good. The Mihdra will rest while we continue in council, and I make further effort to convince you of the reality of our situation."

"See what I mean?" Karlo said with pride at Peritar's reasoned conduct. "Even though he knows we'd back him if he needs our help to remove any opposition, he's using persuasion instead of threats. It's like the saying goes—comes the hour, comes the man."

I wanted that to be true and I wanted Peritar to be the man we needed. But if it was time for adages, I had only one. "The only good communist's a dead communist."

Laughing, Double-K pounded my shoulder with a fist. "You have adapted my saying regarding the Vermeel. And unless Peritar assumes influence, we will need to make many more *good* Pale."

We received hospitality as we had at our first visit to a Vermeel kraal, and were taken to a clean chamber where water dripped from a wall to gather in a natural basin. We took turns on watch, resting little as we discussed whether we could trust Peritar or his people.

After a few hours, Peritar found us, accompanied by an elder woman. "The council wishes to question you more about the treaty offered by your queen."

"Glad to," I said, and everyone made ready to gather their gear and come with me. Peritar stopped us.

"You have seen the unease with which the elders respond. My suggestion is that it is you alone who come to council. As a sign of respect and trust, I invite you to allow this one," he indicated the older woman, "to lead the rest to visit the kraals of the deep home. To see how we live, as you did for me in your home."

Double-K pulled me aside so only I could hear him. "This is an attempt to divide us, Warlord. And besides, I have no interest in seeing how the Pale defecate where they live."

"Peritar," I said loudly, "Khraal Kahlees will accompany me, and the other Korundi will remain here on guard. The Mihdra will gladly view your kraal while we go to council, thank you."

Peritar gestured for us to follow him. "As you wish."

We met back at our cave campsite a few hours later.

"Howzit with the new boss?" Doug asked me.

"Progress," I said. "They had questions about the treaty the queen proposes between us and the Vermeel, but it's clear it's going to be a slog to get the other clans to fall in line."

Double-K huffed, but said nothing.

"Whaddja learn on your tour?" I asked.

Karlo said, "They make the Bedouins of Saudi Arabia look like hedonists."

"Huh?" Doug questioned. "Plain English, professor."

"Living high off the hog," I interpreted.

"Got it," Dougie said. "Yeah, Peritar's people are for sure getting by hand-to-mouth like them folks you'd see on the TV commercials asking you to sponsor a needy kid."

They described what they'd seen—the deepest caverns where water pooled, and the lichens and other plants that grew that were similar to those I'd survived on during my trek through the Korund. And like the Mydreen, the Vermeel penned vereen and gohdahl—animals we likened to rats and goats—for food and milk. They hunted, had rudimentary agriculture, and crafted clothes, tools, and necessities from the materials provided by animals and nature.

Sarkan Sell summed it up. "What you tell us is that in an inhospitable land, the Pale survive, but little more."

Karlo nodded agreement. "As sparse as resources are, the Vermeel have no choice but to live spread over a huge range. There can't be more than a few hundred people in Peritar's clan. It makes me think that the other clans must be about the same size."

Khraal Kahlees frowned. "And what shall be our reward if we shepherd them back to the Furrow, their land of abundance?"

Sarkan Sell answered. "As you imply, clansman, they will multiply."

"To become the Vermeel of old," Jodal Jark said. "With sky hands and driving hands turned against every living thing."

"The wisdom spirit at last inhabits this hatchling," Double-K said, pride layered over his ball-busting.

"One problem at a time, dudes," Dougie said, summing up my own thoughts.

Peritar appeared hurriedly in our cave campsite. "Mihdra friends! Only just now have I learned that Comrade Zero himself was in this kraal not a week ago! Come and hear for yourselves." This time we all accompanied him, loaded and ready to move out.

The council had become even more at ease since their recent questioning of me and when Peritar bade them, Dulak did not hesitate to speak. "Comrade Zero encouraged the elders with news that the struggle continued. He was on his way to the Silent Foot to send a newly readied cell to strike at the Mihdra."

"Dammit," I mumbled, then cursed my cursing. Real officers guarded themselves from such. A minor lapse like my one-word complaint could be as detrimental as a virus. Before I could recover, the disease spread.

"Woulda been nice to know earlier," Doug moaned. "While we were doing nothing."

Jodal Jark joined in with a sarcasm he had to have learned from us. "What do you mean, Douglas Knoblock? Has it not been worthwhile seeing how the Pales cook with dried dung?"

Except for Karlo, the oaks felled one by one.

When will I ever learn? I said to myself. I was ever the private—trapped in the body of a general—with no squad leader to tell me to shut the hell up.

Sarkan Sell growled. "When the hunters rest idle, the quarry gains distance."

Even Double-K complained. "And the innocent will pay the price of our indolence."

It was Peritar of all people who brought everyone from their funk.

"All is not lost! I know well the lands the Silent Foot now occupy. If we leave immediately, there is a chance their operational cell can be stopped."

That was something, at least. We all stood a little straighter. Double-K gave Peritar a look of regard and though Karlo whispered it, he rubbed it in with an industrial-grade buffer. "Did a Pale savage just earn your respect? How about that?"

Khraal Kahlees had learned the one-finger salute from us and gave it to Karlo in quadruplicate.

One of the elders questioned Peritar. "What do the Mihdra say? Do they desire the aid of the Black Tusk? Tell them it is given, Peritar the Eldest."

I was about to give a resounding affirmative when the oddity that struck me came out of Double-K. "Warlord, why are the Black Tusk so eager to see their kinsman destroyed?"

Bingo. In a little over a day, Peritar had turned the People's Committee back to a council of the Black Tusk elders, installed himself as their eldest, and somehow convinced them to help their enemy against their own kind. Maybe Peritar was hoping to spare not only the lives of innocent women and children in Mihdradahl, but also the lives of Vermeel. "Peritar, do you think you'll be able to convince the Silent Foot to abandon their struggle as you've done for your own clan?"

He repeated my query to his kinsman. The Vermeel laugh was no different from that of the other Tarn races, and Peritar joined the rest of the council to gag like chicken bones were caught sideways in their throats.

"The Silent Foot are no better than Vereen. Nor are the Blood Slaked or Sharp Claw. No, we will not try to convince them. We will help you kill them."

✣ ✣ ✣

On arkall we headed north and then skirted east to avoid the inner density of Silent Foot kraals. Peritar felt certain the cell of saboteurs would be taking respite in the outermost village before beginning the long movement east to bring havoc to Mihdradahl.

It had not been a popular decision to split us up, but I'd sent Doug and Sarkan Sell with a handful of Black Tusk warriors to retrieve the cached flitter. It was a necessity we update the operations center with the intelligence we'd gathered, and the only way for that to happen was for them to fly west and back into communication range. Maybe while we'd been gone, Cynar had produced another miracle and perfected the method to detect the rays of the light of the path. I also selfishly hoped I'd be able to piggyback off their wristlets to speak to my wife.

I tried not to think how worried she must be. The guilt I felt for the distress I caused my family would be assuaged if I could tell her the Vermeel insurgency would soon be ended.

I considered these things as Karlo rode beside me, also lost to his own thoughts.

"How're you feeling, Ben?" I knew my earlier lapse into negativity was an indicator of fatigue. Karlo was many things, but his role of team medic had never been lost to him.

"I know I slipped earlier, but it wasn't because I'm getting burned out. I was just frustrated. I actually feel really good. You?"

"Me too. That's what's got me troubled."

Those things didn't go together. "Whatcha mean, bro?"

"We're doing too good, Ben. Our water consumption's way below what we should be requiring. And we're taking in very few calories. Yet I'm not fatigued. I feel strong."

I shrugged. "We've just adapted to the environment, like the Vermeel."

Double-K was just behind us. "I would have expected nothing less. You Thulians have always proven hardy."

There was worry in Karlo's voice. "No, Ben. It's more than that. Haven't you wondered how you were able to tear that Pale apart so easily? I have."

I had, but figured I'd just tapped into the superhuman abilities we had on Vistara. I'd done some pretty incredible feats of strength before, like breaking an arkall's ribs with a punch, but my hand ached for weeks afterward. "It's like I said, I just kinda gave it my all without holding back. Why?"

"Something happened I haven't told you about. Doug and I were watching the Vermeel slaughter a gohdahl. It was interesting to see how they saved the blood, stripped the tendons, you know; they use every part of an animal. They were showing us how they took the marrow and handed me one of their flint knives and a goat femur to try for myself. On a whim, like it was a dried twig, I snapped it in two with my bare hands. Doug tried too and with no effort, he broke one in half."

That wasn't just strange, it was impossible.

Double-K cleared his throat to get our attention. He had a gohdahl shank pulled from his saddle bag. "Not that I doubt you, clansman, but would you care to demonstrate?" Karlo twisted back to take it and he snapped the thick meaty bone in half like a wooden chopstick before handing it back. Only then did he turn to face forward, making his demonstration performed from the awkward posture even more impressive.

His eyebrows lifted, Double-K accepted the two pieces. "I understand what troubles you, Karlo Columbo."

Karlo continued. "We should be worn down, not stronger. Definitely not *that* much stronger. The only thing I can think of to explain it—we used the device."

My head swam. "Cynar's sure the rays from that black stone are deadly! Heck, look how it screwed up those Vermeel!"

Karlo nodded. "It did. But how do those rays affect a Thulian, Ben? I still don't have an explanation for the abilities we've gained on Vistara. If it was the difference of being from a high-G world, we should've lost that advantage by now. But we haven't. If the rays of this device are like a slow poison to Vistaran biology, it's another case where the laws of nature treat us differently."

"You think?"

He nodded firmly. "I don't understand it and I don't like it, but we absolutely can't use that thing again. Besides, how many times can Peritar use it before he ends up toasted?"

Karlo had once again pulled a connection from something that had also been right in front of me, but completely evaded my awareness. Double-K had another of the mutton legs and was testing his strength against the properties of the goat femur.

"How do you feel, Khraal Kahlees?" Karlo asked.

Our friend was distracted. "Eh? Oh, I am well, but neither do I possess the vitality you describe for yourselves. With four arms and all my might, it would snap; no more or less differently than normal." He returned the cured limb to his saddlebag.

Karlo gave a relieved breath. "I think we're all okay, but there's one thing I know for sure—nothing exists that brings only positive benefits and zero side-effects."

Vistara was a never-ending wonder. "Okay. Until Cynar can tell us what's what, no more trips through solid matter. I don't want to grow an extra pair of arms like a Tarn."

Double-K chortled. "That would make you most handsome, but not to the queen's liking, I think."

We encountered Silent Foot in the outer borders of their range. Armed with knowledge of recent events, Peritar told a convincing story that we were called by Comrade Zero to find the local cell and join them for a great strike against the oppressor in the west. With this, we were enthusiastically aided by the locals.

Two days later, we left our mounts with a pair of Peritar's kinsmen and moved in the manner of the Vermeel for the spot he described as ideal. I was hunkered in the bottom of a valley, waiting. Nestled into the crests and dips of the dune above me, Karlo and Double-K watched the mouth of a canyon entrance a kilometer away. From it, a hard plain stretched westward from the gape like a tongue. Five-hundred meters across the plain to the north, a similar series of dunes acted as another jetty wall that defined the channel to the harbor of the kraal. If the cell was in that village, this was the on-ramp for their drive to Mihdradahl.

Peritar and Jodal Jark appeared, silently riding the dune like surf to arrive in the basin, shedding sand from the woven fibers of the suits that were as perfect as any ghillie I'd ever seen.

"The great hunter looks down on us with approval!" Peritar said. "They have not yet departed the kraal."

"How do you know it's the cell?" I asked.

Jodal Jark grinned. "There were arkall and bundles prepared for a long trek. Many Vermeel, armed with the guns made for them by the

Yellow. And," saliva left the corners of his mouth as he bared teeth and tusks, "Mihdra bearing Pale disguise. One of them carried an M4."

"Better than my eyes, this Korundi sees far and true," Peritar said with admiration. "But for good cause was I named Finder."

If there were eyes I trusted more than my own, they were Jodal Jark's. The anxious heat of impending violence must've burned an evil smile on my face because Peritar thrust his tusks at me in an equally devious manner.

"Death to the Silent Foot. Death to the Red Comrades!"

I donned my own net and crawled up the slope, the surface breaking beneath me as I scrambled to not slide back down the slope. Peritar scolded. "The Red Comrades had little to show the warriors of the People when it comes to ambushing an enemy, now do as I taught them Mihdra. Have patience. Our prey will not appear in the time it takes to reach the crest."

I aced all the stalking exercises in sniper school, using every minute of each six-hour time limit to pull myself along by my fingers and push with heels flat, never allowing my discomfort to weaken me into moving faster to hurry to find a final firing position. Even now, I was Type A. My failure was more a question of *how* I moved rather than my speed. I tried harder to distribute my weight evenly as Peritar taught, but lacked the spare arms to do better. I felt like I was finally getting the hang of it when I reached the top. Spotting Karlo's heels peeking out beneath his sand-laced net, I eased into a space not far from him.

At my heels, Peritar grumbled, "The Korundi chieftain and his young clansman prove able to learn. I should have known you Mihdra were doing the best you could by not sliding down the dune. Never mind." He tapped Karlo's heels. "I have erased your trail also, Mihdra."

"Peritar's a badass *and* a ball buster," Karlo whispered.

Peritar returned from making adjustments down the line and settled in to my right, wriggling to disappear below his net like a flounder beneath the sandy bed of a crystal-clear cove.

With Jodal Jark on the far left, the five of us covered a spread of ten meters, tucked into the dips and pockets along the crest of the dune. This part I knew I could do better than Peritar. Juiced by the adrenaline of an impending ambush, I could lie motionless until hell came.

Hell came.

If the rays of the black stone had somehow bestowed me even greater strength, it'd done nothing to ameliorate my need for thermal insulation. What I wouldn't give to have a nylon woobie wrapped around me. The sun set, the temperature dropped, and I shook and shivered, my teeth chattering as the voice inside my head nagged me to consider quitting and backing down the dune while the other, louder voice called me a wussy for even considering missing the kill to come.

You know, the usual.

Every so often we played the telephone game. I whispered to Karlo, he to Double-K, him to Jodal Jark, and back down the line. There wasn't enough candy in the world to entice the most naïve third grader to play the game with us.

"Psst," Karlo shot me. "I caught some thermal activity on the dunes across from us."

"Is it our terrorists?" Night observation devices had become scarce. Besides the thermal binos we brought, we had only a few clip-ons and handheld NODs still working. Needing to pack light, we left them in Shansara in favor of carrying as many K-specs and as much ordnance as we could.

"It was a couple of very small hot spots," he said. "Gone now. Prolly rats."

With no other way to confirm, I whispered to Peritar to ask if there could be rats out there.

"We will soon see very large vereen leave the kraal, indeed. Cease all movement or we will be the ones seen."

He was right, both about the need to be still and that now that sunrise teased, we wouldn't have long to wait. Starlight shone on the sands beneath the arroyo and from its slit, black blobs squeezed out onto the plain. The shapes were too large to be anything but arkall. I cursed that I didn't have a pair of PVS-31s on my head, and my mind composed the picture in the dark. The oblong shapes coalesced into a large pool. I imagined they crowded on the sands, tightening straps and checking loads before beginning their patrol. The large blob split like an amoeba undergoing fission to become so many smaller ones, their shapes changing further as they grew taller with riders mounting. They stretched apart further, forming the single file that aimed to pass right down the middle lane of the superhighway in front of us.

My chest pounded and hot blood surged through my body. The stars twinkled their brightest, the aurora announcing the sun's ascension painted the low horizon in blue pigment, and the sands blanched as if I saw them through eyes powered by white phosphor. At a lazy, lumbering pace, the train of arkall plodded our way, and I practically giggled with thoughts of the kill zone that couldn't be entered soon enough, and of the homicide to come.

Just another hundred meters, I said to myself as the lead animal crossed a line directly in front of me. The last rider was in sight. I counted six of them. The short rider in the middle was sure to be the Red Comrade.

I couldn't wait to walk the kill zone and find him dick in the dirt, his albino-dyed skin crispy and charred.

My rifle was pointed on a vector a few degrees to my right. I moved the last millimeter to get square behind it and waited. When the front legs of the lead arkall touched the invisible trip wire I projected to infinity, I'd light this candle. I tingled with anticipation as I contacted the face of the trigger with the feather touch of impending death.

The scene exploded with flashes like paparazzi snapping photos on the red carpet.

While I was begging the lead arkall to please, please cross the finish line into my zone of death, the ambush kicked off without me. The white-yellow bursts released when K-spec blasts hit a target meant someone had gotten itchy on the trigger, and I was late to the party.

Screw it. This was no time to bitch about being behind the beat when the dance started. I hammered the lead rider and his mount and worked down the line from right to left and back again, just as everyone else did—save Peritar, who was unarmed save the blades I allowed him to carry—making certain everything changed shape to something other than standing.

There were flashes of poorly returned fizzle fire coming from out of the kill-zone, and we relentlessly poured fire onto the scene to finish whoever was still alive enough to fight.

But what I suddenly realized made my heart go into an irregular rhythm as hard to dance to as free-form jazz.

The trails of the energy blasts I thought came out of the kill zone, instead led back to the dunes opposite us. I've been on the receiving end of fizzle fire, but never K-spec blasts. With a sudden epiphany, the difference was unmistakable. And there was only one energy weapon on Vistara so collimated, it could reach across that distance and deliver deadly effect.

My brain ceased to produce any higher function to override my instinct, and I leaped to my feet, spitting sand as I threw my Vermeel ghillie suit off and screamed at the top of my lungs, "DAVE!"

"Are you nuts?" Karlo yelled. "Get the hell down, Ben!"

"DAVE!" I yelled even louder, jumping up and down and waving hands overhead like a man stranded on a tiny Pacific Ocean island flagging down a passing ship.

"Holy smokes!" Karlo proclaimed with thermals held to his face. "They're waving back!"

"Let's go!" I yelled and sprang with all my might.

I flew high, higher than I ever had before. I landed on the compact sand a hundred meters ahead and burst into a run, spraying the dead arkall and riders ahead of me as I leaped over them. I hit the ground running again. Another spring and there, waiting for me with hands on hips, stood the certifiably unstoppable, unkillable, unflappable, most unconventional warrior to ever draw breath.

I would've cried except for the grin he wore, looking like he'd answered the front door to welcome family arriving to share Kahlua pork. Dave shrugged.

"Yo, Ben-dog! What took you so long, brah?"

20

Draped in a Vermeel desert camo net, Dave's cheeks were hollow, his brown face darker than ever, now the color of burnt umber. He removed a pair of NODs revealing sunken eyes that sparkled in the morning twilight. "Fancy meeting you here, brah. Been watchin' you for a while, trying to figure out who the heck it was on that dune."

I hefted him in a bear hug and danced him around with feet suspended and didn't set him down until Karlo was there. He hoisted Dave and joined me to hoot like our home team got the winning touchdown with seconds to spare. Finally, Karlo held Dave at arm's length.

"I can't believe it, though I should've guessed."

Dave hammered a fist into Karlo's chest. "Never count me out till you see the body, brah."

"Why aren't you dead?" I asked, half-joking.

Dave laughed, "Oh, I shoulda been. Our friggin' Black Bird went kaput and if it wasn't for this guy, we'd both be dried goo in the desert." Sliding down the dune, dressed like Dave and also carrying a K-spec was his partner, the co-pilot of Flight Marco Polo, Turv Densman.

"And by the way, brah, you ain't gotta bust my stones about flying no more. I've lost all desire to be a jet jockey."

That the two were not only alive but that they'd been waging a two-man behind-the-lines war against the Vermeel, it was incredible.

But like Karlo said, I should've guessed.

Double-K arrived gasping. "David Masamuni!" He crushed Dave with an all-arms embrace. "Are you a ghost sent to aid us from the afterlife, or are Thulians simply immune to death?"

"Easy, Double-K!" Dave laughed as he freed himself. "I been getting along just fine without a broken spine. But I missed you, too, brah." We welcomed Turv Densman with hearty embraces and when I released him, the pilot-turned-guerilla-fighter snapped to attention and saluted.

"Warlord, we have successfully located Xanalar!"

Dave snorted. "We were screaming for home with the news when the circuit breakers blew like we had too many Christmas lights in the same outlet."

"We experienced a catastrophic loss of power," Turv Densman clarified, then proved he'd been in Dave's exclusive company for some time by exclaiming, "Our shit got weak!"

Karlo puffed. "We know. Been there, done that."

"Got the T-shirt," I added. "We've been sabotaged."

"Sabotaged? By who, brah?"

I was about to give him the quickest explanation ever when I saw his face lose all joy as he surveyed the kill zone.

"Tell me you got more than two Tarns with you!"

I quickly explained who it was checking the kill zone and that Sarkan Sell and Doug were heading west to make commo with the kingdom.

Dave's disappointment was evident. "Why don't you have a battalion here? What's with the terrible getups? Don't tell me you're running a clandestine counterinsurgency!"

This wasn't the time or place but when it was, I'd tell him—"You know what would happen if I'd brought a battalion or two of our highly lethal, aggressive, and conventional troops? Recons would become village sweeps for guerillas, which in turn would become ambushes of our troops, which would build into frustration, which would lead to search-and-destroy missions, which would lead to the wholesale slaughter of the Vermeel. And if that's what I'd wanted, we could've stayed home and just let Khraal Kahlees carpet-bomb the place."

But I didn't say that.

My wristlet buzzed for the first time in a very long time. I expected it to be Doug telling us they'd made contact, and I couldn't wait to show him who was with us, but it was Jodal Jark.

"Warlord, come to the kill zone."

I walked with an arm around Dave's shoulder, afraid he might disappear from my fantasy that he was really here, alive and thriving. He said, "Our gear's nearby. We've got a couple of hovercycle-type things Turv Densman and I cobbled together outta parts from the Blackbird. They may look like what the Clampetts drove to Beverly Hills, but they work. We've been trying to get home, but the opportunity to hit the Vermeel wherever we could just fell in our laps. So, you know, it was time to fish or cut bait."

"Just amazing," Karlo said, correct as usual.

"How have you survived?" Double-K asked.

"We had everything but the kitchen sink crammed with us in the Black Bird—you know, just in case—and a lucky thing, too, it turns out," Dave said.

"And we have maintained ourselves by battlefield recovery," Turv Densman added. "And used clandestine techniques to steal supplies from Vermeel settlements."

"How'd you manage that?" I said, incredulous. We'd experienced how vigilant the Vermeel had been.

"Lessons of thievery taken from time with the Mydreen, no doubt," Double-K said with contemptuous amusement.

"Pfft." Dave waved a hand. "Lessons learned from SERE, Lewis and Clark, and common sense, brah."

Turv Densman shot Dave a funny look. "Do not forget magic, David Masamuni."

That was a weird thing for Dave's partner to say, but I let it go because we'd arrived on the scene. Jodal Jark and Peritar stood over the well-singed body of an otherwise pale Mihdra, dressed in the same costume I wore.

"Good," Dave said with pleasure. "When he gets to Hell, he'll find we sent a buncha his buddies ahead to wait for him."

Peritar gurgled and drool ran from his tusks. Incredulity was apparently a thing in the Vermeel culture. Dave noticed Peritar's stunned manner. He stuck out a hand.

"Name's Dave. I hear you're doing good things."

Peritar found his speech. "Are these *two* Mihdra responsible for *all* the missing operational cells? How?"

Dave snorted. "Missing's right. We've knocked off three Vermeel terror squads *and* their cadres. Our bikes let us cover a lot of ground fast. Once we figured out where the tribes cluster, a mule train heading west —carrying a crew of Pales with a wannabe in a stupid costume—that just stuck out like a band-aid with a fingernail on top of a taco. You guys figure out who these jack-offs are yet?"

Dave and Turv Densman had been running a World War II North African–style hit-and-run operation worthy of David Stirling and the SAS.

"Rat Patrol," Karlo said with awe. "Impressive."

"Warlord," Jodal Jark interrupted to get my attention. "The count is six riders on six mounts. But this is the sole Red comrade among the dead."

Sometimes the Tarn were a little weak in the communication department.

"What're you trying to tell us, Jodal Jark?" I asked.

He seemed put off that I hadn't already grasped the obvious. "Warlord, there were *two* Mihdra in Pale disguise within the kraal. The one bearing the M4, he is not among the dead."

Peritar looked east at the rocky face of the arroyo entrance, a shadow growing from it as the first rays of the morning sun appeared over the plateau.

"Comrade Zero is within."

✤ ✤ ✤

"I heard that name a couple of times," Dave said. "Is that the brains behind these rabble-rousers?"

I gave him a thumbs-up. "Peritar, is there any chance the kraal isn't aware what just happened here?" I asked. Our K-specs were damn near silent. Even when they hit flesh, the sound didn't carry far. If no one was looking, maybe...

He confirmed my fear. "None. The outer watch will be reporting what was observed." With unusual optimism he added, "Perhaps, the belief persists that a tribal blood feud continues."

Karlo said, "If I were Comrade Zero and learned the team I just sent out was ambushed, I'd connect the dots that Mihdradahl's finally come to collect."

We'd both come to the same conclusion. "He's going to run for it," I said.

There was no time to lose.

Karlo and I bounded after Dave at full speed, leaving the rest of the team to catch up as best as Vistarans could.

"Yo, brah," Dave said as we flew. "Sorry for the crack about your strategy. I don't know what I was thinking. You brought a pilot team. It's the right way to do this. That's why you're the big Kahuna."

"No sweat, Davey-Dave. But I think you're right. A battalion would be appreciated right now."

"Next time I promise to be around to help plan, brah."

We reached his hide site. Stashed beneath a net were the two expedient transports.

"Beautiful," Karlo said and named off components. "Deck plate. Vector rings from the drives. Low-yield stones from the accessory modules hooked in series. Have they cut out on you?"

"Nope," Dave said as he stripped bundles off the backs of the contraptions that looked like a kid's go-cart assembled from a junkyard. "Turv-with-the-Nerve figured out the power packs from the control units were still solid and linked them with ones from the cabin pressurizers."

A single seat salvaged from the passenger compartment occupied the front half of the two-meter section of deck plate taken from the passenger compartment. "We can carry one each," Dave said as he untied the last parcel of animal skin bags and threw them aside, leaving the space behind the seat clear. I did the same to the one I stood next to.

Lead by Turv Densman, the rest of our party slid down the dune and landed beside us.

"Peritar, you're coming," I said. "Take us on a route around to the far side of the kraal and the canyon inlet." He'd already described the kraal as being very similar to the one we'd first visited; a rocky plateau inundated with jagged and narrow caverns, but no underground complex of caves.

Dave hopped into the seat of his go-kart. "Ride bitch, Peritar." The Pale complied, whether or not he understood the jesting Dave leveled, same as he would to anyone. Turv Densman took the other bike and I slid behind him to kneel on the bare deck plate.

Khraal Kahlees and Karlo were arguing. Double-K snarled. "The sands will swallow their corpses."

Karlo said, "We'll deter them with precision fire; encourage them to stay inside the canyon."

Double-K growled. "Better we bait all the vermin to come out, thinking to meet us in combat, then exterminate them once the greatest number expose themselves to our ranged weapons. It will be a fine slaughter."

But I bet neither would happen. The Vermeel would stay deep in their kraal. They wouldn't be too anxious to find out who'd wasted their kin, especially when they saw the armed combatants were still out there. They were civilians armed with flint knives, wary and accustomed to surviving by hiding.

"We'll be in touch," I said and slapped Turv Densman on the shoulder. Bomb-'em-Back-to-the-Stone-Age-Double-K and Proportional-Response-Karlo could fight out the best tactical employment for their blocking action.

We lifted and slid behind Dave with Peritar tandem, on a course around the dune. We raced just inches above the sands, flying a winding course through shallow valleys and hopefully beneath the line of sight of any watchers.

As we sped, I ran through every scenario I could, but it all came down to this: if Comrade Zero used the light of the path to escape, we'd have nothing, and the search would be on again. And why wouldn't he? There was only one reason I could think of.

He'd seen how the black stone affected the users. Maybe it'd already injured him.

All we could do was what we were doing.

A Pale family scouring a patch of rocks for some scarce find were left behind us in a blur. I turned to watch them scatter in fear and took note of the obvious—we left no trace of our passing. Dave's guerilla campaign traveled undetected through the midst of the Vermeel, searching and probing, locating villages and ambushing terror cells, hitting and vanishing, creating chaos and fear, and undermining the influence of the Red comrades on this society.

And with each cell they prevented from departing these arid lands, they'd saved untold numbers of innocent lives in Mihdradahl.

All was the unintended consequence of the insidious plot to disable our technology, resulting in the intersection of deadly capability with outrageous opportunity. These two warriors had done more to head off our society's descent into terror than a thousand bombs dropped on the desert.

Dave was a legend. I couldn't wait to hear the full story.

I tried to maintain an orientation to the terrain of the hidden kraal in my overhead map view, complete with the labyrinthine pattern of twisting caverns I imagined, but I had no idea where we were. In the blink of an eye, we broke into flatlands and Peritar thrust a pair of hands ahead. What he pointed at sent a rush of adrenaline surging through me.

There was nothing better than catching someone in the chemical toilet with their pants down, totally unprepared to be tipped over. Three arkall lumbered out of the mouth of a gap in the breaks of the arroyo, riding away from us, oblivious.

Oblivious, that is, until I sent a blast right up their caboose. My first shot went wide and within a millisecond, served to alert them we were flying at their quarter flank. They turned and broke into a gallop for the nearest outcrop of rocky towers that made the colonnades for the wide front porch into the cavern complex. I hammered away as we closed, the only one of us who could shoot as we flew. The rolling motion caused my sights to drift unpredictably side to side, up and down, across and back over my targets, as if I were a stumbling drunkard trying to play pin the tail on the donkey. With a well-timed shot, I finally landed one on the rear beast and as it collapsed, pasted the rider square between the lower shoulder blades, just as his two riding partners whipped their mounts the last few meters to escape behind a column of rock.

"Nice!" Dave congratulated, then warned, "Hard brake!"

We reversed propulsion and flared but before we reached a halt, the air ignited in crackling white fire, and I was reminded of the explosion I'd witnessed from the back of thoroughbred arkall. Blinded and weightless, I was tossed airborne. With no idea which way was up, I tried to make myself round and bounce like a volleyball, but instead hit hard and went end over end like a brick heaved down a bowling lane.

I hurt everywhere but was on my feet. Everything seemed to work, so I shook it off. The bikes were down, noses in the dirt, but upright. Everyone but me had managed to hang on. Note to self: seatbelts are a thing. And when they're not, figure something out. I used to wear a monkey strap hooked to my rigger belt to clip in whenever I got into a helicopter. That might not have helped me here but right now, I swore the fashion accessory was going to make a comeback.

Dave leaped next to me. "Brah, you good?"

"Solid," I lied.

"Those freakin' explosive stones are a bastard!" he said, slapping my shoulder. "C'mon."

Turv Densman and Peritar were trotting behind us, apparently unharmed. We stopped short of one of the rocky pillars. Dave gave me a barrel release to tell me he was with me and just as I was about to move across the line of departure—ready to lead our way behind the wall of K-spec fire I was going to send—chips of stone flew off the rough pillar to the deafening cracks of unsuppressed 5.56 rounds coming at us.

Screw this. I did the desperate thing and thrust my muzzle around the corner and sprayed and prayed a few blind shots and when nothing came back, went for it and barreled in. Dumb, but there it is. I'd managed to wound two arkall, braying in pain on the ground. Over their rotund bodies, I caught a glimpse of a limping Vermeel carrying a satchel and a human—a black rifle in one hand, the other around the waist of the struggling Pale, a pair of costume arms dangling loose beneath. I sent a shot after them, the blast whizzing just behind them as they disappeared around the bend and into the narrow cavern.

"They're hurt," I said, then pointed my muzzle high for the top lip of the canyon. "Let's get above them."

Dave let out a string of curses in a way I'd sorely missed. Then, as if he prepared himself to join me to leap high onto the cliffs, he slung his rifle on his back and tore the cloak open from his shoulders. "I got a better idea."

With one hand, Dave drew his pistol and with the other he stroked the crystals of the chest plate I'd had no idea was even there. The foreboding glow of the black crystal spread like night between the pulsating ring of the smaller multicolored stones.

"See ya." He dashed past me and across the trail, barely slowing to pass through the face of the cavern wall transformed into a rippling waterfall. I was left behind, staring at what was once again unremarkable rock.

How the hell Dave had acquired—much less become the master of the black stone tech—was a question I didn't have time to ponder.

"He knows the light of the path!" Peritar blurted out.

Getting my act together, I launched with all my might, springing high up above the top of the plateau. The labyrinth of jagged paths I'd imagined through the sand-covered table looked like dried veins spread across a broad leaf. I landed and paused, straining for a clue, then heard the *crack-crack-crack* of an M4 ring out from the crevice ahead. I sprang, landing to peer over the edge with my barrel leading my eyes.

The Pale I'd wounded was on the trail below, the satchel he'd carried empty on the ground beside him. Comrade Zero was nowhere to be seen. The dull report of a "blap-blap" from a pair of 9-mm rounds raised from a large gap ahead, and I raced to catch the gunfight I was left out of. I zigzagged back and forth over the gaps above the trail, stealing glances into the chasm beneath me to see Pales scattering beneath overhangs and diving into pockets to avoid the ballistic exchange still going on somewhere ahead.

I came to an abrupt halt above a fork in the trail and waited. In the time it takes lightning to strike, Zero dashed from beneath an overhang and crossed the narrow gap beneath me before I could fire. I leaped back across the crevice to find the angle and raised my rifle, just in time to see the back of a dull metal chest plate vanish into a rocky canyon wall. The empty satchel beside the wounded Pale must've contained the black stone device Zero now wore to broadcast the light of the path.

Like Dave, Zero was not using the trail.

A muffled trio of shots escaped the wavy distortion where Zero had just vanished, and I flinched back, unsure where the rounds were aimed. I thrust back, ready to hammer the trigger, when the shimmer of wavy nothingness evaporated, returning the rough canyon wall to solid. A single unmuffled gunshot rang out from below my feet and a bullet ricocheted off the spot where Zero had just disappeared.

Directly below me, Dave sprinted across the open. "Dave! Above you," I yelled, but he'd already passed through the shimmering wall ahead. I was as lost as a near-sighted racoon bumping his way through a house of mirrors. A running gun battle conducted in and out of the material world was not on my list of things I expected to see today.

My wristlet buzzed and Karlo's face appeared. "Ben, what's happening?"

"Dave's got one of those damn chest plates!" I blurted. "He's chasing Zero through the walls of the kraal!"

The Dave effect was in full swing as Karlo replied, unusually, though most appropriately, "OH, SHIT!"

What else was there to say?

I searched the splay of thin crevices stretching across the plateau, trying to guess where they might appear next. The sharp cracks of Zero's M4 answered by Dave's pistol rang out here, then there, and I played catch -up, dashing ineffectually to where the sounds had come from, only to peer down on canyon trails empty of human or Vermeel.

I found myself all the way at the edge of the kraal, on the rim overlooking the wide plain where we'd just ambushed the cell. Alerted to my appearance, Karlo and the guys waved at me from a distance. I was about to bring my wristlet up when the noise of gunfire filtered through wet paper came from a crevice back in the depths of the maze. I leaped for it, and came down with rifle pointed into the chasm, primed to shoot at the first glimpse of Zero's bleached body hauling ass across the trail. Quite surprisingly, Zero whizzed across the gap below me—flying sideways through the air like a frisbee. His body hit the opposite wall with a crunch that made my testicles retract.

Zero may have had the path of the light, but it was nothing compared to the Dave effect.

I dropped through the gap and onto the sandy trail. In a heap against the jagged wall lay Comrade Zero, limp as a wet rag doll. Dave stepped out from the wavy distortion with a Cheshire cat grin like it was portrait time and the photographer had said, "Cheese."

Dave spit on the sand with victorious contempt. "Dematerialize that! Shithead!"

I was over the wreck that was Zero, mangled in an unnatural repose, still as a corpse, and unarmed. A wet bubble of breath blew from his bloody lips.

"Bastard almost got me," Dave said matter-of-factly from my side. "But he ran dry." He taunted the half-dead man with the gunfighter's adage. "Reloading's a planned event. Amateur."

Dave's arm was bloody. "You're shot!" I exclaimed.

"Nuh uh," Dave denied, until he saw where I pointed. "Damn." He casually examined his shoulder, then dismissed the wound. "Just grazed me. Close but no cigar, asshole," he again teased Zero, who couldn't have possibly heard him.

A disadvantage of assuming the guise we did, I had literally nothing on me more useful for a dressing than spit and sand. I brought up my wristlet. "Karlo, bring it in. We're near your end of the kraal. We've got Comrade Zero prisoner, and he's trashed. Not to mention, Dave picked one up. We need help."

"On the way," Karlo replied. I turned back to find Dave cutting the straps of the chest plate from Zero and tossing it aside.

"He ain't getting away again," Dave said, returning his folding knife to his pocket.

The five W's and an H burst out of me as the means of requesting an explanation from him. "Who? What? When? Where? Why? How?"

Dave chuckled at my word salad and obliged.

"It's weird in there, dig? First, I had to locate the light of his gizmo. Then, I had to get close enough for our wavy-gravy clouds to touch. Having to fiddle with the stones with one hand meant he had a hard time getting good shots off at me with his rifle. I had him dead to rights a buncha times before he finally screwed the pooch and ran dry. I didn't want to kill him, so I went mano-a-mano, brah. I did one of your numbers and just picked him up and tossed him. Funny. I been feeling really strong lately. I mean like, *really* strong." Dave cocked an eyebrow as he looked down on the prisoner. "Guess I overdid it. Anyway, that's that."

I was flabbergasted.

"How in the hell did you learn to use *that*?" I pointed to his chest.

"Oh, yeah, this thing. It's how they been pulling off their hits on us. It wasn't too hard to learn to use. I just figured, these douchers do it, how tough could it be?"

I was still gob-stopped, but managed another question. "How long have you been using it?"

"I dunno. We found it on the first group we nailed. Then it all just kinda came together. Once I had it figured it out, I started sneaking into their camps to steal supplies. Then I got good enough to spy on their meetings and get intel. You know they got some massive-ass underground caves? Pretty amazing."

It was Dave who was amazing. I'd have to let Karlo explain how the black stone had so far benefitted us Thulians—Dave's strength was testament he was clearly experiencing those—but he also didn't know about the negative effects. "Has Turv Densman traveled by the light of the path?"

Dave's bushy eyebrows scrunched. "A couple of times. I've kept him in the real world for the most part. Didn't want him to get killed in case I screwed the pooch and ended up petrified in solid matter. Why you ask?"

I breathed a sigh of relief, then heard Karlo yelling from a distance behind us, "Coming in."

"Come in," I yelled back. Karlo appeared down the trail and took a last bounce to land next to us.

"The guys are behind me, go bring 'em in, Ben."

I returned with Double-K and Jodal Jark to find Dave holding a dressing against his own shoulder as Karlo examined the prisoner with a fretful look. "What's the word?" I asked.

Karlo's voice held concern. "Concussion. Bad. He's got a decent pulse and his respirations are as good as they can be with so many broken ribs. His spine's bruised badly, too. I can't *feel* a skull fracture or any step-offs on his spine, but that doesn't mean much."

I had only one concern. "I at least want him around long enough to answer some questions."

Karlo shot me a harsh look. "I'll do what I can."

Peritar and Turv Densman appeared from the other direction, a group of curious but cautious Pales trailing behind them.

"Is it him?" Turv Densman asked, gesturing at the unconscious and bruised Zero.

Peritar showed his tusks. "It is Comrade Zero."

My wristlet buzzed. With everyone who had a wristlet here next to me, it could only be one person. Doug's face appeared, smiling and proud.

"Yo Ben-dog! I got us some comms! We had to fly about halfway back to Thoria before we got a link, but we're good to go."

"Can you piggyback me onto the net?" I said.

Doug nodded knowingly. "Hells yeah, dude. I'll have Talis Darmon on the cloud in a sec."

This one time Dougie fell short as a mind reader. "Not yet," I said. In less than a minute, a small, sour, and tired face was in the cloud. Tranya Olan looked worn and older than ever I'd seen her, but she perked up at recognizing me.

"Warlord! Have you returned from the eastern wastes? You look frightful!"

"Thanks, Tranya Olan, but I have someone here you might want to talk to."

Dave pressed his face into the cloud. "Hey, baby."

"David Masamuni!" she gasped, then her voice broke. "How I died to see you again! Where are you? How are you? What have you been doing all this time? When will you be next to me again?" She burst into tears.

Dave choked. "I'm sorry, sweetie. Don't cry. I'm fine."

Tranya Olan's distress turned to a scolding. "You don't look fine! You look worse than Benjamin Colt! And he looks terrible!"

Dave laughed through tears. "I love you, Tranya Olan."

As quickly, the temper came out of her sharp sword and she became bendable iron. "I love you, David Masamuni. And I will never fail to tell you that ever again."

I laughed and sniffed a salty tear down my throat before I brought my face back into the cloud. "Okay, Dougie, patch me in to the kingdom."

Doug cackled with joyous disbelief. "Holy moly! Dave's alive! I knew, but I didn't. How? What's he been doing all this time?"

"It won't surprise you. He'll tell you himself soon enough," I said. "Now you can get Talis Darmon in the cloud for me. Then I'm sending for the Black Birds."

"We going home?" Doug asked.

A red mist seeped into my vision. "Not. Quite. Yet."

21

We remained in the kraal of the Silent Foot while Karlo tended Comrade Zero. The Black Birds were on their way. Doug and Sarkan Sell were good where they were, and stayed in place to continue to act as a relay for our comms. After so many weeks of isolation, the sudden return to instant communication with home was the quenching of a long drought.

After Talis Darmon and I showered joyful greetings and assurances on each other that all was well, she got me up to speed on important events, the first being that not long after our departure, another attack had been attempted on Clymaira, and thwarted. Thanks to Cynar perfecting detectors for the rays of the black stone, the infiltrators had been interdicted and killed before a single citizen was harmed.

"Wizard Cynar assures me his latest innovation will also be ready soon," Talis Darmon said through the cloud. She was as perfect and beautiful as ever, but seemed fatigued. I hoped it was from something as mundane as Shara being colicky, but knew it was on my account. "He will explain much better than I, but apparently the rays that join our devices follow a natural path from pole to pole, but less so in the equatorial planes. The Golden Hub produces the towers as we speak.

Once emplaced, we will never need fear similar hindrance to communication again."

"That's great news," I said with as much upbeat energy as I could muster. I was tired and knew I looked like hell, but wanted to appear as wholesome and well as I could to not add to her strain. That she fell morose told me my acting skills had not improved.

"Husband, I promised myself I would not burden you with the hurt I have carried during this separation, but daily it has ground at my soul. I have been unable to resume the impassive apathy we once knew during our antiquity, when all distances were an unbridgeable gulf and the yearning of not-knowing was as unchangeable as the impending death of our world."

"No more," I said. "But will having to suffer Cynar's boasting really be worth it?"

She didn't take my humorous bait. "If Tashara Colt and I must endure an eternity of your absence, at least we will not lay our heads each night to wonder if you are perished, far from us and alone." She wiped at her eyes.

"Whoa, whoa, whoa," I said. "I'm fine. And for what it's worth, our sacrifices have been rewarded. The terror attacks on the kingdom are finished."

"Sacrifice upon sacrifice, never-ending," she lamented, then dried her eyes. "How soon will you be home? Tell me the Black Widows are landing at your location as we speak."

Now for the bad news. "Not just yet. And when they do, I won't be coming directly home."

The disappointment fell over every part of her. "For what reason? I will immediately send diplomats and all means necessary to begin the relocation of the Vermeel to the Furrow."

When I didn't acknowledge that as the solution to my dilemma, the anger came. "Surely, what other tasks may remain can be carried out by your army, or are they all so incapable that the Warlord himself must be there to see it done?"

I knew she was just venting, so I didn't attempt to defend the army.

"It's not that, my princess, but, yes, the kingdom should show good faith and act on its promise to the Vermeel as soon as possible."

Her transfiguration was instantaneous. No longer the wife and mother longing for my return, she amplified into the person with absolute authority and responsibility for the welfare of an entire kingdom. "Then what matter would keep you from returning with all haste? What do you withhold from your queen?"

I didn't know what I didn't know, but I had a grave suspicion time was against us.

"I don't have the knowledge I need. And for the good of the kingdom, my queen needs that information."

Her diminishment came as abruptly as her blaze had ignited. Her sweet voice quavered with distress like the timbers of a ship straining against the storm. All served as an admission as clear as the Vistaran skies.

Her regency was an affliction with no available cure. She sighed.

"I am your princess, forever and beyond. And I am regent to a kingdom that survives by your guardianship. But I promise, Benjamin Colt, I will find an honorable solution for Mihdradahl so its fortune does not eternally rest upon the shoulders of our family. It is with concern of Xanalar that keeps you in the east, is it not?"

Just then Karlo spoke from behind me.

"Ben, our prisoner's conscious."

Anticipating I was going to close the cloud, Talis Darmon begged, "Benjamin Colt, can you not tarry long enough to allow our daughter to see her father?"

"This can't wait." The cloud holding her tormented face turned to static and faded. Unlike the duality of roles that tore at Talis Darmon, the electric charge that ran through me won out over the shame of my cruelty. I followed Karlo into the niche where on a litter, lay the dagger that carried out Brandon Bryant's will to stab at us from beyond his grave.

Zero's eyes darted nervously at the sound of our approach, but his head remained motionless. His neck was expediently stabilized by a thick wrap of rough weave cloth Karlo had scavenged, but it didn't look anywhere near as firm as a real c-collar. Karlo whispered to me, "He has a spinal cord injury, maybe complete. C-5 at least."

"So he's totally paralyzed?" I asked. I had a lot of medical knowledge, but not enough to understand the implications of what Karlo was telling me.

Our best physician was frustrated. "I don't think there's a fracture, but he's for sure in spinal shock. Means the cord's bruised from blunt trauma. He might recover useful arm function, maybe more, but I won't know for some time."

Zero spewed venom into the air above him. "There is nothing wrong with my hearing, Thulian. I am rendered immobile, but do me the least of honors and speak as if I am not senseless."

Double-K watched the supine man with hands resting on the handles of both blades, as if Zero might abandon his feigning and return to deadly volition at any moment. The rest of the crew stood back, revulsion souring their faces. It was an effect I recognized, one rendered on those who'd ever pondered the situation our prisoner found himself, robbed of the ability to raise even a finger, aware that he existed in a virtual living death.

Except for Dave. He looked guilty.

I knelt and leaned over Zero's harsh face, scarred and cracked like the bottom of a dry riverbed. It was then I noticed the misshapen ear, the droop of his eye. He was afflicted with the transformation of repeated exposure to the deadly rays of the black stone.

"What's your name?" I asked.

He didn't give it, instead rasping, "I saw you once, Thulian. And though at the time I knew not who you were, I knew you had to be destroyed."

That was a curious introduction. "Where'd we meet?"

His laugh came out as a weak nasal buzz from the back of this throat. "Had we met, you would not be here." He drew a determined but shallow breath and continued, reminiscing the scene playing in his head.

"It was my final day in Shansara. Your army had at last routed us from the capital." He took a few raspy breaths to feed his tale and as he did, I thought back.

The war to remove Bryant and his Mydreen army from Mihdradahl had been long and bloody. Talis Darmon's brother had taken the throne from their father, and in a manner consistent with its many flaws, the army remained loyal to the new regent and followed his orders to stand against us. Comrade Zero cleared his throat weakly, ready to continue.

"Prince Carolinus Darmon was never a leader but as king, all knew him to have become yet more unreliable, maddened even. When he abandoned the fight to shelter with his witch in the Spectral Hall, none cared to follow. Brandon Bryant had already taken his Mydreen puppet Domeel Doreen with him to Pyreenia. I remained behind as ordered, prepared to make havoc and observe before rejoining in the west to report on what I saw of the conquerors. But I had resolved instead to do all harm possible and if I could, find a worthy target on which to expel my hate and die."

We knew his cadre had come from the hardened gangs of Thoria, but from his speech I intuited that he was a military man, perhaps an officer.

"So you were in the army?"

He took more difficult breaths before continuing as if deaf to my question.

"I watched as you landed on the Concourse of Diasemony. And I witnessed the Princess Talis Darmon at your side. But it was not in her shadow you stood. It was in *your* light that *she* stood. All hailed you with a reverence and awe worthy of the titans that lined the grand concourse. It was to a frenzy I fell when I accepted that I had no means with which to injure this man they worshipped. Then a clarity with which I had never before seen came to me, and I vowed to live. I would gather strength and find means to strike at this victorious general and the princess whom he would place on the spectral throne."

"Delusions of bad-assery," Dave mumbled. "Like someone else we used to know."

If Zero heard him, he took no notice. I returned to my interrogation. "So you escaped and went to Pyreenia to rejoin the renegades?" To that, he responded, his voice weak but harried.

"Renegades? Heroes! And there were many like-minded to me who survived to make the journey to Pyreenia. And when we were welcomed by Brandon Bryant like lost sons, we knew our choice to live was the right one. He told us who it was we had seen in Shansara that last day, and promised he would see our dedication rewarded. He would entrust to us all his knowledge to make our revenge. He was a great man with great vision. He was more than a leader. He was to us a father who shared all with his sons."

The well of Dave's pity ran dry.

"That's all I needed to know. If Bryant treated you like a son, it's because you're as evil a bastard as he was. I gave you what you deserved."

Comrade Zero's eyes rolled up to find Dave. The allegation had sparked an urgency, renewed him. Without gasp or crackle and in his strongest voice so far, he said, "You are wrong, Thulian. The evil was there waiting in Pyreenia. Brandon Bryant saw it for what it was, and adapted brilliantly. When it became necessary to leave the darkness consuming Pyreenia, we made our escape together to Annameria. Such was his genius that he won over the Annamese, and we were welcomed into their fold. And with their approval, we set to work."

I asked him about the nuts and bolts of the operation to build an insurgency against us, and for the first time in our conversation he answered my questions—with delight and pride, as if seeking my recognition as an equal in the elite fraternity of those capable of destroying an enemy from the shadows.

But he told me nothing I hadn't already guessed at.

Bryant had given them a master class in unconventional warfare and most importantly, taught them the manipulative ideology more successful than any other in shaping resentment into a calling for virtuous homicide. He'd turned them loose and went on to orchestrate his larger, more devious campaign against us.

There was only one thing remaining I'd not yet pieced together.

"When did Xanalar come into play?"

His surprise was genuine. "How do you know of Xanalar?" Then he made another weak nasal laugh. "As much as I hate you, it is impossible to deny your ability. You should know, though he despised you, Brandon Bryant felt the same. He always spoke of you with the respect due an equal, never as an inferior."

Even though this man was my enemy, there was some honor in him. Or was it something else?

Our prisoner continued. “I will tell you about our chance collision with Xanalar. It was a disastrous coincidence that instead became the salvation of our purpose to see Mihdradahl tortured.”

The rest of the crew had gathered close, enticed as I was to at last hear something tangible about the mysterious race known to us only by myth and map.

“The Annamese knew not where the Vermeel habited, only that they persisted. After fruitless weeks searching the far wastes, I chose to take us ever farther in the direction of the rising sun. When we sighted the strange flying creatures, it seemed only proof that the desert had damaged our minds. From afar they disabled us with a weapon that caused genuine madness. Stuporous and feeble, we were captured.

“We lay in their dungeons for weeks, tortured in ways crueler than any known to the Yellows or Mydreen. No marks were made on our flesh, but in our heads, they flayed us bare.”

He started and stopped several times as he struggled to describe his captors, then said cryptically, “They are as alike as they are unalike to any other kind on Vistara.” He shook away whatever’d been in his mind and said, “But if ever there were proof of gods who cared enough to intercede in the struggles of their children, our captivity by the Xanalara was that evidence.

“During their probing, they learned our intentions, and it pleased them. To the Xanalara, any and all not of their kind are reviled. They saw that we strayed into their lands not to do them harm, but that we were engaged in hateful purpose against Mihdradahl. The doors of our prison were opened—not with friendship—but with the regard of a master for his beasts of burden. All our belongings were returned to us. But more than returning us to our purpose after so long a delay, they supplied us great gifts. We were given the light of the path, instructed, and told where to obtain more of the precious black stones needed to power the gifts. They wished us well in our endeavors and with exactitude, directed us back westward to the lands of the Vermeel."

I jumped in to ruin any hope that he still held information I didn't already have. "And your first mission was to the Veil of Seriata, to steal as many of the rare stones as you needed to arm yourselves."

Zero fixed Peritar with an accusatory gaze. "You emptied your belly of all our secrets. Were any to betray the cause, I never thought it would be you to turn traitor, Comrade Peritar."

"Comrade? Pah!" Peritar spat. The paralyzed man squeezed his eyelids tight, the only protection available against the force of the rebuke.

Khraal Kahlees growled. "Such hypocrisy! Do not speak of betrayals, Zero, betrayer of all betrayers, cowardly murderer of your own kind! It was chieftain of the dwarves who admitted to us his people colluded with Xanalar, all while soiling himself."

I waved Double-K down and he stepped back, disengaging as if he'd heard all he could tolerate from Zero.

Karlo knelt and wet Zero's lips with a cloth, and he sucked the moistness for a moment. His disfigurement and paralysis tugged at my pity again.

"Didn't the Xanalara tell you using the black stone repeatedly would harm you?" I asked.

His voice grew more fatigued. "No. The damage done by the magic of the stone became apparent, but we cared not. We were under the spell of a more powerful magic. Brandon Bryant's instruction proved more powerful than even the sorcery we had acquired from the Xanalara. Our indoctrination of the Vermeel was rapid and our work commenced in earnest. And intoxicating it was."

Malevolence replaced his infirmity. "For the sweetness tasted in our revenge was greater than any bitterness brought by the magic!"

Peritar menaced over Zero with grinding tusks. "And the people you called comrade became ill along with you! Enough of your deceptions, Zero. I am freed from your manipulation."

Zero smirked. "Only to become manipulated by another, Peritar the Finder."

The warrior we labeled "pale" grew dark. "Shall I tell you wisdom greater than any you shared with us? The youngest hatchling of the People knows the enemy of my enemy is my friend. But a true elder of the People knows an even greater wisdom: when a new friend of great strength offers hospitality, what further use is the old and weak friend? Especially, you. Cripple."

Peritar laughed the deep throaty gargle of a Tarn.

"But I give thanks to the ancestors that you sought us out. For it has led to my ascension, one secured by the might of the Mihdra. I now have the power to rise and become the one true chieftain for *all* the tribes of the Vermeel."

Double-K prodded Karlo with a finger. "How many times have you imbued upon this Pale the quality of an egalitarian? HA! It is *we* who have been used."

Karlo was at a loss for words, and Double-K filled the void.

"I ask you, Karlo Columbo, are we so much different from Brandon Bryant? All we have done is create another Domeel Doreen. Bah!" He threw hands up and Karlo threw his own back in frustration, but I saw in his face a realization.

This wasn't a stalemate. Karlo had lost his last piece on the board in his game with Khraal Kahlees to defend Peritar's trustworthiness.

Zero found my eyes. "Look how the discord within your ranks grows. Not even Brandon Bryant could have foreseen how wonderful our revenge would be!"

The traitorous son of Mihdradahl was miserable, broken, and mutilated, but none of it erased a second of that day in Filestra. My building rage brought a smile to his face.

"And that is your gift to me, Thulian. Though bested, I am not shamed. Because if my ability to bring you pain is at an end, another, greater pain awaits."

He closed his eyes as if that ended our interaction. I grasped his face roughly.

"Speak!"

He opened his eyes and in them was satisfaction.

"You no longer remain in the disregard of an enemy greater and more powerful. Xanalar learned from us of Mihdradahl's rise to prosperity and strength. They are vainglorious, jealous, and powerful. But above all, they are fearful. Your salvation from extinction means they have no choice but to destroy you."

Even Karlo had reached his limit of compassion.

"There were a thousand other ways this could've gone. You could've surrendered that day back in Shansara. The queen would have pardoned you all. You could've returned to a life. Instead, your life's been a waste."

Remorseless, Zero said, "Life is naught but a scramble for a loose knife on the floor."

I knew of only one being more hateful and twisted than Zero. The source of all evil in the universe, met on the sickly plane of existence where she resided. Surely, the Harridan had somehow touched this man. The memory of her foulness caused me to recoil, to distance myself from the sickness that flowed through Zero's veins. I was not alone in being touched by the memory of her. Alert like dogs with hackles raised, the others were fearful at the scent of danger carried from outside the light of the campfire.

Dave spoke anxiously. “Karlo, did you check him for a brand on his back?”

My own hackles raised. Could Zero be one of the cursed we thought had been forever destroyed beneath Vistara?

“No!” Karlo exclaimed, shaking his head. “I never thought to. Could it be?”

Khraal Kahlees huffed with contempt. “Clansmen, this one is indeed a soul-eater. But he is not the offspring of a supernatural abomination. Inside him is an emptiness no amount of revenge could fill. Do not try to understand him, for it will only lead to his darkness seeping into your own light.”

Dave relaxed and shook off the chill not caused by the temperature. “Yeah, no kidding. Screw this guy. He’s done.”

“You are wise for your kind, Korundi,” Peritar said to Khraal Kahlees.

Double-K shrugged away the compliment.

An elderly Vermeel came from out of the group that cautiously watched from a safe distance, and Peritar moved to speak with him. He returned quickly. “A skin-flayer gathers on the horizon. I, too, taste its heaviness growing in the air.”

“How far away is it?” I asked.

“It will strike at dusk.”

I brought up my wristlink. “Dougie, patch me to the Black Bird flight leader.”

“Coming up, homie. Everything cool?”

“We got a sand blaster headed our way.”

“Yikes, dude.”

In a moment I had the grimacing pilot.

“Understood, Warlord. We follow the beacon of the guide party, but I estimate it will yet be a task of an hour or more to locate them. I advise that it will be most unlikely we can arrive in time to evacuate your party. Orders?"

"Ground once you locate General Douglas Knoblock. We'll give you the all-clear once the storm's passed. Hear that, Dougie?"

Doug's face returned. "Good copy, Ben-dog. You guys gonna be okay?"

"Peritar says we're good to hunker down here. It should pass by midnight."

A dry voice croaked with desperate force.

"Take me into the desert."

Karlo returned to kneel beside Zero. "What's that?"

Zero drew another seething breath. "Take me into the desert. Nothing more can I tell you. I am a worthless shell, left with nothing, not even a body fit for torture. Whatever suffering I have caused you, allow mine to end. I have no right to ask favor but, please—leave me to become dust."

Peritar placed his face over Zero's.

"You wish to enter the eternal hunting grounds of the People?"

"Whatever you may think of me, Peritar, I found peace with the Vermeel. I would be grateful to join the eternal hunt."

This pleased Peritar. "You learned as much from us as we did from you, Zero. But of the political conscience you introduced, I thought always that this was *your* greatest wisdom—gratitude is a sickness suffered by penned animals."

His sadistic victory complete, Peritar left to confer with the elders of the Silent Foot.

Karlo was always the check of what humanity demanded. I could count on him to pull me back from whatever retribution my anger begged me to enact. I expected him to object but instead, his face held a calm resolve as he looked to me for permission. If Karlo concluded this was no violation of the good we held dear or, as importantly, our duty to each other, then I was also at peace with it.

We carried the litter into the desert.

From the mouth of the kraal, we watched as the tempest of swirling winds carried clouds of sand—fine, dense, and terrible—across the plain.

The storm's curtain pulled across the desert. We withstood the building furor until the sands tore at our skin. I turned my head to shield my eyes and when I looked back, the wall of the advancing sand-blaster screamed over Zero, and he was gone.

Peritar touched my shoulder from behind. "Come with me, friends. It is time to move deep within the kraal for shelter. All hospitality and protection of the People are yours."

"We never learned his name," Karlo said as we returned into the maze.

"Zero's good enough," Dave said.

Turv Densman was grim. "How could a man of the kingdom have become so twisted?"

"It doesn't matter," I said.

Double-K dismissed our questions. "Let the desert claim him. And with him, the memory of all creations of Brandon Bryant."

Dave said, "Is it time, Ben? Time for the next war?"

"Past time," I said. "On to Xanalar."

Double-K threw back his head and roared. The greatest son of the Korund raised a cry to war that drowned out the windblown sands speeding over the narrow gaps above, so mighty it threatened to bring the rough walls of our protection down around us all.

Khraal Kahlees proved to be the real psychic, and read my mind aloud.

"The time for reckoning has arrived. The justice of the Warlord comes and let all Vistara weep at his judgment, for Xanalar's destruction is at hand."

22

I didn't know what I didn't know. And that's a terrible foundation from which to proceed when you intended to do what we were doing. But above all, I had faith. In our army. In our rightness. And in my conviction that the greatest wrong had been done us. The simplest and best advice on leadership I ever learned was enough.

First, be sure you're right. Then go ahead.

I tried to convince Dave to sit this one out. "You were MIA, bro. You deserve to come off the battlefield. Go to the Veil and be with Tranya Olan. In fact, that's an order."

Dave shot me the one-finger salute. "I got your order hanging, brah. I ain't sitting this one out." He winked. "But thanks."

We arrived back in Thoria to find the *Hope of Vistara* arrived from Filestra, without a single hiccup along the way. Cynar was there as well, insistent he come, too. For once, I accepted without argument and instead gave him a deep bow of gratitude. He repaid my honor in a more typical manner.

"Hehehe. Is it possible you mature into less a dunce?"

So much for dignified gestures.

The last of our forces arrived and our slow journey into the land of the rising sun began. After cruising for days above halcyon nothingness, the tips of the vast mountain range came into sight, growing ever taller, until on the seventeenth day we received the report from our scout craft.

"Xanalar is alerted to our presence and mobilizes."

The Black Bird pilot sent another live feed.

The image was so clear I could pick out individual trees, boughs of purple and red standing out against the green bed of the marvelous city. The many structures reminded me of the ancient Rome or Greece of my imagination, and the crystal towers shone like lighthouses. Rivers spilled from the mountain in waterfalls and cataracts that poured into a checkerboard of lakes. And massing at the boundary between succulence and aridness, an army.

Double-K growled. "Animal-mounted troops in perfect lines. Several hundred, at most. Where are their ranged weapons? Where are their armored columns? Am I to believe those defending this mysterious land are no more advanced than the Mydreen? I remain dubious."

We'd postulated that Xanalar would most likely not maintain a large standing army; their isolation was their protection.

"It appears our estimation is correct," Cynar said. "Luck is with us."

"Wizard Cynar, you of all should know there is no such thing as luck," Double-K said. "There is only loss or victory. And like the Warlord, I believe in total victory."

Doug squinted at the cloud. "What're the things waltzing around over the city?" Schools of gray ovoids swam lazy paths above the city like stingrays over the ocean floor, casting huge rippling shadows beneath them as they flew.

"Them's da kine flying critters," Dave said.

"No other airborne activity," Karlo said. "If they have aircraft, they're not revealing them. Difficult to rate those animals as a high-risk threat, but I wish we had a better look before we have to engage them."

Cynar had spent days pouring over images old and new, interpreting the purpose and significance of the many shapes interrupting the lush landscape in a patchwork of urban planning. He was as fine an aerial image intelligence specialist as we had.

"Warlord, I remain convinced the targets I have identified are essential to their infrastructure. The activity near them I believe is that of defense. I take that as confirmation of their value."

"Agreed," I said. Crippling their city wasn't my first choice, but it would rise to the top of the list if they didn't heed my message. We were literally and figuratively nearing the point of no return as the *Hope*'s commander conferred with Double-K before bringing us to a stop over our first phase line. I cleared my throat.

"Last chance to sound off. Go or no-go for Operation First Contact?" Dave said, "I'm probably not the best person to ask. These assholes put me in a real bad mood. I could sign on to skipping it and just kill 'em all."

Everyone else remained silent.

"I'll take that as a unanimous 'GO,'" I said. "General Khraal Kahlees, please give the order."

"With pleasure, Warlord."

I went to my cabin and prepared. When I returned to the ops center, Double-K snapped a salute.

"Warlord, all sorties have launched. The package has also been successfully delivered. Behold."

A payload with a repulsor bed had been dropped by a Black Bird and remotely guided to land on the sands just beyond the perimeter of Xanalara's defense. An ROV crawled on treads toward the mass of troops, the cloud showing us our first ground-level view of the city rolling up the distant mountain foothills, and our first close look at the mysterious race that inhabited it.

The animals were a close cousin to the sōkoon but the people, they were just as Zero had described: as alike as they were unalike any of the known races of Vistara. Tall, somewhere between a human and a Tarn, but with only two arms and legs. Their hair was silver and shoulder length, falling off narrow skulls bearing tiny sockets with pinpoint black eyes. The noses were short and flat with upper lips cleft like a cat's. They dressed much like the Mihdra—robes and capes, bare bluish skin the color of an Earth sky where not covered by gleaming armor. They carried blades and pikes, halberds and bows, and unmistakably, rifles.

I asked only myself, *Is this a toy army or a real one*? I felt the same doubt as Double-K as to their apparent lack of lethal ability.

"There is a perfect link, Warlord," Cynar said. "You may proceed."

Projecting above the ROV should be a cloud twenty meters wide and in it, they would see the Warlord. I stepped onto my mark and got a thumbs-up from Cynar. Dressed in the full traditional armor of the army of Mihdradahl—gold chest plate and helm, bracers, a purple cape, and for the first in a very long time, the gift of the Warlord Jawn Kurz, my sword Lady Vivamus—I spoke.

"My name is Deacon Benjamin Colt, Warlord of Mihdradahl. I seek to address the leader of Xanalar."

There was the waiting I expected. I repeated myself as the smaller ROV bearing the decipher crawled across the sands toward the mounted soldiers of Xanalar. Finally, a party of three broke from the lines of mounted cavalry and approached. They moved well, as military men of any army should, and from the saddle the point of their formation spoke.

"I am Protector Supreme Mellan," he said in a language my decipher translated from the first. "What is this violation?"

"I come bearing a proclamation for the leader of your people from my queen."

He made no reply, but I hadn't asked a question. I gestured to where the small ROV sat. "The decipher will allow you to understand me." I pointed to my own bicep.

None of them moved to retrieve our gift. This time in flawless Mihdra the leader said, "The Xanalara do not need your primitive device. I ask a final time, what is this violation?"

I collected myself. We'd come up with an opening dialogue that conserved words and used simplified meaning. "We wish diplomacy and friendship."

The Protector Supreme said simply, "That is not possible. Leave or be destroyed."

Dave mumbled at prison yard volume, "Just what I was hoping you'd say."

I kept cool but used my baritone drill sergeant voice. "You have committed injury on Mihdradahl. We have proof of your plot against us."

I believe in the power of the demonstration. The guards followed my command and escorted former First Citizen Granday Fallis into the cloud. Manacled and dressed in prison clothes, he tried to act proud but at seeing the Xanalara, gazed down at his feet.

In their general's face I was certain was revealed a tell of recognition.

"I come to deliver to your ruler an offer of reconciliation from the queen of Mihdradahl."

The Supreme Protector raised a hand high overhead.

"Destroy them."

A voice came into the op center from the lead gunship of our combat patrol. "The flying animals are forming echelon and approach."

From the ROV cloud showing the massed lines of mounted troops, the feline splits in their upper lips widened with grins. Then I got the first real look at one of the creatures that had been flying a graceful easy pattern over the city. It was very much like a giant stingray, the edges of its body furling and unfurling in undulations that propelled it through the air.

On its back stood a soldier, hands on the spade grip of something the size of an M2 .50 caliber Browning.

The view from the eye-in-the-sky command, control, communication and intelligence Black Bird showed dozens more of the living war birds lofting easily to meet us.

We'd soon learn if this enemy were lions or kittens.

"Give the order," I said. "Commence Operation Downfall." I started stripping the useless armor off right there.

Granday Fallis gasped. "You've doomed us all, you madman!"

"Return the prisoner to his cell," I said, putting my desert fatigues back on. "I'm going to observe."

Karlo followed me outside onto the adjacent platform, the only one of the crew besides me without an immediate job. We each had binos and aimed them ahead. The *Hope* remained stationary, our anchor above this first phase line while the two crucial juggernauts of Operation Downfall began simultaneously. It was difficult to decide which to focus on. From twenty thousand feet the precision aerial bombardment by the Black Birds was underway. Bombs rained onto the targets we'd selected, a new explosion rising up every few seconds from all domains across the city. The bombs were potentiated by stones and while less powerful than good-old-fashioned 500-pounders, the Black Birds could carry a dozen of them each. The guidance Cynar created drove them with perfection to wherever the bombardier aimed them.

Karlo sounded much calmer than I felt. "Ben, the big bats are reaching the first of the gunships."

The second portion of our aerial war was about to start. Yes, we were a couple of thousand feet above the ground and no, my natural disinclination toward heights didn't kick in as I braced against the railing and focused my binos.

A kilometer away our gunship squadrons occupied the next phase line, spread wide in a screen for just such a contingency. The wingless animals rose slowly higher and higher to meet them, and I grew anxious. I suddenly regretted my decision to leave the ops center where even if I couldn't see what was happening, at least I'd better hear the traffic between the group leaders and Dave, inside running the air op.

The flyer's massive size became apparent the nearer they came to our small hovering craft. The guns carried aloft the backs of the flying beasts opened fire. Like smoke rings blown from a practiced pipe smoker, circle after circle of white pulses issued toward our airborne defenses. The pulsing rings grew wider and wider, fields of fire crossing and interlocking, until it seemed disaster was sure to engulf our air forces.

"Shoot! Shoot!" I pleaded, just when the gunships opened up.

The fight was across a thousand meters of clear red sky, one opponent flying gracefully like a flight of eagles, the other bobbing clumsily like a swarm of bees. The distance between them filled with streaks of white beams from our deadly K-maxes and staccato lines of the harsh red tracers from our mini-guns, the sizzles and chainsaw buzzes reaching us a few seconds later. Our barrage crossed the distance many times faster than the ghostly rings fired at our flyers, slowly advancing and dreadfully expanding on their path to ensnare our gunships.

Sour bile rose in my throat as I watched.

The first of the flying behemoths was hit, the burst of a K-max impacting squarely on its leading edge. The gray flesh ignited and the giant stingray pitched over, sending its rider on a free fall, the crumpled creature toppling after him. Bright crimson tracers perforated and K-maxes incinerated gray flesh as dozens of the creatures as intriguing as the

Song of Xanalar were knocked from the sky, terrible yet beautiful in their deaths, and we cheered.

The unknown discharges were almost upon our gunships. They broke into evasion—diving, climbing, turning. I watched with horror as a flitter too late in escaping was reached and overtaken by the spread of the strange ray. At first, nothing happened. Then the men on the deck grasped at their heads, mouths wide as if locked in terror. The gunship took a spiral, the pilot still at the controls but not in control; it tumbled and was lost.

"Now we know," Karlo said. It had been the technology Zero warned us about. He was correct. It did indeed cause madness.

Three more gunships fell to the effect, but no more. There were few of the flying stingrays alive and retreating for the city, and I again cheered as our gunships burst into full speed to intercept their escape, gunning them down at their six within inches of the finish line at the edge of their city.

Below, their calvary had the best seats in the house to the demise of their air power.

"Now the mopping up," I said to Karlo, leading us back into the ops center.

"Strafing runs starting now," Dave said to me.

The cloud from our ROV was still broadcasting. Their mounts shifted nervously beneath them, but their riders held fast. It wasn't until the buzzsaw of a minigun ran over their position, bringing eruptions of bloody flesh from riders and animals, that they broke. K-max fire joined and a stray burst took out the link and the image went to static.

Double-K looked to me. "Warlord, I believe we are ready to proceed to phase line Patton to ground the *Hope of Vistara* in order to deploy the assault force."

"Concur, General. Proceed."

We would not be establishing an occupation. The city was massive, and we had nowhere near the size of a force needed to do that, not if I had three *Hope*'s-worth loaded with troops—not that we even had them. But we had enough to fulfill the dual purposes of my operation: there was the physical, and then there was the psychological.

Cynar cackled as he described in verbose detail the damage done to the infrastructure of Xanalar. "Dams and reservoirs spill and flood the lowlands. Rivers divert. Visual signatures confirm the discharges of many centralized collections of stones to indicate I was correct—they served as critical energy producers. Hehehehe." I knew it was that he was proven correct rather than the carnage itself that delighted him.

Dave assessed the destruction of their army with one word.

"Annihilated."

What I intended next was a vital part of my plan to leave the Xanalara with emotional scars to make their sphincters loosen should they ever again think about messing with us.

That, my friends, is one of the purposes of a raid.

I donned full battle rattle and departed below for the hanger. The Warlord was not leading the way this time, but that didn't mean I wasn't going to have my moment.

The *Hope* set down with a single dull thud and the ramp lowered like a massive mouth opening to inhale the light of the world. First out were the Kardans, our fast and light armored cavalry, which would lead the thunder run to reach the mountain foothills where the grand palace awaited, surrounded by tiers of reflecting pools and green terraces. Our tank company floated out next, the sharply faceted surfaces of their armor gleaming in the sun. The company of arkall-mounted Tarn came last, charging after the floating mechanical columns to barrel for the velvety green plains of Xanalar.

Alone for the moment, I ventured down the ramp to stand on the sands of Xanalar, marveling at the city as I thrilled with anticipation of what was to come. Is this how Alexander or Julius Caesar felt at just such a moment? The might of their civilization on the cusp of crushing another? I had no delusions of such grandeur, but how many times in the history of either of my worlds had any man been in such a position?

I was grateful.

My Korundi bodyguards stood beside me. Sarkan Sell raised a hand to shield his brow as he craned his neck back. "Warlord, they depart."

Jodal Jark crowed, "Would that we were with them!"

Raising from the top deck of the *Hope* was the craft we named the flying school bus, and for good reason. It was as un-aerodynamic as one of the yellow rectangular boxes, but instead of high-backed seats of children, packed inside like sardines was our company of Tarn paratroopers, Doug and Karlo with them. The gunships were already raining dragon fire down on the defenders around the palace to clear the way.

I had to admit, Karlo was correct that an airborne assault was as anachronistic as it came, but even he couldn't deny its ability to strike terror into the hearts of those watching helplessly below, as peerless Tarn troopers sank majestically beneath billowing parachutes to appear in the heart of their governance.

It was going to be the wax seal on the glorious document declaring Xanalar as impotent against our kingdom.

A trio of gunships were grounded nearby and I led us onto the one piloted by Turv Densman, who with less insubordination than Dave had likewise refused to sit this one out.

"Take us up," I said to the grinning crew, their guns aimed ahead like ancient harpooners ready to sink a whale.

Though I was a lifelong ground-pounder, I never ceased to marvel at what a bird's-eye view offered.

The Kardans and tanks fired sporadically, prepping the way through, as the mounted cavalry hooted and rode behind them. The madness weapons harried the advance and flanks sporadically, and I listened to the traffic describing how the rays lost effect once the guns were destroyed, which occurred almost instantaneously.

Our unstoppable might drilled through the city, piercing everything in their path as effortlessly as a knife passed through butter.

We suffered no casualties or delays and soon enough, the gunships over the objective pulled back to allow the flying boxcar with our paratroopers to assume its azimuth for the largest expanse of green plain above the palace complex. The palace glistened in the reflection of the surrounding pools and fountains, and in my spine, I felt the green cushion of the drop zone, saying a prayer for soft landings for our vengeful angels.

Two by two they exited the sides of the flying school bus, pale canopies snapping open to stiffly capture air as parachutes filled the sky before sinking to the ground. The complex was surrounded by an impenetrable wall of our armor and into the center of their cordon, our cavalry arrived and spread throughout.

I'd lost sight of the airborne assault force after they abandoned their collapsed chutes. They'd rushed from the drop zone to penetrate the main building and its many subsidiaries. Ground fire hammered the upper palace tiers that layered high like a wedding cake. Balconies draped with flowering vines and ornamented with sculptures more ostentatious even than my queen's own palace were blasted apart, but there was no infamy here. No villainy or perversion as the perfection of artist's hands fell to the violence of my will.

This was justice.

Wide stairs led to a grand concourse above the largest of the reflecting pools and onto it, out stepped Doug and Karlo, surrounded by a mass of desert-camouflaged Tarn. My wristlet vibrated and in the cloud was a grinning Doug.

"Warlord, the palace is ours," he said formally.

"Job well done, General," I replied with equal military decorum. "Have the critical leadership entities been located?"

Karlo stepped close. "Sir, we have them. They await your arrival."

One of the crewmen parted the gunwale gate and I used hand signals to direct Turv Densman to slide into position directly above the concourse, five hundred feet below. My Korundi grimaced but held their tongues as they assumed attention on either side of the opening in the rail, and saluted fists to chest as I stepped to the edge.

I jumped.

The repulsor harness worked flawlessly and after a moment of freefall I assumed the velocity of a feather and descended. I arrived on the white marble of the plaza with feet wide and hands on hips, the furious cheers of my troops coordinated in a deafening stanza with rifles punched overhead to the beat.

"WARLORD, WARLORD, WARLORD."

My name is Colt the Showboat.

I ascended the stairs to join the gathering. Center of the chorus by my brutes was a pair unmistakable for their importance. A thin platinum crown rested above the brows of the man and woman, tall and thin, robed in splendor, and silent in defiance. But from them, I smelled the fear I meant to strike.

Everything I'd done so far was meant not only to overwhelm Xanalar —to make it clear we'd imposed our will on them in a manner absolute —but to strike a terror in them a thousand times greater than had been inflicted on Mihdradahl.

Which meant I wasn't done.

I produced the small cube and laid it on the ground and stepped aside. In all her regal glory appeared Talis Darmon on the Spectral Throne, beautiful and terrible in her serene pose. Her countenance struck me with a fearful reverence, and I bowed.

"Queen Talis Darmon, your Warlord presents you with the conquered regents of Xanalar."

"Whom do I address?" she spoke from atop her throne, appearing as a giantess above us, all as she fixed the captured king and queen in her gaze.

The man spread his chest. "I am Emperor Setultus, the radiance of Xanalar. What insanity inflicts your race to produce such impudence instead of fear! Why have you committed this grievous act on our exalted being?"

Talis Darmon remained regal, aloof, and unbothered by the emperor's insults.

"It is by *your* assault that I have sent my Warlord to punish you." She held up a black stone.

"We know of your support of the murderous reign of terror loosed on my kingdom. We also know how you have conspired with the Veil of Seriata to sabotage the strategic minerals vital to our kingdom. The covert relationship you have enjoyed to likewise supply you with the powerful treasures of their mines is at an end. The Veil is now a protectorate of my kingdom, and you are cut off."

The emperor snarled, "I deny that preposterous claim. If that is the basis for your immoral war on us, it is based on a fallacy."

The queen looked down on him with pity. "I care not if you admit our incontrovertible proof. It is established beyond doubt. But what I have not yet decided is whether there is necessity for your complete destruction. Think carefully as you witness yet further demonstration of our resolve."

I raised my wristlet. "General Khraal Kahlees, proceed with Operation Landmark."

"At once, Warlord."

After almost four years of Earth being consumed in the flames of its second world war, a discussion raged regarding how to bring the last remaining enemy to peace. Rather than unleash the first atomic weapon on the enemy who'd started the war, it was proposed that a demonstration should instead be used to convince them of the devastation that awaited if they did not capitulate. The argument against that was, of course, if there were a fizzle above the waters of the Pacific instead of the cataclysm of a nuclear fireball, the consequences would be devastating.

You're welcome to your own opinions about the choices made then. I'm secure enough in my beliefs to allow you yours.

Our subatomic matter mill was defunct and taking up space in the vault beneath the palace—about as useful as a two-ton paperweight—so discovering the argument that would finally convince Karlo to give us a nuke was a moot point. But he *did* build us the closest thing we'd ever have to a mother of all bombs: a conventional bomb of chemical explosive potentiated with stones, so large it had to be lifted by a specially outfitted Blackbird, stripped of everything but a seat for a single pilot.

And if this boast of mine made us seem like pipsqueaks instead of an existential colossus, well, I'd have more than egg on my face.

But when you have Karlo on your side—not to mention the spiteful genius of Cynar the Magnificent—what was there to worry about?

Still, I said a little prayer before I pointed to the far western horizon, and conjured up the best dramatic image I could by picturing myself Darth Vader.

"Watch and grow fearful."

Timing is everything. The answer to my prayer came with the flash, followed by the mushroom cloud rising from the flat desert. It raced ever higher and rolled outward in a massive bloom of fiery red and blazing white. The thunderous BOOM echoed and behind it, a wave of pressure sped across the barren floor to expel its hot wind against our faces.

Talis Darmon's voice raised to equally destructive proportions.

"This is my promise to you, Xanalar. Should you raise a hand to Mihdradahl again, you shall be extinguished from the memory of Vistara beneath a storm of my will."

Tears streamed from the black marbles of the empress's eyes to coat her gaunt cheeks. Their emperor collapsed, only to be lifted roughly by the Tarn paratroopers.

I bowed to my queen, judging our message had been at last properly received. Xanalar knew our stick, it was time for Talis Darmon to show them the carrot. She wore her most beneficent smile.

"The extermination of your civilization is not my desire. This small demonstration of our might serves as testimonial to our absolute commitment to our defense, and our greatest desire for peace.

"My army now departs your land. Whether they return as destroyers of Xanalar, that is up to you. The bridge for communication between our kingdoms is in place. My Warlord leaves with you the device by which we can embark together on a journey of diplomacy, rather than an exploration of malevolence. I await your efforts, eager to know you better. If not to establish friendship, then at least, to cement the recognition that we are capable of coexistence on Vistara, with hope that all our peoples may live without fear of obliteration visited by the hands of the other."

The cloud extinguished.

The emperor quivered. I nodded to the Tarns to release his arms and I moved to depart the land and people of fable to whom we'd laid waste.

“Warlord.” The soft voice implored my attention.

I turned back to see the empress with her hand extended to me in plea.

“Would your queen truly leave us in peace?”

I nodded.

“Was it you who conquered the kingdom of the Yellows?”

I nodded.

“Was it you who has exterminated the White gods beneath Farnest?”

I nodded.

Tears came to her anew and she sobbed. “Your cruelty is greater than that of any vengeful god to ever exist beneath or above.”

The stolen words came to me.

“Like all of our enemies before you, surely your sins must have been great. Otherwise a punishment as terrible as I would not have been visited upon you.”

23

Loaded and underway, westward bound, I bestowed a praise on our task force, one inadequate to how I truly felt about their performance and its importance in securing for our kingdom the future it deserved.

But I decided we could skip the slow boat ride home.

Fuming next to me in the back of the Black Bird, Double-K said, "How I wish I had stood beside you to witness the groveling of the Xanalara!"

Doug turned from the cockpit. "It was another Ben-dog classic, Double-K. I got the chills when Ben laid his spiel on them. I think I peed a little. That speech gets chiseled on the pedestal beneath your statue, duder!"

Next to him in the cockpit, Karlo groaned painfully. I knew *he* knew who I'd plagiarized. Genghis Khan was not the role model for the man I aspired to be, but was a role model nonetheless.

Turv Densman and Dave were flying their own bird to the Veil to pick up Tranya Olan, and after a brief rest, I expected us all to reconvene in Shansara. On the jump seat between Khraal Kahlees and I, Cynar pored over one of his devices, oblivious to the cramped discomfort. "Whatcha working on, Cynar?" I asked.

Without looking up from the slate he said, "I gathered the rays discharged from our experiment."

"The MOAB, you mean?" I asked.

He lowered the slate in a huff. "Of course the MOAB, you dipshit!" His obligatory dig at me out of the way, he proceeded. "Hehehe. Quite successful, I think. But as always, there is room for improvement."

"You want to make a bigger one?"

Rather than take another shot at me, he grew serious.

"I was deeply affected by the queen's words to Xanalar. The might of our defense is indeed a measure of our commitment to peace. With what life I have remaining, I wish to dedicate all efforts toward an ever greater ability with which to defend Mihdradahl."

I heard in him a recognition of his mortality, long it had been, and that perhaps, it was truly nearing the end for him. It brought a lump to my throat. "Cynar, do you feel well? I know we've been asking a lot of you. I should've kept you back," I said, regretful I'd surrendered and let him come with us.

He ate sour persimmons. "Never better. Stupid oaf."

"Then what's got you talking like that?"

Cynar stroked his scraggly long beard as he considered.

"You know me to be a man of science, Benjamin Colt, but I continue to doubt you understand what that means. So, for as many times as there are stars, once more will I attempt to explain. Idiot.

"Objective observation of phenomenon, impartial examination of all gathered evidence, the development of theorems and models to explain the results—all of these are a part of a process as necessary to me as the organ that supplies my heartbeat.

"When considering the evidence I have collected these years since you abducted me away from a blissful isolation spent exploring the workings of all the universe, I have come to a conclusion.

"With all objectivity, there exists true evil. And, indeed, there is also good; imperfect and rare though it is, its presence is undeniable. And within the strife and turmoil I have lived at your side, it is almost singularly present in the works of our queen."

Then he crooked a snarky glance my way.

"And by extension, in yours, also, I suppose. Nitwit."

The lump in my throat grew larger. Cynar went on.

"Mihdradahl prospers, not simply by the science that restores the life to our land, but by the ideals of those who lead the way to shape this wonderful future of ours. If the laboratory for this experiment of righteousness is not protected, what will become of Vistara? If I fail in my dedication to see this continued beyond the mortal coil attaching me to this world, then my science is without justification.

"It is for this reason I have taken an oath; I must ensure our goodly queen has the tools needed to continue to build this better world, and perhaps, Vistara will allow it.

"And when it does not, you are there with your clod-headed schemes and equally imbecilic friends to see it done.

"So there."

✠ ✠ ✠

I don't know who squealed louder, Shara, my wife, or me as we gathered in a squeezing embrace with our little daughter between us. Her cheeks were still the softest thing in existence and her hair retained the baby scent I couldn't bear to think of disappearing as I smooched her over and over.

Beraal stayed with us until I sent her to her father, leaving me alone with my nuclear family for the first time in the longest time. My wife sighed loudly.

"Promise me this will never end, Benjamin Colt. That we will always be together, without fear of peril."

"I could play along, sweetheart, but you and I both know there's no predicting the future. We could ask the Mists of all Time, but they're never correct."

"That is true, beloved husband. But we make the future. It does not unfold without our permission."

"Then I promise to do my best to forge a future we can be proud of."

"That is all I can ask, Benjamin Colt. And I also promise... I *will* find a way to surrender the regency."

But as I thought about Cynar's heartfelt conviction—the same as mine—that I held in my arms the living embodiment of all that was good in our world, I kept it to myself that our promises were the sweetest of all self-deceptions.

✢ ✢ ✢

The next day was business and topping my list was a burning question that could only be answered by a predictably unpredictable and unreliable ally. It was most likely he was incapable of the honesty we were about to demand.

"Hello, Eidolon Sah," I greeted him, semi-surprised the old boy hadn't yet been offed by one of the conspiracies he feared.

"Well, if it isn't Benjamin Colt. What's shaking, my old friend, you Thulian death dealer, you!" Just then he noticed the queen beside me and corrected his comportment by donning the guise of statesman. He stiffened and bowed.

"Queen Talis Darmon! It is most humbling to be in your majestic presence again. I remain your greatest admirer and student."

"I greet you in kind, good friend," she replied with the wry mirth only a queen could get away with.

Eidolon Sah raised from his seated bow. "How may I serve the queen of Mihdradahl?"

She cleared her throat. "I have report from my ambassador there have been recent, shall we say, difficulties in Aetheria?"

The leader of Annameria played it cool.

"None that I am aware of. All proceeds splendidly."

"Cut the shit, buddy," I said. "Did you just rub out a bunch of your council?"

Eidolon Sah put on his shocked face.

"Knock it off, already," I said. "We're not calling to ball you out, but it's time for plain talk. What happened?"

Eidolon Sah spoke to someone just outside of the cloud. "What'd you say, Tom-Tom? I thought you were on board?"

Tomellan Cart moved into view. "It is so, Warlord, that there was a plot to murder the Most Benevolent Protector of Annameria. And against my counsel—as it was unacceptable behavior from a partner to Mihdradahl—the conspirators were dealt with harshly and without judicial process."

Eidolon Sah threw up innocent hands. "See, Benjy? Look what I have to put up with. I'm dragging these folks kicking and screaming into a new age, and for all my hard work, *this* is how they repay me. A man's gotta do what a man's gotta do. You of all people should understand."

Talis Darmon lifted an eyebrow. "Eidolon Sah, it is with understanding of the realities of your environment that I shall overlook this incident as we continue our arrangement. With that in mind, it is with grave seriousness that I insist you now answer the Warlord's next query with complete candor."

Eidolon Sah relaxed as if all were already forgiven and forgotten. "Of course. Like you said, we're partners."

I hit him with it. "We know you've been cutting deals with the dwarves."

"Okay," he said flatly. He hadn't denied it, which seemed like a good first step.

"Are you in contact with Xanalar, too?"

"Xanalar?" he splurted. "Oh, hell no, Benjy!"

I aimed a knife hand at him. "Did you know Bryant and the dragon lady's secret police were running an operation to infiltrate Mihdradahl with Vermeel terrorists?"

"Whoa, whoa, whoa! No way, Ben, no friggin' way! I knew nothing about that."

Seeing my scowl he tried harder to deny it.

"C'mon, man! I was just the first consort! You know I wasn't privy to everything that was going on!"

I made fists and the knuckles of both cracked loudly.

"I mean, at least, I didn't know *that's* what they were doing. I remember when Bryant first showed up with a bunch of rough-looking Red characters in tow. I heard through the grapevine the Yellow Roamak took them off to their special place in the Kublana province, but I had no way of knowing what the heck they mighta been getting up to. Annameria's a big place, you know? Kublana's a helluva lot farther away from Aetheria than Pyreenia is from *your* capital, buddy. And we all know there was stuff going on *there* you guys had no idea about."

Talis Darmon nodded to me. I also accepted his admission as truth, or at least, that it was as much as he was capable of giving. Eidolon Sah leaned forward.

"What's Xanalar got to do with anything, Benjy? Everyone knows they're some kinda screwy weirdos who've kept to themselves the last few thousand years."

I choked. "Well, it might've been nice to know they were even there —buddy."

Eidolon Sah made a scrunchy face. "You never *asked.* Buddy!"

Talis Darmon took charge. "Eidolon Sah, I appreciate your forthrightness. It is not with accusation that we discuss these matters. The Serians supplied Xanalar with the products of their mines, including rarities unknown to us that enabled the technologies used to terrorize my kingdom. I bring this to your attention to make you aware that Xanalar may not be the isolated civilization of its reputation. They assisted the campaign of terror that was launched from your borders."

"Queen Talis Darmon, I swear I had no idea about any of that," Eidolon Sah said with unusual sincerity.

She made her slight smile of regal dispensation. "And I believe you, friend. We have severely punished Xanalar for their crime. Going forward, we mean to be ever vigilant for their intrusion. Your farthest borders lay closer to theirs than do ours. I ask you to join with us in monitoring for their appearance, overt or clandestine it could be."

Eidolon Sah stroked his chin in deep thought. "I may need to do some digging around in the Province of Kublana. So far from the throne, they've always been a little *too* out of sight, out of mind—I mean to say —so far from the seat of the Benevolent Protectorate's governance."

Ambassador Tomellan Cart smiled approvingly at the revision.

"One more question," I said. "Has our shipping guild been involved in carting stuff from the Veil to Aetheria?"

Eidolon Sah recoiled down as if whacked on the top of the head by a nun's ruler.

"A little, here and there," he said, meekly.

"Thank you, Most Benevolent Protector of Annameria. That is all for now." The cloud closed and she turned to me. "What do you think?"

I groaned. “Their guild’s been playing all sides against the middle for too long. I’ll tell Zaylin Twee to add it to her list of things the Guard needs to investigate. And, I’m going to give her my solemn promise not to interfere. I’m hoping that’ll repair some of the trust she lost in me.”

My wife smiled approvingly. “I leave it to you, husband. But tonight is our celebration marking the beginning of another annual. I wish it to be a joyful gathering. Though I know it cannot be completely avoided, perhaps we can limit the intrusion of too many worldly matters.” She fluttered her lashes at me.

“I’ll do my part to make it a barn burner of a hoedown, baby.”

“I have no idea what you mean, husband, but it invokes an image of something raucous, which is not what the occasion requires. As we have not before celebrated this day together—as we seem to have always been engaged in some dire unpleasantness—you do not know. The celebration of the start of a new annual is meant to be spent with family and close friends, an occasion to gather and enumerate the fortunes encountered during the past year, both good and bad. It is how we give voice to the recognition of each other’s importance in how we endure and prosper.”

“So serious,” I teased. “Maybe after that’s done, us Thulian savages can show everyone how to party like it’s 1999.” I busted one of my bad dance moves.

She giggled at my verve, then turned pensive.

“Husband, Karlo Columbo seems troubled. I thought his return to martial pursuits was meant to alleviate his fatigue?”

“Like everything, baby, it’s a mixed bag.”

“Did he not perform admirably?”

“Oh, that he did! And I think I’ve got just the assignment to cure his current blues.”

"Then I await to bear witness to the work of your healing powers, Warlord."

✠ ✠ ✠

We met at our apartments that afternoon and proceeded on foot, the Amber Quarter our destination.

Our mob melded with the many others on their way to the historic district of Shansara. It was a quaint and charming borough of winding and narrow cobblestone streets, as Bohemian a place as existed in Mihdradahl. A gentrified mishmash of bars, eateries, arts, and entertainment—and today it was as crowded as Bourbon Street on Mardi Gras.

If New Years was supposed to be the sober event Talis Darmon described, no one else seemed to know that's how it should be celebrated.

Our large party did not stick out, if you can imagine such a thing. Thulians, Mihdra, and Tarns. Men, women, a toddler, and one gadron, all in one group. And though we were famous—not the least among us being the queen (who, as usual, was so stunning she could have caused a riot on a Brazilian beach)—we were treated by our fellow citizens to respectful privacy.

I faded back and threw an arm around Karlo's neck. "How you doing, brother?"

He gave a subdued smile. "Doing good. Glad to be here with everybody."

"Don't keep it in, bro. What's eating you? You might as well tell me or I'll call Dave to get it out of you."

Walking just ahead, there wasn't room to slide a piece of paper between Dave and Tranya Olan.

Karlo chuckled. "Ah, you know me, Ben. I can overthink a ham sandwich."

"You're fretting about Peritar, and Double-K calling you out for being naive."

Karlo nodded. "He got it right and I got it wrong. I made a rookie mistake and projected my own values onto Peritar's actions, like someone on his first A-team mission with indig. Ben, we may have backed the wrong horse."

"Ah, you know better than that, bro. If we only dealt cards to players as on the up-and-up as us, we'd have no one to gamble with."

"S'pose." He shrugged.

"I got an offer for you, bro. We have to roll out the relocation of the Vermeel to the Furrow. No one in the governance has any experience with something like this. How about you run it like a Civil Affairs operation? You'll have a civilian deputy from the council, and I've got a military deputy in mind, someone I want you to train up and leave with Peritar once you're ready to come back. Remember that young platoon sergeant, Kezan Strahl?"

"The one who ran the ambush that nabbed Peritar? Sharp guy!"

"I've thought about it, and I want to give him the bump to officer. You and him choose your men, and you give them the on-the-job experience to run a stability op, just like an SF A-team. Does that appeal to you?"

Like the notions Karlo had for engineering gadgets, I knew he had a vision for the Vermeel.

He perked up. "It does, Ben! Thanks."

I didn't tell him that post-relocation of the Vermeel, it was back to the coal mines for him. It was nearing time for him to rejoin Cynar and get back to innovating even more things with which to outclass whatever danger waited somewhere on Vistara, or elsewhere.

But that could wait.

Pleased with myself, I threaded my way to rejoin Talis Darmon and took Shara from her. She wasn't quite big enough yet, but I was looking forward to showing her the world from atop my shoulders. Dougie was surrounded by his ladies. Double-K and Beraal walked side by side. Cynar and Dureen Zell strolled with Perrin Halser, who like Karlo seemed content to be romantically unattached. All I cared was they knew they were a part of this family and would never be alone.

Zaylin Twee tagged behind; close enough to be with us, far enough to be apart. I vowed that when the next opportunity presented itself, I'd pull her aside and fix what I'd broken.

From down the street floated the melodious mix of sharp twangy and flat buzzing notes made by an orchestra of the stringed instruments of old Mihdradahl. The sunken amphitheater lay ahead, the only really open spot in the Amber Quarter, and the obvious source of the racket. I was about to lead us in another direction when Talis Darmon turned to me with a thrilled look.

"Shall we take in the performance?"

I knew she loved the symphony, but elevator music was more appealing. The plucking and strumming of instruments that sounded like dozens of cats being strangled with their own guts was a thousand times worse than Muzak versions of Led Zeppelin or the Beatles. If there was anything good to say about the local tunes, at least I didn't find myself humming them long after returning from the grocery store.

I would walk across fire for her. I could tolerate this.

"Doubt there'll be seats left, but we can find some standing room," I said, handing the baby back to her.

I led our way onto the concourse and we filled in with the rest of the mob stuck on the SRO flats overlooking the bowl. The stage was small and the musicians were just as closely packed as were the people in the tiers, red skins and colorful silks jammed shoulder-to-shoulder to fill every bench in the amphitheater.

The music stopped and there was applause, and I selfishly hoped we'd arrived just in time to have caught the end of the encore.

Onto the stage strode Shaera Kōall.

"Fellow citizens of Mihdradahl, I bring you warmest greetings and wishes for the commencement of a splendid new annual around the sun."

"What the hell's she doing here?" Doug said, drawing scolds from annoyed spectators, turned to see who'd made the rude outburst.

The aristocrat stood in a soft spotlight, its rose tint chosen to complement her pink skin and shade her platinum hair to rose gold.

"And in keeping with our traditions, I wish to share my own enumeration of fortunes for which I am so deeply indebted to you all, my dearest fellow citizens."

Hearty applause rang out.

"But first, I must delve into matters that I know weigh on us all. The kingdom has suffered greatly this annual past. And it is by the misuse of the gifts we have been graced with by our privileged position on Vistara that such calamity has returned to us.

"Though our might has preserved us, its legacy has also harmed us. The terror levied against us was unjustifiable, but the bitter roots of that poisonous vine grew from a seed sown by our own hand, planted with our cruel treatment of the Vermeel.

"And with the same aggression we decry in our enemies, we have seized the lands of our neighbor in the Veil of Seriata. And rather than extend the hand of diplomacy to a new friend, we have brought war to a peaceful and sedate kingdom of riches and mythical splendor. And to what end?

"To secure the safety of our kingdom? Or to establish an empire, ruled from Shansara?"

Khraal Kahlees exploded. "The witch contradicts herself! She paints us in infamy for that which only weeks ago, she herself made impassioned plea to the council! All at a time before we had knowledge demanding the necessity of our actions! And now she decries them! The hypocrisy! The audacity!"

We'd been the only ones to hear him, as the thunderous applause drowned out even his mighty bullhorn.

Shaera Kōall basked in the adoration of the crowds.

"A promise has been made to see our kingdom evolve in its governance. Yet, that promise has not seen a single foot placed on the path toward that imagined destination. Instead, we see entrenchment, and the building of the greatest force for conquest to ever exist in the history of Vistara. And though some may think that to be a shield for our protection, holding it are hands I fear could be used against Mihdradahl's greatest asset—her free citizenry.

"Are we to forget the nightmare we were plunged into by King Osric Darmon's incompetence? Only to be followed by our near destruction at the hands of his first heir? It is by fickle grace that Queen Talis Darmon has brought us to such prosperity, but I ask you—by what divine providence do we pray it continue? Especially in light of these foreboding events that steer us away from peace and instead, aim the kingdom towards a militaristic domination of all that is known?"

Someone in the stands—no doubt her agent—leaped to his feet and pumped a fist high as he bellowed, "No to aggression! No to silence! No to tyranny!"

The crowd erupted, taking up the chant.

"Everything she says is a lie!" Karlo screamed at the top of his lungs.

But no one heard him.

Beraal was there. "I shall not let her past denouncements of the queen's move to establish a republic vanish from the public ear! My next information campaign begins immediately! Shaera Kōall's own words will expose her as naught but a contrarian and a deceitful seeker of power."

The crowd roared ever louder.

Tranya Olan, Keshin Tellest, and Shasa Karin had drawn in close.

Dave was at my side. "Brah, say the word. I'll have a gunship here in a flash to scatter this riot and lift the queen out."

Zaylin Twee countered. "No! That would play into *her* hands."

The decision as to what to do next fell on me.

Apache looked up at me and wagged his tail. He was enjoying himself. I took a cue from him and assessed the many strangers surrounding our party. They all smiled meekly back at me, seemingly embarrassed. Whether their looks were sympathetic—affected by the aspersions being cast at our queen—or their looks held the seeds of the doubts Shaera Kōall had so astonishingly planted, it was hard to tell.

At the least, there was no aggression.

We were in no danger.

"Let's just walk back out the way we came," I said. I moved to take Talis Darmon's elbow, but she resisted, remaining with eyes fixed on the spectacle.

"Talis Darmon," I said. "What do you want to do?"

She was not anxious. She was not disturbed. Nor worried, nor perturbed, nor concerned. She rocked our daughter against her bosom and turned to me bearing a contented smile.

"There is nothing to be done at this moment, my fierce love. Let us return to our home. All unfolds, just as my theory predicts.

"The age of the Nomad's influence is upon us."

✚ ✚ ✚

We gathered together on cushions, just as we had the night we pondered the inadequate image Karlo saved from the Whites' navigation system. A photo, a poem, and a possibility, weaved together by this family into a belief that Xanalar was real, a place where incomparable beauty survived, preserved and hidden on Vistara.

But the wonder that had brought us all close that night was now a shared bereavement: for the dream that had been Xanalar, and for a kingdom poised to abandon reason at the call of a poisonous siren.

"Be not heavy of heart, my cherished family," Talis Darmon said. "It is still the celebration of the new annual around the sun, and we are together to see it commence. Healthy, prosperous, happy, and most importantly, safe."

Beside Doug, Selvin Wharran brushed a stray lavender tress behind her ear. "I also am filled with gratitude," she said with uncharacteristic boldness. "It has been an annual marked by great strife but also by even greater gifts. I am with egg! And so are my sisters!"

Bandra Lang and Faahl Saleen squealed and lay hands on their own abdomens.

"Dougie! You dog!" Dave howled. "Congrats, brah!"

Doug was beaming. "Get ready, Unca Davey-Dave, 'cause you gotta be there to help me train my new fire team! All of you!"

"This is propitious news indeed, my Thulian brother," Khraal Kahlees said. "I shall send for the finest mounts in all the Korund as gifts to bestow on your seed, awaiting the day I shall teach them to ride."

"What about you, Double-K?" Dougie asked. "What're you grateful for, duder?"

Being put on the spot seemed to catch the fearless warrior off guard. "Err, there are of course many things for which I am grateful. That I have such close bond with my daughter is first among them."

Beraal lay her head on her father's shoulder, and I felt the saline build in my eyes.

"But I must say, a close second is this," said the green giant. "That my discernment regarding the Pale was proven greater than Karlo Columbo's! Gah, gah, gah!" He hacked an uproarious laugh that deafened us all.

Karlo threw back his head and joined to laugh at his own roasting. "Man, have you ever learned to bust stones."

Cynar's cackles became a coughing fit that brought laughter from Dureen Zell. Perrin Halser covered his face.

"What about you, sweetheart?" I teased, placing a hand on Talis Darmon's tummy. "Do we need to get the creche out any time soon?"

My wife shrugged. "I had thought to tell you when we were alone."

My heart skipped a beat.

"Are you serious?"

She nodded and I drew her into my embrace. From moments spent together in despair to sharing the greatest joys I'd ever known, she carried me with her in a life spent living an unimaginable fantasy.

Shara was showing off her latest ability. Her balance had improved to the point where her chubby little legs propelled her into a run that threatened to turn into a wipeout at any second. She delighted in her new game, pausing every so often to look back for the inevitable chaser.

Zaylin Twee played along, gleefully pursuing as Shara double-timed an escape for the kitchens.

Zaylin Twee sang, "Tashara Colt, come ba-ack."

"Shara," my wife sang louder, a first of her use of my pet name for our daughter. "Come sit on my lap beside your new brother or sister!"

At that, Shara halted. She broke into a silly grin, then reversed course. She took a few steps, then crouched. She sprang, flying past Zaylin Twee and over the heads of all our friends. She made her splash-down in the center of my lap.

"Like Dada!" she squealed, then crawled into the lap beside me and patted at her mother's tummy. "Baby."

My wife shrieked, "Benjamin Colt! What does this mean?"

If I knew, I couldn't say. Like everyone around us, I was robbed of speech.

Dave's mouth fell open, then he burst out, "I'll tell you what this means! We're in for trouble!"

Tranya Olan took Dave's hand and placed it on her belly. "How wonderful is this adventure called life."

Laughter flowed up to the ceiling and spilled from the open windows to spread across Shansara bathed in splendid lights and wrapped in the warmth of the tranquil night sky. Suddenly, I knew what it all meant.

No matter what comes, be it a future wondrous or unraveling, it was one of our making.

My name is Deacon Benjamin Colt.

I am Warlord of Mars.

ABOUT THE AUTHOR

Doc Spears is a veteran of the United States Army and works as a consultant and trainer in the defense industry. Writing has been the worst vice he's found yet and doubts he'll be able to stop even with help, which he refuses to seek. When not offending the sensibilities of all decent peoples everywhere, he can be found with Nick Cole and Jason Anspach plotting to infiltrate all realms of sci-fiction.

To be notified about Doc's upcoming books, including the sequel to this title, visit **www.WarGateBooks.com**

www.ingramcontent.com/pod-product-compliance
Lightning Source LLC
LaVergne TN
LVHW100505110826
845146LV00002B/526

* 9 7 9 8 8 8 9 2 2 0 6 6 4 *